A SHOT IN THE DARK

Johnny Edwards is fishing when he gets Tony's letter from Cuba. Tony is in trouble and urgently needs Johnny down in Havana. But Johnny stalls—ashamed to admit to his former war buddy that he has been living a life of indifferent ease and indulgence—and when he does arrive, he finds Tony has just been murdered. His boredom replaced with thoughts of revenge, Johnny decides to find the murderer himself. And that's when he runs into Ellen McCarter—trim, slim, with sun-streaked hair—a helluva distraction. But not enough to sidetrack Johnny, who continues to follow the murderer's trail up to Fort Myers, Florida... where the first person he runs into is slim, trim Ellen!

SHELL GAME

Bill Stuart is vacationing in Florida, collecting shells, when one evening he stumbles upon a beautiful young woman hiding under a fishing pier on a deserted beach. Undaunted by her cock-eyed story, he offers her a lift into town. Valerie agrees if she can drive. When she discovers they are being followed by a gray sedan, Valerie breaks every law to shake them; and just as mysteriously does a quick disappearing act when they arrive at the bus station. The local chief of police isn't interested in tracking his missing person, so Bill heads back to the beach to retrace Valerie's footsteps—which just happen to lead to a cabin that is occupied by the body of a very recently murdered man!

RICHARD POWELL BIBLIOGRAPHY

Mysteries

Don't Catch Me (1944)

Lay That Pistol Down (1945)

All Over but the Shooting (1946)

Shoot If You Must (1946)

And Hope to Die (1947)

Shark River (1950)

Shell Game (1951)

A Shot in the Dark (1952)

Say It With Bullets (1953)

False Colors (1955)

Novels

The Build-Up Boys
(as by "Jeremy Kirk," 1956)

The Philadelphian (1957)

Pioneer, Go Home (1959)

The Soldier (1960)

I Take This Land (1962)

Daily and Sunday (1964)

Don Quixote USA (1966)

Tickets to the Devil (1968)

Whom the Gods Would Destroy
(1970)

A Shot in the Dark

\- \- \-

Shell
Game

Two Mysteries by
Richard Powell

STARK
HOUSE

Stark House Press • Eureka California

A SHOT IN THE DARK / SHELL GAME

Published by Stark House Press
2200 O Street
Eureka, CA 95501
griffinskye3@sbcglobal.net
www.starkhousepress.com

ISBN: 1-933586-18-4
ISBN-13: 978-1-933586-18-2

Text set in Figural. Heads set in Brazilia.
Cover design and layout by Mark Shepard, home.comcast.net/~shepdesign
Proofreading by Rick Ollerman

The publisher wishes to thank Dorothy Powell Quigley
for all her help and persistence on this project.

First Stark House Press Edition: June 2008
0 9 8 7 6 5 4 3 2 1

The Powells
Discover Ft. Myers
By Dorothy Powell Quigley

The earliest memory I have of my father is a sunny day, standing with my mother and brother, watching him walk away from us, up a long flight of steps and disappearing through the door of a huge building. I was four years old. The building was the Pentagon in Washington D.C.; the time, World War II, and my Dad was on his way to serve in the War Department of Public Relations, eventually as a Lieutenant-Colonel and Chief Censor for General Douglas MacArthur in the Pacific.

It was in the service that my father, like so many others, discovered the "perks" of Florida living: good weather, sandy beaches and plenty of fish to be caught. Discharged from the Army, he called Mother to meet him in Miami. She liked it too, and together they began a search for a nice little house in what was then real-estate-boom-time Miami. Sticker shock, followed by a thirst for adventure, drove them west through the Everglades along the Tamiami Trail, then north where they stopped for lunch in the sleepy small town of Fort Myers, population twenty-five thousand in 1946. They noticed in the local paper that real estate prices were much more to their liking there, and that is how and why and the day they settled on a nice little house on the Coloosahatchee River, to fish, to grow mangos, and live the life of a free-lance writer.

It was here that he wrote so many of his mystery and crime stories. In this book you will read two of his favorites: *Shell Game* and *A Shot in the Dark*. My Dad loved to write. He was so witty, so fresh, and with all the research he did, his books are really informative, too. While living in Fort Myers he noticed many newcomers grabbing up state land on the causeways and setting up little boat and bait businesses and he thought then that this sort of modern pioneering might make an interesting novel. But that thought was put on hold. A handsome offer from the prestigious N.W. Ayer Advertising firm in Philadelphia called the family back to the city where my father's family had lived for seven generations.

For twenty-five years, since his marriage to Mother, a Vassar graduate from Cleveland, Ohio, he had wanted to write a story about his hometown whose social traditions his bride had found "quaint." *The Philadelphian* was published in 1957 and immediately sky-rocketed to Number 1 on the bestseller list. Film rights were bought and the movie, *The Young Philadelphi-*

ans, was a box-office hit. Two years later *Pioneer, Go Home* was published; the story he had seen in those little boat and bait businesses under the Fort Myer causeways. Another best-seller, another box-office hit, *Pioneer* was re-titled *Follow That Dream* and starred Elvis Presley. With those two big successes Mother and Dad decided to follow their dream, and as Dad said, "We raced back to Florida."

In 'retirement' he wrote six more novels, nineteen books in all. Mother died in 1979. After that he wrote no more. Dad was ninety-one when he died in 1999. I wish he could know that within eight years a new generation of readers have discovered and are enjoying the books he loved to write.

ARDMORE, PA
OCTOBER 2007

A Shot in the Dark

By Richard Powell

CHAPTER ONE

It was stupid to go on needling the customs officer at the Havana airport, but the guy irritated him. When Johnny Edwards arrived on the night plane from Miami, the officer had glanced at his clothes and motioned him to stand aside while more prosperous-looking passengers were cleared through customs. Ordinarily Johnny would have shrugged it off. But he had spent the last twenty-four hours being angry at himself and it was a relief to get irritated at somebody else.

The customs officer said in a worried tone, "I do not understand, señor."

"You asked why I came to Cuba," Johnny said politely, "and I told you I was here on a fool's errand."

"People do not say they come to Cuba for such a reason," the man objected. "They say they are the tourist. They say they are the businessman. They—"

"I couldn't get away with claiming I'm a businessman. All my friends would laugh like hell."

A few feet away, the Cuban girl slanted a look at him through eyelashes you could use for feather dusters. She was quite a number: black hair that probably uncoiled to her waist when the braids were loosened, sleepy dark eyes, a figure that rippled like smoke rising from a cigarette. He had tried to make a little yardage with her on the New York-Miami hop, just to pass the time, and had been thrown for a loss. That look was the first she had given him. It was queer; you could break your neck trying to impress a dame and then a casual remark would catch her interest. She was hanging around now to listen.

The customs man was poking through Johnny's battered satchel as if he hoped to find plans for a revolution.

"People who are not the tourist or the businessman are sometimes the workman," the official said sternly. "You must understand, señor, that the visitor to Cuba must not work without the work permit."

"I've never been so flattered in my life," Johnny said. "What makes you think I'm a workman? Nobody else has ever thought so."

"The hands, señor. We of the Customs notice things. The hands are those of a workman."

"Well, let's see," Johnny said, spreading out his hands palms up and studying them. "Are these ridges across the first joints of the fingers bothering you? They come from putting in overtime with a set of golf clubs."

"Ah. So? But these on the palms?"

"Hauling on ropes."

"Ah, ropes! That is work."

"It sure was. No more New York-Bermuda yacht races for me."

"How long ago was this Yacht race, señor?"

"About a month."

"Ah! Then how does the señor explain this red place with the blisters on the left palm?"

"Fishing rod. I was working the Restigouche yesterday. That's a salmon river in Canada. It's no use, chum. Nobody has ever been able to pin a charge of working on me."

"I do not understand," the man grumbled. "Señor, it will be necessary for me to—"

A rustle of Spanish words interrupted him. The Cuban girl was taking a hand in things. She was telling the customs officer she knew the young American quite, quite well. It was true that his clothes were old and faded but what could one expect from a fisherman? It was simply that he had tired of catching small fish in the United States and suddenly decided to catch some of those great ugly fish—what did one call them? Ah yes, tarpon—in the waters of Cuba. Being a young man of impulse, he had not paused to get proper clothes. One might call him a rather useless young man and certainly not of much intelligence, but his family had much much dollars and there were connections in high places in Cuba.

"Ah," the man said. "Dollars. Connections in high places." He gave Johnny a bow and said in English, "Señor, Cuba welcomes you." He handed the battered satchel to Johnny and waved him grandly on.

Johnny started to say something but the girl slipped an arm through his and led him away. "Idiot!" she whispered after they walked a few steps. "One should never try to joke with men who have a little authority. Perhaps you think it was bold of me to do all this."

Johnny grinned. "I thought it was swell. But I don't know why you bothered. You certainly didn't bother about me back on the plane."

A trim shoulder tilted in a shrug. "On the plane," she said, "you were just another man. I meet a great many. They all think so highly of themselves and are so very dull. As I listened to you talk to the customs officer you did not appear to think highly of yourself. That interested me. Is it true?"

"You seem to know all about me and I don't know a thing about you. What do you do, besides rescue guys in distress?"

"I am a singer. Light opera. Concerts. Perhaps you attend concerts?"

"You already know the worst about me," Johnny said. "So I'll admit I avoid things as educational as concerts."

"I think I like you, señor. Would you share a taxi with me into Havana?"

"Wish I could. But I've got an errand to do first. You know, that fool's errand I mentioned."

The black eyes gave him a glittering look. "A woman, naturally."

"Matter of fact, a man. A friend of mine got in a little trouble down here and yelled for help. Probably it isn't anything much. I'd like to see you after I straighten it out."

She dug into her handbag, brought out a card and scribbled an address and telephone number on it. "I would like that, too," she said, giving him the card. She beckoned to a taxi, stepped into it and then leaned out and said gravely, "I will try not to be too educational."

CHAPTER TWO

He hailed a taxi and got in and groped in his pocket for the letter that had yanked him out of the crisp June weather of Canada and set him down twenty-four hours later in a sweating tropical city. He found the address and read it to the driver. Then he settled down in the back seat, intending to put away the letter and take a nap during the ride to the address Tony Mendoza had sent him. He didn't put it away, though. He found himself reading it again, just as he had done a dozen times since it arrived.

Querido Johnny, it began.

That was an emotional way for one man to write to another. But the Spanish were emotional people. They wrote the way they felt. To a Spaniard, a friend wasn't just a guy you liked to have a few drinks with. He was a guy who could have your house and the shirt off your back. He went on reading, picking out words in the glow of the light above the cab's rear seat:

You will be surprised to hear from your old Tony. Who would think to find me in Havana?

Well, Johnny, there was nothing left for me to do in Manila. The plantation on Panay was no good after the war. It could have been farmed again but a Spaniard is no longer welcome. The Philippines for the Filipino! I could have gone back to Spain, but I had been away twenty years and did not wish to go back to that tortured country.

Your country seemed like the one good place left in the world. I had no way to get in from the Philippines and so I came to Cuba thinking it would be easier. Unfortunately, Johnny, we Spanish nationals who lived in Manila under the Japanese are looked on with some suspicion and we must prove that we were not collaborators. I do not say this is unreasonable and of course it is true that once your country and mine were enemies. So your officials here in Havana would not give me an immigration permit until long investigations could be made.

Johnny, it was not pleasant to wait. One is not given a work permit in Cuba. One waits and waits and every day the money gets less.

I tell you this because I have done something very foolish. A man said he could get me in your country without a permit. I should have refused to listen, but I was weak. Then later, when affairs had gone much too far, I became frightened. You know how easily I get frightened. In this case I ran away just when I was about to board a boat to be smuggled into your country.

It became at once very clear to me that it is not permitted to change one's mind after learning something of the system. Shots were fired after me and the next day

certain men visited the place where I had been living. The good Cuban woman with
whom I had been boarding told them nothing. She knows where I am hiding, how-
ever, and will guide you if you can come to help your foolish old Tony....

A guy like Tony got scared easily, all right. Almost as easily as a guy
named Johnny Edwards.

He closed his eyes and watched some pictures flickering in front of his
eyelids. Newsreel stuff. There ought to be an announcer telling you
solemnly: "This... is Manila. February, nineteen forty-five. Driving in from
north and south, MacArthur's men have closed a trap on twenty thousand
Sons of Nippon. Now the Japs must be blasted out, street by street, house
by house. A job for the heroic G.I. For the foot soldier..."

Yeah, and here comes that heroic G.I., S/Sgt. Edwards, John C., of the
11th Airborne. There he goes, all alone, tommy gun in hand, slipping past
the corner of what had been a house. Is he out to silence a Nambu machine
gun? Is he seeking water for his thirsty squad? Rescuing a wounded com-
rade? Hell, no. He's looking for souvenirs. There he goes, bright-eyed and
bushy-tailed. Watch closely. Hooray, he found the souvenirs!

Unfortunately the souvenirs are still in use.

That sound you hear, folks, is one of those Nambu machine guns. It is
stitching bits of metal through the legs of our hero. This is a very ineffi-
cient way to collect souvenirs.

Now we dissolve to a night scene. That dark spot you see is a smashed
house. In it is S/Sgt. Edwards, John C. He has remembered what he was
told about pressure points and so he hasn't lost more than a quart of blood.
He expects somebody to come for him at any moment. Not his squad,
though. They don't know where he is. He expects Japs. He dropped his
tommy gun while crawling into the house and only has a knife. He hears
somebody feeling around for him. He jabs blindly with the knife, wondering dully why the Jap keeps dodging and sobbing and talking Spanish
at him. Fortunately he blacks out, because the Jap is a horrible scared little Spaniard named Tony Mendoza who has been hiding in the cellar and
saw the heroic G.I. get his and came up to help him.

It turned out that he was four hundred yards and three days inside the
Jap lines. The scared little Spaniard carried him down into the cellar and
kept him alive. So naturally, when the little guy got in trouble some few
years later, he thought maybe his American friend would help.

Of course that sort of stuff was strictly from Don Quixote. Americans
were practical people. The guy named Johnny Edwards had his own life to
live. He was living it fishing for salmon on the Restigouche in New
Brunswick when the letter reached his home. When it was forwarded to
him it made him frown. Manila was a long way back. Let's be sensible

about this thing. Send the guy a nice hunk of change so he can buy off his playmates. Besides, the salmon were hitting well.

He went out fishing with the letter in his pocket. The salmon were rising nicely but he had forgotten how to take them. He kept thinking of Manila. He remembered waking up in the cellar of the smashed house with Tony wiping sweat from his face and talking to him in soft musical Spanish the way you might croon to a baby. At the time he hadn't realized what chances Tony was taking. First the guy had crawled upstairs where he could have been shot by a Jap patrol. Then Tony had to get in close and take a knife away from him and carry him to the cellar and nurse him through a delirium in which he moaned and talked and yelled. Any one of those yells could have brought Japs, and let's not pretend that any visiting Jap would have considered Tony a neutral.

What made a scared little guy like Tony take those chances for somebody he didn't even know? And what made a guy like Johnny Edwards hate to admit he owed Tony anything? Was it because, if somebody took a lot of risks saving your life, you ought to try to prove your life was worth saving? It was a complicated subject and he couldn't figure it out.

So here he was in Havana, irritated at having his salmon fishing interrupted, calling his trip a fool's errand, trying to convince himself that Tony was being frightened by shadows.

All right, Edwards, let's admit what's the matter. You're afraid Tony will ask what you've been doing since the war. Then you'll squirm and say, well, Tony, you know the family has a lot of money and they let me do what I want and so I've just been bumming around the country playing golf and fishing and going in yacht races and drinking too damn much and making passes at dames. Tony will be too much of a gentleman to say you're not doing much with the life he went to a lot of trouble to save, but you'll be afraid that's what he'll think. Of course you can explain to Tony that being thrown down by your girl, while you were overseas wrecked your life and gave you a license to be a bum, but a guy like Tony probably won't believe anybody has a license to be a bum.

"Señor," the driver said, "this is the street and I think that is the house."

They were parked in a narrow street where houses jammed close on each side, leaning at slightly tipsy angles. Wet cobblestones steamed in the glow of the headlights. He had forgotten how hot it could get in a tropical city after the rains began. The air was so moist it was almost a liquid. When you took a breath you could taste flavors in the air: the ripe taste of garbage, the mustiness of earth that seldom received any sunlight, the tang of salt from the harbor not far away. He paid the driver and climbed out of the cab and watched it slosh away down the street. After it turned the corner, darkness clamped down over the street like a lid.

He walked to the house the driver had indicated, rapped on the door. Nobody came. He rapped again and told himself not to get impatient. Tony was the only one who had a right to be impatient. It had taken Tony's letter three days to reach his home, and two days more in being forwarded to the fishing camp. Then he had wasted almost a day carrying it around in his pocket, trying to find excuses for not helping Tony. The plane trip had taken another day. Seven days altogether. Six of them weren't so bad. But he didn't feel good about the day he had wasted.

The door creaked open about a foot. A white blob of a face floated into the dark opening and a woman's voice asked in Spanish what he wanted.

"I want to see Tony Mendoza," Johnny said. "I'm a friend of his from the United States. He—"

The door slammed shut. Through it the woman called shrilly, "Go away. I know nothing of this. Go away at once!" There was a sharp note of panic in her voice.

"Wait a minute," Johnny yelled. "Give me a chance to talk, will you?"

There was a shuffling sound beyond the door. It faded, died away. Johnny got out matches and struck one and looked around the doorway. He located the faint traces of a house number. It checked with the address in Tony's letter. Probably it was only natural for the woman to be suspicious. Still, Tony had written that she would be looking for him, and you would have expected her to listen for more than a couple of sentences. He began knocking, quietly and politely, at intervals of a minute or so.

Finally something squeaked above his head. A window. He stepped back and saw the white blob of the face swinging out over his head.

"Go away," the woman called. "I will not open the door. I will not talk. Go away. Cheat! Liar! Bandit!"

"I have a letter," Johnny said quickly. "Don't take my word for it. A letter from Tony. He said you'd be expecting me. Read it and see if I'm not telling the truth. I'm his friend, I tell you. Look, here's the letter."

"Everybody has letters," the woman said in a queer tight voice. "I will not open the door."

"I'll shove it underneath. You don't have to take any chances. Just pick it up and read it."

The fat white face looked down at him for a few moments and then vanished. The window squeaked shut. Johnny went back to the door and listened. It was hard to catch sounds through the slow heavy thud of blood in his head. Finally he pushed the letter under the door, leaving a corner sticking out so he could get it back if nothing happened. He waited. For a long time the white triangle stayed the same size. At last it gave a tiny twitch. He held his breath. The woman's fingers were nibbling at the letter like a fish working timidly at a bait. The bit of paper on his side of the door moved slowly, getting smaller, smaller. Suddenly it flicked out of sight. Nothing happened for minutes. Then abruptly the door opened and a fat hand reached out and gripped his arm and pulled him into the house. "Stand still," the woman said shakily. "I will make a light."

A switch clicked and an electric bulb set in a wall bracket began to glow feebly. The face he had seen as a white blob took on detail: eyes like raisins pushed into dough, a small twitching nose, a series of chins oozing onto a black dress. She looked very frightened.

"Señor," she said, "I think I have done something wrong. You really are a friend of Señor Mendoza's?"

"Yes, sure," Johnny said soothingly. "Want me to describe him?"

"No, no, please do not bother. I am not clever about descriptions anyway. Señor Mendoza described you to me and yet I am not clear at all. He said you would be an American and young and about so tall—" She made a vague gesture above her head, compared it with his height and lifted her hand a little. "But it is still very confusing. Señor, would it seem discourteous if I said that all Americans look very much alike to me? As, perhaps, a foreign race such as the Chinese might look alike to you? I have seen very few Americans in my life."

"I can understand that. Don't worry about it."

"But I do worry, señor. You see, the other man was an American too."

Johnny frowned. "What other man?"

"The other friend of Señor Mendoza who came earlier tonight. I knew Señor Mendoza was only expecting one friend from America, so when you came just now, I was sure there was something wrong. I did not trust you."

"How would anybody else know Tony was expecting a friend from America?"

The rabbit nose twitched nervously. "Señor, as you know from the letter, Señor Mendoza was hiding. Perhaps four days ago there came a small thin man, asking for his good friend Señor Mendoza. This one was not the American, you understand. Perhaps he was a Cuban, perhaps a Spaniard, perhaps almost anything. He was the sort of person one sees and does not really notice. He did not seem dangerous, not like other men who had come looking for Señor Mendoza and so perhaps I made a mistake."

"You didn't tell him where Tony was hiding?"

"Oh, no. I said with great firmness that Señor Mendoza had left word only a certain American friend of his was to be told where to find him."

A small dull pounding started in Johnny's stomach. It made him slightly sick. "And so tonight," he said, "that certain American friend came around."

"Yes, señor," the woman said huskily. "And it is possible that I did wrong to tell him where Señor Mendoza could be found."

"How long ago was he here?"

"An hour before you came."

"Where do I find Tony?"

"Señor, there is a church. You go out the back and through an alley and across the street. The church burned several years ago. But the walls and floor are stone and remained. Also there is the cellar. One climbs through a window and finds a door up near where the pulpit used to be and then one finds stairs behind the door and goes down them into the cellar. At least that is what Señor Mendoza told me. It was he who found the place when it became necessary for him to hide."

Johnny nodded. Anybody who lived through the assault on Manila knew how to hide in smashed buildings. He borrowed a candle from the woman and went out the back door and down the alley she pointed out. It was a black tunnel between two houses, patched with gray at the end where the next street crossed. He found himself moving in a slight crouch, setting his feet far apart so he could swing fast in any direction. It was queer; set a guy down at night in an old Spanish city and throw a scare into him and click!—there he was back in Manila in 1945. It was ridiculous. There was nothing to worry about. That business of the other American didn't mean anything. In a few minutes he'd be telling Tony about it and having a good laugh. It was silly to run, bending low across the street as if a machine gun might throw a burst down it. It was a waste of time to creep up to the black skeleton of the church, watching the scars of windows for the glint of metal or the blur of a face. He shouldn't let old habits come back to haunt him.

He swung in through a window opening and stumbled through piles of rubble until he found the door. It swung open as if the catch was broken or it had been slightly ajar. Behind it lay a solid chunk of blackness. He held the candle in his left hand and struck matches with his right. It wasn't easy to light the thing. His mind seemed to be a little mixed up and part of it kept screaming that if he went on striking matches some Jap would blow his head off. Finally he got the thing lighted and started down a corkscrew of stone steps. Now he felt better. You couldn't be tricked into playing war games while you pattered downstairs with a lighted candle. A candle flame was a pleasant normal thing. It—

It went out. He stood motionless while his legs tried to pretend he was drunk. That was idiotic. He had merely reached the bottom of the steps and a flutter of cold air had snipped out the flame. There was no reason to get that Manila feeling back stronger than before, no reason for a throb to start in his legs where the bullets had skewered them. It was only imagination that made his nostrils quiver and pick up the raw fresh smell of smokeless powder.

He forced his drunken legs to step onto the cellar floor and carry him around the stairway shaft. There was light up ahead, seeping toward him through a distant arch and around a couple of stone pillars. He stumbled toward it. A lamp stood on the floor: an old-fashioned kerosene lamp with a wick that was turned up too high and made the flame glare and smoke in the chimney. Beside the lamp lay a man who slept restlessly, with little nervous twitchings. His face looked very tired.

Johnny's throat tightened. "Tony," he called. "Tony!"

A flicker of expression touched the man's face and a whisper came back to Johnny—a deep sighing whisper that slid off walls and vaulted roof and trailed away into silence. It wasn't the right whisper, though. All it said was *Tony... Tony... Tony.* And that wasn't an expression changing on Tony's face. It was a shadow from the leaping flame in the lamp, the same shadow that made Tony seem to stir and twitch. Johnny moved forward and saw the dark stain on the coat and shirt and the three tiny glints that came from the empty cases of .45-automatic bullets on the floor near his feet.

You thought of odd things at a moment like that. You thought of another cellar in Manila. You thought of how you had gone out fishing with Tony's letter jammed angrily in your pocket, trying not to let it bother you. You thought of how, not long ago, Tony heard footsteps and turned up the wick of his lamp and called happily to his American friend and heard three shots from a .45 automatic. Or maybe he only heard the first one.

Another whisper crept through the vaulted cellar. It might be almost anything: the quick shuddering escape of a long-held breath, the faint scrape of a foot on stone, the click of a safety catch sliding out of its notch. The sound came from behind him. A shiver crawled up his back and stopped at his left shoulder blade and made it begin twitching. Funny, though. For once he wasn't scared. He didn't feel dull or numb any more. Something in his head was sending little hot spurts of energy through him. Something in his head told him to kneel slowly as if to examine Tony's body and to reach out carefully and grip the lamp and get ready to whirl and throw it.

He knew exactly what would happen when he did that. Somebody was going to get killed. For some reason he didn't care who.

He gripped the base of the lamp and spun and threw it. Flame cut a brief comet streak in darkness. Glass crashed. Sound bellowed at him and jets of fire squirted twice and bullets howled off stone. He lunged into blackness. A body should be there. A body that would jolt and go down under his rush and lie there screaming while he went to work on it. But it wasn't there. He tried to stop his driving rush and knew he couldn't and felt the solid crash of stone against his head and shoulder.

He was down. He was down on the stone floor flopping and gasping.

Somewhere a man was running away—a man who still had at least one slug left in his automatic but who wouldn't come back and use it no matter how you screamed at him. He staggered to his feet and saw a distant flashlight and tried to follow it but lost the light immediately in the sparks fizzing inside his head. Stone blocked his way again. Wherever he turned there was more of it.

Anyway it was no use now. The clatter of footsteps racing up the stairs floated back to him. Echoes picked up the sound and multiplied it until the arching spaces filled with a hollow, ghostly applause. He listened to it carefully. It seemed to be meant for him, all right. It was applause for an ironic little drama that began in a cellar in Manila and ended in a cellar in Havana. It was applause for a guy who couldn't be bothered.

CHAPTER THREE

The hotel where he was staying had one of those bars where the light is kept dim so that you can't see what brand of liquor or woman you're getting. He went in and ordered a double Scotch and carried it to a booth in the corner. It didn't taste badly, as a matter of fact, but maybe anything would taste all right after you had been living on coffee and cheap rum and benzedrine for two days. He hadn't had much sleep. He closed his eyes for a moment and immediately a series of words began unreeling like ticker tape against the purple screen of his eyelids. *Querido Johnny*, it began. *You will be surprised to hear from your old Tony....*

That wouldn't do. That wouldn't do at all. In the first place the writing was in a queer edgy script that scratched his eyelids. In the second place it drove a guy nuts to see that letter every time he closed his eyes.

A good subject to keep his mind off Tony's letter was the Cuerpo de Policia Nacional de la Habana. Maybe, since he knew them so well by now, he could get familiar and call them the Havana cops. For the first twenty-four hours after the murder, the Havana cops had been very interested in him. They were so fond of him they wouldn't even let him out of their sight. But then they found that his story checked perfectly and that he hadn't killed Tony Mendoza and that he wanted to camp on their doorstep yelling for immediate action in solving the case. So for the last twenty-four hours they hadn't wanted him *in* their sight.

In truth, Señor Edwards, one does not solve a murder so quickly. In fact one is not certain that it will be solved. Who was this man named Antonio Mendoza, after all? Merely an unimportant Spaniard who came to our city hoping to get an entry permit for the United States and refused to await the proper course of events and became involved with smugglers and lost his courage at the last moment and ran away and, since he might have talked, was killed. One might be forgiven for saying, señor, that your friend should have known better. And of a certainty the Cuerpo de Policia Nacional de la Habana cannot be expected to take any interest in the smuggling because that does not involve the breaking of any Cuban laws. So we will be grateful, Señor Edwards, if you will go about your business.

He finished the Scotch and got a refill and put that away and began to feel pleasantly drowsy. He took a chance and closed his eyes once more. The letter started unreeling again but this time it was blurred and didn't scratch so much. It was pleasant to relax....

His eyelids opened slowly and with a great effort like windows that had been painted shut. He realized that he must have been asleep for quite a while. He didn't understand why they hadn't thrown him out; a drunk sleeping in a booth was a poor advertisement for any bar. He started to get up, looked across the table, blinked. A girl was sitting there smiling at him. She didn't look like the brand of girl for whom bars kept their lights dim. He was seeing her through a slight haze but he got the impression that you could turn a searchlight on this dame without destroying the effect. Rippling blond hair, skin tinted a faint golden color by the sun, a face with soft misty features. Below the face she wore a string of pearls and some more golden tan and one of those evening gowns that just barely manage to rise to the occasion.

"Hello, Johnny," she said.

He tried to get his eyes into better focus. "Hello, Jane," he said.

"It's not Jane."

"Hello, Betty."

"It's very drunk out tonight, isn't it, Johnny?"

"It could be drunker," he said, "and I think it probably will be. If you'll give me a minute to get my eyes screwed back in, I'll look through a bunch of names and phone numbers I keep in my wallet and see if I got any names you like."

"I already looked in your wallet and didn't find any that appealed to me."

"This is very refreshing," he said, still getting her face through a blur. "I've known a lot of girls who felt like checking on a guy's wallet before they played up to him, but you're the first who ever did it to me."

"What especially impressed me in your collection," she said, "was the name of that Cuban girl, Conchita somebody-or-other. According to the receipt for your plane ticket you've only been in Havana forty-eight hours and you've already lined up Conchita. Of course you've always been pretty good at that sort of thing, I suppose."

He didn't feel like playing this game any longer. "If you'll excuse me," he said, "I'll run along. I'm not myself tonight so that makes us strangers."

She gripped his arm and said crisply, "I'm not going to sit here for an hour watching you sleep it off and then let you walk out on me. Johnny, it's Claire!"

He seemed to be wearing two sets of eyelids tonight. That remark snapped open the second pair. Her face came into sharp focus. It was Claire, all right. "Funny thing," he said. "You remind me of a girl named Claire Allison. I was engaged to her before I went overseas in the war. You know how absence makes the heart grow fonder? My absence made her heart grow fonder for a guy named Fenway and she married him. Hello, Mrs. Fenway."

"Well, well," she said. "I thought you were carrying a torch for me all these years and it turns out to be just a pail of ashes."

"Don't kid yourself. All these years I've been giving you official credit for wrecking my life."

"You were perfectly capable of wrecking it all by yourself."

"I know. But everybody needs an excuse and you were it. How's good old Chuck Fenway? And when did you dye your hair blond? That helped throw me off when I was trying to recognize you."

"I can answer both your questions at once. I decided to get rid of my brown hair and my husband two months ago."

He stared at her. "You seem to treat the whole thing very lightly."

"Not at all," she said coolly. "It's a very serious thing to have your hair bleached."

"Just hell on men, aren't you?"

"Oh, nonsense. Chuck doesn't even feel it. All he wants right now is to be admitted to practice before the U. S. Supreme Court and to be elected president of the Civic Orchestra Association. He doesn't need a wife. He needs an official hostess."

"He always was a guy with ambitions. You must have known that before you married him. So why did you?"

One of the bare golden shoulders lifted in a shrug. "I thought I was one of his ambitions too. And maybe you don't realize, Johnny, that an ambitious man can be very attractive to a woman. Not just because he seems to promise security, either. It's because he also gives the impression of being more of a man than other men."

"Other men, in this case, being a character named Johnny Edwards."

She said casually, "I could have been wrong." Her voice went up a notch at the end of the sentence so that it was almost a question.

This was tough for him to handle. His head wasn't in good enough shape right now to analyze nuances and tones of voices. He had grown up with Claire. Once she had been a clear-eyed laughing kid with whom he had romped like a puppy. He had always planned to marry her. Maybe he hadn't wanted very badly to marry her, because after all he had never wanted anything very badly, but at least she had meant a lot more to him than anything else. So being tossed over had left him wanting just about nothing at all and he had gone to a lot of trouble proving it to people.

He edged away from the subtleties into which the talk had been drifting and said, "How come you're down here?"

"Establishing a legal residence in Florida. For a divorce, you know."

"I mean, how come you're in a bar in a hotel in Havana all by yourself."

She laughed and said, "If you're worrying about me running around without an escort, I did have one. We happened to come in here and I saw you and told my escort I wanted to talk to you and sent him away."

"You seem to use up guys about as fast as a draft board."

"Have I used you up, Johnny?"

You couldn't tell how she meant remarks like that; her voice and eyes and her faint smile put a dozen different meanings into it. Perhaps she wanted him to choose the meaning he liked best and then if she didn't care for the choice she could claim she meant something else. Right at the moment he wasn't prepared to make a choice.

"There never was much to use up, was there?" he asked.

"I think I'm being kept at a distance," she murmured. "All right, let's change the subject. Johnny, I've heard rumors you're on the outs with your family. I don't mean disowned or anything like that, but have you had an argument or something with them?"

"Yeah. I keep telling them I'm a no-good bum and they shouldn't give me another cent, and they keep insisting I'll snap out of it and that they'll stand by until I do. It's quite an argument. Too bad they haven't a chance of winning."

"That's an annoying conscience you have."

"I didn't think it was a conscience. I thought it was just a matter of looking at myself with my eyes open. I don't like what I see, but if I had a conscience I'd want to change it."

"I see. You're just a low character. No sense of duty or anything, hmm?"

"Sense of duty? What's that?"

She said calmly, "That's what brings you down from New York or somewhere to help a person named Tony whom you met in Manila and who seemed to be in trouble."

He didn't like that. He had been trying not to let Tony and Claire get connected in his thoughts, because between them they summed up just about his whole past life and he hadn't wanted to face the whole business all at once.

"In addition to going through my wallet," he said, "you took Tony's letter from my pocket and read it."

"Should I feel badly about it, Johnny? I was desperately curious about you. Yes, I read your letter. I wish I could read your mind, too."

"That wouldn't take much of anybody's time."

"Well, did you clear up your friend's trouble? Are you free now?"

He picked his words carefully, because her reaction might be important to him and said in a flat voice, "I cleared up his trouble, all right. I was fishing when I got his letter and I didn't want to stop just then so I lost about a day's time and I got here just in time to tell the cops there had been a small murder."

She frowned slightly and twitched her shoulders as if a man she didn't like had tried to paw them. "I wonder why you threw it at me that way," she said.

"I wanted to see how you'd take it."

She reached across the table and touched his hand. Her fingers were long and lovely and felt as if they had just come out of a quick-freeze unit. "But I don't know how to take it," she said. "I don't know whether you're blaming yourself for it or trying to shrug it off or what. Why don't you tell me everything—how you met this man and all about it."

"I think I could manage it on two drinks."

She turned and beckoned to the bartender. Obviously she was a very valuable person to take to bars because people were always watching her and so you got immediate service. He poured the two drinks of Scotch down his throat and waited for the warmth to spread out through his body. When he finished the story, she sat for a moment without any expression on her face.

He said irritably, "Doesn't that get any reaction from you? Can't you start bawling or something?"

"You're being awfully dramatic, Johnny."

"I know, but it's not often I have a chance to blame myself for a murder."

"You don't have to blame yourself! It's just one of those hideous coincidences that come along in life. A thousand things happen to go wrong and a man gets killed. Suppose the Cuban woman hadn't been so stupid? Suppose your taxi driver had known a short cut? Suppose your friend had gone for a walk? Suppose the letter hadn't taken so long reaching you? Suppose—"

"Suppose I hadn't taken so long reaching Tony?"

"Johnny, you've been leading an aimless life and not doing anything that really interested you, and this comes along and it's dramatic and tragic and so naturally you can't stop thinking of it."

"What I need is another interest in life, huh?"

She said in an odd husky voice. "Would you like a shoulder to cry on, Johnny?"

He had never heard Claire use that tone of voice. It sounded like deep notes plucked from a cello and it sent little answering vibrations tingling over his skin. He stared at her smooth polished shoulders and said, "Are you offering one of those?"

"If you like."

He tried to grin but his face was too stiff. "After a guy got next to one of those shoulders," he said, "he might forget he just wanted a good cry."

"Would that be bad, Johnny?"

"You know, Claire, you were so subtle at first that I didn't catch on. But I get the idea now. I didn't have to tell you my sad story to rate this offer, did I?"

"No," she said slowly. "I guess not."

It was a very queer feeling to have had a wonderful excuse for wrecking your life and then to have the excuse snatched away. "I'm not sure I can count very well right now," he said. "So would you tell me about how much money I had in my wallet?"

"Around six hundred dollars, Johnny. Why?"

"I wonder if that's enough?"

"I have plenty of money. Do you want some?"

"I was just thinking," he said. "There has to be a fairly big gang back of this murder. Any time you get a big gang, you have hangers-on. You know, guys who are on the edges and know something about it but aren't in on the real chips. And you often find guys like that hanging around in drinking and gambling joints looking for a way to make a fast buck. Or maybe I ought to say a fast peso. Suppose I started offering six hundred bucks right out in the open at those places for information about the murder of Tony Mendoza. I wonder what would happen."

"You're not serious. You can't be."

"That's right. Guys like me are never serious. But I think I'll do it just as a hell of a big joke."

"Johnny, listen to me. I—"

"Sorry," he said, getting up. "I got to see a man about a murder."

She grabbed his arm again. "Johnny," she gasped, "you can't do that to yourself. I know it was a horrible affair but I could make you forget it."

"I think you could," he said. "But it might be a bad trade." He twisted his arm away from her and went out.

CHAPTER FOUR

Everybody thought he was drunk but he wasn't. His head had never felt so clear in his life. Some of the effects of that concentration were interesting. Take the case of the taxi driver. After leaving Claire a short time ago he got a cab and told the driver to take him to a good tough night club section in the waterfront area. Ordinarily he wouldn't have noticed that the man's glance flickered over him as if pricing his clothes and wrist watch. He noticed it this time, though. Then, when they reached the waterfront area and the taxi stopped, he was perfectly aware of the fact that the driver tried to peek in his wallet as he paid the fare. After that, even though his back was turned, he heard the quick hiss of Spanish as the driver whispered to a man lounging on the sidewalk.

He lit a cigarette and watched the cab move slowly away down the street and looked around him. It was quite a section. Through doorways came the blast of juke boxes and shrill cackles and brays of laughter. Sailors were all over the place. They tacked drunkenly down the street arm in arm. They eddied in little groups at the entrances to bars. They floated in and out of places as aimlessly as driftwood. Cubans in dirty white pants and shirts sidled through the groups drumming up trade for one joint or another.

Johnny studied the setup and was pleased. Probably there wasn't a better spot in Havana for his purposes. Behind him the whisper that the cab driver had started was spreading. Feet shuffled. A man laughed softly. Johnny turned and walked up to the four men who had gathered behind him, stopped and said politely in his best Spanish, "In case the driver of the taxi did not get a good look into my wallet, it holds about six hundred dollars."

Four pairs of black eyes shifted uneasily, glanced at him, looked away.

"Anybody who wants it can have it," Johnny said. "All I want is a little information."

All of a sudden the four Cubans started to understand Spanish. "Very interesting, señor," one said, crowding him a little. "And what is the information the señor wants?"

Any other time in his life Johnny's knees would have started shaking. Not now, though. It was just a matter of not much caring what happened. He blew smoke slowly into the eyes of the man crowding him and said, "I'm interested in a certain gang that smuggles aliens into the United States. I figure that down here along the waterfront you men or some of your friends know who goes in for smuggling. The particular gang I'm interested in murdered a friend of mine two nights ago. His name was Tony Mendoza. Here's the six-hundred-dollar question. Who killed him?"

Four pairs of eyes went blank. Four Cubans drifted away down the street as if they didn't know he existed. One of them peered back over his shoulder, however, and saw that Johnny was still watching.

The hell with them.

He started down the street, stopping beside every lounging Cuban to repeat his offer. It was funny how the pattern repeated. Johnny frowned. Things weren't going right. He worked his way down the street for a couple hundred yards without finding anybody who seemed to want six hundred bucks. At that point he reached a narrow alley cutting back toward the harbor. It was nice and dark and had a few turns that would keep everything private. He sauntered into it, whistling softly. Maybe the boys merely needed a little encouragement.

He paused after turning the first bend in the alley, treated himself to a final cigarette and waited. Nothing happened. It was ridiculous. He gave everybody a good chance by staying there to finish his cigarette, but he couldn't have drawn less business if he had been crouched there behind a flame thrower.

He walked back out of the alley feeling more in a mood for a fight than anything else. He looked both ways when he came out and scowled. Not a Cuban within fifty feet of the alley. He crossed the street hoping to find a better class of crooks, but it turned out that the other side was even worse. Now he couldn't even get near a Cuban. They simply melted away as he approached.

He saw another alley and turned down it, without much hope. Nobody followed him this time either. He kept on wandering down the alley and found that it swung around behind some houses and angled back toward the main street. As he approached the exit, he saw a group of men huddling there whispering. He crept toward them hoping to pick up what they were saying. They had their backs to him and it wasn't hard to get close.

"... not for six thousand dollars," one of them was saying.

"But Pablo," another argued, "it would be so easy."

"How does one know it would be easy?" a third man said. "Obviously the American is crazy. How does one know what he might do? How does one know he does not have a gun?"

"Are we to be afraid of a crazy man? Are we to be afraid of a gun? No, no," the first man whispered. "It goes deeper than that. Who knows who might not belong to this smuggling gang? If a man is seen following this crazy American, those who belong to the smuggling gang may think that he plans to betray them for the six hundred dollars. Then—poof!—it is too bad for that one. No, no, my friends, it might be worth one's life to be seen even talking to the crazy American. It—"

Johnny walked into the middle of the group and said irritably, "Don't be so yellow. I don't have a gun. I—"

He didn't have a gun and he didn't have an audience, either. The Cubans took off as if he were selling chances to win a zombie. The whole business was utterly fantastic. He had done the wrong thing from the moment he reached the waterfront area. He walked angrily down the street, looking for trouble. There were still plenty of sailors on the street, but the most you could hope for with sailors was a wild brawl with fists and maybe some clumsy knife work. He began getting out of the honky-tonk area and kept on walking aimlessly and then with a sharp jerk of nerves realized he was being followed. Sweat came out on his forehead. For a while he had been all set for anything, but as time went on and nothing happened, his beautiful clear concentration on a single idea had slipped. He was beginning to feel tired. A guy couldn't stay keyed up forever. He wasn't in the mood now but it would be stupid to change his plans.

He picked the next alley and moved slowly into it and stopped and waited. Funny how his heart was pounding.

A guy slid up to him. A thin young Cuban with a spotted face and lips drawn back over horse teeth. He moved in a jerky way that made you think he was high on reefers. Something glittered faintly in his hand: a cheap small-caliber revolver that wouldn't be a good buy even if you got it for box tops.

The whole idea started to seem very annoying. The kid didn't know enough to keep his gun out of reach. Johnny slapped it aside with his left hand and slugged him in the stomach with a hard right. The kid's head jerked down. Johnny brought up a knee. It smashed into the kid's face and he crumpled. Johnny took the revolver from a limp hand and walked disgustedly out of the alley. He headed back toward the honky-tonk section and after walking a block suddenly realized that maybe the kid really belonged to the smuggling gang instead of being just a loner on the make. He returned to the alley. The kid was gone.

He started back to the honky-tonks once more. All he wanted was a drink. He had been wrong a while ago, thinking that he wasn't drunk. He had been, but good. But he had been drunk on an idea, not on alcohol, and ideas left hang-overs that kept driving spikes through your head. They—

Brakes squealed beside him. A car. A big black car. Guys were piling out of it. For a moment he thought this was it, but then he saw the badges and uniforms. Hands locked on his arms, dove in his pockets, grabbed the cheap gun.

"Señor," a cop said politely, "you are under arrest."

Johnny began laughing. He was still laughing as they bundled him into the car and raced off down the street. It topped the whole mad evening to end up by getting arrested. It was really funny. He had never done anything with his life and it turned out he couldn't even get rid of it when he tried.

CHAPTER FIVE

He awoke feeling that nothing was wrong with him that a blood transfusion couldn't fix. He was in jail, but if this was typical of jails a lot of guys were missing the boat by staying honest. There were bars at the windows and door, but judging from the looks of the place they were intended to keep people out rather than in. This was a suite no less, with a bedroom, living room and bathroom. It looked like the sort of place where they might put a political prisoner who had a chance of winning the next election. He got up and was only mildly surprised to find his baggage had been brought from the hotel. Somebody had washed and pressed his faded old clothes while he was asleep, too. He felt he would disappoint people by not living up to all this splendor, so he took a shower and shaved.

Breakfast was served. A silent messboy in a starched white jacket brought it in and watched him eat and refused to answer any questions. Johnny lit a cigarette. They gave him exactly enough time to finish it and then two guards came in and scooped up his baggage and told him politely to follow them.

"This is very nice here," Johnny said, trying to draw them out. "Maybe I don't want to leave." That didn't even rate a shrug. "Okay," he said, "I'll go quietly."

He followed them down corridors and up steps and came into an office where a brisk-looking guy who was a lieutenant of something requiring a sharp uniform sat behind a polished mahogany desk.

"Ah, Señor Edwards," the lieutenant said in English. "I trust you are well?"

"Wait till I get back to the States and tell them about Havana jails," Johnny said. "You'll have a made-in-America crime wave."

"We hope there will be no rush. Not all our guests are treated as you have been. But I would like to establish very clearly that we have treated you well. You admit that?"

"Sure. The only complaint I have about your jails is you don't have enough people in them. Especially murderers. I'm interested in one particular murderer who—"

"You need not tell me," the lieutenant said, patting a thin folder on the desk. "I have all the facts here."

"Not quite all the facts. Not the fact of who killed Tony Mendoza."

"You must let us handle these police matters."

"Be honest, now," Johnny said. "Do you think you'll catch the guy?"

"Who knows, señor?"

"Yeah. That's what I was afraid of."

The lieutenant moved restlessly and said, "A moment ago you said, 'Wait till I get back to the States.' If you will pardon my use of American slang, señor, I would like to reply that I can hardly wait."

"That's too bad. I like it here."

"You might not like our other jails."

"That's interesting," Johnny said. "You must have me charged with something."

"Not yet, Señor Edwards. But last night you were armed with a revolver which, of course, you have no right to carry. We could put you in jail for a year and then deport you."

"Lieutenant, you're losing your reputation for hospitality."

"We would be even less hospitable if we reserved a place for you in the morgue, señor. And the reports I have received show that you almost went there last night."

"All right," Johnny said. "I admit I was in a crazy mood. But I'm over it now. Let me stick around Havana and I'll try to stay out of trouble."

"I do not believe you could. And it is bad, both for the tourist trade and for the good-neighbor policy, to permit the sons of wealthy American families to be killed in our city."

"You've been busy investigating me, haven't you?"

"Yes, Señor Edwards. And it also appears that you are the nephew of a United States Senator. Sometimes the personal feelings of one of your Senators can upset delicate international affairs. Such as, for example, the quota limits on Cuban sugar. A thousand pardons, but we must act accordingly. A reservation has been made for you on the morning plane to Miami. Adios and good luck."

"In other words, you're throwing me the hell out of your country and saying don't come back."

"In the words of your countrymen," the lieutenant said gravely, "you said a mouthful."

A police car took him to the airport and a couple of detectives loaded him on the Miami plane. He slumped into a seat and fastened the belt and watched land move away beneath the wing and jade-green water slide into its place. A lot of queer things had happened to him in Havana. When you found you had let a guy like Tony be murdered it hit you pretty hard. You started by feeling numb. Then you began trying to shrug off the blame. But every time you tried that you picked up a little more blame, until finally you didn't quite know how you could go on living with yourself. There was one excuse, however, that you could still cling to. A girl had thrown you down and naturally that had wrecked your life and so from then on you had a wonderful way to dodge the blame for everything you did wrong.

Unfortunately the girl turned up and wanted you back. That really fixed things. No more excuses. So you found yourself wandering crazily down a Havana street trying to coax somebody to knock you off. Toward the end of the evening you began to admit what you were doing and then of course you couldn't go through with it.

The question before the house, Edwards, is who can we blame now?

A girl moved into the seat beside him. A girl with pale gold hair and long slender nervous fingers. Guess who.

"I've given you fifteen minutes alone with your thoughts," she said abruptly, "and I'm sure my company can't be any worse."

"Fancy meeting you here," he said. "It's a small airplane, isn't it?"

"How are you, Johnny?"

"I think I'll live."

"That's good. There seemed to be some question about it last night."

"I'll bet I've been handing the Cuerpo de Policia Nacional de la Habana too much credit," he said. "For a while I thought they could give the FBI lessons on how to check up on people. But in this case their check-up system was named Claire Fenway, wasn't it?"

"I wasn't going to let you get killed."

"You must have had a reason. I don't quite see you as a charity worker."

She shrugged, and said casually, "Will you be staying in Miami very long, Johnny?"

You might think that was a change of subject but it wasn't. He took a good look at her face. At a quick glance it was still the same lovely glowing face he remembered from the old days. But when you looked closely you saw there were lines of strain around the mouth, a droop at the corners of the lips.

"Me?" he said. "I don't stay long anywhere. Why?"

"Oh, I just wondered. I established residence in Miami. For my divorce, you know. So I have to stick around."

"Probably all that trouble you went through in Havana wasn't worth it."

"Johnny," she said earnestly, "is anything left at all?"

"You mean, am I still a wide-eyed kid with illusions about the one and only girl? You can't expect that, can you? For that matter, would you even want it?"

"I want some fun out of life," she said, almost fiercely. "I want to go to dances and swim and play golf and visit amusing places. I want to do all the things you've been doing since the war. We're an awful lot alike, Johnny. We could have fun together, couldn't we?"

He stared out of the window. The plane was cruising up the curve of the

Florida Keys and there was a shining necklace of cumulus clouds strung in the air above the bits of land. From a distance those clouds looked bright and glittering and attractive, but they had very little substance and if you flew inside them it would be damp and gray with a lot of air currents to toss you around.

"I don't think we could," he said finally.

"But Johnny, what are you going to do? You can't just sit around and blame yourself because that man was killed in Havana."

"That's right, I can't. And furthermore I don't have to. Did you ever happen to realize there's a guy involved in this business who's more to blame than I?"

"Of course. The man who shot your friend."

"Yeah. The guy who walked up to a complete stranger, cut him down and ran. I think about him a lot."

"You ought to try to forget the whole thing."

"Well, I can't. And you know what? The more I think about the guy who killed Tony the less I'm forced to think about myself."

"Johnny, why don't you see a psychologist? In thinking about the murderer aren't you just looking for a way to throw the blame on somebody else? Maybe a psychologist could show you an easier way out."

"I don't want an easier way out. I like this one."

"But don't you see the danger in it? Merely thinking about the man won't be enough. The next step will be feeling you have to do something about it."

He said softly, "I already took that next step."

"You can't!" she cried. "You'll end up wanting to hunt him down and kill him!"

He closed his eyes for a moment. Words could produce queer results. You found the right words and it was like turning the key in a fire alarm box. All of a sudden bells started to clang and sirens began howling. You wanted to chase a fire. You wanted to kill a man. You didn't have to argue whether it was right or wrong. All you needed to know was that you wanted it badly and that you had never wanted anything else badly in your life. It was quite a thing to want something that way. It made you feel alive.

"You know," he said, "I think you're right."

She stared at him. "It doesn't seem to worry you."

"I never felt less worried in my life."

"It's ridiculous! You don't know who he is and you haven't a single real clue and you can't even go back to Havana to look for any."

"That's going to make it interesting."

"It would take all your time! You'd have to make a career of it! You couldn't do anything else! You—"

"Just think," he said, "after all these years, Johnny Edwards has a career. He's got a goal."

"You won't stick to it. You've never stuck to any idea very long."

"I don't really want to talk about it."

"But—"

"Let it go, will you?"

She stopped talking and stared angrily ahead. Finally she got out a piece of paper and a pencil and scribbled something on it. "I'm going back to my seat," she said. "After you get this wild idea out of your head, maybe you'd like to give me a call. Here's my address and phone number." She dropped the scrap of paper in his lap and left.

He looked at it for a moment, smiling. Then he pulled out his wallet and removed the other scraps of paper and put them all together and tore them into bits. He was starting a different kind of collection now. He shoved his hands into a coat pocket and felt the new collection. There were three items in it. They were small and cylindrical and hollow, and they had been flipped onto a cellar floor in Havana by a .45 automatic.

CHAPTER SIX

He lounged on a bench overlooking Havana's Plaza de la Fraternidad, a razor-lean young man in a loose white suit and tight shoulder holster. He didn't think very highly of shoulder holsters, especially when worn under a shirt. If he ever needed the gun fast it wasn't likely that people would watch him do a strip-tease reaching for it. Still, it didn't seem right to go after a murderer equipped with nothing more deadly than a scowl.

It was a nice day in Havana. The steam-room weather of hurricane season was over and palms were doing a rumba in the busy trade wind. The sunlight had just the right amount of warmth, like a shot of good Bacardi. He relaxed and tried to look every inch the American tourist. Apparently he succeeded. Twice he had to chase away lottery ticket peddlers and once he turned down a guide who claimed to know some of the best places in Havana and all the worst. Nobody came along, though, to tell him who had knocked off Tony Mendoza.

He didn't expect anybody to hand him news on purpose, but he hoped someone would give him a lead without meaning to. It worked like this. You ran a blind ad in a couple of Havana papers offering a reward for any information about the death of one Antonio Mendoza five months ago.

You gave a post office box number. On the face of it, how stupid could you get? It was like walking into a crooked casino and asking the roulette wheel croupier to please tramp down on his pedal so your number could hit.

But the trick was, when you acted very stupidly, people began worrying about you. Finally one of them wrote to your box number saying he would meet you in the Plaza de la Fraternidad on such-and-such a date to discuss this most interesting subject. And would the señor please, since he was unknown to the writer, sit on a bench with his left shoelace untied so that he could be identified and approached with confidence? You had stupidly asked in public for information about a murder so naturally you would be stupid enough to wait on a bench with your left shoelace untied. Somebody would saunter by and study you and whoever had killed Tony could decide how best to get rid of some of the stupidity in the world.

He crossed his legs casually and made sure that his left shoelace was firmly tied. So far, he hadn't been able to spot any stroller who seemed unusually interested in shoelaces.

As he lounged in the sunlight, watching people through half-closed eyes, something began nagging at his attention. At first he couldn't tell what it was. He concentrated on it, finally found the answer. Somebody was paying too much attention to him.

He shifted uneasily on the bench. Of course there had always been the chance that he might be recognized, shoelace or no shoelace. Five months ago, in offering six hundred bucks for the name of the murderer, he had been about as public as a street-corner revival meeting. A lot of people had taken a good long look at him and maybe some of them had belonged to the smuggling gang. They would remember that he was tall and lean, that he had brown hair and gray eyes and a face that ordinarily wouldn't hold your attention very long unless you were shaving it. Those angles of his appearance hadn't changed, but he had counted on other changes fooling people.

Last time, for example, he hadn't been wearing good clothes. In his three days in Havana he hadn't eaten or slept much. Now he was cool, clean, rested. He wore a white linen suit and white suede shoes and one of those Panama hats they weave under water and give away for ninety bucks. A clever disguise, Edwards. Too bad it hadn't worked.

He began checking everybody in sight to find out who was watching him. Maybe he had been making a mistake up to now. Maybe he had been looking only for guys with bulges in their hip pockets. Let's look for bent old women and ragged kids chewing gum and—

That girl. The one who had just sauntered by. Had she passed him once or twice before? Had she peered at him every time? She was an American girl. Nice long legs, trim flanks that rippled instead of jiggled as she walked, slim waist, shiny brown sun-streaked hair with a wave at the end—all the standard equipment. To be fair, a lot of deluxe equipment, too. You found the type all over the country. Guaranteed to dance well, keep the conversation going, be a good sport, let you make a little polite love under the right conditions. Step right up and order yours, gents. Only one to a customer. They last a lifetime... not like the girl he had once planned to marry.

She was coming back now, around the park. As she approached he looked squarely at her for the first time. That was a mistake. He had met her before, and she had been wearing grooves in the pavement trying to meet him again just by accident. When she spotted the flicker of recognition on his face she smiled gaily and made a bargain-counter beeline for him.

"I do know you, don't I!" she cried happily. "I'm Ellen McCarter. We met last week in Miami."

Maybe a brush-off would work. "Sorry," he said. "Afraid I don't remember."

"Oh, dear. And I did try so to make an impression."

"It must have been another guy. I'm sure he was impressed."

"This has never happened to me before," she said firmly, "and it isn't going to happen now. Your name is John Edwards. You're the new trainee of the Miami Border Patrol Sector."

In a minute she'd be checking his fingerprints. "I remember that much too," he said, "but—"

"I met you about three-thirty Thursday afternoon a week ago in the office of Chief Patrol Inspector Ed Brian. He introduced us. My brother is Tim McCarter, Senior Patrol Inspector over in Fort Myers. I'm a rather nice girl and don't go around picking up strange men."

He gave up. Next thing she'd be handing him letters of recommendation from her minister. "Oh yes," he said. "Now I remember. I must have had something else on my mind that day I met you."

She tilted her head on one side and studied him. "You have something else on your mind now, don't you? Is she pretty? Are you meeting her here?"

"I never have just one woman at a time on my mind," he said coldly. "I always think in terms of harems."

"I'm sorry," she said. "It was rude of me to say that. And for all I know, you're here on orders and I'm sticking my snub nose into Border Patrol business. Shall I run along?"

He almost took her up on the hint about Border Patrol business. In a way his business did concern the Border Patrol, although the Border Patrol didn't know it. But if he used that excuse it might get back to the Chief Patrol Inspector and then he'd have some explaining to do.

"I'm just playing tourist," he said. "Had a few days off and decided to see Havana."

"Wonderful!" she said, as if that made them soul mates. "I've been taking a week off. I flew here on Monday with Jean Atkins—she's my best friend in Fort Myers—and we've been doing the town. Of course," she said, frowning, "Jean would have to go and meet a man last night and desert me. So you see, when I spotted you I was desperate. I told myself, I, too, can meet a man. And I did, didn't I?"

"I'm not sure you got a bargain."

"I'll take a chance. Anybody who gets into the Border Patrol is a pretty good risk. Let's sit down, shall we? I've worn my high-heeled shoes down to loafers, parading by hoping you'd toss me a kind word."

He sat down. If you could train this girl to be a detective, no eligible criminal would be safe.

"Did you know," she said, "that you're already a marked man in the Border Patrol? You only took your Civil Service exam four months ago. You got your appointment two weeks later. You went through Training School at El Paso with terrific grades. You've only been a trainee in Miami a month and they're already talking of sending you out to a unit."

"How do you know all this?"

"Oh, we're a pretty close family. Everybody hears about everybody else. Besides, I was especially interested because Tim—my brother, you know—hasn't had a partner in Fort Myers for months, and I've been wondering who we'd get. Anyway, what I wondered was how you did all this so fast."

"I didn't know it was fast."

"You didn't know there's quite a waiting list? That it can take months and months to get an appointment? There's a general impression around that you're quite a guy."

Yeah, he thought, I'm quite a guy, and by sheer coincidence my uncle is a United States Senator. He could hear his uncle's voice now. *What's all this nonsense about the Border Patrol? Why don't you settle down and take that job, with your father?* Then later. *All right. ALL RIGHT. But don't come whining to me if they throw you out of their school.* Much, much later. *All right, so you passed at the top. Now what do you want. Miami? Hell, boy, do you think this government's run just for your benefit?* A little later, and wearily. *All right, they'll send you to Miami. I could have swung two appointments to Federal District Court for the trouble you've caused me.*

"Have you been hearing a word I said?" the girl asked. "I get the queerest feeling that something is bothering you."

He ought to tell her it was only a murder. You'll have to pardon me, he might add, if I don't show the proper school spirit about the Border Patrol. I'm just hitching a ride with the boys. It turns out that you need a license to play tag across frontiers with a murderer. Since this particular killer is in the alien smuggling racket, it seemed like a good idea to move heaven and earth and even a Federal Bureau to get in the Border Patrol. So honest, honey, nothing else is bothering me, and let's sit here talking for hours, shall we?

He said abruptly, "Let me give you a ring sometime."

It might have been more diplomatic to have slapped her. She jumped up looking like a kicked puppy. "I'm very sorry," she said. "That's what a girl deserves for acting desperate, isn't it? I still think you're probably a nice person. But I've decided I'm not a very nice girl." She gave him a weak smile and walked away.

No doubt he had spoiled her whole day for her. She would go back to her hotel room and throw herself on the bed and weep and decide that he was a nasty brute. After all, she had been engaged in the important project of getting a date for the evening and what right did a man have to interfere?

Yeah, you're a beast, Edwards. You and your dull old murder. It's making you coarse. You start by slapping girls around and pretty soon you'll be putting the slug on children and—

Speaking of children, what was going on?

He stared down at the black-haired Cuban kid kneeling in front of him and busily getting an assortment of rags and polishes from his shoe shine box.

"Hey," Johnny said. "What do you think you're doing?"

There was a flash of bright black eyes and white teeth.

"Shine, señor," the kid said, flourishing a rag.

"I don't want a shine. Beat it."

The kid gave him some double-talk in Spanish. That was an old act. Chatter at the tourist in a foreign language until the sucker gives up. This was really getting to be his day. He ought to put up a turnstile and charge admission. He threw some sharp Spanish at the kid and won a resentful stare.

"Besides," Johnny added, "these are white shoes."

The kid pulled out a bottle containing a very small amount of gray fluid and waved it triumphantly and went into a sales talk.

Johnny dug into his pocket and flipped the kid ten centavos and said, "All right. Now beat it."

The kid shrugged, pocketed the money, gave the shoes a farewell pat and began gathering his things.

Johnny caught his breath. Was it imagination, or had he really felt a slight tug at his left shoelace? He leaned slowly forward, glanced down. His left shoelace was untied. He watched the kid reach for a can of black polish. He moved his right foot quickly, pinned the small groping hand to the pavement. He didn't put much weight on it—yet.

"Don't move it," he said softly. "You could lose a hand that way."

The kid looked up. Black eyes glittered. Let's not be sentimental, Edwards. This could get you a knife in the ankle. "Who told you to do it?" Johnny said. The kid tensed a little. Johnny increased the pressure. "Don't move," he said again. He reached into his inside coat pocket, slid out his wallet, eased a ten-dollar bill from it. He crumpled the bill and let it drop and put his other foot on it. "A smart kid would speak up and get me to lift both feet," he said gently.

There was a different glitter in the eyes now. "I do not know him," the kid whispered. "He said it was for a joke. How many pesos are under your foot, señor?"

"More than you see in a week. Describe this man who liked to joke."

The kid frowned slightly. "It... it is difficult, señor. This man, no, I do not think he is Cuban. Or of the United States. He is small. The face is thin. He wears a dirty white suit. But for the peso I would pass him on the street and not see him. How many pesos did you say?"

Could a kid make that up? It wasn't likely. He'd be more apt to invent a guy who was five feet seven and one-half inches tall, weighed one twenty-nine, had four gold teeth and a scar on his right cheek. And besides, the description sort of matched that vague description he had picked up, five months ago, of the guy who had apparently been the finger man in the killing.

Johnny lifted his feet.

The crumpled bill flicked out of sight in a grimy hand and the kid swept up his stuff and sauntered off.

The Havana cops, Johnny thought, undoubtedly had his best interests at heart in throwing him out of the country. If he could keep on improving his mind he might work up eventually to be a moron. He had let that girl come up to him and talk about the Border Patrol in a voice that anyone snooping around could hear. The boys in the smuggling gang wanted to find out who was offering a reward for information about the death of Antonio Mendoza. They had tried to trick him into sitting stupidly in the Plaza with his left shoelace untied, so that they could identify him without giving themselves away. He hadn't done that, but he had identified himself by talking stupidly out loud about the Border Patrol.

The guy who spotted him may have worked things out like this: *The señor was supposed to sit on a bench with his left shoelace untied. Since the señor did not do this, perhaps he is not quite as stupid as we thought. Perhaps he has been trying to set a trap for us. Let us therefore show the señor that we know all about his trap by hiring a boy to untie his left shoelace. That should upset the señor very greatly. It should make the señor realize that he is dealing with very clever and dangerous people, and that the safest thing he can do is forget the unfortunate death of Antonio Mendoza and return with great speed to the United States.*

Of course he hadn't been expected to catch the Cuban kid at work. He was making real progress. He was getting part of this racket pinned onto a guy nobody could describe. The way he was going, give him time and maybe he could prove there hadn't even been a murder.

He wondered whether the man you couldn't describe was still around, watching. It was possible that he had found something very interesting to do, such as trailing an American girl along the Prado. He wouldn't know that the girl had merely been looking for a date; he might figure she was playing detective. It began to look as if, one way or another, Ellen McCarter wasn't going to be lonely during the rest of her visit to Havana.

Johnny got up and walked rapidly across the park and down the Prado. As he walked he kept looking for men who fitted the description the Cuban kid had given. It wasn't very profitable.

He walked for block after block and finally spotted the girl. She was looking at hats in a shop window. When things went wrong in a girl's life there were always hats.

He paused beside her and said, "I like that second one from the right, with the broad brim."

Her head jerked around toward him. She blinked.

"In case you don't remember," he said, "the name is Johnny Edwards. We met about three-thirty Thursday afternoon a week ago in the office of Chief Patrol Inspector Ed Brian in Miami. Eight days later, which happens to be today, we had an unforgettable ten minutes in the Plaza de la Fraternidad in Havana, which happens to be here. I was going to give you a ring, remember? But you haven't been answering your phone."

It would be interesting to see what kind of act she put on. The average girl would make a real production job of it. First ice the guy thoroughly—

She said happily, "I don't know when a nicer thing has happened to me."

This girl was either very naïve or a fast operator. Either way, she was the kind you could only handle safely at long range. That was great. Here he was weaving in for a clinch. "You'd make me feel better if you tried on a few sneers for size."

"I thought of that," she said, "but then I realized how awful it would be if in the middle of a sneer I broke into a delighted smile."

"When you get a chance like this you ought to make the guy grovel. How soon are you going to ask why I suddenly chased after you?"

She studied his face. There were a lot of conventional ways in which girls looked at men. There was the straightforward, let's-be-pals way. The timid, I'm-so-little-and-you're-so-big way. The over-the-shoulder glance, in either the come-on or ooh-you-scare-me versions. Hadn't she learned any of them? It was upsetting to have a girl just plain look at you.

She said finally, "I don't think I'll ask why you chased after me until I can figure out an answer I'd believe."

"I suddenly realized you're a mighty attractive girl."

"I like that answer the best but I believe it the least. Do you have any others?"

"I was sorry I acted rudely."

"Is it all right if I call you Johnny? That's not a bad answer, except that you weren't rude and aren't sorry."

"I was trying to keep this from you," he said, "but somebody came by right after you left and said you were going to inherit a million dollars."

"That's one I didn't think of. Shall we let it go at that? Besides, it gives me the right to invite you to lunch."

"Sorry. I'm inviting you."

She said quite firmly, "Either I buy the lunch or I'll have to refuse your invitation."

A girl like this could keep you pretty badly off balance. "You'll be sorry," he said, "when I order filet mignon."

"And you'll be surprised when what you get is plain old arroz con polio. At my little restaurant they never heard of filet mignon."

Women could find the most delightfully inexpensive places to eat when they were paying. During the meal she chattered happily about Fort Myers and the Border Patrol and her brother, all of which were wonderful. Her brother was much older than she was. When their parents died she was only five and her brother had insisted on raising her. Wasn't that wonderful of him? He had been in the Border Patrol (wasn't it a wonderful organization?) since shortly after it was started in 1924. They had been living in Fort Myers on the lower west coast of Florida for the past ten years. Had he ever stopped in Fort Myers and what did he think of it?

"I thought it was wonderful," he said.

"I hope you choke on a chicken bone," she said cheerfully. "You're poking fun at me. I do use that word wonderful a lot, don't I?"

"Oh, some. Look, I've enjoyed lunch with your brother very much. How about letting me have dessert with you? Do you ever talk about yourself?"

"Ordinarily, not more than once a sentence. But I thought, just for fun, I'd wait and see if I could make you talk about yourself first. You haven't told me a thing."

He thought about that. If he gave her the story of his life it would go like this:

I was in college when World War II came along, see? I went into it believing in the Ten Commandments, the Four Freedoms and the One and Only Girl. You know what I believe in now? I believe that a tommy gun is better than a bayonet. What does a tommy gunner do with himself between wars? Well, if your family has money, like mine, and handles you with kid gloves, like mine, you drift around the country picking up knowledge. For instance, did you know that Merion Golf Club's East Course is no place for a guy with a wild slice? Did you know that after a sailfish hits the bait you need to give him slack line for about ten seconds? Did you know that no two bartenders make a whisky sour the same way? Did you know it almost never discourages a girl to learn I may inherit a lot of money some day? I got quite an education bumming around the country, didn't I?

While I was bumming around, people kept telling me I needed a goal in life. They said I'd stop being bored and footloose if I could find something I wanted very badly and couldn't get easily. You know what? They were right. I got a nice little goal now. I want to track down a guy and kill him. Greatest little cure for boredom ever invented....

The girl said, "You've gone into one of your trances again. if I snap my fingers do you come out of it?"

"I was just trying to boil down the story of my life for you. It came out

awfully small. I had a year in college and the war came along and I put in
five years in the Army and afterward I just fooled around until I managed
to get in the Border Patrol."

"Didn't you finish college after the war?"

"Seemed like too much trouble."

"You should have finished," she said earnestly. "You—no, I haven't any
right to say that. Kick me when I start to preach, will you? Because I certainly haven't done much with my life, so far. Here I am twenty-three and
all I've done is go to school and keep house for Tim and fool around with
a little orange grove. I'm trying to bring back an old grove by top-working
the trees over to Temples. Do you know anything about oranges?"

"I often find a slice in an Old-fashioned."

"You won't be angry if I say something?"

"No. What?"

She looked at him solemnly and said, "You could stand a little top-working too."

This was getting to be quite a date. You pick up a girl in whom you have
absolutely no interest, except that you want to keep her out of trouble, and
you have to put on a show of liking her a lot and so that gives her a license
to reform you.

"What I mean is you don't seem to be happy about anything."

"I'm happy about meeting you."

"Good. How soon do you throw caution to the winds and give me a faint
smile?"

He couldn't help grinning. "Stand back," he said. "This is it."

"Not bad for an amateur. Can you remember how you did it?"

"I'll have to practice in front of a mirror," he said. "Look. I have some
errands to do this afternoon. But how about tonight? I'll put on my patent-
leather hair and a knowing leer and take you to a few rumba joints."

She thought that would be wonderful, and he arranged to pick her up at
six. He took her back to her hotel, asking about her plans for the afternoon. She was going shopping. It sounded safe enough. Nobody was likely to bother her in broad daylight unless she wandered off the tourist beat.
He dropped a few casual hints about the trouble a girl without an escort
could get into if she roamed around carelessly. She said it was wonderful
of him to worry about her. He would have to watch that stuff. Some girls
became grateful much too fast. According to the books, back in ancient
times you had to rescue women from dragons before they felt they had a
first mortgage on you. There must have been a surplus of men in those
days. In modem times a mouse would do.

CHAPTER SEVEN

He went outside and got a cab. Just in case anybody was tailing him he had the cabbie do some broken-field driving. When they reached the Malecon he paid off the cab, cut across the boulevard and hailed another cab going in the opposite direction. He told the driver to head for the building that housed the U. S. Embassy and Consulate, and to park down the avenue from it.

Now that his trap had failed he didn't have much to work on. But there was one clue. According to the Cuban woman, Tony had gone to the Consulate almost every day hoping for news about his immigration permit. Finally, one day, Tony returned looking very excited. He wouldn't tell the woman what had happened, except that he had met a man and hoped to enter the United States very soon. That sounded like Tony's first contact with the smuggling gang.

What Tony had stumbled into was no ten-centavo racket. Only a well-organized gang that was in the business for keeps would have gone to so much trouble to knock off an alien who might have talked. They must be handling aliens in wholesale lots, and a good place to find them in wholesale lots was the Consulate. If he could get a line on who was in the gang and how it operated, maybe he could pick up the trail of the American killer. He didn't figure he would ever get enough evidence to send the guy to jail. All he wanted was enough to send him to the morgue.

The taxi halted down the avenue from the Embassy-Consulate building. Johnny told the driver he just wanted to sit there and watch for a friend. The driver accepted the explanation and a five-peso note, pulled his hat down politely over his eyes and took a siesta. Johnny settled into a corner of the back seat and began watching the steps leading up into the gray building.

In the Border Patrol they taught you how to spot aliens. There were a lot of different ways but in this case you had to go by appearance and actions. You looked for men in coats that were too heavy for Havana's climate, and for women who didn't know how to use make-up and wore faded and much-washed dresses. On that basis quite a few of the people entering and leaving the building could be classed as aliens, but you could rule out the ones who looked brisk and confident. That left people who seemed to be very unsure of themselves. When they entered the building they looked nervous and humble. They moved out of other people's way. They paused to straighten clothing and to brush off specks.

He sat for two hours watching them. At the end of that time he was ready to swear it was possible to go in business as a recruiter right outside the building. Not on the basis of a two-hour study, of course. But if you watched day after day you ought to begin recognizing people who came back time and again and who always had the same nervous, timid manner. Then you would sidle up and say—

Unfortunately, nobody was sidling up to anybody. No one was even watching. He had a nice theory but nobody was using it. He roused the driver and had the man drop him a few blocks away from the building. Then he walked back. He was going to visit the local intelligence unit of the Immigration and Naturalization Service. That sounded impressive, but what the unit consisted of at this moment was one Senior Patrol Inspector of the Border Patrol. The unit must give Havana smugglers a lot of sleepless nights.

He found the office on the second floor of the Consulate, put on an eager-beaver expression and walked in. A nice-looking guy in civvies was behind the desk. "My name is Edwards," Johnny said, giving him a shy grin. "I'm a new trainee over in Miami." He dug out his credentials and slid them across the desk.

The other man glanced at the credentials, got up. "Glad to meet you, Edwards," he said, shaking hands. "I'm Harmon. Nobody told me you were coming."

"I wasn't sent over. Just had a couple days off and wanted to see Havana and couldn't resist dropping in to say hello. Hope you don't mind?"

"Glad you did. Sit down. How do you like the outfit?"

Johnny sat down. The problem was to get Harmon talking about the Border Patrol and then ease the conversation around to the present setup in Havana. Maybe a good way to do that was to take the role of a wide-eyed recruit and coax Harmon to play the part of an old campaigner. Harmon didn't look like a very old campaigner but that didn't matter. In any line of work men felt like old campaigners if they had ten days on the new guy. And all old campaigners loved to talk.

"Gee, it's a wonderful outfit to be in," Johnny said. "I never thought I'd make it." That was the right touch, so far. Harmon was nodding indulgently. "They almost scared the life out of me at Training School with all those courses. It was good stuff, though."

"Yeah, that school's a good idea," Harmon said.

"I figure what a guy learns out there will come in mighty handy later on."

Harmon grinned. "You're telling me," he said. "Getting it in school's a lot better than learning it the hard way. Why, back when I came in—"

We're off, Johnny thought. He sat on the edge of his chair and listened, keeping the eager look on his face and tossing in admiring comments at the right moments. Under all this attention Harmon became a very old campaigner indeed. You got the impression he had personally organized the Border Patrol back in 1924.

Johnny worked hard not to yawn. He had heard all this stuff dozens of times. The Border Patrol was a small-time outfit. It had a few men and little money. Nobody paid much attention to it, except maybe aliens. Whenever the Border Patrol cracked a good case, somebody else usually grabbed the credit: the FBI or state troopers or local cops. The outfit was so young it didn't have many traditions and had to work hard on the ones it had. No wonder a guy like Harmon talked his head off when he got a chance; nobody would listen to this Border Patrol stuff except a member of the outfit.

Harmon finished with the glorious old days and reached the drab present. This was the moment to switch him onto the proper track. "Yeah," Johnny said sadly, "I guess I got in too late. Looks like nothing happens nowadays. Just a matter of picking up guys who jump ship and rounding up people who overstay their visitors' permits and—"

"Wait a minute," Harmon said. "Maybe they never told you there are a hundred thousand aliens in Cuba trying to get into the States."

"So they want visas. That isn't our business."

"All right, they want visas but they aren't getting visas. Maybe they have criminal records, or were tied up with the Reds or Nazis. Maybe they aren't healthy. Maybe they have no money and nobody in the States to put it up for them. Or maybe there just isn't room for them on their nation's quota. They still want in, visa or no visa. Don't they teach you kids that in Training School or over in Miami?"

"Well, yes, but everybody knows they don't have a prayer of sneaking in. Oh, maybe one or two will stow away on a ship. Or a charter boat from the Keys will pick up a couple. But—"

"In case you never looked at the figures our sector picked up about six thousand aliens last year."

"But what I mean," Johnny said, "is none of that is organized. You couldn't call it big-time crime."

"Oh, you couldn't, huh?" Harmon said irritably. "I don't know why you kids always get the idea you know all the answers. It just happens I sent a report to Ed Brian about that last night. You'll be hearing about it when you get back. And it just happens that some gang or other is getting the racket damn well organized."

He got up and began striding up and down the room, talking. There was hell to pay. It had sneaked up on him slowly. First there was the business of the aliens who were regular visitors to the Consulate downstairs. The clerks got to know them. And so, when some of the regulars stopped showing up, the clerks noticed it. What had happened to them, huh? They didn't have U. S. visas. They couldn't get work permits in Cuba. If you checked at their addresses they were gone. Vanished. Dozens of them.

And take the Chinese. Part of the job was to watch for bunches of Chinese who came in on freighters from the Orient. They couldn't work in Cuba, either. Chances were ten to one that some Chinese beneficial society in New York or Chicago or Frisco had put up the dough and was hoping to run them into the country. Three months ago a bunch of twenty-four arrived. By last week they had vanished.

Johnny said, "Got any idea who's behind it?"

"An idea!" Harmon cried. "How would I have an idea? I got nothing to work with. No men. No money to speak of. All I can do is hire a lousy stool pigeon named Rankosci and buy a few dollars' worth of news from him every week. Mighty little news I get for the money, too. So—" He stopped suddenly, whirled toward the door. "Who told you to come in?" he shouted.

Johnny swung around. He hadn't heard a sound, but a third man had entered the room. He stood just inside a closed door: a thin little guy in dirty white clothes. He had pale, mild eyes and bleached hair. The kind of guy you'd never look at twice.

"I am sorry," the man said humbly. "I had some information for you, Inspector. As I came near the door I heard you call my name and thought you saw me."

"I can't see through the door," Harmon growled. "And you know perfectly well nobody ever hears you coming."

The man shrugged. "Perhaps that is fortunate," he said. "If people noticed me I would never learn anything."

"Just remember not to learn anything around here."

Johnny got up. "I better go," he said. "Looks as if you have business."

"Stick around," Harmon said. "They'll send you over here some day to see how we operate. Might as well pick it up now. This is the man I was telling you about. Works for us—some. Rankosci, this is one of our new men, Edwards."

Rankosci bowed and said, "I am honored to meet Inspector Edwards."

"That's an unusual name of yours," Johnny said. "How do you spell it?"

The man smiled faintly. "On your records," he said, "it is spelled G-e-o-r-g R-a-n-c-o-s-c-i."

"Polish?" Johnny asked. "Rumanian?"

"Well, yes and no."

"Don't be shy," Harmon told the man. "Give him the spiel."

Rankosci said, politely, "It is a large world with many fine countries in it. I like to feel that I belong to a number of fine countries."

Harmon chuckled. "It works like this, Edwards. Our pal here changes his country depending on who he's talking to. He can be a Pole or Russian or Czech or Hungarian or most of the languages I've ever heard of. He switches his name around to match. If he ever met an American Indian I bet his name would be Rancocas and he could talk Ojibway."

"That's interesting," Johnny said. "But what does it say on your Cuban visitor's permit?"

"Please," Rankosci said. "That is a personal question."

"Yeah, but don't the Havana cops ever ask it?"

"They do not bother me," Rankosci said. "I do not cause them trouble and sometimes I am quite useful."

Harmon said, "You won't get anywhere pumping him. All right, Rankosci, sit down and spill your news."

Rankosci pulled up a chair and sat down. "Do you have a cigarette?" he asked.

Johnny slid a pack across a corner of the desk to him. Rankosci's thin yellow fingers fluttered over the cigarettes and carefully extracted one. For some reason that seemed to reduce the number of cigarettes amazingly. Johnny shook his head admiringly, wondering how Rankosci had done it. This was quite a guy. You wouldn't think it to look at him. In fact if you didn't know his background you wouldn't get around to looking at him.

"This is my news," Rankosci said. "Last night a seaman from a freighter was drinking with friends in a café and boasted that he was going to jump ship when they dock in Miami next week and go to live with a cousin in Detroit. He is a Czech national."

Harmon began asking questions and making notes. Johnny didn't pay much attention. He was trying to identify a vague feeling of uneasiness that was creeping over him. He wondered if he could have seen Rankosci before. That idea seemed to fit in with the uneasy feeling. A guy nobody noticed...

"Well, thanks," Harmon said finally. "Anything else stirring?"

"Things," Rankosci said, "are very quiet."

"Yeah. Too quiet. What about those Chinese?"

Rankosci puffed out a small cloud of smoke and seemed to vanish in it. "Chinese?" he said, as if the word was a new one.

"Don't play dumb with me. What happened to those twenty-four Chinese who vanished?"

"Perhaps they have been hired for work outside Havana in the sugar cane fields."

"Try again," Harmon said irritably. "They all had visitors' permits. They can't take jobs here."

"Perhaps," Rankosci said, "they have—"

He stopped suddenly. There was a moment of silence.

That was queer, Johnny thought. Rankosci had started to say something and then changed his mind. Or had he? The guy wasn't the type to talk first and think later. And nothing had happened to distract him. Nobody had moved or spoken or... wait a minute. Somebody *had* moved. A guy named Johnny Edwards had crossed his left leg over his right. Johnny looked down. A few hours ago his left foot had been important to a man nobody noticed. He swung the foot gently, watching Rankosci. Was it imagination, or did the man's pale eyes glance at the moving foot? Johnny began sweating a little.

Rankosci said, "I was thinking that perhaps they have gone back to the Orient."

"Sure," Harmon said. "They got homesick. Now look. Has one of the local gangs organized this racket?"

"I do not think they would do that."

"Every other racket in town is organized. Why not aliens?"

Rankosci said, "When a Cuban must leave this country quickly, because of some local disagreement, where does he wish to go? To the United States. He does not want to find himself in trouble when he arrives. So, he does not engage in activities which would make him unwelcome in the United States."

"Yeah, I know they used to figure that way. But I wonder if they still do."

Rankosci got up. "I will try to find out," he said. "Now if you would be kind enough to look out of the window and see if the back street is clear...."

Harmon went to the window. "There's a Cuban lounging in a doorway across the street."

"I thought there would be," Rankosci said. "People are always interested in who enters or leaves the United States Embassy and Consulate by the back way. However, I do not think he will see me." He bowed politely, opened the door eight inches and slipped out.

"What a character," Harmon said. "I want to see how he works this. Usually he won't come in here at all. I meet him outside, at night. Let's watch this, huh?"

Johnny joined him at the window and they stared down at the quiet back street. On the other side, a Cuban with lank black hair was draped in a doorway like wash on the line. As they watched, a girl with side-wheeling hips came down the sidewalk. She was on the Cuban's side of the street, and as she came toward him the limp figure in the doorway began to look more starched. The Cuban turned his head slowly to watch her pass. Apparently Rankosci had been waiting for something like that. Suddenly there he was on the near side of the street, drifting along going nowhere and doing nothing. A guy nobody noticed. By the time the girl reached one end of the street, Rankosci reached the other. Each turned a corner and vanished at the same moment.

"Nice timing, wasn't it?" Harmon said.

Johnny nodded. He wondered if there had been nice timing in the fact that he had met Rankosci in the office. He hadn't seen anybody tailing him but that didn't prove much. If Rankosci had been the guy in the Plaza de la Fraternidad and had tailed him ever since and finally saw him go into the Embassy and enter Harmon's office, Rankosci might have decided it was a good moment to pay Harmon an official visit. And if all that were true, Rankosci would be waiting out front to pick him up again.

He looked at his watch and said, "I'd better run along. Thanks for letting me sit in on that."

"Don't mention it, Edwards. See you in Miami some time. Pick up those twenty-four Chinese for me when they check in, will you?"

"Yeah, sure," Johnny said.

He walked back to the desk to get his cigarettes. Then he swore under his breath. He should have known. The pack of cigarettes had vanished as completely as Harmon's twenty-four Chinese. And quite possibly in the same way.

CHAPTER EIGHT

Johnny went downstairs and decided to leave by the rear exit, on the theory that Rankosci had circled the building and was watching out front. Of course there was a Cuban watching the rear exit but Johnny didn't think that had any connection with him. He went out the back way. Across the street the Cuban was scratching his shoulder blades against the doorway and hardly wasted a glance on him.

He walked rapidly down back streets for a few blocks and finally circled up to the main avenue and sauntered back toward the Embassy. There was no sign of Rankosci. He passed the Embassy and went on for another block. Still no sale. Of course Rankosci might be thinking circles around him. He turned off the main street and walked on two more blocks and turned a corner. He stopped, waited ten seconds, stepped quickly back around the corner. Nobody was in sight on his side. Across the street, though, light and shadows from the setting sun dappled a whitewashed wall, and if you looked closely some of the patches of light and shadow began to resemble a dirty white linen suit and a faded Panama hat. Another patch might be a newspaper hiding a man's face. It seemed likely that if you looked over the top of the newspaper the man might begin to resemble Rankosci.

Apparently the thing had worked very simply. Rankosci hadn't risked guessing which exit he would use. Rankosci had gone out the back, walked around to the front, entered the building and waited downstairs to tail him. Very clever. But maybe from now on Rankosci might wish he had been stupid.

Johnny crossed the street, whistling, and sauntered toward Rankosci. The newspaper in front of the man's face quivered. Johnny stopped, ten feet away, leaned against the wall, stared up at the sky and waited. He had an interesting plan. If it worked, he would find out whether or not Rankosci was the man nobody could describe. He would also find out whether or not the quickness of the hand always deceived the eye. In this case the hand would probably be holding a knife.

Ten feet away, the newspaper rustled. Rankosci folded it and put it carefully in his pocket. He gave Johnny a hurt look.

"Don't do that," Johnny said. "You'll make me cry. What I'm doing is bad form, huh?"

Rankosci said in a sorrowful voice, "Havana is a large and evil city. I saw you wandering through the streets and merely wished to make sure you came to no harm. I will see you some other time." He turned and walked slowly away.

Johnny followed at a slight distance, whistling. The thin shoulders ahead of him cringed slightly.

Rankosci stopped and said, "I do not understand."

"Havana is a large and evil city," Johnny said. "I don't want you to come to any harm, either."

"What harm could come to me?"

"I don't know yet. But I'm hoping to find out."

Rankosci licked his lips with a liver-colored tongue, and walked away. Johnny followed a few steps to the rear. If he could stay with the guy a while it ought to get on Rankosci's nerves. Maybe it would scare him to a point where you could make him do some talking. It was queer that Rankosci didn't try to run. He kept on at the same slow, shuffling pace through a residential section and into a business district and then over toward what had been the old walled city. You might think the guy couldn't make himself run.

In half an hour Rankosci stopped again. His face had a yellow glaze, and sweat rolled down it like melting wax. "It is very dangerous for you to follow me," he said.

"For me?" Johnny asked.

"No. For me. I never permit myself to be seen with certain people. Such as the Havana police. Or Inspector Harmon. Or any Americans. In the circles in which I move, it would not be understood."

This was interesting, Johnny thought. He had hoped that would be the case. His whole plan was based on it. "You're a good guy, Rankosci. I'll quit tailing you. We can saunter along arm in arm."

"What for?" Rankosci whispered. "What for?"

"We have things to talk about."

Rankosci wheeled and started off again. He cut through side streets and came out on an avenue lined with cafés and bars and rumba joints. Only a few people were around; this was a tourist section slowly getting ready to make a night of it. Down the avenue a man and girl got out of a taxi and headed for a restaurant. The girl had good legs and Johnny suddenly remembered he had a date with the McCarter girl.

Sorry to stand you up, Ellen, but I got to see a man about a murder.

Rankosci drifted up one side of the avenue and back down the other and then crossed again and drifted up once more. You might think he was looking for somebody. You might—

A whisper floated back to him. It came as Rankosci shuffled past a slick-haired man lounging outside a café. Johnny couldn't catch what was said. He walked by the lounger and stared at him but the man pretended he wasn't there. That was a bad sign.

Rankosci turned off the avenue. That brought them into an old section of town where houses crowded close on each side and sometimes pushed you off the sidewalk into the street. You could smell fish and salt air. Not far away a tugboat whistle grunted. It was getting dark. A change was coming over the man he was following. Rankosci was moving more confidently, more alertly. You got the feeling that it might not be smart to crowd him. He was a different person in the dark than in the light.

As they went on Johnny began to realize that they weren't going anywhere now. They were winding in and out of the same section. He didn't like that. They were killing time, maybe until it was really dark. He thought about the slick-haired lounger and glanced around and saw a shadow flicker out of sight a little way back. That made it all very clear. He reached inside his coat and unfastened two shirt buttons and loosened the revolver in his shoulder holster. It was a .38 on a .44 frame. You didn't get much recoil, and at rapid fire he could put four out of five slugs in the kill zones of a silhouette target.

There wasn't any time to waste. He quickened his pace to cut down Rankosci's lead. Up ahead loomed the dark slot of an alley. He leaped forward, grabbed Rankosci, yanked him into the alley and twisted him around with his back to the street. His left hand gripped the guy's shirt collar, tightening it around his throat.

"Now let's talk," he said softly.

The face in front of him was a pale blur. Rankosci made a hissing noise as he breathed. "I still do not know what to talk about."

Johnny tensed. This was the pay-off. This would prove whether it was worthwhile turning the heat on Rankosci. He had tailed the guy all this time for just one reason—to get him so shaky that he would act without thinking when a certain question was thrown at him.

"Talk about this," he snapped. "Who shot Tony Mendoza?"

His left hand tightened on the shirt collar, trying to pick up the tiniest twitch of muscle in Rankosci's body. He wasn't quite alert enough. He missed the twitch. Below his left arm steel made a watery flicker driving in toward his heart.

CHAPTER NINE

Because he was so keyed up everything seemed to happen in slow motion. The knife floated toward his chest. His left arm straightened lazily in an effort to shove Rankosci back. His body began a ponderous turn out and away from the blade. None of his actions meant anything. He was much too late.

Something tapped his chest lightly. His brain waited for pain to flash up through nerves but nothing happened. The message center in his head sent out a high-priority demand for news. His body paid no attention. It had ideas of its own and was busy with them. All his brain could do was sit up in his head and peer out through his eyes and watch his crazy body complete its spin away from the knife. His right arm moved without orders and locked a hand on Rankosci's wrist. His left arm dropped and came up under Rankosci's arm, and his hands played a clever little game of leverage.

All of a sudden there was Rankosci backed up against his chest and the knife was clinking on stone at his feet. Somebody was starting to scream in pain. The wrong guy. It was Rankosci screaming. How unreal could things get? He studied the situation and found that he had an armlock on Rankosci. His left hand and arm were applying the leverage and his right hand was free to grope inside his shirt and find out what went on. His fingers touched a broad band of leather. A thin cut started in the leather over his heart and sliced toward his side and stopped abruptly where the revolver bulged outward. That was a big relief. Now he could stop worrying about falling over dead. There was nothing like quick thinking and fast reactions and a .38-caliber breastplate for avoiding a knife thrust at the heart.

It was certainly nice that he wasn't fast on the draw.

"Shut up," he told Rankosci.

The thin scream choked off into a moan. He relaxed the armlock. In the silence after the moan faded he heard a rustle of feet at the mouth of the alley and saw a shadow flutter across the opening. He jerked back against the wall, shielding himself with Rankosci's body, and yanked out the .38.

"Rankosci," he said, "you're just before losing a pal. Unless you want to call him off."

The man locked against him took a deep breath and let out a gabble of words. It took Johnny a few seconds to realize he couldn't understand what was said. Rankosci was jabbering one of his other languages. He cut off the words with a twist of the armlock. "Talk to him in Spanish," he snapped. "Tell him to stay clear or you'll both get shot."

Rankosci obeyed. The shadow whisked back across the mouth of the alley and footsteps rattled away into the distance. That was better. But of course he still had no idea what Rankosci had told his pal in the strange language. He marched Rankosci to the cross alley and used armlock pressure to force his head out past the corner. Nobody blackjacked it. He stuck his own head out. The street was empty. He ordered Rankosci to head back to the tourist section and kept the armlock on him as they walked. It turned out that they were only two blocks away. The section was in business now, throbbing with rumba music and filled with raw chunks of neon color. As they reached the lighted area Rankosci cringed and began flopping along like a rag doll. It was queer how he hated the light.

"You know what?" Johnny said. "We're going to be pals tonight. It might look odd for old pals to saunter down a street, armlock in armlock. So I'm turning you loose. Maybe you think you can outrun a bullet?"

Rankosci twisted his head around. "Please," he gasped. "This has all been a horrible mistake. I do not even recall what you said that made me do such a terrible thing. Naturally I will not try to run away."

"Good. Now let's find a quiet place to talk."

"I will be glad to apologize most humbly," Rankosci chattered. "Otherwise I do not know what to talk about."

"That's all right. I'm good at making conversation. Which is the best bar up here?"

"Need we go into one of these places? They are very public. As I explained, it can be dangerous for me to be seen in public with an American."

"You walked me through here on your own. Why get scared now?"

"I... I took a chance. You see, I did not know why you were following, and sometimes an acquaintance of mine can be found here, and I thought perhaps he might help me get away. Besides, it was early in the evening and few people were around. Some very unpleasant people may be here now. The tiniest thing can make them suspicious."

"Did you ever hear that expression, into every life some rain must fall? Well, you just got caught in a cloudburst. I like the looks of this café across the street."

"I am sure," Rankosci said, sweating, "you will not shoot me if I refuse to enter."

"I don't have to shoot you. All I have to do is start raising my voice louder and louder like this and talk about the Border Patrol."

He spoke the last two words quite loudly. Apparently he might just as well have shot Rankosci. The man went pale and sagged. Johnny gripped his arm tightly to keep him from falling and led him across the street to a café with the gaudiest neon sign in the block. The place had a dance floor and rumba band and looked like a popular tourist spot. That ought to make it a safe place for a talk. He picked a booth toward the rear, shoved Rankosci into the bench facing away from the door and took the opposite place. He felt more comfortable watching the entrance even though he didn't expect trouble inside the joint.

He ordered two shots of rum and drank his. Rankosci drank in quick sips, peering up and around like a scared jungle animal at a water hole. You couldn't say that the rum brought color back into Rankosci's face because apparently he never had any color, but it did darken his skin one or two shades of gray. Johnny ordered another round.

"Please," Rankosci said. "My limit is one drink."

"Gotta keep me company," Johnny said carelessly. He took out a pack of cigarettes and slid them across the table. Rankosci's yellow fingers fluttered over the pack. Then he stopped and looked embarrassed. "Go ahead," Johnny said. "I want to see if I can figure it out."

Rankosci gave him a wan smile and took a cigarette. "How many did you get?"

"Five," Rankosci said, opening his hand and showing them. "I... I am really very ashamed that I do it. But American cigarettes are expensive and one gets in the habit of stealing them and finds it hard to break."

The second round of drinks came. Johnny drank his quickly and began talking casually about liquor and brands of cigarettes. Across the table Rankosci sipped his drink and peered over the top of the glass with pale wary eyes. The idea was actually very simple: get Rankosci just drunk enough so he couldn't think fast, then start a cross-examination. The right moment for asking questions ought to come when Rankosci started fumbling the cigarette trick. He had to match Rankosci drink for drink to keep him from realizing what was happening.

After the second drink Rankosci did the cigarette trick and palmed seven. He had loosened up and improved his work. After the third drink, though, he only got two cigarettes. The fourth round was the clincher. Rankosci's hand moved so slowly that Johnny could count the three cigarettes being palmed, and even then Rankosci dropped one. Johnny smiled and told the waiter no more drinks for a while and moved over beside Rankosci.

"Now that we're friends," he said gently, "you're going to help me, aren't you?"

The pale eyes squinted to bring him into focus, and Rankosci mumbled, "I do not know how to help you. I do not know anything."

"Okay. Then let's talk about you. You're a recruiter for the gang. But you like to play both ends against the middle and you're also an informer for the Havana cops and for us. All you do is steer prospects to a contact man. You probably aren't supposed to know how the gang operates but I bet you do."

Rankosci was crying a little. "I am just a harmless person who—"

"I'm harmless too when I'm treated nicely. All I want is the guy who killed Mendoza. I'm not interested in breaking up anybody's racket. Now look. You recruited Mendoza. Ordinarily you'd step out of the picture right there. But Mendoza got scared and ran away and the gang told you to find him. They were afraid he'd sing. You found out that Mendoza would only come out of hiding for a certain American friend. You reported that to the gang. So they got an American killer. Exit Mendoza."

"I know nothing of such evil things."

Johnny took a deep breath. There was no use turning on all the heat right now. Rankosci would only lie. The idea was to coax him to tell a little harmless bit of information, and then a bit more.

"Let's be practical," Johnny said. "If I don't get anything at all from you, I'm going to stand up and give a drunken lecture about the glorious Immigration Border Patrol of the Immigration and Naturalization Service of the U. S. Department of Justice. Probably I'll end by presenting you with a medal for faithful service."

Rankosci said, gulping, "I know very little to tell you."

"You're learning fast. A minute ago you didn't know anything. What's the going rate for smuggling in a European alien?"

Rankosci's eyes flickered. He seemed to be studying the question from every angle, like a guy checking on a booby trap. Finally he decided it wouldn't explode in his face and said, "Six hundred dollars."

"How about a Chinese?"

"Fifteen hundred dollars."

"Discrimination, huh? How come?"

"One can dress a European alien in American style. One can teach him to avoid obvious mistakes once he enters your country. But a Chinese is always a Chinese. He is more dangerous to handle until he reaches his final destination. So the charge is higher."

"Why handle them at all, then?"

Rankosci said anxiously, "Please remember I am merely repeating what I hear. A Chinese is dangerous to handle *before* he reaches his destination. But afterward he drops out of sight. He never talks. The European alien is easier to smuggle in but may talk *after* reaching his destination."

"Very interesting," Johnny said. Actually he wasn't at all interested. The questions were merely designed to loosen up Rankosci. "Now let's get down to cases. This guy I'm looking for, the American, is he one of the mob or did they hire him just for the job?"

Rankosci cringed. "I do not know," he whispered.

Johnny studied him carefully. It was hard to tell when Rankosci was lying. It was also hard to tell how much he knew. But it was likely that, even though he worked on the fringes of the racket, he knew a lot more about it than he was supposed to. He ought to know whether or not the American was a member of the gang. And if he didn't know that much he wouldn't be any use. So this was the time to shoot off the fireworks.

"I don't like that answer," Johnny said. "So brace yourself. Here comes your medal." He got to his feet and said in a loud drunken voice, "La-deez and gen-nemen. I wanna make a speech!"

The gourd player in the band missed a couple of beats and three couples stopped dancing to peer at him. He felt a series of frantic tugs at his coat.

He bent and heard Rankosci gasp, "Please do not! I will tell you what I know."

Johnny waved to his audience and called, "Changed my mind." He sat down and said, "Okay. Give."

It took Rankosci a few seconds to get the words up his dry throat and past numb lips. "The... the man you want is in the organization. I believe he operates the American end of it."

"What's his name?"

Rankosci gulped and said miserably, "I do not know."

"What's he look like?"

"I do not know that either."

"I'd better start my speech again, huh?"

"Please," Rankosci cried. "I really do not know! And I did not realize they planned to kill your friend. I was not there. My part was merely to find where he was hidden but all I could learn was that he could only be seen by an American friend who he was expecting and all I did was report that to Carlos and—" He stopped, horrified at what he had blurted out.

"Good old Carlos," Johnny said.

"I—I think I meant to say Manuel."

"Or Jorge or Esteban or Paolo. Look, I'll give Carlos back to you. I'll even take your word that you don't know this American. But I want one more hunk of information out of you. Where's the American end of the racket? Where do they land aliens? Where do I find this guy I'm after?"

"If I tell you, you will not ask any more questions?"

Johnny thought: Let's not be stupid about this, chum. You ought to know you won't get off that easily. However, if you want me to play along....

He said aloud, "That's the last question."

Rankosci gave a sigh. "I understand," he said, "that the aliens are landed at Key West."

"I must be drunk," Johnny said. "Because you know what? I thought you said Key West. Outside of the fact that the only land route out of Key West is the Overseas Highway, which happens to be one hundred and seventy miles long and has toll houses and all kinds of bottlenecks where the Border Patrol can set up check points, Key West is a swell place to land a big bunch of aliens. So let's draw a map and see what place you really said."

He took out a pencil and drew a rough map of Florida on the back cover of the menu. After sketching the outline he lettered in the names of Key West and Miami and Fort Lauderdale and Stuart and Jacksonville going up the east coast and then Tampa and Bradenton and Sarasota and Punta Gorda and Fort Myers and Naples and Everglades coming down the west coast.

"Now," he said, "we're going to play a game. Did you ever hear of a thing called a ouija board?"

Rankosci said nervously, "Perhaps I did not mean to say Key West. Perhaps—"

"Let me get it my way, chum. A ouija board has numbers and the letters of the alphabet around it. And it has a gadget you put your fingers on and move until it reaches a number or letter. When you want the answer to a question, you close your eyes and concentrate hard and move the gadget around and it spells out the answer for you. Cute, huh? We're going to play it with this map and a pencil."

"But I am ready to tell you—"

"This is how we're doing it. Take hold of the pencil. That's it. Now we put the pencil point right here on Havana. Now I close my hand over yours like this, see? Now you shut your eyes and keep them shut. Ready?"

This wasn't any ouija board nonsense, of course. It was lie detector stuff. It was crude but it might work. Rankosci's nerves were short-circuited and he was drunk and thinking slowly. Rankosci was sure to peek to see where the pencil was going; if he saw it was going in a dangerous direction he ought to react very simply and try to push it in a safe direction. Anyway that was the idea. He couldn't think of any other way of double-checking on the guy.

He squeezed Rankosci's hand tightly around the pencil and said, "Keep those eyes shut, now. Bear down on the pencil. Move it very slowly. Start pushing it straight away from you. Here we go!"

The pencil point began creeping on the map. Rankosci's fingers felt stiff and brittle under his hand. The pencil quivered and you got the feeling that Rankosci's muscles were tied in hard knots up his arm and across to his neck. The black line headed across the Florida Straits toward Key West, made a series of tiny jags like the graph line of an earthquake and started strongly up the east coast of Florida. Rankosci's fingers seemed to relax.

Johnny yanked Rankosci's hand and the pencil up from the map. "Open your eyes a minute," he said. "You know what? See those little zigs and zags off Key West? I got a definite feeling that the pencil was trying to circle to the west and head up the Gulf of Mexico. But a cramp hit my arm and that pulled the line east. Let's try it again, shall we?"

"I am sure this proves nothing at all," Rankosci said weakly. "Couldn't we—"

"Nope. Close your eyes. Here we go again from Havana."

There was no doubt about it this time. As the pencil line neared Key West he had to work hard. Rankosci was making a real bid to get up the east coast. Johnny tensed his forearm and forced the pencil line to swing wide to the west through the ship channels off Dry Tortugas. Then he pushed Rankosci's hand and the pencil north, aiming for the long coast line from Everglades and Naples to Tampa Bay. The thin fingers gripped in his hand were getting slippery. He didn't know whose sweat it was. This was a workout. Rankosci wanted to go lots of places and none of them were on the west coast of Florida.

He forced the pencil line in near the coast and drove it slowly northward. Every nerve in his body was strung tight, trying to pick up and interpret vibrations from Rankosci's hand. The line crept north. Past Everglades. Past Naples. Past Fort Myers. Past... whoa! They hadn't quite reached Punta Gorda and the pencil was beginning to move a shade more easily. Rankosci was starting to loosen up. Johnny gripped the thin fingers hard and stopped the northward push and began slowly forcing the line back. He could hardly budge the pencil. He wrestled silently with Rankosci's hand and gained a quarter-inch and then suddenly the pencil point snapped and left a jagged mark right beside Fort Myers.

Johnny relaxed. If he needed any more proof all he had to do was look at Rankosci. The guy was staring at the wig line on the map as if it had turned into a coral snake. Johnny said, "Fort Myers, here we come!"

"It is of course quite silly," Rankosci said in a sick voice. "Fort Myers is not the place at all."

"I'll tell you how you can prove that."

"Yes?" Rankosci said eagerly. "How?"

"I'll get you a visitor's permit tomorrow. We'll take the first plane to Miami and then fly to Fort Myers and we'll walk arm in arm all over town and I'll get you back here Sunday. Oh, by the way, I'll be wearing my Border Patrol uniform while we're in Fort Myers. You like that idea?" He peeked at Rankosci and saw that the guy would just as soon jump into Havana Bay and count how many teeth the biggest shark had. "No?" he asked gently.

"I—I do not think it would be wise. I would like to leave now. I do not feel well."

"A little more talking will fix you up."

"You said that was the last question."

"Yes, but you didn't answer it. I did. If you can't tell me anything more about this American, or about the Fort Myers angle, we'll have to start on Carlos."

Rankosci began sniffling. "All my life," he said, "people have been bullying me because they are bigger or stronger or braver than I am. Now you are bullying me. It is not fair." He put his head down on the table and wept.

Johnny took out his cigarettes and lighted one. Rankosci ought to be easy to handle after this. He leaned back, feeling very good, and glanced around the café. The place was beginning to fill with tourists. A nice-looking American girl and her boyfriend were being guided to a table near him. The girl had sun-streaked brown hair and clear brown eyes and—

"Oh, brother," he muttered.

The clear brown eyes belonged to Ellen McCarter. He tried to shrink down out of sight but it was no use. An ordinary run-of-the-beauty-shop girl would have given him the queen and peasant treatment. But with Ellen that was too much to hope for. She turned and came directly to his booth.

"I wish you'd tell me," she said, "whether there's something wrong with me or wrong with you."

It took him a few seconds to get up; the booth was cramped and drinking on an empty stomach had put an extra joint in his legs. He didn't know why he was feeling guilty.

"I guess there's something wrong with me," he said. "I got drinking and after a while decided I'd be no bargain on a date tonight."

"I wish you'd be frank," she said. "I don't believe that at all. The whole thing was my fault, wasn't it?"

The guy who had come in with Ellen stepped around her and tapped him on the chest with his index finger. Johnny peered at him. Either he was drunker than he thought or this was quite a hunk of man. Hormones had run wild to create him. He was better than six feet tall and had shoulders that could only go through a door sideways. He had golden hair chopped in a crew cut and blue eyes and a face that only a woman could love.

The guy said, "Are you the fellow who stood Ellen up?"

If you were smart, you picked smaller characters to dislike on first sight. This just wasn't one of his smart nights. Johnny said, "Is this your finger poking me? Do you want it back, or shall I break it off and throw it away?"

"Oh, a tough guy, are you?"

"This conversation is getting nowhere," Johnny said. "Both of us ask questions and neither of us answers them. Just who are you, chum?"

"I happen to be a friend of Miss McCarter's from Fort Myers. My name is Bob Tate. I ran into her tonight at her hotel and found she was being stood up by some drunken bum—"

"You're being unfair to me," Johnny said. "You didn't know at the time I was a drunken bum."

The girl tugged at Tate's sleeve and said, "Please, Bob. Let's sit down and forget it."

"You sit down, Ellen," Tate said. "This fellow at least needs a good talking to. What's your name, fellow?"

"My name is Bob Tate," Johnny said.

"You're a drunken bum."

"You're in a rut, Bob. You're repeating yourself."

"You ought to be ashamed of yourself."

"I am," Johnny said. "I got this way on only four shots of rum. Usually I can do much better. How much rum can you handle before you get to be a drunken bum, Bob? Be honest, now."

Bob Tate looked at him sternly. "I don't drink," he said.

"This will be a big evening for Ellen. Tell me, Bob, do you smoke?"

"It just happens I don't. And—"

Ellen stepped between them and said angrily, "I want you both to stop this idiotic business. I apologize to both of you for starting it. Will you both sit down?"

Johnny turned away from them and started to slide into the booth beside Rankosci. Rankosci had stopped sitting there and crying. The bench was empty.

That hit him like a kick in the stomach. He had been standing right in front of the booth, so Rankosci couldn't have slipped past him. And it didn't seem likely that the guy could palm himself like a handful of cigarettes and vanish. But wait. The back of the benches didn't reach all the way to the floor. Rankosci could have slid under the table and crawled off.

Johnny whirled around to start looking for him and ran into something large and solid. The large object made a growling noise. Two big hands slammed him back onto the bench. He shook his head dizzily and listened to voices arguing.

One was saying, "You let me by, Bob Tate. You hurt him."

Another voice said, "What did he mean by suddenly starting to push me around?"

Johnny worked his eyes carefully back into focus, as if they were a pair of strange binoculars and peered up at Bob Tate and Ellen. That morning she had probably wrecked any chance of his trap working. Now she had popped up just in time to let Rankosci escape. Any time he needed bad luck he would certainly send her a rush order.

Johnny got up slowly. There might still be a slight chance of catching Rankosci if he could get past the guy with too many hormones. "Excuse me," he said mildly, trying to squirm by. "I got business."

"Want to run, do you?" Tate said, grabbing his arm. "You were tough enough a minute ago. Sure, you can go. You can make a real apology to Miss McCarter and then you can get down on hands and knees and crawl out."

"Bob!" the girl cried. "You mustn't—"

"I'm sorry, Ellen. This is out of your hands. This fellow thought he could stand you up and push me around and I'm going to teach him a lesson. Either he crawls out of here or goes outside with me and gets a lesson."

Johnny sighed. He could make about as much yardage through this character as he could make through the Cleveland Browns. "All right," he said. "Let's go."

He pulled out his wallet, paid the anxious waiter and walked slowly toward the door with Tate. This was going to be rugged. Ordinarily he would give himself about three rounds with Tate. Sober, that is.

"I ought to tell you," Tate said. "I used to win amateur boxing contests."

Johnny corrected his estimate. Make that half a round, sober. Right now he would be lucky to get in one punch. It would be nice, though, to get that in. There was only one way to do it. As he stepped onto the sidewalk he pivoted and threw a hard right hook. It slammed into Tate's jaw and sent a shower of sparks up his arm. Tate fell back against the wall of the building. He melted slowly down it and ended by sitting on the sidewalk, looking tired.

"No one," Johnny said, "was more surprised than I."

"I hope you're ashamed," the girl cried. "I hope you have the decency to feel badly about doing that."

"I do feel badly. But if he had hit me I'd feel worse." He looked at Tate and said, "Want me to stick around?"

"What for?" Tate mumbled.

"I thought maybe you would want to show me your press clippings. You know, about those fights you won. I thought maybe you still might want to win this one."

"In a ring," Tate said, "I'd have won this on a foul. Why don't you beat it? I'll see you sometime when we can start even."

Johnny shrugged. He turned to the girl and said, "You all right?"

"Yes," she said. "Is that bad? Do you feel I ought to be knocked down too?"

"You won't believe this, but I'm sorry I couldn't keep our date."

"And you won't believe this," she said, "but I'm glad."

He walked down the street and got a cab. It had been quite a day. He had been close to learning a lot of things but he had ended with nothing but a name: Fort Myers. It must be an interesting place. It seemed to be peopled exclusively by slick killers and pretty girls and handsome clean-living heroes. He hoped there was room in the town for a heel named Johnny Edwards.

CHAPTER TEN

Johnny checked his appearance in the mirror of the washroom at Border Patrol headquarters in Miami, gave his campaign hat a tilt and went upstairs to report to Chief Patrol Inspector Ed Brian. When he reached the door he paused until he caught the glance of Brian's secretary and beckoned her to join him in the hall. When she slipped out, he asked, "How do things look?"

"I think all right, Johnny."

"I owe you a lot, Grace. You've been swell."

"It's all in a good cause, even though what I did was sort of irregular. So if it works, good luck in Fort Myers. Ellen's a nice girl and if she turns you down, let me know. I'd better go back. You wait a minute out here until the chief finishes the morning mail."

She went back in the office. She was a good kid and she had been very useful. When he returned from Havana a week ago he had faced a big problem: how to get transferred to the Fort Myers unit. Of course McCarter needed a partner but getting the assignment wasn't a matter of just asking. In fact, asking might have killed his chances. Chief Patrol Inspectors liked to make their own assignments instead of having trainees make them. And, of course, Brian might have discussed any such request with McCarter in Fort Myers; that wouldn't have worked out well if Ellen McCarter had told her brother what a heel she met in Havana.

So he had gone at it indirectly. He had taken Brian's secretary out to dinner and told her a long sad story about how he had fallen for Ellen McCarter and just had to get transferred to Fort Myers. One thing about girls: you could count on them for any match-making project. So Grace had promised to drop hints to her boss very carefully so he would think the Fort Myers transfer was his own idea.

From inside the office Grace wigwagged to him and he marched in and snapped to attention in front of the chief's desk.

Brian looked up. He was one of the old-timers in the Border Patrol, a solid guy built along the lines of a bulldozer. He ran a hand through clipped gray hair and said, "Hello, Edwards. How are you this morning?"

"Fine, sir. And you?"

"Buried under this lousy paper work, as usual. Never could handle the stuff."

Johnny grinned. Throughout the Miami Border Patrol Sector, Brian's howls about paper work were a standing joke. Actually the guy was good at paper work, but he hated being tied to a desk. Brian lived in constant fear that somebody higher up would learn that he was good at paper work and promote him to be Alien Control Officer in Chicago or some place where he would have to sit at a desk all day.

"Got to thinking about you this week," Brian said. "How would you like to go to Fort Myers?"

"That'd be swell, chief."

"You aren't ready for it," Brian grumbled. "But it's like this. Those reports from Havana about aliens dropping out of sight have me worried. Maybe something big is up. And we have a hole in the dyke over in Fort Myers. Tim McCarter's been working it alone, and I gave him orders not to go out looking for real trouble on account of he could meet the wrong guy on a dark night. So Tim needs a partner. You met him?"

"I might have seen him here once or twice."

"Sit down," Brian said. "I'd better give you a fill-in." He brushed papers aside, leaned back and dropped a couple of pickax-sized feet on the desk. "Tim and I been around this man's outfit a long time," he said, getting a faraway look in his eyes.

Johnny put on his eager-beaver face. They were going to play old campaigner.

Brian said, "Tim broke me in along the Mex border, twenty years ago. We were a team, see? Those were fancy days out there. Some clown had the idea of building high observation towers near favorite crossing spots of the Rio Grande. You laid up there on a platform in the open, and sometimes across the river Mexicans crept out onto roofs and took pot shots at you with high-powered rifles. If you shot back, you started an international incident. One night I got mad and sneaked across and sorta discouraged a few Mexicans. When I came back, Tim McCarter damn near killed me. You know why I'm telling you this, Edwards?"

"Yes, sir," Johnny said. "You want me to know what kind of a person he is. You don't want me going to Fort Myers acting reckless and getting him down on me."

"That's it. Tim won't go for any boy wonder stuff. He's a responsible guy. I don't suppose you know when his parents died he took on the job of raising a kid sister. Fussed over the girl like an old hen. Still does. Maybe you ought to know that a couple of guys who got interested in Ellen McCarter found Tim hard to get along with. It's not jealousy, see? He doesn't think most men are good enough for his sister. So take it easy along that line."

Johnny thought fast. This might be a good moment to set up an alibi, in case Ellen had talked about him to her brother. "Gosh, chief," he said, "do you think something that happened when I was in Havana could put me behind the eight-ball? You remember I met Ellen McCarter here in your office. Well, I ran into her in Havana. Didn't have a date, really, just lunch together. That wouldn't make her brother sore at me, would it?"

"Don't see why it should. I—" Brian looked hard at him. "This girl doesn't mean anything to you, does she?"

"Just another nice girl, chief. I like lots of girls." Johnny added anxiously, "You wouldn't call off the assignment just for that, would you?"

Brian muttered, "I was trying to remember how I got the idea of sending you to Fort Myers. I was trying to think if you put it in my head. But you weren't around when I thought of it. I remember I was sitting here and... and... well, it doesn't matter. Now look. I want to give you a slant on the job you'll have to do." He went to the big map on the wall and moved his finger from the North Carolina border down the shore line to Key West and up the west coast to the Apalachicola River in Northwest Florida. "That," he said, "is the Miami Border Patrol Sector. Know how long that shore line is?"

"More than two thousand miles, chief."

"Two thousand three hundred and seventy-one miles of sea frontier. I have fifty-eight inspectors to cover it. Some day when I'm not swamped with paper work I'm gonna figure how many times fifty-eight goes into two thousand three hundred and seventy-one. Well, anyway, this is the point. You fellows can't cover that shore line. If you watch one beach, they can land aliens forty miles away. So what's the answer?"

Next to paper work, this was the chief's pet subject. Johnny said promptly, "We have to develop informants."

"That's it. Informants. Got to have friends to help you watch—fishermen, tourist camp owners, storekeepers, bus drivers. Right?"

The chief played this record every day. "Right."

"I keep pounding away on this because I know what you kids like to do when you get out on your own. You want to pull grandstand stuff. You want to run for touchdowns without lockers. In this business what happens is you get thrown for a loss. Lay off it, see? Just make a lot of friends who can do you some good."

Johnny thought: We will now all join hands and sing *Brighten the Corner Where You Are*. While the Border Patrol had been out making friends, he had been out making enemies. And guess who knew where the smugglers landed their aliens? The Border Patrol system was all right in most cases but his own system had worked better in this one. He hoped the chief didn't get the word about Fort Myers until everything was over. Because if the chief got the word, he would throw a lot of extra men into Fort Myers. Then one of two things would happen. Either the guys in the racket would realize the heat was on and lie low, or they would be caught. And if the killer was caught nothing worse would happen to him than a few years in jail. It was too hard to knock off a guy who was in jail.

Aloud he said, "Yes, sir, I'll try to make lots of friends."

"All right. Let's go send the word to Tim. He ought to be out on the road about now."

They walked down the hall to the radio room. Brian tapped the radio operator on the shoulder and said, "See if you can raise Tim McCarter for me. I'll write out the message."

The operator nodded and began chanting into his mike:

"MI 3 from WWMI. Attention Inspector McCarter. Come in, please... MI 3 from WWMI. Attention Inspector McCarter—"

MI 3 was the Fort Myers patrol unit. Somewhere out on the road the call was crackling into the receiver in McCarter's sedan.

Brian paused in his writing and said, "How soon can you report to Fort Myers, Edwards?"

"I can get there late this afternoon."

The loud-speaker on the wall began to chatter Morse code. "WWMI from MI 3," the dots and dashes said. "I am receiving you. Over."

Brian said to the operator, "Send him this," and handed over the message he had been writing.

The operator chanted it into the mike: "MI 3 from WWMI. Attention Inspector McCarter. Message follows from Chief Patrol Inspector. Assigning Trainee John C. Edwards to Fort Myers patrol unit. He will report to your home late this afternoon. Message ends. Acknowledge, please. Over."

Johnny said, "How come McCarter uses CW instead of voice?"

"They have queer radio conditions around Fort Myers," Brian said. "Lots of times one of those low-powered auto transmitters won't get a clear signal to us here with voice. I've known times when Tim had to relay to us through Tampa or New Orleans, even with CW. What's holding up his acknowledgment?"

The loud-speaker woke up. Johnny listened to the snap of Morse code and felt blood starting to tick in his head. McCarter was sending: "WWMI from MI 3. Attention Chief Patrol Inspector. Request another trainee be sent in place of John C. Edwards. Over."

Brian said angrily, "What the hell's wrong with Tim?" He told the operator, "Ask him why he doesn't want Edwards. Tell him I'm right here."

The operator sent the message. McCarter apparently took a little time to think about it. Finally he replied that he thought other trainees were more experienced. Brian's face took on the color of a Glades fire. He whipped back a message that if Inspector McCarter wanted to discuss the running of the Miami Border Patrol Sector, or had some things to say he didn't want to put on the air, he'd better get to a phone fast and say them.

The loud-speaker was silent for what seemed like a long time and Johnny held his breath. Then at last a string of curt dots and dashes said, "WWMI from MI 3. Will take Edwards. Over and out."

CHAPTER ELEVEN

A little before five o'clock Johnny reached Fort Myers and found the section, downriver on the outskirts of town, where McCarter lived. It was a quiet neighborhood of widely scattered white houses and shell roads and orange groves. He located a house all by itself on a lane near the river that might be the McCarter place. Nobody was home. A man was working in a grove back up the white shell road and Johnny walked toward him to check the address. It was a nice-looking grove: clean aisles between the trees, shiny dark green leaves, heavy fruit. The grove worker had an old jeep equipped for spraying and wore dungarees and a homemade mask.

The two-cycle pumping engine was making a lot of noise and Johnny yelled, "Is that the McCarter place down the way, doc?"

The grove worker bent to switch off the engine, yanked off the hooded mask. Shoulder-length hair spilled into the light. It was brown hair into which sunlight had bleached creamy streaks of gold and silver. The effect was as if you had kicked a moldering box from the sand and saw smooth old coins tumble from it. Pretty, all right. It belonged to Ellen McCarter.

She looked at him, did a double-take.

"It's me all right," he said.

"I didn't recognize you," she said, "without your scowl."

"I just washed my face and can't do a thing with it. Look. In view of the reception I'm getting, would you mind turning that spray nozzle the other way? I happen to know it's loaded."

"Don't worry. It only works on small insects, not on large ones. Did you have something to ask me? Or isn't there anything on your mind but a superiority complex."

"I wanted to ask, is that the McCarter place down the lane. You know, Tim McCarter of the Border Patrol. He has a sister named Ellen. Lovely girl if she didn't have such a temper."

"That's our house," she said. "But I'm sorry, we don't sell rum or allow drunken brawls." She climbed down from the jeep, frowning. "What do you want to see him for?"

"The glad news," he said, "is I'm going to be his partner."

"Oh, no," she said faintly.

"I have a feeling you're understating things."

"Now see here, Johnny Edwards," she said fiercely, "if you're going to be Tim's partner, we're going to stop acting this way right now. I'm not going to have his life spoiled by any childish feud. As far as I'm concerned, I never met you until this moment. I've forgotten everything else that happened."

"Since you've forgotten," he said, "maybe I shouldn't remind you that you gave me quite a reputation with your brother. In fact he tried today to block my transfer."

"I never said a word to him about you!"

It was just as well that her spraying outfit wasn't a flame thrower. She said in a shaking voice, "I don't have any idea why Tim didn't want you. I never mentioned you to him. There were always more pleasant things to talk about. I can see you're not going to believe me. So let's drop the subject for now, shall we?"

"Yes, ma'am. Clunk. Jarred the ground, didn't it?"

She ignored the comment. "Now let's go to the house and get a room fixed for you."

"A what!"

"A room. You know, one of those things with four walls and a ceiling and a door and bedroom furniture. People often sleep in one."

"Thanks just the same, but I couldn't think of it."

She said with a grim smile, "We hardly ever murder guests in their beds."

"As soon as I see your brother I'll check in at a hotel."

For some reason her eyes began to get damp. "We simply aren't going to start off this way," she said. "I don't think you realize how closely you and Tim will have to work. You've just got to get along together. But if Tim thinks you and I have had trouble, he won't be very good company. And he'll be sure to suspect it if you don't stay with us until you get settled."

They were pretending again that McCarter didn't know about the feud. Johnny shrugged. "What's wrong with a hotel?" he said.

"What's wrong is that everybody will know when you come off duty and go on. All your calls will go through the switchboard. The sensible thing is to stay with us until you find a room with people we can trust."

"Okay," he said. "But I still think when your brother gets home he'd rather find termites."

By the time he carried his luggage into the bedroom she assigned him, a Border Patrol sedan eased into the driveway. He went onto the porch and saw a square, solidly built man get out; he looked like the sort of ex-fullback who back in the Twenties would have been called Five-Yards McCarter. His face had been roughed out by a sculptor who tired of working with such hard material and gave up. His campaign hat sat so squarely on his head that you might think he adjusted it each morning with a builder's level.

This was not the kind of guy you lounged up to and said, "Hi, Mac. I'm Johnny Edwards." Johnny clicked to attention and said crisply, "Patrol Inspector Trainee Edwards, reporting for duty, sir."

"Hello, Edwards," McCarter said. He shook hands, cleared his throat with a noise like gears stripping and muttered, "I see you got here on time."

This was like boxing carefully with a guy in the first round to see what he had. "Yes, sir," he said.

"We don't have to use that sir stuff."

"Right."

McCarter took off his campaign hat. His head was bald and the hatband had left a red circle around it. "Hot day," he said. "For November, that is. Did Ellen meet you when you arrived? I understand you know her."

Apparently Ellen hadn't had a chance to brief her brother on the party line. "Yes, she did," Johnny said. "She seems to think I ought to stay here until I can get settled. I'd feel much better going to a hotel."

"Trouble with hotels is that everybody in town can keep track of when you're on duty and when you're off. You know that situation Harmon reported from Havana. We have a lot of work to do and I'd be happier if nobody knew when we were doing it. So if you don't mind bunking here until we get you located right..."

McCarter sat down and dug out a pipe and began filling it with attention to each grain of tobacco; he seemed to find a pipe handy when he didn't know what to say. Judging by the number of pipes in the living room, not many words need be wasted around the place.

Ellen came onto the porch carrying a tray with three tall glasses. "Hello, Tim," she said. "I thought we might have a drink to celebrate or something."

Tim McCarter looked up. The bleak look thawed out of his gray eyes. "Swell idea," he said. Then he added, almost like a kid looking at a wrapped present, "What's in it?"

"Oh, some of my best limes," Ellen said. She carried the tray to Johnny.

Good old limeade. They must have some big nights around here, harmonizing around the harpsichord. "Thank you," he said gravely. He tried a swallow, couldn't help grinning. "If these old taste buds don't deceive me," he said, "this is a Rum Collins."

Ellen's face got pink. "I thought you ought to taper off gradually."

"What's this about?" Tim said.

"Just a little joke we had," Ellen said.

Tim looked at each of them in turn, and frowned. A joke had made an illegal entry into the conversation. He said, "I'll finish my drink while I clean up," and went to his room.

Dinner that night brought long periods of silence. Everybody acted as if whatever he said would be held against him. Afterward they went into the living room and settled down in chairs like reluctant witnesses taking the stand.

"Cozy, wasn't it?" Ellen said abruptly.

Nobody answered her.

"What I mean is," she said, "let's all have a good swig of embalming fluid and then crawl back to the morgue."

Tim cleared his throat.

"Frankly," Ellen said, "I don't regard that as an intelligent comment. So let's drag things out in the open. Tim, I met Johnny last week in Havana. Jean Atkins had deserted me and I was lonely. I'm afraid I threw myself at Johnny, hoping for company. That turned out to be a poor idea. We didn't get along. Today you tried to block Johnny's transfer here. He thinks it was because I went bleating to you about the squabble we had in Havana. Now who's going to confess next?"

"What does she mean, you didn't get along?" Tim snapped. "Just what happened between you two, Edwards?"

"I made a date with her and didn't keep it," Johnny said. "She happened to run into me that night when I'd had a couple too many. A guy named Bob Tate from here was with her and we had a few words and finally I smacked him in the jaw when he wasn't quite ready."

Tim considered that for a while. He seemed to be relaxing. Maybe it wasn't as bad to break a date with his sister as to keep one. Finally he said, "You didn't show up very good there, Edwards."

"You don't have to tell me."

"I do have to tell you! You're in the Border Patrol whether you're on duty or off, in uniform or out."

"Before this gets out of hand," Ellen said, "let's clear up the main points. Did I tell you anything about meeting Johnny in Havana?"

"The only time you mentioned him was a couple of weeks ago, after you met him in Ed Brian's office."

"Oh, dear. I'd forgotten that, and I told Johnny I'd never mentioned him to you. Anyway, that takes care of the Havana angle. Now don't you have a little contribution to make, Tim?"

"I don't intend to be bullied about this."

Ellen said sweetly, "Nobody's bullying you. But, since all of us know you didn't want Johnny, it might be fun for all of us to know why."

"All right. I don't regret what I did. All I'm sorry about is that Edwards learned of it." He turned to Johnny and said, "I didn't want you because I didn't like the way you got into the Border Patrol."

"That's ridiculous!" Ellen said. "He made terrific marks in his exams and passed at the top in his classes."

"Sure," Tim said. "But how did he get a chance to take those exams and to get in the school? Want to tell her, Edwards?"

"Why not?" Johnny said. "Political pull. Is that bad?"

"The guys you skipped over might think so."

"It was about the first time I ever wanted anything badly. So I pulled every string I could reach to get it."

Tim said, "You're right about never having wanted anything else badly. I looked over your record once when I had a moment in Ed Brian's office. You didn't do much in the Army, didn't do much afterward. What sold you on the Border Patrol?"

The only thing to do was slug it out with this guy. Johnny said coldly, "I like the pretty uniforms."

Tim started to get up from his chair and Ellen jumped up and pushed him firmly back into it. "You had absolutely no right to ask the question that way," she said.

"What I don't understand," Johnny said, "is why the political angle bothers you so much and doesn't bother the chief or anybody else."

Tim shrugged. "They don't know," he said. "I got the word from a friend in Washington. I didn't see any reason to pass it on."

"Oh. Well, thanks for not telling them. But where does that leave us?"

"It leaves you at bat with two strikes on you. It leaves me willing to see you hit a homer but not willing to bet on it."

Johnny said gravely, "Look, coach, I'm just up from the bush leagues. Is it all right if I merely bunt?"

A tiny smile wrestled with the corners of Tim's mouth. "I'll even settle," he said, "for a base on balls."

Ellen said in a plaintive voice, "Nobody has asked where this leaves me. It leaves me playing umpire, as in the phrase, kill the umpire. It also leaves me with the dishes to do. Kindly do not spike each other while I'm gone."

Johnny watched her go into the kitchen and muttered, "That's quite a sister you have there."

"Yeah," Tim said. Then he added, surprisingly, "You could have done worse than keep that date with her."

"I get that idea, too. What happens if I try to do something about it?"

"She makes her own decisions, Edwards. All I do is back her up. I kind of think she's made one in your case. I don't think it's one that leaves me any worries."

Johnny got up, stretched lazily. "You never know," he said. "Wait till she sees how I can do dishes."

He went to the kitchen and tried to be very helpful and charming. Ellen accepted the help but didn't buy any of the charm. A very difficult girl to handle. Maybe she was waiting for an apology.

"Thanks a lot for clearing things up between your brother and me," he said. "He and I understand each other now."

"Or anyway, you understand him. I'm quite sure he doesn't understand you. I don't either."

"I will introduce you gradually," he said, "to my many good qualities. Then it won't be quite such a shock. Look, what I'm trying to do is apologize for thinking you were the reason why Tim didn't want me."

"All right," she said. "I'll accept the apology. And you get credit for a good quality. I could probably brace myself for one more good quality today."

"I'm not sure you'll think this is one. Would you like to go to the movies or something tonight?"

"Yes," she said. "In fact I *am* going to the movies. With somebody else."

"Pardon me while I restrain some bad qualities. Maybe another night?"

She put away the last of the silver and hung up the dish towel and said finally, "I really think it would be better if we didn't. Do you mind? And now I have to hurry to get ready." She gave him a pleasant smile and waltzed off to her room.

Johnny went back to the living room and found Tim buried in a western story magazine and pipe smoke. He picked up a copy of the Fort Myers *News-Press* and glanced through it restlessly. The movies at the Fort Myers theaters didn't look very interesting, anyway.

He dropped the paper and said, "What does a guy do around here at night?"

"You mean," Tim said innocently, "if he doesn't have a date?"

The big stiff was actually enjoying this. "You know I don't have a date," he snapped.

"What's the matter, Edwards? Losing your dishwashing skill? I thought no girl could resist you in the kitchen."

"She already has a date."

"Might surprise you to know," Tim said, "that happens quite often." He puffed out a cloud of pipe smoke and peered through it like a big happy gnome. "You—" Tim paused as somebody knocked on the front screen door. He got up and opened it. "Hello, there," he said in a voice that seemed to hide a chuckle. "Come on in. Ellen will be ready in a minute."

A big guy, turning his shoulders a little to get through the doorway, came in. He had close-cut yellow hair and blue eyes and a clean profile and the kind of jaw that felt just right at the end of a solid punch. Next to smallpox, Johnny thought, this was all he needed to make it a really big evening. The guy was Bob Tate.

"Hiya, Tim, old boy," Tate was saying. "You're looking good. That is, for a guy who poisons himself with those pipes of yours. Maybe...."

His voice trailed off slowly as he saw who else was in the room. He balanced carefully on his feet, let his shoulders sag a little to free the long hitting muscles across his back.

Nobody was going to beat him to the punch this time. Johnny got up and checked the position of the furniture that might get in the way.

"I understand you two know each other," Tim said. "Edwards is my new partner."

Johnny waited, his skin going hot and prickly as Tate looked him over. The guy turned back to Tim and said deliberately, "What do they have against you at headquarters?"

Johnny said to nobody in particular, "Funny he doesn't have anything to say to me. He had plenty to say last time."

"The first guy who starts anything," Tim said pleasantly, "can take me on too. In fact, the first guy who makes another crack can get out."

They stood there for a few moments like puppets waiting for somebody to pull the strings and then Ellen came dancing in and threw smiles around like confetti and took Bob Tate's arm and rushed him outside. Tim sat down and began filling a pipe, grinning like a gargoyle.

"I thought you said you were careful who you let your sister go out with," Johnny said.

"Nope. She's careful."

"What does she see in that character?"

"Maybe she sees a guy who doesn't stand her up. You know, if I weren't enjoying this so much, I'd tell you it wasn't any of your business. But just for the laughs, go ahead."

"What does he do besides keep all the girls happy?"

"He has a local flying service. Ferries people out to Boca Grande and Captiva and the other islands, does some crop dusting, takes aerial photos. When I want to look at some boat offshore he's always willing to help. For free, too. When you're in charge of a Border Patrol unit and have no money to spend, that comes in handy. So lay off, see?"

"Next time we meet," Johnny said, "I'll ask him for his autograph." He walked to the door. "See, you."

"Going somewhere?"

"Yes. I decided to have a big night. I'm going for a walk down to the dock."

He went outside and headed across the lawn toward the river. Behind him, in the house, there was a sound as if somebody were rolling empty barrels downstairs. Probably it was just McCarter laughing. He told himself not to let it upset him. It was ridiculous to get involved emotionally with these people. All he had to do was keep his mouth shut, locate the man who had killed Tony, settle with him, and then resign from the Border Patrol and clear out.

He walked onto the dock and stared out at the broad dark river. It was a quiet night. You could hear the rustle of the tide coming upstream and the sigh of a porpoise rolling up for air. A cabin cruiser slid into sight, feeling its way out into the river with the exhaust tapping like a blind man's cane.

Apparently the pilot knew every ripple of sand on the bottom; it was too dark now to see any unlighted channel markers.

Just as he had that thought, a searchlight beam knifed out from the boat. It fingered the surface of the river, failed to pick up any markers, swung back to shore to get a fix on some landmark. The beam brushed over Johnny's face in a quick glare and swept down the bank. Then, oddly, it leaped back at him. Johnny frowned into the blinding glitter. He hadn't been around this dead town long enough to be considered a landmark.

A thought jabbed him. Back in a Havana night club he had left a crude map with a sort of arrow pointing to Fort Myers. And that morning, on a short-wave broadcast that anybody could monitor, his transfer to Fort Myers had been announced. He didn't stop to work it out any further. He threw himself flat. Something snapped in the air above him. Something else ripped splinters from the dock and went off into the night with a banshee wail. Out in the river the light snapped out and the mutter of the exhaust lifted to a roar.

As he lay there he heard pile-driving thumps on the lawn as Tim ran down from the house. "Edwards!" Tim was yelling. "Where are you? What happened?"

Johnny peered out at the river. Nothing was left of the boat now but a throbbing in the distance and the wake hissing along the shore. He jumped up, ran back to the shelter of the coconut palms at the edge of the lawn.

"Among the things a guy can do here at night," he said, "you forgot to mention that he can get shot at."

CHAPTER TWELVE

Johnny went to the rear of the black Border Patrol sedan, unslung the whip aerial and raised it. Inside the car Tim stepped on the accelerator to power the battery, flipped down the lid of the glove compartment to reach the sending key. His fingers jerked a few times on the key. Signal 82. The Fort Myers unit was going into service. No orders came from WWMI. Tim waved a hand, Johnny telescoped the fifteen-foot sending aerial and locked it into place, climbed into the front seat and they were off for another day.

"Join the Border Patrol," Johnny said, yawning, "and see Lee County, Florida."

A month in Fort Myers with nothing happening was telling on him. Things had looked promising that first night, but apparently the boys in the racket had changed their minds and everybody had run for cover like fiddler crabs scuttling into holes. The new party line was to bore him to death instead of shooting him. It was working well, too.

At first Tim had been very worried by the shooting. But Tim hadn't been able to figure why it had happened and had worked around to deciding it was an accident: a guy was doing some illegal gigging along the shore and saw a uniform and thought a conservation agent was after him and threw a couple of 30-30 bullets in his direction as a hint to lay off. Just as a precaution, though, Tim insisted that Johnny continue living in the McCarter house.

Johnny sighed. They had been together, all right. Morning, noon and night, ten days a week. The only trouble they had found was strictly home-grown; they got along together like a couple of Florida real estate salesmen working on the same prospect.

"What," he said, "is the breath-taking program for today?"

"We'll visit Fort Myers Beach," Tim said. "And on the way we can drop in at Punta Rassa."

Punta Rassa was a tiny fishing village at the mouth of the Caloosa-hatchee, where the ferry connected with Sanibel Island. "Don't tell me what we're going to do there," Johnny said. "Let me guess. We're going to make some more friends."

"You don't like making friends, do you, Edwards?"

"I need a good enemy to bring out the best in me. Bob Tate would do nicely if you'd let me at him. Why your sister wastes time on him I don't know. She was out with him twice last week."

"Three times," Tim said. "Tuesday, Thursday, Saturday."

"Thursday he just ran her into town for a book. Why do you want to count that?"

"Why do you want it not to count?"

"We'd better quit this," Johnny said. "I'm not getting in the right mood to make a lot of friends today. Let me practice thinking nice thoughts. Let's see now, in Punta Rassa I will make a lot of friends by talking about fishing and tourists. At Fort Myers Beach I will make more friends by talking about real estate and tourists. Maybe as a treat we can stop at Iona on the way back and talk about crops. That's the place where they don't give a hang about tourists."

"Some day," Tim said, "you'll make a couple of friends by mistake and you'll learn something about a few tourists who forgot their entry permits when they came in from Cuba."

"If I could count on that, nobody would be safe from my winning ways."

The car rolled into Punta Rassa and Tim parked and went into the general store to talk about fishing and tourists. Johnny walked up the sandy ruts to the fishing shacks that straddled out from shore on pilings. At least it wasn't so bad when he could talk about fishing, and there was a Cracker in one of the shacks who could remember back in the Nineties when sportsmen were just learning how to take tarpon. The old man was on his rickety porch, making a crab net from a ball of twine. He had a face as brown and wrinkled as a dry coconut husk, and when he grinned all his features seemed to vanish in the wrinkles. Johnny sat down and talked about crab nets and how the snook were running. Jenks told him to come down some night and try cane pole fishing for snook. It was pleasant sitting there, looking across the blue flicker of San Carlos Bay at the distant shadow of Sanibel. It wasn't often he managed to relax so completely.

The old man said idly, "I seen Howard Pingree late yestiddy. He docked at the ferry landing to pick up supplies."

"Pingree?" Johnny said. "Do I know him? Oh, yes. Charter boat captain, isn't he?"

"That's him. He's got a nice little ole charter boat. I don't see him taking out many parties, though. But he said he had a good charter coming up. He was on his way to Everglades to pick up some rich guy and take him down to the Shark River country."

The old man didn't often ramble that way. Well, keep him happy. "Good fishing down there," Johnny said.

"Uh-huh. Man needs good tackle and lots of it for those big reds and snook."

"Sure does."

"Howard had me on his boat going over charts so I could show him some of them tricky channels down around Lostman's and the Shark. So I happened to see his tackle. Can't say I thought much of it. You wouldn't think a couple moth-eaten feathers and one little ole rod would be enough."

Johnny sat up. The old man hadn't been rambling after all; he had just been easing around to get downwind of his subject, the way he would do hunting in the Glades. Subjects like this were tricky and you didn't go crashing through the palmettos right toward them. "I suppose," he said casually, "he could pick up tackle at Everglades."

"I wouldn't be surprised. Even though a feller might think tackle was easier come by in Fort Myers."

"You know those waters down through the Ten Thousand Islands and Lostman's and the Shark pretty well, huh?"

"Well as any man can know them. Fished there all my life. And seeing it can't do no harm now, I don't mind saying back in Prohibition I may have used some of them channels coming back from Cuba with maybe a drap of liquor."

"I wonder what Howard would want to check on those channels for?"

The face in front of him went blank. "Come a storm out in the Gulf," Jenks said, "it would be handy."

There was a cold note in the old man's voice and Johnny knew what it meant. His last question had gone crashing toward the subject like an untrained hound. Jenks didn't like that. "Yeah, sure," Johnny said. "I guess a man would have to take a lot of supplies and gas on a fishing trip to the Shark, wouldn't he?"

That was a good enough question but the subject had already been frightened off. "Some do, some don't," Jenks said, getting up. "I figure I'll take me a nap."

"Right. See you again, Mr. Jenks. That is, if you don't mind a dumb damyankee coming around."

An extra wrinkle that could have been a smile creased the old face. "You're learnin'," he said. "You made that sound like just one word." He paused at the door of his shack, and seemed to be working on an idea. Finally he said sharply, "Howard Pingree's got a 30-30 rifle," and let the screen door slam behind him.

Johnny walked down the steps of the shack wondering if his legs or the flimsy boards underfoot were doing the quivering. It had been quite a visit. It was like still-fishing in the waters of a pass and suddenly feeling your line start to run with deep quiet power. He tried to picture Howard Pingree. A thin guy. Somewhere between thirty-five and forty. An anxious, hungry face with a wide mouth and small chin that made you think of a catfish working the shallows.

This was a weird country and amazing people. A month ago and ten miles upriver, a guy out in a boat at night squinted along a rifle barrel and ripped a couple of high-velocity bullets that could have been 30-30's at a Border Patrol trainee on a dock. A month later and ten miles downriver, echoes of the shots were still barreling around. How did things like that get known? Did Tim or Ellen mention it to somebody or did the rifleman have a few drinks too many or... well, you couldn't figure it out.

Johnny went back to the car and tapped out AA AA AA on the horn in Morse code to get McCarter's attention. Tim came out of the general store and walked over.

"What's the matter?" Tim said. "You restless?"

"Yeah," Johnny said. "I want to go catch a smuggler."

"Imagine that. Just tell me what smuggler you want to catch and we'll go get him."

"I want to catch one named Howard Pingree and I'm not kidding."

Tim's face went red. "You could have said that right off and saved me from making a fool of myself."

"I wouldn't want to interfere with a man's life work."

"Some day we're going to have it out, aren't we, Edwards? Do you figure this is the day?"

"Today I'll take a rain check. All right, maybe that crack was a little rough. But you're going to needle me about having finally made a friend so I thought I'd even things up ahead of time. Old man Jenks tipped me off." He briefed the talk for McCarter.

"Not too much to go on," Tim grumbled. "That's like putting two and two together and getting twenty-two. Just because Pingree didn't have much fishing tackle—"

"Much? For fishing around the Shark he doesn't have any. The guy's going to pick up some wet cargo. You can't shrug it off."

"I wouldn't do that," Tim said, climbing into the seat behind the wheel. "Might discourage you so you'd never make a second friend. Let's run down to Everglades."

This was the first time he had ever seen Tim drive steadily at forty miles an hour. In less than two hours they reached the town of Everglades, on the edge of the sawgrass country sweeping south to Cape Sable. They visited around the docks and the Rod and Gun Club and found that Pingree had not put in to Everglades recently. Nobody knew of any wealthy sportsman who had chartered Pingree to guide him to Shark River. Tim drove back from Everglades at forty-five miles an hour, stopping at Naples on the way. Nobody knew anything of Pingree's charter there, either.

They got back to Fort Myers at fifty miles an hour to check on Pingree's activities before he left. Pingree had bought thirty gallons of gas at the Yacht Basin. By itself, that fact meant nothing. But when you added the twenty gallons he bought at a second pump and forty at a third, it began to add up to a lot of gas. Pingree had bought a new engine a few months ago for his thirty-six-foot cabin cruiser. The owner of the boat yard where the engine had been installed thought Howard must be doing well these days charter fishing, but several of the other charter boat captains couldn't remember seeing Pingree out with many parties.

Late that afternoon they drove as close as possible to the little cove on the lower Caloosahatchee known as Pingree's Landing. Just off the road an old coupé registered in Pingree's name was parked in the bushes. They followed a footpath through a tangle of mangroves and reached an unpainted wooden shack, beyond which a sagging pier teetered out over the water of the cove. Pingree lived alone and the shack was deserted. They peered through windows.

"Do you see what I see?" Tim asked.

"You mean four hundred bucks worth of television set?" Johnny asked. "Yes, I see it. Twenty more years and he can get a program on it. Nearest station's in Miami. Is he nuts?"

"Sometimes a Cracker does queer things when he gets in the chips. Back in Prohibition a guy down here bought a Cadillac and then knocked the side out of his shack so he could push it inside. He didn't want to drive the car, he just wanted to live with it. Well, let's go turn in a report."

They drove back to the McCarter house, making fifty-five miles an hour in places. Tim telephoned the chief in Miami and reported that Pingree might be on his way to Havana to pick up some wet cargo.

After that things went into low gear for several days. Johnny's nerves began to feel like hot wires strung through his body. The way this was working out, the Border Patrol was likely to mess up his private business. It looked as though Pingree might be the man he had been stalking all these months, but there was no way to make sure unless he could have a few quiet moments alone with him.

On the fourth morning WWMI flashed a coded lookout to all units. Pingree had left Havana late the night before with, it was believed, two aliens. The Havana police said he had left in a hurry because somebody took a shot at him. As Johnny and Tim finished decoding that message, WWMI sent another coded report. The Border Patrol's converted Army crash boat, snuffling along south of the Marquesas, had spotted Pingree's cabin cruiser and then lost it in an early morning fog when the lighter-draft boat cut across the shoals of the Quicksands.

After that message, Pingree dropped out of sight. All along the coasts of south Florida, Border Patrol units stayed alert. There was no way to figure where Pingree might land. He could either come up the west coast or slip through the Florida Keys to the east coast. Tim picked out some special friends and asked them to let him know at once if they saw the Pingree boat. He spent hours hunched over maps figuring out plans to cover anything that might happen: plans for road blocks, for co-operation from the Highway Patrol and local police and the sheriffs of Lee and Collier counties.

Three more days passed. Nothing happened, although Pingree could have made the run from the Marquesas to Fort Myers in less than half that time. On the third night Johnny and Ellen were sitting alone in the McCarter house. Tim was out, visiting people who might know whether Pingree had any friends farther up the coast. He had left a list of telephone numbers of people he expected to see, in case Johnny needed to locate him.

Johnny slumped in an easy chair and stared at the Fort Myers *News-Press*. He wasn't seeing the type or pictures. He was seeing the lower west coast of Florida the way it unrolled below you from a plane. Bob Tate had flown them down to Cape Sable and back that afternoon in his amphibian, and it had been quite an experience. From Cape Sable north for fifty miles lay the drowned shore line of the Everglades, laced with tidal rivers that coiled in and out and back on themselves like so many black water moccasins. Mangroves along the banks reached the fantastic height of sixty and seventy and eighty feet. You could hide all the boats in Florida in those rivers.

Above the river country came the Ten Thousand Islands. They fitted into each other like pieces of a jigsaw puzzle, separated by narrow channels that appeared at high tide and vanished at low. Pingree was probably somewhere in that green labyrinth, waiting for things to cool off. From the northern end of the Ten Thousand Islands he could make a night run to Fort Myers in a few hours.

There was something queer about the whole setup. You started looking for a bunch of smooth operators who did things in a big way and found a riverbank character who left a trail like an alligator going through mud as he bought gas all over the place, forgot to carry enough fishing tackle to back up his story and checked with old man Jenks about inland channels. Then he reached Havana and picked up two aliens and somebody took a shot at him. That didn't sound like a big-time operation. It sounded more as if Pingree were on his own. Maybe he had been a small-timer in the gang, and got restless about lying low and decided to go in business for himself. Maybe—

Johnny took the phone. "This is Edwards," he said.

A thin voice said, "I wanted to know why you ain't been down yet to go cane pole fishing for snook."

"Been kind of busy. But I'll make it."

"Maybe I could fix things so you wouldn't be so busy. Friend of yours just went by going upriver. Man we talked about the other day. Thought you might want to see him so I traipsed over to the shore to phone. He was easing along without running lights. Probably you could beat him to that place he hangs out if you don't argue with me too long. You owe me a dime for this call, too. Now get goin'."

"Okay. Thanks a lot."

He dropped the phone, ran into his bedroom, slipped into the Sam Browne belt, buckled it, checked the revolver in the holster.

Ellen blocked him as he came out. "What is it?" she cried.

"Pingree. He just slipped past Punta Rassa."

"You'll want Tim. Here's the list of phone numbers he left."

"You track him down. I don't have time if I'm going to beat Pingree to his landing."

He brushed past her and ran out to his car. Behind him he heard the frantic clatter of the telephone as Ellen started flashing for the operator. He spun right onto McGregor Boulevard. The ghostly gray columns of royal palms flickered past, then curved lines of coconut palms, then scrub pine and palmetto. He swerved down the road to Iona Cove, drove a mile, turned back upriver toward Pingree's Landing. As soon as he made the turn he switched off his headlights. The road was just a track across sand, faint and blurred in the starlight.

Bushes lifted a solid black wall ahead and he saw the glint of Pingree's parked car. He skidded to a halt, ran stumbling down the long black footpath to the river. Mangroves brushed his face and flung cunning loops at his feet. He reached the cove and saw the dark bulk of the shack and the pier staggering out drunkenly on its pilings and the empty black water. For a moment he was afraid he had guessed wrong, and might stand there helplessly while Pingree cruised upriver to another landing place.

Then he heard the exhaust. It came tapping closer and closer like the sound of a blind man's cane. He would never forget that sound. Five weeks ago a man in that boat had squinted down the barrel of a 30-30 rifle and squeezed the trigger a split-second too late.

A boat drifted into the cove as quietly as the reflection of a cloud on water. Bow and stern lines squeaked tight on pilings. Voices whispered. A man climbed onto the dock, padded along sagging planks, shuffled through sand. It was Pingree. Watery glints rippled along the rifle in his right hand. Johnny flattened himself against the wall. The revolver sat up easily and lightly in his hand. Inside his chest his heart sent out pulses as slowly and heavily as a bell buoy. Either this was the man who killed Tony, or he knew who had. One way or another he was close to the end of the long hunt.

"Drop it, Pingree," he called. "This is the Border Patrol." The man froze like a dog taking a point.

The rifle fell to the sand.

Without any warning feet clattered on the deck of the boat and men leaped into the water. Johnny went cold. He heard the desperate churning of water. The swimmers were heading for the bushes along shore. He didn't know what kind of characters Pingree had picked up in Havana. They might be tough babies. If they were armed and started working on him from different points along shore things wouldn't look good.

He yanked out his handcuffs: "Get in the shadows here," he snapped. "Then hold out your right hand."

Pingree didn't budge. Either he was scared stiff or was stalling. Bushes crackled as the aliens scrambled ashore. Johnny stepped out into the open, shot once at the sound. Pingree still hadn't moved. His face looked heavy and white, like a skinned ham. Johnny was tempted to clip him with the barrel of the revolver and put him away, but then Pingree couldn't do any talking. And he didn't know much how time he had before Tim would come roaring along.

"You have one second to hold out your hand for the bracelet," he said.

Pingree moved his right hand slowly forward. This was the wrong way to handcuff a person. The right way was to make your prisoner stand at arm's length from a wall and lean forward until his head touched it. Then, when you made him put his hands behind his back, the guy was off balance and helpless. There wasn't time to make Pingree do all that. Johnny leaned forward to snap on the cuffs, keeping his revolver back against his body and watching Pingree closely. There was one dangerous moment when he had to concentrate on Pingree's right hand to get the bracelet on it.

That was the moment when a wave of blackness started at the base of his skull and washed up quickly through his head.

CHAPTER THIRTEEN

He was struggling to awaken from a nightmare. He seemed to be floating in black water at the bottom of a very deep well. Far above him, somebody was leaning over the edge of the well dropping stones into the water at regular intervals. The plunk of each stone set up echoes inside his head. He tried to climb the sides of the well and found himself teetering on hands and knees, staring at sand lying gray and rumpled in the starlight.

Several objects glittered near him. He balanced himself carefully, because the sand was tilting like the Gulf in a ground swell, and reached for one of the objects. Handcuffs. He stuffed them into a pocket, wondering how he happened to drop them. The second object turned out to be his revolver. He was upset about that; it did revolvers no good to be dropped into sand. The third and last object was tiny, and lay several feet away from him. The thing was an empty .45 cartridge case.

That was queer. It couldn't have come from his revolver, because revolvers didn't eject cartridge cases when you fired them. Only automatics did. And besides, his revolver was a .38 not a .45. He had dropped everything else that had been lying on the sand, however, so perhaps he had dropped the cartridge case too. He put it in a pocket, crawled to a nearby cabbage palm and hauled himself up by the trunk until he was standing.

Suddenly he remembered everything that had happened.

He stumbled out to the dock. The boat was gone. He swung around and stared at the shack and the rumpled sand and the mangroves that reared up like frozen black surf around the clearing. He took out his flashlight. Its beam probed shadows, flickered over empty sand and over water as smooth as tar. There were not even bubbles on the water to show that a boat had recently left the cove. He looked at his watch. Half an hour had passed since he reached out to snap the handcuffs on Pingree's wrist.

A lot of things didn't make sense. Pingree had tried to kill him a few weeks ago. Tonight Pingree had a chance to do the job right and more reason to do it, but he had cruised off leaving him alive. Something was phony. He stared at the .45 cartridge case.

He walked back to the footpath to where he had left his car. As he started to get in, he heard the hum of another car racing toward him. He crouched beside a fender.

The car swished to a halt near him and he saw that he was right in not hoping. It was a Border Patrol sedan. He stood up and called, "They got away, Tim."

Tim jumped out of the black sedan and ran to him. "You hurt?" he asked.
"No."

The spotlight of the sedan flicked on, touched him briefly. Another voice
said, "The hell he isn't. Sand all over him and rocking like a boat." The
spotlight faded and the Lee County sheriff got out and joined them.

"Pingree slugged me, was all," Johnny said. "Rabbit punch. I'll be all
right."

"What happened?" Tim said.

"Pingree came off the boat and when I hailed him, other guys jumped in
the water and made it to shore. I started to handcuff Pingree. I was working too fast and got sloppy. He must have chopped down at the back of my
neck. I was out for half an hour. The boat's gone. Everybody's gone. Any
time you're ready you can start telling me what a great job I did."

"You don't mind if we catch a couple aliens first, do you? Get the aerial
up." He turned to the sheriff and said, "Block the Beach Road junction for
us, will you? Take Johnny's car. I'll call one of your deputies to take over,
soon as I can."

The sheriff drove away. Johnny raised the aerial and Tim sent the flash
to WWMI. Then they started back to Fort Myers. Johnny hung on as they
took curves; you wouldn't have thought McCarter could make like a dirt
track champion when he was in the mood. They screeched onto McGregor Boulevard in a turn that left hot rubber on the road, raced to the outskirts of town, skidded to a halt.

"Road block," Tim said.

Johnny pulled out the big sign from the luggage compartment, planted
it on the road where the sedan could spotlight the words: STOP. U. S.
OFFICERS. Tim raised the aerial and began sending more details to
WWMI. He finished, hauled out his pipe.

"What do I do?" Johnny said. "Just keep braced until you're ready to tee
off on me?"

"I have nothing to say right now."

Johnny shrugged. When it came it ought to be good. So long, fellows.
Nice to have been with you in the Border Patrol.

The funny thing was, he was beginning to work up a little respect for
the outfit. Apparently the boys really went to town when something
broke. Radio signals were jerking through the night and a net was spreading over south Florida. At first the meshes were large and loose. In Miami,
a patrol unit swung west and reported it was blocking the Tamiami Trail
at city limits. Up in Sarasota another unit cut Route 41.

An inner and outer net was starting to form. A patrol unit was racing
west from Miami to block the Tamiami Trail at Naples. A Florida Highway
Patrol car whisked out of the Fort Myers station and halted where the

Beach cutoff road met the Trail. A Fort Myers police car hauled off to the side of the road at Edison Bridge across the Caloosahatchee. The meshes of the net closed slowly.

Two hours later their own mesh of the net suddenly caught a bit of news. A truck driver for one of the gladiolus farms, coming out of town, looked back at their sign and then stopped to see what was happening.

"Aliens," Tim said. "Did you happen to see a couple of strangers in wet clothes around town tonight?"

The truck driver thought a moment. "Look, Tim," he said. "We been friends for years. If a guy picked up a couple guys down the road earlier tonight and gave them a lift into town, not knowing a thing about them, would he be in a jam?"

"Hell, no. Did you pick them up?"

"Well, yeah. They didn't look like aliens, see? They talked just like you or me, only sort of tough. Their clothes were wet, all right. They said they'd been in a friendly tussle and fell off a dock."

"Give it to me fast and straight," Tim said, opening the circuit to WWMI.

Twenty minutes later, after some quick checking by the Fort Myers police, everybody on the radio net knew that two aliens, who had probably lived in the United States for a long time and then had been deported, had hopped a ride into Fort Myers before the net was formed and got out of town on a Trailways bus heading north on Route 41.

Half an hour went by. Then the Sarasota unit called WWMI and said in a cheery and not very official way, "Easy one hand. Just pulled your boys off the Trailways bus. Where do you want them delivered?"

"Lee County jail in Fort Myers," WWMI said. Then it added, "MI 3 from WWMI. Attention Inspector McCarter."

Tim flipped down the lid of the glove compartment and checked in.

"What do you think about Pingree?" WWMI asked.

Tim tapped out, "Everything indicates Pingree escaped in his boat. His car still parked near his shack."

"MI 3 from WWMI," the receiver said. "Chief Patrol Inspector will meet you at Lee County jail at approximately 0300. To all other units: nice work, everybody. Return to normal assignments."

At ten o'clock the next morning Johnny sat in the living room of the McCarter house and tried to shrug off the sick throbbing in his stomach. He was disgusted with himself. You might think he was a school kid worrying about being thrown off the team. He watched Chief Patrol Inspector Brian come in and sit down heavily. Across the room Tim McCarter cleared his throat with a noise like a wagon crunching over glass.

The chief said, "I've been over things again with those two aliens. They were deported as habitual criminals in 1947 and slipped back to Cuba a couple months ago. They met Pingree in a Havana bar and made a deal to be landed here and driven to the bus station. Their friends in New York had sent them drivers' licenses and other fake identification and they figured they had no worries once they landed. So when Edwards grabbed Pingree, they made a break for it and that's the last they saw of Pingree."

Johnny fingered the .45 cartridge case in his pocket and said, "How many shots did they hear after the hassle started?"

"I suppose one," Brian said. "You only shot once."

"Yes, but I found a .45 cartridge case on the sand when I came to."

"It could have been lying there for days," Tim said.

"Yeah, sure," Brian said. "Well, things have popped so fast that I haven't had a chance to get the whole story of how this started. Let's have it, Tim."

Johnny braced himself in the chair.

Tim said, "Last night at eight o'clock I was out talking to people I thought might have a line on Pingree. Edwards was here. A friend of his—the same old Cracker who gave him the tip to start with—phoned and said Pingree had just gone upriver. Edwards figured Pingree would land at his shack and decided it would take too long to locate me. So he took off for Pingree's Landing while Ellen checked around for me."

Johnny was mildly surprised. McCarter had had a good chance to go to work on him with brass knuckles, and instead was taking it easy.

The chief said, "How long did it take Ellen to locate you?"

"About twenty minutes. The way I figure it, Edwards had a tough decision to make. If he waited to notify me, Pingree might land and get away. If he went alone, he was one guy against three.

"He got there a couple of minutes before the boat came in. Pingree came ashore carrying a rifle. Edwards drew on him and told him to drop it. The two aliens jumped in the water and got ashore. Edwards stepped out to handcuff Pingree and while he was doing it, Pingree sneaked in a rabbit punch. When Edwards woke up, it was half an hour later and everybody had disappeared."

Johnny took a deep breath. The brass knuckles were there under the gloves. McCarter realized something could be said in favor of his action in starting after Pingree alone and cagily said it first. But all the time McCarter had been waiting to slug him with the charge that he walked up to a disarmed smuggler and let himself be rocked to sleep.

Brian hadn't missed anything. He said, "Edwards, this Pingree had dropped his rifle, hadn't he?"

"Yes sir."

"Exactly how did you go about handcuffing him?"

"Now wait a minute," Tim said in a harsh voice. "Don't forget two tough characters had just reached shore. Edwards didn't have time to handcuff

Pingree the way the book says. He had to take a chance and he didn't quite get away with it."

"All right, Tim, all right," the chief said. "I was just asking. I wasn't going to take your boy apart."

"Okay, then," Tim muttered.

This was really something, Johnny thought.

Brian said, "Edwards, do you have anything to add to all this?"

"Well, I could have told it so I looked a lot worse."

"Just leave it the way it is," Tim said irritably.

Brian got up. "Suits me," he said. "Edwards, you have nothing to worry about. And I'm not forgetting that you got the tip originally. Well, what do we do about Pingree?"

"He must be low on gas and supplies," Tim said. "He can't hide out long. I don't suppose you could spare us any help in running him down?"

"Wish I could, Tim. But we still have this big Havana deal to worry about, with aliens dropping out of sight by the dozens. I don't dare stretch things too thin anywhere in the sector. You two boys see if you can clean it up. Better get some sleep for now. So long."

After the sound of his car faded, Johnny moved cramped muscles and said, "I don't get it, Tim. You know I'd have rushed off alone to Pingree's Landing even if you'd only been two minutes away."

"Yeah, I know that. Whatever headaches I have about you, they're mine and not Ed Brian's."

"You know something? I like you a lot better than I did. I wish I thought we'd get along from now on. But frankly, I think you're still going to need aspirin."

"Don't let it worry you. I don't expect people to change overnight. Speaking of headaches, you got any bad effects from that rabbit punch?"

"I'm all right. Sleepy is all."

"You feel up to a little workout?"

"If I have to. What kind of workout?"

"A while back," Tim said, "you were acting tougher than usual and I said we'd probably have to have it out some day. I asked if you wanted to make it right then. You said you'd take a rain check. I'm collecting that rain check now."

Johnny stared at him. McCarter's face looked as blank as his bald head. "You're kidding," he said.

"No I'm not. Unless you claim you're still rocky from that rabbit punch, we're going outside and I'm going to take some of that tough-guy recklessness out of you."

"Oh, I get it. Years ago when Ed Brian was a kid you cooled him off that way, didn't you? He told me about it. But look. It won't work with me. The setup is different. It would be silly."

"Aw come on," Tim said softly. "Let me be silly if I want to be."

"I'm not going to fight you."

Tim said regretfully, "This may be hard on the furniture," and began unbuckling his Sam Browne belt.

Arguing with this character was like trying to stop a bulldozer by lying in its path. "It would probably be my chair that got broken," Johnny said wearily. "All right, let's go." This was one of the most ridiculous things that had ever happened to him. Just when he started to like the guy, he had to fight him. Unfortunately he couldn't explain to Tim that it was a waste of time trying to beat some sense into this heel Edwards, on account of Edwards was busy with a small private manhunt that kept him from being lovable.

They went outside and Tim suggested that they stay on the river side of the garage so that Ellen, working in her orange grove, couldn't see them. Johnny took off his belt and jacket, tested the footing in the sand.

"You ready?" Tim said politely.

Johnny put up his guard, and nodded. He felt oddly helpless, watching the big man facing him. How did you begin a thing like this when you didn't want to begin it? He started circling slowly to his right, waving a feeble left jab at Tim.

Something clipped his forehead and set him back three feet. Oh. You began it like that.

The punch hadn't hurt. Enough power in it to move a piano but not much jolt. Still, nobody likes to be tossed around. He came back fast, slipped a hook that steamed at him like a slow freight, whipped in a hard right. He could feel the impact right up to his ear. Bob Tate had gone down under a punch like that. It bounced off Tim's jaw and the guy didn't even blink. A lot of slow-freight hooks came back at him and he had to weave fast. Slow or not, the way those hooks kept trundling at you from all directions you could get in trouble playing on the tracks.

He moved back and tried to figure what to do. He hadn't really meant to throw the right that hard. He didn't want to knock the guy cold. And to be honest, quite possibly he couldn't. The sensible way to handle a man as rugged as McCarter was to stay at long range and cut him up with jabs and right crosses.

When you came right down to it, apparently you couldn't get a draw with Tim. It was either take him or be taken. He drilled in a hard jab, feinted another and got a quick opening for a right cross. He didn't throw it. He slipped a hook over his shoulder, got another opening, passed that up too. Quick, somebody, lend this guy Edwards some killer instinct. Or anyway lend him some brains. You know what this idiot is going to do? He's going to ask for it. He's going to poke his profile right out on the tracks and derail some of those slow-freight hooks, just to get this dull business over.

The hooks slammed into him, rolling him back and back and then flapping him down on the sand.

A girl's voice, clear and furious, said, "Why don't you get down on hands and knees and bite it out with him?"

That startled Johnny into opening his eyes. Beyond Tim's legs, planted like a couple of tree trunks in front of him, he saw Ellen.

Tim swung around and mumbled, "I didn't know you were here."

"Don't let me interrupt. Can I bring you a flint ax or some other primitive weapon?"

"Now listen, Ellen, this is none of your business."

"Whose business is it? The coroner's?"

"You know Edwards and I have been working up to this for a long time. And that stunt he pulled going after Pingree was the pay-off. So after Ed Brian left I decided we'd settle things and—"

"I've been watching for five minutes and all you've settled is the fact that you're forty-five years old."

"You don't have to tell me nothing else is settled yet," Tim said grimly. He turned and looked down at Johnny and said, "I don't see you getting up."

It was a little late to try playing dead again. "Just prop me up against the garage if you want to take a few more swings."

"Don't kid me. You're not that bad off."

"All right. I'm fine. I just like it lying here—"

"You were talking about Bob Tate once and saying he quits easy. And I said lots of guys quit easy and asked how fast you get up when you get knocked on your can. This looks like the answer."

"Look, Tim, you just won a fight. What do you want to prove it, a death certificate?"

"You know something, Edwards? I didn't care whether I won this or not. Main thing I wanted was to see if you could take it. I wondered about that business at Pingree's Landing. You bobbed up without a scratch and claimed you'd been knocked out for half an hour. Well, now I've stopped wondering. That empty .45 case you found. Somebody shot at you and you turned yellow and ran."

Johnny got up. This was bad stuff. "Maybe we'd better have a rematch."

"I'll give you one," Tim said, "but it won't prove anything. Now you're more scared of what I think of you than you're scared of getting hurt."

Ellen walked up and shoved them firmly apart. She faced Tim and said, "If we weren't related I'd say you came from a long line of morons. Tim! Be sensible. A child could tell you what happened. Johnny threw that fight to you."

"He what!"

"He threw it to you. I was watching for five minutes. I didn't try to stop it because nobody was getting hurt. Johnny had several chances to hit you and didn't take them. And you were too slow to hit him. Then before I could move, Johnny walked right in and let you knock him down."

"Look, Ellen, you're talking in your sleep."

"Don't forget I saw Johnny hit Bob Tate. All he did was wave at you."

Tim looked at Johnny and snapped, "What do you say about all this?"

"I don't think anything I said would matter."

"You got something there," Tim muttered. He thought for a few moments, jamming his hands into his pockets as if he didn't trust them out in the open where they could turn into fists. "Well," he said finally, "I'll give you the benefit of the doubt. But just remember it's Ellen's doubt. I can't seem to work up any." He turned and walked heavily toward the house.

Ellen sighed. "I don't suppose," she said, "any man likes to think a fight was thrown to him."

"I didn't do a very good job. Maybe he's right that I can't take it. I never really had a chance to find out."

"You took a few cuts on your face. If you want to come in the house I'll fix them. Do you know something, Johnny? You could make a good friend out of Tim. What keeps you from trying? I've known that something very important is bothering you. What is it?"

"It's a long story and I forget how it starts."

"All right," she said. "It's just the cuts on your face you want fixed. Come on."

He sat on a chair in the kitchen and let her dab at his face with bits of cotton. She had long cool fingers. It made him remember the time in Havana when he had watched her helping Bob Tate.

She stuck an adhesive bandage under his left eye and said, "There."

"Thanks for everything."

"Don't mention it," she said coolly. "Letting Tim win that fight was a very fine gesture. It's a point in your favor. I wish I could think of another." She got up and left.

CHAPTER FOURTEEN

Johnny folded the Sunday newspaper and rose from the breakfast table and said, "Hope you haven't changed your mind about this being a day off."

"No," Tim said. "I haven't changed my mind."

Johnny counted the words. Six. In the week since the fight that was the first time Tim had wasted six words on him when one would do.

"I thought I'd go to the beach," Johnny said. "Planned to meet somebody there."

"Oh," Ellen said. She added lightly, "The same somebody you had a date with twice in the last week?"

"Don't grill people that way," Tim snapped.

"I merely wondered what she was like," Ellen murmured. "Can't I ask Johnny a simple little question such as what is she like, Johnny?"

"It looks as if nobody can stop you," Tim said.

"She's just a girl," Johnny said. "Little redheaded kid who's staying at the beach for the season."

"It must be nice," Ellen said, "to have hair all one color, not bleached into streaks like mine. What's her name, Johnny? And—"

Tim said, "You already asked one question. Why don't you lay off?"

Johnny walked out of the room. It took more than Tim McCarter to stop Ellen when she set her mind on something. And, since there was no red-headed girl, he might have trouble keeping up his end of the conversation. He collected his bathing suit and a towel, wrapped his .38 in them so it wouldn't show and left the house.

He had spent those two evenings during the past week poking around Pingree's Landing. He had gone through the shack until he almost had a census of the termites working through its wood. That put him one up on the Lee County sheriff, who had made an official search without finding termites.

Today he was working on another idea. It was so vague that he couldn't describe it to himself. What happened was that you tried to fit disconnected facts into a pattern and suddenly got a flicker that came and went so fast that you couldn't remember the pattern.

He drove to the cove at Iona, a couple miles downriver from Pingree's Landing, rented a flat-bottomed boat with an inboard motor and cruised slowly up the Caloosahatchee. At Pingree's Landing he switched off the engine and began poling upstream close to the bank. He was looking for the cabin cruiser. Pingree's brain couldn't have been working very well if he had hidden the boat anywhere near his shack; however, his own brain wasn't working well either and maybe this was a good way to give it a day off.

When you looked at a mile of riverbank from a distance it looked like a mile of riverbank. But when you came close it turned out to be several miles of riverbank, because of the way coves and sloughs cut the shore line into lace. Here and there, as he poled along, the pale copper water deepened and he saw the rakish shadows of snook. Dense mangroves waded tiptoe on their roots into the water. Sometimes they almost enclosed a small pool that couldn't be seen until you looked at the bushes from a certain angle and caught a glint of water behind them.

By noon he had poled nearly a mile upriver, and turned back to search along shore below the landing. In mid-afternoon he saw a white glint back among the mangroves. It might be merely a faded leaf but he decided to take a look anyway.

Bushes parted like a theater curtain. Deep in the pale green shadows loomed the cabin cruiser.

For a minute he couldn't move. His boat drifted across the hidden cove and the blank eyes of the cruiser's portholes seemed to watch it coming. Nothing stirred. He reached slowly into his rolled-up towel and eased his fingers around the butt of the revolver. The bow of his boat squeaked against the cruiser. There was no answering sound. Johnny snaked forward and slid aboard Pingree's boat.

It was deserted. Below in the cabin the bunks were rumpled and smelled stale, and the galley held dishes on which food had dried hard. Above deck, lines angled from bow and stern to clumps of mangrove. He hauled the boat close to the bank and went ashore, balancing on mangrove roots to avoid leaving footprints in the muck. Pingree hadn't been as careful; here and there the muck showed where he had stepped. Johnny started following the footprints. As he went along he noted that branches had been snapped at intervals. The breaks were at waist level, as if the man had blazed a trail to help him find the boat again. The trail hit the sandy road a few hundred yards downriver from the footpath leading to Pingree's Landing.

He returned to the boat and searched it carefully. It looked as if Pingree had only taken two things away with him: his 30-30 rifle, and the cruiser's big bow anchor. He searched still more carefully. There were a couple of new scars in the wood of the stern transom, as if the point of a heavy anchor had been dropped there. And, quite close to the scars, you could see where a dark stain had oozed over the paint.

His right hand came from his pocket carrying an empty .45 cartridge case. The vague pattern he had glimpsed and lost stood out glaringly. He had been right in suspecting that Pingree wasn't the killer. The guy was a small-timer in the smuggling gang. He didn't like lying low, and slipped off to Havana on his own. The gang had somebody in Havana take a shot at him to scare him out of business, but Pingree got his two aliens aboard and headed back to Fort Myers. The boys were waiting for him. There was only one complication: a character named Edwards who came boiling up at the last moment.

Johnny nodded. He had been right in deciding that Pingree's brain hadn't been working very well if he had hidden the boat near his shack. Because, natch, Pingree's brain hadn't been working at all. Pingree hadn't carried the big bow anchor far. Probably just down to the bottom of the river.

Things were looking up. For the first time, he had cut across a trail leading directly to the man who carried a .45 automatic and had killed twice with it. It wasn't much of a trail—just a line of broken branches leading from the boat to the sandy road paralleling the river—but fortunately he didn't have to follow it. All he had to do was sit in the boat long enough and the killer would come creeping back through the mangroves. The guy intended to use Pingree's boat again; otherwise he wouldn't have snapped the branches.

The killer intended to use something else again, too. That was the rifle. Up to now, Johnny knew, he had been lucky. The gang hadn't wanted to kill him and bring half the Border Patrol down on Fort Myers. Of course Pingree had taken a couple of shots at him originally but that didn't count; Pingree must have acted on impulse, without orders. Now things were different. If somebody happened to be killed with a 30-30 bullet and Pingree's rifle were found nearby, Pingree would be blamed.

A shiver about the size of a black widow spider crawled over Johnny's skin. If he wasn't careful, and lucky, that rifle would be found near him.

It was very dark in the little cove walled by the mangroves. The only light came from the green goblin face of his wrist watch. It was nine-thirty. He settled down quietly in the cockpit of Pingree's boat to spend the next three or four hours. That would make a total of almost thirty hours he had spent in the boat since finding it more than a week ago. Every time he had a free night he slipped away from the McCarter house, hid his car off the sandy road and crept along the trail of broken branches to wait in the boat.

Spending night after night in the boat was no fun. He was getting jumpy from strain and lack of sleep. Back at the McCarter house they thought he was dating a girl these evenings. Tim McCarter had even broken a moody silence to lecture him about not going overboard for a woman. Tim would have done better to give his sister a lecture, because she seemed to be going out a lot in the evenings, too, to meet Bob Tate. Some girls liked to go slumming.

What Ellen did, however, wasn't his problem. He had plenty of his own. Right now there were a million sounds to identify. Insects wove a net of shrill vibrations around his head. The tide made sipping noises among the mangrove roots.

Some night, one of those sounds would have a meaning he'd better catch fast. The killer might not stroll casually into his trap. Several nights recently he had noted headlights keeping pace behind him as he drove down McGregor Boulevard. Each time he had swung into back roads to break his trail and the headlights had vanished. The whole business could be meaningless but this time he wasn't taking chances. If the killer ever trailed him here, things would happen—

He listened. Actually it was a number of old sounds strung together in a new way. Something was coming through the mangroves. It didn't sound like a small animal or bird or snake. The small animals made a rustle, stopped to listen, came on again. Birds moved in quick fluttering bursts. This was a longer, heavier sound, made up of leaves rustling and branches scraping and mud sucking at feet. A big confident 'gator could be coming. Or a man, not quite so confident.

He crouched, eased back the hammer of the revolver. Something flickered among the mangroves. It could be a pen-sized flashlight, pricking the darkness and vanishing. The winks came slowly closer. He gripped his own flashlight in his left hand, aimed it, waited. For a few thuds of his heart there was only blackness and silence. Then the light winked ten feet away. He began taking up trigger slack, flipped on his flashlight.

The white beam drilled through the dark with almost physical force. It gleamed on hair laced with pale streaks of gold and silver. It showed a girl's body frozen in long tense lines of terror. Ellen's body.

Ellen stared blankly into the light. "Johnny?" she said in a soft wail. "Johnny?"

CHAPTER FIFTEEN

That wasn't blood in his head any more. It was pink steam. It fogged his eyesight and built up pressure until the top of his head jiggled like the lid of a kettle. Right from the start she had made confetti of his plans. First she helped wreck his trap in the Plaza de la Fraternidad in Havana. Then she came along with her boyfriend at just the right moment to let Rankosci escape. Now she would mess up the boat deal. And just a moment ago—although it probably wouldn't impress her at all—she had almost interfered with the trajectory of a bullet.

"By an odd chance," he said harshly, "it is Johnny. It could just as easily have been a guy with a 30-30 rifle."

She gasped in relief and said, "I'm so glad it's you. I was getting scared."

"You shouldn't have been. I was only going to shoot you once."

He pulled the boat close inshore, stretched out a hand. She jumped aboard with a flash of slim bare legs. In snake country, bare legs. High-heeled shoes, too. Her legs were scratched and the shoes were blobs of mud.

"I bet it's quite a sight," he said, "to see a bare-legged girl in high heels kicking it out with a snake."

She said in a faint voice, "I wish I thought this would amuse you. I was dressed to kick it out with that redhead you claimed to be dating."

"Was it your car trailing me several nights lately?"

"Yes. I kept leaving the house before you did and waiting along your route, until last night I saw you driving back from Iona Cove and I parked near there tonight and followed you here without lights."

"The Border Patrol needs you."

She sighed and said, "I wish you did."

Next to this dame, Little Red Riding Hood was a woman of the world. Some night she was going to be out with the wrong guy, and one of her naïve actions or remarks would win her a double helping of trouble. It would be a good turn to throw a little scare into her. "Of course I need you," he said, putting a juke-box croon into the words. "It gets lonely here. Now you just slip out of your inhibitions and into something soft and clinging and we'll play house. Or do I mean boat?"

"Don't be ridiculous," she said calmly.

He frowned. He reached out and took hold of her shoulders and said, "I'm ridiculous, am I? Did anybody ever tell you that no man likes his wolf call tagged as a bleat?"

She gave a queer sort of irritated laugh, twitched her shoulders to shake off his grip. That pink steam was building up pressure again in his head. Did she think she could get away with treating every man she met like a case history in social service work? She didn't seem to realize what might happen. He had tried to give her a hint but words didn't impress her. Maybe a little action would teach her a lesson. He slid his hands down her arms, grabbed her wrists, jerked them behind her back. Her body curved in helplessly against his. She gasped. The white blur of her face tilted away from him. All right, he thought, now beg or cry or fight.

She didn't move. She wasn't even breathing quickly. She was merely waiting for him to get tired and go away. That wouldn't work. Frankly, he was getting less tired every second.

He clamped both her wrists in one of his hands, slid his free hand up to the back of her head. Her lips felt cool and childish, as if she were being taught how to play post office and didn't like it much. For some reason it hurt not to get any reaction at all from the girl. It was senseless to go on hurting himself but he was in a senseless mood, like a kid falling off a toy wagon and getting up and kicking the thing and screaming you old wagon you. He grabbed violently at the neck of her dress and started to rip it off her shoulders.

That made her begin crying. She didn't sob or anything but merely let the tears come in a quiet steady stream. If that was intended to make him feel like a rat it was a waste of time because he already felt like one.

He let her go and stepped back. "All right," he snapped. "Take it easy. The all-clear just sounded."

"Was it fun?" she said in a choked voice. "You were trying to prove something, weren't you, Johnny? Did you manage to do it?"

He wished he could watch the expressions on her face but it was too dark. "I was trying to prove when a girl keeps chasing a man she can catch herself some trouble."

"According to the best authorities," Ellen said with a tiny laugh, "she can often catch herself a man, too. I often wondered if you might be worth catching."

"Now you know. I'm worth catching like malaria."

"You mean that act you just put on? You were about as convincing as if you'd put on a cardboard mustache. I don't know a thing more than I did before."

"What do you want to know?"

"Oh, lots of things. I'd like to know why you're such a grim person. If you want to tell me anything you might start by explaining what you're doing here."

"Believe it or not, I'm waiting for a ferry boat."

"All right. If you won't give me any answers I'll give you some. This is Howard Pingree's boat. You kept hunting until you found it. If someone really made you answer, you'd say you figure Howard Pingree will come back to get his boat some night and you hope to be waiting for him. You'll claim you're doing it because you and Tim had that fight and you want to show Tim how wrong he was about you."

She was smart. That was just what he had planned to feed her. "Got it worked out pretty well, haven't you?"

"I have it worked out better than that, Johnny. I know this country and its people and Tim fairly well. Howard Pingree could never walk ashore here and hide for two weeks without Tim learning about it. So where is he?"

She was a little too smart. "What happens if I stick to that first story you dreamed up for me?"

"I don't believe it and Tim won't either."

"You're going to tell him, are you?"

"You haven't given me any reason why not."

"Let's get this straight," he said. "I always like to know exactly what the deal is when I'm being blackmailed. If I give you the full story, will you keep it to yourself?"

"I doubt it very much, Johnny. Look at it this way. Suppose Tim started searching through the mangroves here, when you're on the boat. Each of you thinks the other is somebody else, and starts shooting. That leaves me holding a double funeral. So don't tell me a thing unless you want to."

For some strange reason he did want to tell her. The hunt had been a lonely job. Nobody hoped he would win, or would feel badly if he lost. For more than seven months he had been locked up inside his own head and he wanted to get out. Maybe Ellen couldn't help, but it was worth a try.

He started talking. At first it wasn't easy. Some of the ideas that had been slinking around inside his head didn't look pretty when he dragged them out for somebody else to see. He went through the whole sickening business of how Tony had needed help but he hadn't wanted to be bothered and so Tony was murdered. He told her about the manhunt and where it stood now.

He finished and peered through the gloom to see how she had taken it. She was curled in a corner of the seat like a kitten trying to get warm, or maybe like a girl trying to get as far away from him as possible. She was crying again.

"It might be interesting to know who you're crying for," he said. "For Tony? For Ellen and Tim McCarter?"

"I'm crying about you. Johnny, it's such a waste. All that drive and energy of yours concentrated on one horrible idea."

"What's horrible about catching the guy who killed Tony?"

She said faintly, "You don't want to catch him. You want to murder him."

He didn't like the sound of that word. He didn't like it at all. But maybe it was just as well to understand right now what he was willing to do.

"I could dress it up in fancy words about making the guy pay his debt to society and saving the courts trouble," he said. "But all right. Let's just say I want to murder him."

"Johnny, you could do so much with your life if you put that energy into something else."

"Sure. I could break seventy in golf or catch a record salmon or invent a drink that would make Johnny Edwards as well-known a name as Tom Collins. But you know what? I've already tried those things and all they do is help pass the time. This is the only thing I've ever really wanted."

She whispered, "Johnny, it's not much of a career, is it? It can end awfully fast. Then what will you do?"

"I think I'll invent that drink I mentioned. The Johnny Edwards. And after inventing the thing I can stay drunk on it."

"The trouble is you have a guilt complex. You're trying to punish yourself."

"Now that you've tagged it with a name, I just forget my guilt complex, huh?"

Ellen got up slowly, as if there were a lot of aches in her joints. "I think I'll go home," she said.

"And give Tim an earful, naturally?"

"I'm not going to tell him anything. Will you pull the boat in so I can get ashore?"

"Wait a minute," he muttered. "I'll go with you. If I stay on this tub and hear a rustle, I'll start thinking it's Tim and be afraid to shoot."

He switched on his flashlight, cleaned up the mud that had flaked off her shoes and made sure the boat looked as if nobody had been aboard.

By the time they reached the McCarter house it was after eleven. The door to Tim's bedroom was closed; on an impulse Johnny opened it quietly and peered in. The guy was sleeping. Light filtered into the room and waxed his bald head.

He left the room and closed the door and found Ellen standing there. "All right," he muttered. "I'll tell him."

"Thanks, Johnny."

"It may take me a while to work up to it. Don't expect me to start right off at breakfast. I get bored with my life story that early in the day."

"If you're not too tired," she said, "I have an idea that might be worth trying tonight. We could write down all the information you have about the man you've been hunting and see how many people around Fort Myers it fits."

He shrugged. When it came to detective work, everybody wanted to get in the act. Anyway it couldn't do any harm. They sat at the dining room table and Ellen began making mysterious charts.

"Now," she said finally, "you talked to one person in Havana who actually saw the murderer and who isn't a member of the gang. The Cuban landlady who was helping your friend hide."

"I went all over it with her and she couldn't describe him. She never had much contact with Americans. As far as she was concerned, most Americans sort of look alike, the way Chinese do to us. She was expecting a tall young American to come along asking where Tony was hiding and one dropped by to ask the question and that was it." Ellen began scribbling busily on one of her charts.

He said irritably, "Where do you think that gets us?"

"It gets us looking for a tall young American."

"Great. There can't be more than a thousand around Fort Myers."

"That's right. So now we've eliminated most of the population of Lee County. Out of our thousand suspects, how many might have been in Havana when your friend was killed? And how many could have been in Havana when I met you? The Havana gang must have told your man about that trap you set and he must have wanted to run over and take a look at you."

He hitched his chair around closer to her. "You're starting to interest me," he said. "Got some more ideas?"

"Oh yes. Now we look for a man who is smart enough to run the Fort Myers end of the operation and that will eliminate more people. He's got to have a job that apparently lets him make an honest living and yet gives him time to handle smuggling. He also has to be somebody you've met more than once around here."

"You're pulling that one out of a hat."

"Suppose you were in his position, Johnny? A man comes to Fort Myers to kill you. You know who he is but he doesn't know you. Would you avoid him or not?"

"All right. You win. Sure, I'd want to keep my eye on him as much as I could without making him suspicious. Look. I can answer some of these questions but not all. Do you know people well enough to answer the rest?"

"When you grow up in a small town," Ellen said, "what you learn about your neighbors would fill a book. Get the telephone directory and we'll be scientific."

They made out a long list of names of men he had met in the Fort Myers area. Some names weren't in the book, but as they went through the alphabet one thing or other reminded them of the missing names.

As they went through the T section, Ellen said, "You just skipped one. How about Tate, Robert J.?"

"Oh. Did I miss him? I'm giving him to you as a present."

"That's very charming of you," she said. "But we won't play favorites. His name goes in."

When they finished there were about two hundred names. He stared at them and felt a shiver skate over his body. Until now the hunt had been an impersonal affair, but having names to work on made the killer seem very real and brought him close. In fact—

He looked around at the black rectangles of the dining room windows. It was a mild evening and most of the windows were open. It was merely imagination, of course, but when you were in a mood like this you thought something flickered and vanished beyond one of the screens. He got up, knowing it was silly, and took his revolver and went outside and circled the house. Naturally there wasn't anything suspicious. He went in and apologized for being jumpy and then on a stubborn impulse shut all the windows and lowered the shades.

So far, the list was a broad one. It covered men in their twenties or thirties who were tall and whom he had met more than once. He and Ellen started applying the other tests. Was the first man on the list smart enough to run a big smuggling racket? Did he have the right kind of cover job or hobby? Could he have been in Havana those two times? It was a long job and by one o'clock they had only tested the first ten names.

Ellen stood up and rubbed tired eyes. "I can work on this tomorrow," she said. "I'll leave everything over here on the buffet. Tim won't go poking through it. Do you know what, Johnny? I found out one nice thing about you tonight. I found out that you were avoiding me in Havana not because you disliked me at first sight but because you were busy. The way my mind works, that turns you into a much nicer person."

While he was wondering how to answer that, she walked around the table, bent down and kissed him. Her lips didn't seem quite so cool and childish this time. His face started roasting and he said, "What's that for?"

"That," she said calmly, "is so I can remember something else nice about the evening." She smiled and went off to her room.

She was a funny impulsive creature. He shrugged, put the incident out of his mind. He got ready for bed, found he wasn't quite sleepy enough and decided to relax on his bed to think about the list. It really might turn up something. Ellen had been smart to think of it. She wasn't as naïve as she seemed. Maybe she would make a fairly good Little Red Riding Hood after all. Give her enough time and she would have the average wolf baking cookies for her. She—

Wait a minute, chum. The list, remember?

Oh yes, the list. If Ellen worked on it all during the coming day she might finish checking all the names by night. She was a handy person to have around. It wasn't easy to keep her at arm's length, though. You started doing that and then you found your elbow joints bending treacherously and all of a sudden she was breathlessly close. You—

The list, bud, the list.

He got up irritably and crushed out his cigarette and switched off the light and went to bed. It was a silly list of names that just read Ellen McCarter, Ellen McCarter, Ellen McCarter.

CHAPTER SIXTEEN

Someone was shaking him roughly. He groaned and opened his eyes and saw a kid's balloon decorated with a threatening face floating over him. It turned out to be Tim's face.

"What a sight to greet a man when he wakes up," he said.

"Never mind the cracks," Tim said. "Get up, will you?"

He rolled out of bed and saw that it was just getting light.

"How come so early?" he complained. "The alarm clock hasn't gone off."

"Sometimes this job doesn't go by alarm clocks. One of the guide boat captains just called me. He wants to talk to us just as soon as we can get to Matanzas Pass. This guy is taking a party out after kings in about an hour and we have to get to the dock before he leaves. This may interfere with your rest, but once in a while the Border Patrol comes ahead of those late dates of yours."

Johnny washed, shaved, dressed and was ready in nine minutes. That gave him sixty seconds to gulp a cup of coffee which Ellen had ready. Amazing how a girl could look so bright and cheerful and pretty at short notice. He didn't have a chance to talk to her about last night because Tim was there, but Ellen patted the papers on the buffet and hummed the *I've Got a Little List* song from *The Mikado*. He remembered that Ellen McCarter-Ellen McCarter-Ellen McCarter list he had gone to sleep grumbling about. That was quite a list, too.

He and Tim climbed in the Border Patrol sedan and started down McGregor toward the beach. The speedometer needle swung up to forty. At that rate they would get to the beach in fifteen minutes, hardly enough time to start giving Tim the autobiography of Johnny Edwards. He peered at Tim's profile. It was as friendly a thing to have poised near you as the edge of a war club. Later in the day might be a better time to talk. He settled down in his corner of the front seat and fumbled in his blouse pocket for a cigarette. There was only one left in the pack. He took it out and crumpled the empty package and suddenly remembered a strange thing. Last night before going to bed he wanted a cigarette. He opened a new pack, took one, left the pack on his bureau. So why was only one cigarette left now?

He tried to smooth the crumpled package. It was hard to tell now whether it had been in his pocket a long time or not. He studied the cigarette. Usually after you carried cigarettes around for a while they lost grains of tobacco and thinned out at one end. This one was plump and straight. Of course anybody with sense would know that the almost-full pack was still on his bureau, just as anybody with sense would never have had the feeling last night that a man was peering in through the dining room window. He tossed the empty package away and lighted the cigarette. It was a perfectly ordinary cigarette and tasted very good.

They parked at the bridge leading over Matanzas Pass to Fort Myers Beach and strolled to one of the docks where a guide boat captain was warming up his engine. The man glanced up, waved casually.

"Nice morning," Tim said.

"Fine morning," the man said loudly. Then he lowered his voice and said, "If you don't mind I'll play with this engine while we talk, in case anybody wants to watch. Hope I didn't get you here on a wild goose chase."

"Once in a while," Tim said, "we even catch a wild goose. What's the deal?"

"You know Jake Bentz?"

"Sure. Commercial fisherman. A well-known bottle-a-day man."

"Yeah, well, I thought you might like to know Jake has just gone on the wagon. When he goes on the wagon he doesn't fool. He even loaded it on his boat when he went out fishing today. He left about six o'clock with more than a hundred gallons of drinking water. He figured on getting real thirsty."

"Did he figure on getting hungry, too?" Tim asked.

"Not too hungry. I wouldn't say he took more than a couple sacks of potatoes and a dozen cases of canned goods."

"Thanks."

"You haven't seen me, if Jake asks. And I don't know where he went except he claimed to be heading after them kings that are running fifteen miles out in the Gulf."

Tim nodded, and they walked back to the car.

"What do you make of it?" Johnny asked.

"No use guessing," Tim said. "We'll just have to hang around and meet Jake when he docks. Let's get some breakfast."

They entered one of the lunch places at the bridge and ordered breakfast. Johnny said, "I'm going to run across the road and phone."

Ellen's voice drifted across the wire, faint and pleasant.

"Hi," he said. "This is Johnny. A little matter worried me and I thought I'd check. In my rush this morning did I leave a cigarette burning on the edge of my bureau? If I did it might start a fire. It ought to be right beside an almost full pack of cigarettes on my bureau."

"I'll take a look, Johnny."

He waited, drumming his fingers slowly.

"Hello," Ellen said cheerily. "No cigarette burning. There was only one in the whole room, crushed out in your ash tray. It was nice of you to worry."

"Did you look right beside that nearly full pack of cigarettes on my bureau?"

"There wasn't any pack on your bureau."

His fingers were starting that drumming again. "Oh. This is my day for forgetting things. How's the list?"

"Well, I haven't started on it yet, Johnny. But I will as soon as I straighten up the house."

"Look," he said. "I was sort of wakeful last night and I got up and fooled around with those papers, not writing anything but just studying them and I was so foggy I could have mislaid some. Are they all there?"

"Just a moment." After another pause she came back and said, "Everything is there."

"I guess that's all. Thanks."

"Do you know this is the first time you've telephoned me, Johnny? Do you remember that first day in Havana growling that you'd give me a ring sometime? I'm glad you got around to it. Well, take care of yourself."

He repressed an urge to tell her to take care of herself, because he was afraid of using too much emphasis. There was no use passing on a completely formless fear to a girl who was all alone in a house on the outskirts of town.

He went back across the road to the other lunch room. Tim frowned at him and said, "You took long enough. Now you got cold fried eggs to eat."

"It's all right. I'm not hungry."

"If you have any ideas about slipping off to see that dame of yours while we're hanging around here, just forget them."

"Whenever I get tired of living my own life I'll call on you to do it for me."

"I don't think your life would interest me much," Tim said.

"That's too bad. I was just working up to telling you all about it."

Tim grunted, and didn't say anything more. The funny thing, Johnny thought, was that he *had* been trying to work up to it. There couldn't be a worse time. He bought cigarettes and began smoking one and found himself taking the others out of the pack and counting them. There were nineteen left.

Tim gave him a queer look and said, "How many did you expect to find?"

"I expected to find one from twenty leaves one. Look, are you in the mood to listen to a long story?"

"No. Let's finish and get out of here."

All through the morning they hung around the docks, and a good moment to talk to Tim never came. Tim prowled up and down like a heavy old watchdog worrying about cats. Jake Bentz and his boat were still missing. At noon they returned to the lunch room. Johnny ordered the Fishermen's Special and when it came pushed it around on his plate without eating much.

Tim pulled a quarter from his pocket and flipped it across the table. "I'll buy you a call to your redhead," he growled. "Then maybe I can eat in peace."

Johnny got up silently and went across the road and put in another call to the McCarter house. The phone rang and rang. It had an empty sound, and he began to sweat. Then suddenly there was a click and Ellen said hello. He took a moment to change the air in his lungs, and said hello.

"Is, uh, everything all right?" he asked.

"Why of course, Johnny. Why wouldn't it be?"

"How's the list coming?"

"I just finished charting everybody up to K. And do you know something queer? I've eliminated everyone so far."

"You've been going fast."

"I think I could have done one more letter," she said, "but I ran out of cigarettes and had to drive downtown to get some."

His left hand began to ache from gripping the receiver. "You ran out of cigarettes?" he said slowly.

"Yes. I was sure I had several nearly full packs lying around. I'm always forgetting one pack is open and starting another, but none of them had more than one or two left and so—"

"You're working too hard on that list. Why don't you go to a movie this afternoon or something?"

"But I'm fine, Johnny. And I wouldn't want to quit now. I keep feeling I'm getting closer to the answer."

"You sound tired, though."

"You're the one who sounds tired. Is anything wrong?"

It wasn't right to scare her to death with nothing to go on. "Nothing's wrong," he muttered. "Must be a bad connection."

"Johnny, I hate to ask this, but have you told Tim yet?"

"We've been so busy I haven't had a chance. I will, though, don't worry."

"I know you will, Johnny. Good-bye."

He said good-bye automatically and heard the connection click off and then realized that he wanted to keep talking to her because every second she was on the phone meant that she was still all right. He sat in the booth and brought out his cigarettes. The pack was half empty now. He tapped it so that four cigarettes stuck out. He took one openly with his right hand and tried to palm the others. They spilled on the floor. He wasn't very good at it. There was a character named Georg Rankosci who was a kleptomaniac about American cigarettes and who was very good at that trick.

Rankosci was over in Havana. He hoped.

He went back and joined Tim and said, "I don't feel so hot. Could you get along without me this afternoon?"

Tim said, "I couldn't and your redheaded dame can."

"Tim, I want to tell you something. It will take a while."

"We don't have time now. I want to ask around and see if anybody has an idea where Bentz could have gone."

Johnny picked up his lunch check and muttered, "Let's go, then."

They asked for news of Bentz at all the roadside places near the bridge and at the fish packing house and at the two docks. By mid-afternoon they had worked around to the drawbridge tender, without learning anything. At that point Jake Bentz came back. They went down to the dock and watched him leave paint on the pilings with a sloppy landing. He made his lines fast, came weaving down the dock toward them.

Tim said, "How were the kings running?"

Bentz stared at him like a mullet out of water and then giggled. "Never did catch up with them. Have a drink with me, boys?"

"Where did you take the supplies?"

"Supplies?" Bentz said vaguely. "Supplies?"

"What's the matter?" Tim said. "You need time to think about it?"

"I done nothing to worry about," Bentz said. "I was out after kings yesterday, see? They're running ten, fifteen miles out in the Gulf. This Cuban fishing schooner is out there, see? You know how they follow the schools up and down the Gulf. Well, it seems they got low on supplies and so they give me some dough to bring stuff out today."

"Ordinarily you report things like that."

"I was going to report it, Inspector. Only I stayed out there killing a bottle they broke out for me and I ain't thinking very straight. I didn't bring in nothing off that boat, honest. Go ahead and look."

"Believe I will," Tim said. He and Johnny searched the boat but no Cuban goods were aboard. Tim pulled a chart out of the rack in the cabin and asked Bentz to point out the exact location of the Cuban schooner. He jotted down the compass bearing and distance. "What's the name of this schooner?" he asked finally.

"The, uh, the Dolores M. out of Havana. You don't think I done wrong, do you, Inspector? It was just a little favor and I made forty bucks out of it. A guy could yank in three hundred pounds of kings and not clear that much."

"I'll let you know," Tim said. "Come on, Johnny."

They started walking back to the bridge and Johnny asked, "Is he telling the truth?"

"How do I know?" Tim said. "I sure wouldn't pick a lush like Bentz to run errands if I was cutting inside a few laws. But maybe with Howard Pingree hiding out, somebody had to go to the bottom of the barrel and get Jake."

"You think Pingree is hiding out?"

"What do you think?"

"I might make a guess if you would listen to a long story."

"You still trying to peddle that long story? Lay off until we have nothing to do. And anyway, guesses are no good. We don't have to guess about this schooner. I'm going to phone Bob Tate and see if he will fly us out."

They went to the place with the phone booth and Tim went in and closed the door and made his call. Johnny waited, fidgeting. He could run across to the other lunch room and call Ellen, but Tim would be sore and the phone was out where everybody could hear.

Tim finished and came out. "Okay," he said. "He'll take us. But he has to get the four-place amphibian down the ramp to the water and then warmed up, so we'll drive back to his place and save a little time."

They got in the car and started back. Tim was feeling pretty good about the plane angle. Assuming there was a schooner, they would reach it before anybody ashore could send a warning, assuming anybody wanted to. It was mighty nice of Bob Tate, Tim said. The guy was always ready to help. And usually there was no way to pay him, although in a case like this a voucher could probably go through for ten or fifteen bucks. A guy like Johnny, Tim said, would do worse than take a lesson from Bob Tate. There was a fellow who came out of the war with nothing, and got a couple of surplus planes and built up a good business crop dusting and flying people to Boca Grande and Sanibel and taking aerial photos.

Johnny didn't argue. Maybe, if he listened solemnly to the lecture, Tim would talk himself into a good mood. There was a small favor he wanted to ask. Bob Tate's hangar was upriver a quarter-mile from the McCarter house. So they would be driving right past the lane leading to the house.

He nodded gravely and said yes, he was changing his opinion of Bob. As they approached the lane he said, "How about dropping by the house just a minute? I want to pick up some cigarettes and things."

"All day you been like a cat looking for a place to have kittens. Settle down, will you?"

Tim stamped irritably on the accelerator. A little farther on they made the turn into the road leading to Bob Tate's hangar. They parked and went in.

Tate's mechanic, Jocko Stearns, peered down at them, jerked a thumb at the ramp. They went out and found Bob Tate waiting. He was wearing an old leather flying jacket decorated with the Flying Tigers' patch.

"All set?" Bob asked.

"Yeah," Tim said. "But before we start, have you any cigarettes? Johnny ran out and I only smoke a pipe."

"You're forgetting I don't smoke," Bob said. "It would do Johnny good to lay off a while."

"Maybe Jocko has a couple he can spare," Tim said.

Bob shrugged, went inside the hangar.

It was a complete waste of time. Johnny had cigarettes in his pocket. He had mentioned them merely as an excuse to stop and make sure Ellen was all right. But Tim meant well.

Bob Tate brought out the cigarettes and they boarded the plane and took off. For just a moment, as they banked to head downriver, Johnny caught a glimpse of the red roof of the McCarter house. It seemed like years since he left it that morning.

CHAPTER SEVENTEEN

In the front seat Tim and Bob checked the compass bearing and estimated the ground speed. Five minutes went by. Ten. The plane started flying a search pattern. Finally Tim tapped Bob Tate's shoulder, pointed off to starboard. The plane nosed toward the horizon to investigate a speck.

The speck grew and became a schooner, lying on the pale green water like a toy boat in a bathtub. Two men moved lazily on deck, mending a trawl net. Across the stem were faded letters: Dolores M., Havana.

Tim shouted over the roar of the engine, "How about landing so I can board her?"

"I don't like coming alongside a boat way out here," Bob complained. "If I bust up a wing we got a long swim home."

"There isn't any breeze or sea running. Come on, Bob."

A guy like Tate, Johnny thought, couldn't even have done kitchen police for the Flying Tigers.

Bob Tate frowned and brought the plane down about as gracefully as a clam shell bouncing across water. He seemed to be nervous. A Cuban in a dirty white cap ornamented with a shred of gold braid watched them.

Tim called, "This is the Border Patrol. Heard you ran out of supplies. If you're in distress you can put into the bay or river and I'll okay it."

The Cuban smiled. He had more gold in his teeth than on his cap. He said in a soft, slurring voice, "I am Luis Madero and this is my fishing boat, the Dolores M., out of Havana. Thank you, we are not in distress."

"How's the fishing?"

"Some mackerel. Some grouper. It is most good of you to fly out. Perhaps you will come aboard and have coffee?"

"Mighty nice of you," Tim said. "Maybe we will."

Johnny climbed onto the plane's right float, grabbed the line that snaked out from the schooner, drew the plane alongside and made it fast. A rope ladder tumbled down to him. He climbed to the schooner's deck, hoping that they could get the visit over fast. All he wanted was to hear Ellen saying in a surprised voice that she was all right.

He greeted the captain politely and looked around. One thing was sure; the schooner wasn't carrying all the aliens in Cuba or even a good catch of fish, because it was riding much too high in the water. The Dolores M. was an interesting boat. It had a new radio aerial and an old patched trawl net. Fish scales were scattered around artistically but there wasn't the odor of fish you might have expected. The hatches leading to the hold were battened down as if a hurricane were coming, or maybe a visit from the Border Patrol.

Tim and Bob Tate came aboard and the captain led them below to his cabin and served thick black Cuban coffee. They talked politely about hunting and fishing and Bob Tate told a rambling story about hunting wild turkeys in the Glades. Like all Bob's stories, this one put across the idea that he was pretty good at something. In this case, he turned out to be one of the few men in Lee County who could creep up on a wild turkey. Johnny wished the guy would shoot the turkey and announce its record-breaking weight so they could start back. It would be getting dark soon and probably Ellen wouldn't think to pull down the shades.

After they finished the coffee, Tim fingered a stack of magazines on the table and said, "I see you go in for western story magazines, captain."

"Very fine," the captain said. "Cowboys, sheriffs, guns. It practices good my English, too."

"You keep right up to date on them," Tim said. "There's a new one I haven't seen yet."

"Ah yes. The fisherman from your town, I asked him to bring me all the new ones."

First they wasted time shooting turkeys and now they were going to shoot rustlers. "Look," Johnny said, "if we wait much longer we'll need radar getting back."

"Yeah, it is late," Bob said. "How about it, Tim?"

"They're twisting my arm," Tim said to the captain. "Well, thanks for the coffee."

They left the schooner and began flying back to Fort Myers. Bob Tate looked back and said, "What about those magazines?"

"Magazines?" Tim said innocently.

"You're not kidding me," Bob said. "I know how you work, Tim. That dumb captain made a mistake leaving them out. You looked through them and saw greasy fingerprints and other signs that they had been pretty well read. Can anyone tell you Jake Bentz delivered them a few hours ago and the Cuban read them since then?"

"That's very interesting," Johnny said. "But all it proves is Jake or somebody made a trip to the schooner before today. Where does that leave you?"

Bob said, "Spell it out for the guy, Tim. I know you didn't stop with just noticing the fingerprints. What were you doing, memorizing the names of the magazines and the dates on them?"

"Oh, nothing much."

There was a smug note in Tim's voice, and Johnny said irritably, "You don't have to act so mysterious about it. You just memorized them so you can buy copies for yourself."

Tim's face got red. "If you had any brains," he snapped, "you'd know I'm going to all the dealers in town and find out who bought those magazines. There were eleven new issues of western story magazines in that stack. I have all the names and dates. I figure any magazine dealer in Fort Myers ought to remember who bought eleven western story magazines all in one bunch within the last few days. Does that satisfy you?"

"I'm sorry," Johnny said. "I didn't think it through."

"All right," Tim growled. "And I'm sorry I spoke up, only sometimes your needling gets to me. Now look, Bob, just forget what you heard, will you?"

"You know me," Bob said. "As far as I'm concerned, all the guy had on board was a set of Shakespeare."

Tim nodded and settled down again in the front seat. The red color in the back of his neck slowly faded.

Suddenly the plane banked left and Johnny braced himself. Bob Tate was peering out through his window, looking at something below. He leveled off and said, "That's a queer place for a boat."

The plane banked and wheeled back. They seemed to be heading for the fuzz of green where Howard Pingree's cabin cruiser was hidden. The plane roared in. Bob tilted the wing out of the way and a blur of gray-green flickered below them. There might have been a flash of white in the blur.

"See it?" Bob yelled.

"I caught something," Tim said. "I don't know if it was just water or not. How about it, Johnny?"

This was no time to fool around with Pingree's boat. "All I saw were mangroves," he said.

Tim said, "What did it look like? Could it have been a cabin cruiser?"

"It not only could have been," Bob said, "it damn well was."

Johnny said quickly, "You saw a fancy arrangement of branches, or light on water and dead mangrove leaves. Where could you hide a boat down there?"

Bob Tate turned his head and said, "A guy might think you don't want anything more to do with Pingree's Landing. Had a little trouble there, didn't you?"

Bob Tate certainly had the chin you loved to touch. With a right-hand punch, that is. "I don't mind trouble," Johnny snapped. "You want to give me some?"

"Shut up, you guys," Tim growled. "You really saw a cabin cruiser down there below Pingree's Landing?"

"That's right. Look, Tim, I can fly around and see if I can pick up that same angle for you."

Muscles twitched along Tim's jaw. For him, that was wild excitement. "Don't fly over it any more," he said. "If that's Pingree's boat he'll get suspicious. Can you find that place from the ground?"

"I think I could."

"Pour it on, then. Let's get back to your place fast."

Johnny sat tensely, the seat belt cutting into him. When they landed, Tim wouldn't want to lose a minute—not for a phone call or for a stop at the house or anything.

The plane dipped and creased the water and skated to the ramp. Bob Tate jumped out, calling to them to moor the plane.

Johnny went through the hangar and climbed in the car and started the engine. Tim and Bob came out in a few seconds. Tim headed for the driver's side and then saw that Johnny wasn't moving and got in on the right. They whipped by one intersection. Another. The lane branching to the McCarter house loomed up and Johnny stamped on the brake and whirled the car into the lane. The sudden jerks flung Tim forward. Before he recovered they were half way to the house.

Tim yelled, "What the hell you doing?"

Stopping at home. I want to see if Ellen's all right."

"Why wouldn't she be all right? Why—"

The car slid the last few feet on locked wheels. The house was dark. Johnny jumped out, raced up the walk and into the house. His feet set up hollow echoes. "Ellen!" he yelled. "Ellen!"

More echoes. He flipped on lights, ran into the dining room. Not a paper in sight. You could see where she had worked, though. She had sat in a chair with her back to the kitchen doorway. On the dining room table in front of the chair were two pencils and an ash tray. The tray held five cigarette stubs and a long unbroken ash where a sixth cigarette had burned without being touched. Beyond the ash tray was a cigarette package. It was empty. A little farther down the table was Ellen's purse.

He stood there with his heart thudding slowly and sullenly, like surf after a storm. It would be nice to think that Ellen had taken the lists, fourteen cigarettes from the package, left her purse and gone to visit a friend. But you had to be crazy to think that.

Footsteps came slamming into the house and Tim cried, "You got some reason for this, Edwards?"

Johnny turned slowly. For a moment he had forgotten Tim. "Ellen's gone," he muttered. "She's been kidnapped!"

Tim said in a horrified voice, "You must be out of your mind."

"I am. I'm trying to smuggle an idea into yours. If you'd taken time to listen to me today you'd understand. But if you'd listened this wouldn't have happened. I tell you she was working on a list of suspects we cocked up and she was getting places. I know. Those phone calls I made today were to Ellen to find out how she was doing. But the guy we're after must have been watching and moved in on her. So—"

Bob's voice cut him off. "What's the delay?" he said, peering into the room. "I thought you were in a hurry."

Tim made a helpless gesture. "Edwards says Ellen's been kidnapped."

Johnny cried, "Would she go out shopping or visiting without her purse? And why would she smoke five cigarettes and leave a sixth burning and what happened to the others in this empty pack and..." His voice trailed off.

Tim said, "Do you make anything of it, Bob? He said something about lists of suspects Ellen was working on and some guy spying on her."

Johnny said desperately, "You've got to listen to the whole story before it will make sense."

Bob Tate yawned. "I have all the time in the world," he said. "I only hope Howard Pingree does too."

"You got something there," Tim said. "Edwards—"

"Pingree isn't on his boat," Johnny shouted. "You won't find him there. You—"

"I bet you hope we don't find him there," Bob drawled. "Guy scares you, don't he?"

Johnny took a quick step forward but ran into Tim's hand, "That's enough nonsense," Tim said coldly. "Yellow or not, you're going with us. You can talk on the way."

This was like trying to flounder through quicksand and sinking deeper every second. You couldn't blame Tim. A guy you think is yellow starts giving you a lot of wild reasons why he shouldn't go on a dangerous job and what do you believe—the wild reasons, or that the guy is yellow? He decided on one more try. "Give me fifteen minutes to explain everything," he said. "Then if you don't believe me I'll shut up and do anything you want."

Tim's grip on the blouse slackened a notch.

Bob Tate said lazily, "Fifteen minutes, huh? So long, Pingree. Maybe Johnny wants to give Howard Pingree time for a getaway. Not because he's yellow, either. He let Howard get away once, remember. Might be an angle."

Johnny began to have a little trouble breathing. Tim had the blouse in a bear-trap grip. That was quite an angle Bob had mentioned. A guy lets a smuggler get away and comes back with a story of being knocked out but without a mark on him. Later the guy keeps running off to telephone when Jake Bentz gets into the news. The guy doesn't want to spend much time on the schooner. He can't see the cabin cruiser that Bob Tate points out. He doesn't want to go looking for Howard Pingree.

Does that look as if Johnny Edwards had been bought off by Howard Pingree and a smuggling gang? Brother, it does.

Johnny walked, shoulders sagging, to the hall. Then he whirled and drove his shoulder into Tim and broke past him. He ran into the kitchen, flinging a chair back at the doorway. He leaped the steps and raced across the yard. Light glared suddenly. A floodlight.

Tim shouted, "Edwards! I'm going to shoot!"

He ran dizzily toward the dark orange grove. He wasn't likely to reach it, though. Not with Tim bringing the big revolver down until the notch and the front sight and the running figure came into line.

CHAPTER EIGHTEEN

Behind him the .38 let go. His body jerked. He stumbled and almost went down and then knew that he was trying to drop dead before he was hit. Any time Tim missed three in a row it was on purpose. Those shots were just for the record. They were aimed high. Tim didn't know whether he was yellow or a crook and had given him the benefit of the doubt by six feet.

He plunged, gasping, into the orange grove and twisted among trees until he was out of sight.

Johnny sat down. There wasn't much point to rushing about with nothing in his head but a lot of hollow roaring sounds. He wanted his head quiet and empty so there would be room for ideas when he got around to moving them in. Gradually the roaring faded.

That was good, he thought. That was progress. Now we start by thinking of Ellen McCarter, age 23, height five feet six inches, weight 118, hair brown (that sun-streaked business is too poetic for police blotters), eyes brown. Ellen McCarter, a name under the classification Missing Persons. Question: Is this Missing Person alive or dead? Answer: Take your choice, bud.

Frankly, bud, since you give me a choice, I'll say that since there was no blood or signs of great violence, and since nobody likes to kill a girl until he absolutely has to, this Missing Person is still alive.

Now that we have settled that point, the first problem is to rescue this Missing Person before somebody regretfully knocks her off. Very well put, Edwards. Now let's have some of those brilliant ideas.

Now listen, you jerk, you've been playing detective for months and you have all kinds of clues and now you got to stop playing and put those clues together so they make sense. You end up with a clue you had absolutely nothing to do with collecting. You end up with a shred of knowledge that big dumb Tim McCarter picked up on the schooner. What it comes down to is this: If that western story magazine clue doesn't get you the killer and get you there fast, you've had it, but good.

He got up and crept toward the house. He wasn't worried that Tim had set a trap, because Tim was anxious to get to Howard Pingree's boat and wouldn't let himself be sidetracked. But it was quite possible that whoever snatched Ellen had come back. It would simplify matters if he could run across the guy right now. If he wasn't careful, however, it might simplify matters for the wrong person. He moved quietly through the shadows to the garage. The doors were open and his car was there, heading out. For a moment he was tempted to wait in a dark corner and hope for a visitor. He had done enough waiting, though. Night after night of it on Pingree's boat. It didn't seem to bring him any luck. He slipped into the garage and got in the car and started it and took it out like a bronco bursting out of a rodeo chute. Nothing happened.

Five minutes later he was downtown and had parked and was starting on the rounds of magazine dealers. He walked to the shop near the Arcade Theater on First Street and asked if anybody had bought a lot of western story magazines lately.

The proprietor said, "Would it have been about a dozen?"

Johnny began sweating. "Yes," he said. "Who was it?"

The guy was maddeningly deliberate. "Would it have been, say, the day before yesterday?"

Johnny tried to take it easy. You couldn't rush things in Fort Myers. "It could have been," he said thickly.

"Wait a minute, Johnny. The answer you want comes in two words. You want it?"

Johnny whirled. "Yes, I do," he said. This had better be good. It had better be awfully good.

"In two words," the man said, "Bob Tate."

CHAPTER NINETEEN

He went into the booth and closed the door. Bob Tate, the perfect gentleman. The guy who didn't smoke or drink or have any little vices. The hard-working business man. The guy anyone could count on for a favor. It was incredible.

But brother, once you got the idea, things fit like new skin on a rattler. Bob Tate matched all the specifications. The right height and age and looks. A job that let him make an honest living but gave him plenty of time for smuggling. A couple of planes to use ferrying aliens from the schooner. Smart enough to run the racket. Doing favors for the Border Patrol so he could keep an eye on them.

The Havana angle was perfect. Not only *could* Bob Tate have been in Havana at the time of the Plaza de la Fraternidad trap, but he *was*. Bob had breezed over to Havana to see how the Havana gang handled the trap and found a cute little trick named Ellen McCarter from his own home town buzzing around the guy who had set the trap. So Bob dated her that night to see what the score was. Just before or at the start of the date, word was passed to Bob that amateur detective Johnny Edwards had backed Rankosci into a corner and was trying to grill him. That worked out nicely. All Bob had to do was take Ellen to the café where Edwards was working on Rankosci, and pick a fight to let Rankosci get away. He had a good alibi for starting a fight because of the fact Edwards had broken a date with Ellen.

Later Bob got another good alibi, by accident. Probably Howard Pingree had been told to watch the McCarter house and see what Edwards did on his first night in Fort Myers. Edwards wandered alone down to the McCarter dock and Pingree decided to get rid of the trouble-maker right then, and took two shots at him. Bob Tate was dating Ellen and couldn't be suspected.

The shooting business undoubtedly put Pingree in the doghouse with the rest of the gang and after awhile Pingree got impatient and tried to go in the smuggling racket for himself.

Right there was the first time Bob Tate had no alibi, Johnny thought. It must have been Bob who rabbit punched him at Pingree's Landing and then shot Pingree. Bob must have been tempted to do a little more shooting that night, too. But when you start knocking off Border Patrol inspectors you want hurricane-proof alibis and there were a couple of aliens loose that night who might have seen him. So Bob decided to hide Pingree's boat and take Pingree's rifle—in itself a mighty nice alibi—and wait for a better time.

Bob Tate bought the magazines and flew them to the schooner. Bob was startled when Tim wanted to go aboard the schooner. Bob kept telling long dull stories about creeping up on wild turkeys while they were aboard, to prevent Tim from asking too many questions. Bob was so alert to the danger of the pile of new magazines that he followed every thought Tim had. Bob didn't want anyone checking on who bought the magazines so, on the flight back, he pretended to discover the Pingree boat. That was supposed to keep everybody so busy that Tim would forget the magazines or the storekeeper would forget who bought them.

Probably it was Georg Rankosci who prowled outside the dining room last night and learned about Ellen's list of suspects. Later, when everybody was asleep, Rankosci sneaked into the house to pick up information, and incidentally to pick up most of the cigarettes lying around. During the day somebody had undoubtedly watched the McCarter house and caught glimpses of Ellen working on the lists. Eventually the gang must have decided that they couldn't take a chance that Ellen might hit the right answer, and they had moved in on her.

It must have been quite a day for Bob Tate. First he had to sweat out the lists and then he had to sweat out the schooner. You had to hand it to the guy, though: he did a smooth job. He managed to get Ellen out of circulation. He decoyed Tim away from the dangerous magazine angle. He tied that idiot Edwards into knots and almost arranged to have him shot by Tim McCarter. That would have been the perfect crime.

It had been quite a day for Bob Tate and it was going to he quite a night.

He dropped a coin in the phone box and asked the operator for the chief of police.

"Hello, chief. This is Edwards of the Border Patrol."

"Well, hello, Johnny. This is a pleasant surprise."

"Look, chief, I got troubles. I need your help."

"Sure, Johnny, anything you say. Where are you calling from?"

"Right in town. Now here's the setup—"

"Where did you say in town?"

"I can give you the story faster if you don't interrupt."

"You'll find us very sympathetic."

An ugly little idea began gibbering in his head. This wasn't one cop talking to another. This was a cop playing cute with a suspect. "What will we talk over?"

"Whatever you want, Johnny. We're all your friends. The sheriff and the Highway Patrol and, of course, Tim McCarter."

That did it. "Tim called you, did he?" he snapped. "What did he say?"

"Don't get excited. There's nothing to worry about. He said you were badly upset and if we ran across you, would we please look after you until he finished working on a case."

"Who else is looking for me? The sheriff? The Highway Patrol?"

"Tim tried to call the sheriff but he's out of town. So he called me. But don't use the wrong words, Johnny. We're not looking *for* you. We're looking *after* you."

"I don't feel like being looked after in jail."

"Johnny! Hang on and let's talk and—"

"So you can have the call traced. I'll save you trouble. I'm calling from the gas station at Five Points. Come on out alone and I'll talk to you."

He hung up, walked quickly out of the store. Maybe the chief would buy that Five Points gag, maybe not. If not, he had to move fast. Tim had used those two minutes at the house to call the chief, who in turn had probably tipped off the Highway Patrol and the sheriff's office.

He had almost reached his car when he heard the siren wailing along First Street. It kept on going past the store toward Five Points at the other end of town. That would give him enough head start so the chief wouldn't know where to look. He climbed into his car and headed out McGregor. What had he been thinking just before calling the chief? Oh, yes. He'd been thinking that it would take more than one guy to raid the hangar looking for Ellen and then to go hunting for Bob Tate around Pingree's Landing. Anyway it would take more than one guy like Johnny Edwards.

He turned out his lights when he reached the road leading to Bob Tate's place and drove down it a little way and parked off the road. A couple hundred yards ahead, the hangar cut a black chunk out of the horizon. He had hoped to see lights. Lack of them was a bad sign. It either meant nobody was there or that they were waiting for him. He wasn't sure which was worse.

He reached the hangar. The door near the driveway hung ajar, almost invitingly. He moved cautiously around to the river. Bob Tate's amphibian still floated at the ramp. Maybe it had been left there in case somebody wanted to skip to Havana. Or maybe Jocko Stearns had been too busy with other duties to take care of it. Jocko had taken time to close the big sliding door leading to the ramp, however—and all the windows too. He finished circling the building and studied the partly open door. That was inviting, all right. It appealed to him like an invitation to drop dead.

He tried to picture the setup of the building. The office and storerooms were to his left. The doorway led directly into the main hangar. There was a clear space beyond it where the amphibian at the ramp was usually parked. To the right was the smaller plane; earlier in the day, Jocko had been up on a portable steel platform working on the engine. If the open door was a trap, he was expected to creep in slowly and get a fast reception. It might be smart to go in fast and get a slow reception. He walked up to the door and suddenly flung it wide and leaped through.

Light ripped the blackness: a long thin spear of light that slanted down and grazed his body and plunged into the doorway. An engine started roaring and backfiring. Flame winked. Small angry things went screeching off concrete and clanging through metal. Johnny dodged blindly. He crashed into an object and spun aside and fell and rolled and thudded into a wall. For a few moments he didn't move. His head was fogged with noise and shock. The hangar had turned into a crazy house in an amusement park. The floor tilted and the walls leaned in and sounds jumped at him from unexpected places.

The roaring stopped abruptly. The long beam of light began an angular dance around the hangar. Johnny shot at it fast, without aiming, and started to roll out of the way. Before he finished his roll the light flicked out and flame winked again and the small angry things howled into the spot where he had been.

Silence again. Something hard was creasing his left shoulder and the ceiling had come squashing down on his head. He felt around carefully. It wasn't the ceiling. He was under a work bench and one of its legs was jammed against his shoulder. He couldn't see and in the scramble he had lost all sense of where he was in the hangar. He began working out answers slowly. That had been a spotlight probing for him. Something else had been aimed at the doorway, too. A chopper. A sub-machine gun, with the button set for full automatic fire.

The light had come from a source several feet above his head. He remembered the portable steel platform Jocko Steams used in working on the planes. The spotlight was probably clamped onto its railing. Jocko was up there with the chopper and with a nice comforting steel floor under his feet. The light had gone out just before the chopper cut loose the second time. His own shot hadn't hit it, so quite likely Jocko was up there alone and got scared and switched it out. The spotlight made a good target; Jocko might be nervous about turning it on.

A voice called, "Hey, Rankosci. Where are you?"

That was Jocko. It was hard to tell where his voice came from.

Somebody whispered, "I am all right."

That was Rankosci checking in.

"You're all right, are you?" Jocko said bitterly. "You mean you're all wrong. When you called me from near the magazine store you were going to follow him and if he came here you were going to nail him before he even got inside."

Rankosci said, "I couldn't get close. However, he is dead."

"No he isn't dead! He came in here like a bat out of hell and I never got the light on him. What do you say to that?"

"I think I will say good-bye."

"You yellow rat," Jocko screamed. "If you duck out now you won't live long. If we don't get you here, Carlos and his boys will take care of you back in Havana. You don't look very good right now anyway. It's your fault Edwards got to Fort Myers."

There was a long pause and finally Rankosci whispered, "What do you want me to do?"

"Where are you?"

Rankosci said sadly, "I am just outside the doorway. If the inspector tries to run I am in a good position."

"A good position for what? For stepping aside? You get in here and lock that door!"

"But I do not like to be shot at."

"Get in here!"

There was a faint sniffle. After a long interval the door squeaked. Johnny glared into blackness and tried to locate the sound but it went wriggling all over the place. Something clacked. That would be the lock.

Rankosci's voice was louder now but more unhappy. "I have done it," he said.

"There's a switch beside the door. Turn on the lights."

"That would be dangerous."

"Don't worry. I can take care of myself."

"Ah. But who will take care of me?"

Johnny said quietly, "The undertaker will."

Rankosci said, "You see? He will shoot at me first."

"Turn on that light!"

"No. I am happier in the dark. I like the dark."

"So what do we do?" Jocko snarled. "Sit around chewing on our big toes?"

"If I could make a suggestion," Rankosci said, "perhaps we could make an arrangement with the inspector."

Jocko thought that over. Finally he called, "Does that make sense to you, Edwards?"

Johnny broke open his revolver quietly and replaced the empty shell. There were two dangers in doing a lot of talking. The first was that he might be located by the sound. That wasn't very likely, considering the way echoes played ping pong against the walls and metal roof. The second danger was that Rankosci would work up enough courage to creep around looking for him, planning to make up for that time he had bungled the knife thrust in Havana. But that could happen even if he kept quiet. He didn't have much to lose.

"You know what, Jocko?" he said pleasantly. "The smart thing for you to do is throw down that chopper and point your spotlight straight up and quit. The city cops will be here any minute."

"How corny can you get, Edwards? You're in bad with everybody. Tim McCarter asked the cops to pick you up. I tailed you guys to Tim's house an hour ago. While Tim was phoning, Bob gave me the word. You better hope the cops *don't* come. They'd shoot you. Now, what'll we talk about?"

"Let's talk abut Ellen."

Jocko said, "Your dame's all right. Bob was jittery about those lists, see? He told us to grab her if anything looked wrong at all—you know, like her running to the phone to yell copper or something. Rankosci happened to be peeking in and sees her jump up with a little cry and he thinks she hit the jackpot. So he sneaked in the back and got behind her and grabbed her throat and put pressure on that big artery and she blacked out and never even saw him. We got her wrapped up in a room here. She don't know who snatched her or where she is or anything."

Johnny's fingers relaxed a little on the revolver butt. "She knows about Bob, doesn't she?"

"That's the funny part of it. She went right by his name without a tumble. Reason she jumped up was she came to the end of the list without tagging anybody. Does that give you an idea, Edwards?"

"Yeah," Johnny said slowly. "You mean a trade."

"Sure. Drop your revolver, feel around until you reach the lights, turn them on and we'll let the dame go."

"The world's full of dames. Make me a better offer."

"Maybe I had you tagged wrong," Jocko said. "If you're gonna be sensible, we can talk sense. What if I said we could use another good tough guy in this racket? What if I said, forget this screwy yen you have to kill Bob Tate and make yourself a half-million bucks."

This was interesting. Jocko couldn't be serious, of course. The idea was to make him fall for a phony offer, and then catch him off guard and stitch a few slugs through him. It would be worth while playing along. At least he would learn how the crowd operated. At best he might convince Jocko he was taking the offer and might get a chance to catch Jocko off guard. But to be convincing he'd have to play hard to get.

"You guys don't make that kind of money," he said. "How can you?"

"How can we? Listen, this is big stuff, not peanuts. All right, we started small but just before you barged in we had worked up to forty-five aliens a month. The schooner makes a trip a month, see? Mostly Bob flies them in from the schooner. We don't fool much with motorboats, only for emergencies. People get too curious about motorboats coming and going."

"One of your aliens will get caught and talk."

"Let 'em talk. They can't even describe the schooner. We bring 'em in with their eyes taped. We got two guys delivering them up north in house trailers with the windows blacked out and the drivers have dames up in the front seat with them and look like tourists and nobody bothers them. And Bob's got a little ham radio station here to keep in touch with the schooner. This thing's foolproof."

Jocko sounded serious. It would be funny if he really meant the offer and thought it might be accepted. "Forty-five aliens a month, huh?" Johnny said. "Let's say five hundred a year. Six hundred dollars each for the ordinary ones and fifteen hundred for the Chinese. That's not even half a million bucks a year. And look how many guys get a cut. Look at the expenses."

"Yeah, we got a big overhead. A guy like you might pull down thirty grand in the next year."

"Then it would take me fifteen years to make that half-million. You can't get away with it that long."

"We ain't trying," Jocko said in a satisfied tone. "One more year and we quit."

"One of us is lousy at arithmetic. Where's that half-million?"

"It's there. This is the fattest and safest racket any guy ever dreamed up. You know your law. After we quit, how long is it before nobody can touch us?"

"You mean for running aliens? You're safe after three years."

"And how about the aliens we run in?"

"They won't ever be in the clear," Johnny said. "They're not protected by any statute of limitations. They can always be arrested and deported. What's all this about?"

"What we're taking in now is chicken feed. Look! In three years we're in the clear. The aliens aren't. We got their photos and fingerprints. Three years after we quit, we move in on those clucks. They ought to be starting to make good money by then. Guess who they'll be making it for. Us! If they squawk, they get deported."

A shiver iced Johnny's skin. "You're missing an angle, though," he said. "You'd be in the clear on the smuggling charge but on the books they still have a crime called blackmail."

"Blackmail!" Jocko sneered. "We even have that figured. We get these aliens to sign a promissory note for five grand each. They don't know what it is. We tell 'em it's an application. They're so used to signing applications and all kinds of papers they think probably you have to sign things in this country even to break a law. Okay, Edwards, count it up. We got a hundred fifty aliens in already. In a year we'll quit with seven hundred aliens in. Each has signed a note for five thousand bucks besides his passage. That makes three and a half million, don't it?"

"How many guys will cut in on the big money?"

"Just a few of us. None of the lugs will."

A plaintive voice spoke up from somewhere in the darkness. Rankosci. He said, "I did not know of this angle."

Jocko snarled, "You're one of the lugs, see?"

"Oh," Rankosci said.

Johnny listened carefully to the echoes of that syllable. Rankosci hadn't said "Oh" in a disappointed way. He said it thoughtfully. He ought to be thinking: *They weren't going to cut me in on the big money. They aren't going to like remembering that I know about it.* Yes, Rankosci ought to be worried. Maybe it would pay to worry him some more. That might give him another chance to get away. He said smoothly, "Now that Rankosci knows the whole setup, maybe you ought to cut him in. I wouldn't trust the gut. He might spill it. Look what he spilled to me."

"That was a mistake," Rankosci cried. "You made me drunk and—"

"But you're on the wagon now, ain't you?" Jocko crooned.

"I will never drink again! I will not talk. I—"

"Shut up," Johnny said. "Look, Jocko. You have a proposition there. But what about Bob Tate? I've been a little rough on him. All right, so he knocked off a pal of mine and I felt bad about it, but I can do a lot of forgetting with half a million bucks. The thing is, will he lay off me?"

"Sure, sure," Jocko said soothingly.

"Let me think it over a minute."

That was just a stall. He wanted to listen. If he had a lot of luck he might hear a key scraping in a lock and the door creaking open. About now Rankosci ought to want out, but bad. He ought to realize he had no future in the racket. The trouble was, it might be a toss-up in Rankosci's mind: Did he have more future if he ran, or if he stayed and hoped?

He listened. Nothing stirred in the big echoing hangar. There was only one change. His eyes were getting adjusted. He could see faint gray slabs where windows cut into walls. That meant Jocko was seeing better, too. It meant Rankosci could probably see well enough to move around. Rankosci might figure a knife in the right place would square things for him.

He said, "I have just one more question. What about Tim McCarter?"

"You worried about Tim? Don't."

"What do you mean, don't? The guy has it in for me. When he finishes at Pingree's Landing and comes back he'll report me to headquarters as a deserter."

Jocko said in a coaxing tone, "Look. The story he put out on you was you went to pieces. He only put it out on the phone to the local cops. What if we twisted that story around and said Tim went to pieces instead of you? What if Bob Tate swears Tim went nuts and forced him to go down to Pingree's Landing? What if you rescue the girl out in the woods somewhere and prove you had the right angle all the time? She won't know the difference. We dump her out there and tell you where to find her."

"You got to do better than that," Johnny said, trying to put just the right amount of suspicion in his voice. "At headquarters they'll take Tim's word over mine."

Jocko said, "Tim won't be giving out any words."

That wasn't a throat he was trying to use for swallowing. That was an old hunk of garden hose and he was trying to force rocks down it. "I don't get it," he said hoarsely.

Jocko cried, "You don't think Bob's just out for a stroll, do you? He's going to take care of Tim! He has Pingree's rifle hidden down there. Pingree did it, see? Pingree snatched Ellen McCarter, see? A month from now we show you where to drag the river for Pingree and you bring up what the crabs left and the case is all washed up. How do you like it?"

"I like it fine," Johnny said. "Just fine. I'm your boy."

He crept out slowly from under the work bench. Tim might be dead already. Or there might be a little time.

"It's a deal," Jocko said. "Turn on the light, Rankosci."

"I—I am a little nervous," Rankosci said. "I have moved since I came in. I am not sure I could find it."

"Shut up," Johnny said. "I'll turn it on." He moved out a little, crouching. He turned to bounce his voice off the wall so it would be hard to follow. "I'm moving across the room," he said. "Keep an eye on Rankosci after I switch on the lights. He knows too much. I—"

"Everybody can trust me," Rankosci wailed. "We are all in this together."

"I'd sooner be together with a coral snake," Johnny said. "We'll get the light on you and see if you look worth trusting. I'm—"

"I do not like light!" Rankosci screamed. "Nobody trusts me in the light. People bully me in the light. They—"

"Brace yourself," Johnny yelled. "I got the switch. I'll count three. One—"

Something scurried. Something made little squeaking ratlike noises. A shadow wavered at the gray blob of a window, clawing at it.

Twenty feet away, high up in the hangar, squirts of flame leaped out and the tommy gun roared. Johnny swung around. The revolver jerked three times against his hand. The spurts of flame blacked out.

Johnny straightened and crept to a wall and felt slowly around until he reached the light switch by the door. He didn't know whether he had won or not. He braced himself against the wall and flipped the switch. Jocko was draped over the railing like an old mattress. The chopper lay below on the floor. By the window was a heap of old clothes, badly torn.

It was queer, he thought dizzily. He hadn't expected that. Nobody would ever know why Jocko had started shooting. Maybe he was trigger-happy. Maybe he couldn't stand seeing Rankosci skip out. Maybe he thought the shadow was a guy named Edwards. Maybe he just hadn't done any thinking.

CHAPTER TWENTY

He started through the section of the hangar that had been partitioned into rooms, flipping on lights as he went. There was a ham radio outfit in one room. The next room had a heavy lock on the door. He opened it; all it contained was a pile of Army cots. Beyond was a storeroom containing one opened cot. There was a long slim bundle on it, draped with a blanket. He threw back the blanket and saw Ellen. She had been tied and gagged and her eyes had been taped shut and she had no idea who had removed the blanket.

He worked on the gag first. It came loose and Ellen tried to scream for help. Actually she couldn't. There were blue marks on her throat where Rankosci had clamped down on her jugular and all she could put out was a croak. "Take it easy," he said. "It's Johnny. I'll have you loose in a minute. Listen. I have to work fast. This tape's going to hurt coming off. Squeeze your eyes shut."

She nodded. There were four pieces of tape across her eyes. He ripped them off, trying not to watch. When it was over she lay there with welts rising on her face and tears popping out under her eyelids.

"Yell if it makes you feel better," he muttered.

"I can't yell," she wailed, "I can't do anything but squeak. Where am I, Johnny?"

"In Bob Tate's hangar," he said, working on the ropes. "He didn't snatch you but he runs the racket."

"I can't believe it! I checked his name on the list and he seemed all right and... and— Oh! I *didn't* check him at all! I was so sure he couldn't be the one."

"So was I. But his boys were watching you and thought you tagged him, so they moved in."

She said faintly, "I heard a lot of noise. Did you kill him?"

"No. Two of his guys are dead, though."

"I'm so glad you didn't kill him," she gasped. "Not that he means anything to me. But I don't want you to be a killer."

Her wrists were free now, and he started on the ankles.

"You're too late," he said. "I already qualified."

"But that was in self-defense, wasn't it?"

"I'll try to take care of Bob in self-defense, too."

"Johnny, don't. Please don't. It will do something to you. Really it will. I—"

"When you hear the full story you may cheer me on."

"Johnny, is Tim all right?"

He cut the last cord around her ankles. "Can you sit up? Can you walk?"

She sat up slowly, watching his face. "You didn't answer when I asked is Tim all right."

"There isn't any soft way to break this to you," he said. "I messed things up. Tim thinks I deserted. He's out with Bob Tate around Pingree's boat. I think Bob plans to shoot him."

Her face looked as if he had kicked her in the stomach. She tried to push herself up from the cot. Her legs crumpled and he caught her before she dropped to the floor. "I'm sorry," she said in a tight, flat voice. "That wasn't a faint. My legs are asleep. What can I do?"

He picked her up and started carrying her and telling her the whole story. He talked fast as he stumbled through the main hangar where Jocko hung over the railing and the heap of torn clothes lay under the window. When they reached the road he helped her walk to the car. He finished the story by the time he drove to the lane leading to her house.

"Got it straight?" he asked. "First call the local cops, then the chief in Miami."

She nodded and climbed out of the car and then said in a rush, "I hope you come back safely. I hope Tim does. I hope something else. Do you know what I mean?"

"If you get your first hope," he said, "you won't get the third." He sent the car howling down the road.

His headlights began washing over the sandy ruts leading to Pingree's Landing. Something glittered ahead in the bushes. Glass. Window glass. The rear window of the Border Patrol sedan. He jammed on the brakes and the car rushed to a stop in the sand. He sat for a moment, lights on, listening. The radiator of the car ticked softly. No sound came from the jackstraw jumble of trees and bushes to his left. There was no way of telling whether or not Bob Tate had found a good chance to use Pingree's rifle, so he had to play this by ear. That meant assuming Tim was still alive. He didn't dare try to yell a warning, because Bob would catch on at once and Tim wouldn't.

What he had to do was decoy Bob away from Tim. It wouldn't be easy. Right now Bob considered Tim the most dangerous person in Fort Myers, because Tim would check on the magazine angle. So the idea was to make Bob think he was in the clear about the magazines and then give him some reason to come running breathlessly to knock off a guy named Edwards.

You worked the horn by pushing a ring inside the steering wheel. He began rocking the ring, jerkily. Sound blared into the night. Dot-and-dash sound. As a pilot and ham radio operator, Bob Tate must know Morse code.

He sent a message slowly. "McCarter from Edwards," he signaled. "Your magazine lead no good. Repeat. Your magazine lead no good. I checked news dealers and none remembered selling western magazines."

He paused. Around him the mangrove jungle was quiet. Everything seemed to be holding its breath.

The dots and dashes said, "E-l-l-e-n s-t-i-l-l m-i-s-s-i-n-g."

Tim wasn't in the clear yet. Not by plenty. Bob Tate wasn't dumb; he would wonder why Johnny Edwards had come back and it would take a good explanation.

"Need your help fast," he signaled. "Caught guy tailing me. Have him here in handcuffs. Will talk if heat put on. This more important than Pingree. Guy is member of gang, named Rankosci, from Havana."

He stopped. That should do it. That ought to bring Bob Tate faster than a million bucks; Bob already knew where he could get a million bucks if guys like Rankosci could be kept from talking. Now he'd better get out of the car before Bob and the 30-30 bullets arrived. He paused as an unpleasant idea began haunting him.

When the horn stopped sending messages, would Bob get suspicious and decide it was a trap? And then would Bob start shooting his way out of it? And wouldn't the nearest and easiest target be Tim McCarter? That was an angle he had overlooked when the plan first popped into his head.

Of course some people might suggest sitting there playing with the horn. That would be crazy. Fun was fun and Tim was a nice guy, but nobody could expect him to do that. Or could they?

Maybe he could make a deal with himself and send one more message and then dive into the bushes. He slid down until he was lying on the floor with his legs outside the car.

He reached up along the steering column and hit the ring before he knew it. The vibration tingled through his body like high voltage.

He got himself under control and signaled, "Am sure Rankosci knows whole story."

It was an odd feeling to lie there like a chicken with its head on a chopping block. He had his revolver out of the holster but before using it he would have to untangle himself from the frame of the car and the door and pedals and steering column. He was gambling that Bob Tate would start shooting from a little distance, instead of creeping right up to the car.

He sent another very slow message: "W-h-a-t a-r-e w-e w-a-i-t-i-n-g f-o-r? W-h-a-t a-r-e w-e—"

A high-pitched sound drilled through the blaring. *Spanggg!* His hand froze. *Spanggg!* He gripped the ring and jerked out the words: "Get-Bob-Get-Bob-Get—"

He yanked down his arm and hooked his heels under the side of the car and went squirming and tumbling out of the car and into a heap on the sand. As he straightened, a final shot starred the windshield and Bob Tate leaped from bushes a dozen yards away and ran toward him. Johnny dug his right elbow in sand. He swung the revolver down with a slow squeeze on the trigger and watched the sights dip below Bob's collar and felt the jolt come back through wrist and forearm and saw the running figure spin with the impact and go down.

He got slowly to his feet and walked to the crumpled figure. Then suddenly his throat went dry and ice started freezing in his stomach. The body was moving. Bob Tate wasn't dead. He was pawing at a dark stain high on his right chest.

He lifted the revolver and lined the sights up neatly. Bob turned his hand around palm up as if to hold off the bullet and began babbling for a break and swearing to tell everything. He had waited a long time for this. It was tough that the chance had to come in this nightmare way but—

He had waited a long time, all right. Too long. Now he didn't want it any more.

He bent and picked up the rifle and reached inside Bob's shirt and got the .45 automatic from its shoulder holster. If he hurried he could step to one of the bushes and get over being sick before Tim arrived.

CHAPTER TWENTY-ONE

He sat in the living room of the McCarter house with Tim and Ed Brian. They had wanted the whole story and had gone after it with hard, slugging questions. They had it now. They looked a little punch-drunk.

Ellen brought in more coffee and gave him a small twisted smile and went out again. The welts across her eyes looked like a pink mask. She ought to be in bed with a cold compress on those welts but she wanted to be in on everything.

It had been a long night. Bob Tate was in the hospital, slightly hoarse from telling everything he knew and probably a lot of things he didn't know. A couple of bodies were not telling anything to the local undertaker, and in a few hours boats would start grappling for another candidate in the Caloosahatchee near Pingree's Landing. A Border Patrol squad was camped around a filing case full of photos and fingerprints in the office at the hangar and a lookout had been flashed for the men who drove the cars and blacked-out house trailers. The schooner, too far offshore to be seized or boarded, was heading back for Havana with a Coast Guard boat tagging along in her wake.

"I wish I could figure it," the chief said in a tired voice. "When you had a chance to kill him, you didn't. Nobody would have tried to prove murder. I keep looking for the answer to that."

Johnny said, "Let me know if you find it before I do."

"What are your plans for when all this is cleaned up, Edwards? Go to work in your family's business? Head back to your salmon streams? Stick with us?"

"I wouldn't have expected that third choice."

"I didn't give it to. you. I just asked what you wanted to do. I haven't made up my mind." The chief rose. "I'll look in at the hangar and then catch some sleep. I'll be around tomorrow. You two take it easy, hear?"

Tim watched the chief leave, then said abruptly, "Where do you want me to start apologizing, Edwards?"

"I want you to start apologizing in Miami while I'm here in Fort Myers. This is going to be quite a letdown for you," Johnny said. "I think you're a swell guy. I only dislike one thing about you. You drive a car so slowly it gives me the jitters."

Tim got up. "I'm going to bed," he muttered. "It will take me a while to get over that one. Don't think what you said makes me feel all of a sudden that you're a great guy, too. Because it doesn't." He walked to the doorway and then turned and growled, "If you stick around you can drive the car, though." He went into his bedroom and slammed the door.

Johnny lit a final cigarette and wondered how long he would feel empty. Most of his life he had never wanted anything very badly, and so there had been a lot of dull times when he had just gone through the motions. Then, of all things to pick, he found that he wanted very badly to kill a man. There was no use kidding himself: he had come alive for the first time. He had a goal. But when he got there everything went flat. The trouble was, of course, you could only kill a guy once and then you had no place to go. You might think he wanted to go somewhere else now. He looked up and saw Ellen moving around the room, straightening furniture and cleaning ash trays. That was odd. This was where he had come in, a couple months ago, in Havana. A girl had been wandering up and down trying to catch his attention. An American girl. Nice long legs, trim flanks that rippled instead of jiggled as she walked, slim waist, shiny brown sun-streaked hair with a wave at the end—all the standard equipment. To be fair, a lot of deluxe equipment, too. You found the type all over the country. Guaranteed to dance well, keep the conversation going, be a good sport, let you make a little polite love under the right conditions. Step right up and order yours, gents. Only one to a customer. They last a lifetime.

She happened to glance at him and said, "I heard what you told Tim. It was very nice of you."

"It was really a dirty trick," he said. "I could have broken the news more gently."

"He'll change his mind about you, Johnny. But it will take time. He's about as good at changing his mind as a freight train is at zigzagging."

"Just out of curiosity," he said, "how good are you at changing your mind?"

"Me? Worse than Tim, I'm afraid."

He had figured that. Fortunately he hadn't let himself get out of hand. "If you're going to insist on cleaning all the ash trays now," he said, "let me help."

"Why do we have to change the subject to ash trays?"

"I'm not changing the subject. You came in here to clean ash trays and straighten up the room and—"

"I came in here to straighten up my personal affairs. They happen to be in a tangle."

"But I looked up and there you were cleaning ash trays—"

"Isn't it lucky," she said wearily, "that there weren't any ash trays around the Plaza de la Fraternidad that day in Havana. Otherwise you'd have watched me parade back and forth in front of you and decided I was just taking a few ash trays for a walk."

"That's funny. I was thinking about that time in Havana, too. But you were actually trying to attract my attention that day."

"I told you I'm even worse than Tim about changing my mind."

He caught his breath. There might be possibilities here, if a guy went about it slowly and in the right way. Let's not get too excited, though. A thing like this could build up to an awful letdown. "You know what?" he said cautiously. "I wish we could start all over, back at the point where we met in Havana."

"That's a long way back."

"Would you be willing to try, though?"

She sighed and said, "If you insist. But I've forgotten some of my lines. I may get them mixed up."

He walked over to her and said very seriously, "I'd like to give you a ring sometime. Do you remember me saying that?"

"Yes, Johnny."

"Well, what's the answer?"

"Yes, I will."

"That doesn't make sense," he complained. "I ask if I can give you a ring sometime and you say, yes, I will."

"I told you I might get my lines mixed. I was answering another question. It comes along later, I hope."

His legs started wobbling, and he grabbed her. "What question was that?" he said. "What one?"

She moved close. Her voice sounded calm but her body quivered against him like a flame. "Any old question," she said. "Any old question at all."

His arms locked around her. It was quite a thing to feel alive again. Like the one-to-a-customer angle, it could very easily last a lifetime.

THE END

Shell Game

By Richard Powell

Chapter One: THE GIRL ON THE BEACH

Most of my friends in New York like to spend energetic vacations. They go offshore in charter boats and attach themselves, with seventy-five-pound test lines, to large and angry fish. They rush out happily in hunting season to exchange salvos of double-O chilled shot with other sportsmen. In summer they put on crampons and race up mountains, and in winter they put on skis and race down mountains. They can have it. Personally, I like to saunter along a beach adding to my collection of sea shells and bathing beauties.

I had no reason to suspect that my stay on the lower west coast of Florida would be any less pleasant than other vacations. In fact I thought it would be more pleasant, because the beaches I planned to visit are famous for their shells. And, of course, Florida publicity gave me the idea that all the palm trees in the state would fall down if they weren't propped up with bathing beauties. I didn't realize that I was letting myself in for something that would make fishing and hunting and mountain climbing and skiing look like rest cures. Because, as it happened, my quiet little hobbies introduced me to trouble in coffin-size lots.

Many interesting objects wash up on the Gulf beaches of Florida. A few days after my arrival, it began to seem likely that these objects would soon be joined by the body of a person named William J. Stuart. I wouldn't have worried quite so much about the idiot except that William J. Stuart is my name.

Everything started the night I was collecting shells a couple of miles below the town of Gulf City. I chose early evening for the trip because there was a new moon. At new and full moons you get unusually high and low tides; very low tide is excellent for collecting shells. The tide was far out, and I splashed happily along, probing the shallows off the beach with my flashlight. I was having good luck. My burlap sack was getting heavy with nice specimens of Chinese alphabets and heart cockles and angel wings, and I had even found a lettered olive in a rare golden shade.

Just ahead of me were the pilings of an old fishing-pier. I waded to them and flashed the light at the base of a piling. Something made a quick swirl in the water, darted behind the piling. For a moment my toes wriggled uneasily and I thought about sharks. Then I told myself, *Look, Stuart, you can handle any shark that likes to swim in four inches of water.* I poked the light forward. This time the object in the water didn't retreat. I blinked. I was staring at a girl's foot.

"Well, what's the matter?" she said crossly. "Do I have six toes?" Her voice had husky vibrations, like cello notes.

"Your foot would be worth looking at," I said admiringly, "even if it only had three toes. What's it doing out here?"

She snapped, "I'm waiting for the tide to go down, so I can walk ashore without getting my feet wet."

That was supposed to wither me. I do not, however, wither easily. Ordinarily girls don't swoon when I first approach. They're more likely to start thinking up insults. I can't croon or swell my biceps to sixteen inches or dance divinely. My body is put together as loosely as an old stepladder, and my limp brown hair keeps flopping in my eyes, and usually both my hat and my profile look as if they need reblocking. But I have learned that if I stick around and grin at the insults, I make out all right. The average girl is likely to decide finally that half a man on the beach is better than a man-and-a-half out catching giant tarpon. What I mean is, I don't have much but I have it there.

So I said cheerily, "I'm waiting for the tide to come in, so I won't have to walk so far when I get ashore. Does the rest of you live up to your foot?"

"No," she said, keeping in the shadow of the piling. "I bulge. I have buck teeth and a squint. Please turn out that light. It hurts my eyes."

"Yes, ma'am," I said, turning it off. I edged forward until I could see her in the starlight. She was wearing gray slacks rolled up above her knees, a white shirt, a bandanna wrapped around her hair, and she carried a big white purse slung from one shoulder. She was medium height and slender. I studied her face and saw a firm chin, slight hollows in her cheeks that trapped shadows, cool dark eyes under gull-wing eyebrows, a nose just the right size for sniffing disdainfully at me, lips curved in a slightly derisive smile. "It's not true about the bulges and the squint," I said. "In regard to the buck teeth, if you'll just smile a little more and let me check those upper incisors—"

"Did anyone ever tell you it's rude to stare at a person's face?"

"Well, I tried staring at your foot and you didn't like that either. I should think you'd be used to men staring at you. You have an interesting face. In a four-color ad it would get a lot of readership. Your face might not sell the product, though. People might think you were looking down that nose of yours at the box of Munchy-Wunchies."

"I'm not in the least interested in how my face would look in an ad."

"Sorry," I said. "I can't break myself of the habit of talking shop. You see, I'm in the advertising game, in New York."

"Oh, yes. A huckster. The Super-Chief, gin rummy at ten cents a point, glamour girls, double Scotches."

"Oh, no. The Long Island Railroad, penny-ante poker, nice girls my friends want to marry off to me, coffee with two lumps of sugar. I work at Baldwin and Bond. On my door it says, 'William J. Stuart, Art Director.' What," I said, hinting politely, "does it say on your door?"

"It says, 'Do Not Disturb.'"

"If you really mean that, I'll splash away and collect some more shells. But—"

"Is that what you've been doing? The beach is littered with shells. Why go wading out here?"

"The ones on the beach have been picked over. And by the time a shell gets washed ashore it's often cracked or chipped. Are you interested in shells? I picked up a lettered olive in quite an unusual golden shade."

"My opinion of shells," she said coldly, "is that they make an excellent surface for secondary roads."

"You do shells an injustice. They built these west Florida beaches. They provide savage tribes with an inflation-proof currency. They lay down deposits of limestone. In their lighter moments they create pearls and the basic ingredients for clam chowder. They—" She ducked suddenly behind the piling, and I said, "I don't seem to be holding my audience."

At that moment a long beam of light lashed out from shore. It glared at me coldly across the wide tidal flats, then flicked out. It was a car's spotlight. I heard the engine hum as the car moved on down the beach. Probably a fisherman heading for the deep-water pass at the southern end of the beach.

The girl came out from behind the piling and said, "Why do people have to do that? It hurts my eyes."

"A likely story," I said in a cheerful tone. "I suspect that you escaped from a prison camp and that's the sheriff looking for you. You waded out here so the bloodhounds would lose the trail. By the way, what color are your eyes?"

"Do you ever talk sensibly, Mr. Stuart?"

"Uh-huh. I was just trying to cheer you up. You seemed in a mood to bite things out with the nearest barracuda."

"I'm sorry. But everything's been so maddening. I came out here this afternoon with a crowd to go swimming and have a picnic supper, and it got to be a dull party, and I wandered off down the beach alone, and when I came back the idiots had left. I suppose they all thought I was in somebody else's car."

"Must have been a hen party," I said. "I can't imagine men overlooking you like that."

"My shoes were in one car, too, so I don't have any, and I cut my feet on some of your nasty old shells. I saw your light and waded out here and hid behind a piling to see what you looked like. I thought if you looked human I'd ask for a lift back to town."

"Stuart, old boy," I said, "the answer to whether or not you look human is that she's been trying to drive you away."

"I haven't! I mean, not really. It was just that you were so cheerful I could hardly stand it."

"I will reform. I will look on the dark side of things. About that lift into town, I have a car parked up the beach where the road ends. I know I'm a sinister-looking character, but—"

"At this point I'd bum a ride from Dracula. But I don't think I need worry. I suspect that women trust you, don't they?"

"Yes," I said, "and I wish they wouldn't. It brings out the best in me. Someday I'd like to find out what the worst is like."

"Maybe you'd be disappointed. Let's go, shall we?"

I took her hand and we started wading toward the beach. She had a nice hand, but her slim fingers trembled and felt cold. She was quite nervous. Her fingers tightened on mine every time a mullet jumped in the shallows, and when we reached dry sand she kept peering back over her shoulder. Of course it was natural for a girl to be upset after finding herself alone on a beach at night, miles from home.

I began chattering to help her relax. I told her that old Joe Baldwin, my boss, had lent me his family's winter place on the beach in Gulf City for my vacation. The Baldwin place was called the Casa del Mar, and it was so big and Moorish that I kept looking around hopefully for a built-in harem. I told her that my car was a convertible and only two months old and that the dealer had made me take several hundred bucks' worth of accessories I didn't want but that I was no pushover; I had held out firmly against two-way radio and television. I talked a lot of nonsense about this and that, and gradually her fingers stopped trembling and she even laughed a few times. She told me that she lived in Gulf City all year round and that her name was Valerie Wilson.

When we reached the car she looked at it admiringly and said she had never driven a convertible and would I let her try it. I said sure, and stowed my shells in the luggage compartment, and put on my shoes, and lowered the top of the car. We eased along over the rough shell road for a quarter mile, passing a few isolated beach cottages, and then slid onto the concrete road leading to the business center of Gulf City. I relaxed against the seat. It was shaping up as a nice vacation. Pretty girl, warm tropic night, soft breeze, gentle hum of tires—I sat up suddenly. There was nothing gentle about the noise the tires were starting to make. They were beginning to yowl. I glanced at the speedometer. Forty. Forty-five. Forty-eight—

"This road," I said mildly, "is a lousy runway for a take-off."

"Don't you like to drive fast?"

"Sure. Anything up to thirty-five."

She laughed softly and turned off the dashboard lights. "It doesn't seem so fast," she said, "if you don't look at the speedometer. Are you as cautious about everything as you are about driving?"

"Not at all. Once I pick up a mysterious girl on a beach and let her drive my car I lose my head about women. Within reason, of course."

She seemed to be concentrating on driving and didn't answer. The hum of the engine climbed slowly up the scale. Houses flashed by. We were getting well into Gulf City. "They have a sign at the outskirts of Gulf City," I murmured. "It says, 'Drive Slow and See Our Town, Drive Fast and See Our Jail.' I hope it's a nice jail. Probably there's a cop flying formation with us right now."

"Nonsense," she said.

I looked back. As a matter of fact there was a pair of headlights a couple hundred yards behind us, apparently going at least as fast as we were. I told her about it.

"If it was a cop," she said, "he'd have caught us long ago."

"You mean that car's been keeping pace with us all along?"

"Oh, no. Just a little while."

"We've only been driving a little while. We—"

Just then she stamped on the brakes. The car almost stubbed its radiator cap on the street, swung into a side road.

"You live down here?" I asked.

"No. I just thought you'd like to see this section. Pretty, isn't it?"

"Nicest blur I ever saw. That car behind us made the turn, too. I hope it's a coeducational jail."

"If he was a cop he'd have blown a whistle or a siren or something."

"Yes. If he was a cop. Is there any other reason anybody else would chase you? Are you sure that car using the spotlight on the beach wasn't looking for you?"

"Ridiculous. I'll prove he isn't following us."

She began whipping the car in and out of back streets, making fast skidding turns, and racing down straightaways with the accelerator nailed to the floor. I had never realized that a car could do things like that. The next time I took her for a drive we would go by oxcart. The headlights behind us kept pace for a few turns, then vanished.

Valerie glanced at the rear-view mirror and said, "See, he's gone. I proved it, didn't I?"

"Maybe you only proved you're a faster driver than he is. Or maybe he switched off his headlights and is still following. Or—"

"I wouldn't have your imagination for anything," she said. "It must be like living in a haunted house." She made another turn and came out on the main business street of Gulf City, heading for a traffic light.

"The light's red," I muttered, without much hope.

She made a quick left turn in front of a truck coming out of the cross street. "Did you say that light was red?"

"Yes. We went through it. Do you mind if I mention something else? We're headed the wrong direction on a one-way street."

"You should have told me before I made the turn. I can't read your mind, can I?" She made another turn—legal, for a change—and braked to a quick stop in front of a bus terminal.

"If the cops in this town are awake," I said, "my license number is probably as well known right now as the winning number yesterday in bolita."

"Whatever bolita is."

"It's Florida's version of the numbers racket. If you live here how come you don't know that?"

"I don't go in for things that are against the law," she said, looking at me with wide, innocent eyes. "Well, thanks awfully, Mr. Stuart. I'm sorry I wrecked your nerves. If you get in any trouble about my driving let me know. Valerie Wilson. I'm in the book." She gave me a bright smile and a pat on the hand, and jumped out of the car.

I came out of my side of the car fast and caught her as she reached the sidewalk. "Look, honey," I said. "I don't have one of those greased-lightning brains. Mine works more like a wet match. But even a guy like me can work this out. That car on the beach was hunting for you. And he tailed us into town. Why?"

"What nonsense! He was heading in the other direction when we got back on the beach. I saw his spotlight way back of us."

"I know. I wondered why you kept turning around. Well, he decided you couldn't have walked or run that far and he came back and saw our footprints. You asked to drive the car for fear he might do just that. And you did all that fancy driving and turned against traffic on a one-way street to throw him off."

"Well, honestly! I bet you peek under the bed every night for burglars."

"And about that beach party. What kind of a beach party is it that breaks up right after eating? Usually they keep going for half the night."

She said, rather breathlessly, "There was a dance in town. We were just going to stay on the beach long enough to watch the moon come up over the Gulf."

"When you live on the lower west coast of Florida the moon doesn't come up over the Gulf. It sets over the Gulf. You say you live here all year round?"

"Yes," she snapped. "But I'm just a working girl, not an astronomer. Why are you acting this way? What are you trying to prove?"

"I think you're in trouble."

"That's ridiculous. But if I were, just what would you do about it?"

"That depends. If you're in a jam and it's not your fault, I'd like to help."

"And suppose it was my fault?"

"Valerie, I think women are wonderful. I worship them. But when they go shopping for bargains in trouble, I want to worship them from afar."

She said in a jeering tone, "Galahad with his fingers crossed. Romeo asking Juliet for her character references. I don't think I can be very irresistible tonight."

"You're quite a number. But usually it takes me longer than an hour to fall hopelessly in love with a girl."

"Then I'd better rush off before you reach your time limit and start feeling reckless. Good night, Mr. Stuart, It's been dull knowing you." She walked toward the entrance to the bus station.

I kept pace with her, and said, "I know you don't live in a bus station. I think I'll bore you a little longer and make sure you get home safely."

"Oh, I could scream!" she said. "There's nothing wrong with me that an aspirin and hearing you say good-by won't cure. I—" She bumped into the doorway of the bus station and her white plastic shoulder bag flew open. The contents scattered all over the pavement—a lipstick and compact and bobby pins and cigarettes and matches and a half-used package of fruit drops and a small tin of aspirin and a pencil and all the other junk women carry. "Look what you made me do," she cried.

"Sorry. I'm afraid I've made you jumpy."

She stooped and began picking up stuff. "Me jumpy?" she said indignantly. "You're the one who's jumpy. Probably it's just as well I spilled all this. Now you won't suspect me of carrying a small pearl-handled automatic."

I retrieved two nickels and handed them to her. "What brought pearl-handled automatics to your mind?" I asked. "Nobody mentioned guns. Thoughts don't just pop into people's heads. One thought always suggests another. You must have had an interesting chain of thoughts."

"I did. I thought how ridiculously upset you are, and I wondered what would upset you more, and I decided that a small, deadly weapon in my bag would have done the trick."

"Don't sell me short," I said. "In my younger days many a tin can bit the dust before my air rifle."

"I don't think you had any younger days. You act so middle-aged now. Collecting shells, driving thirty-five miles an hour—I think my compact rolled into the gutter."

I crawled over to get it, pausing on the way to collect a pair of three-cent stamps, stuck together, and an empty paper of matches. "I have a theory about girls' handbags," I called over my shoulder. "I claim you can figure out a girl's character from the contents. You've been keeping these stamps because you intend to soak them apart someday. But the stamps look faded, as if carried a long time. That indicates a nature full of good intentions but with poor follow-through. The empty match paper hints that you don't pay enough attention to details. You left irregular stubs when you tore out the matches, a sign of impulsiveness and quick decisions. No charge for the analysis. And here's your compact and a coin purse."

I turned to give her the articles. I had certainly been right about the quick decisions. She had made one, and vanished.

I took a fast look around the bus station. Nobody was in it but an old guy sweeping the floor. He hadn't seen anyone. A sign in the rear said, *This Way to Buses and Taxis.* I hurried to the parking area beyond the sign and found a taxi driver tilted back in a chair beside a call box, reading a comic book. He hadn't seen anyone. I returned to the waiting-room and saw a thin Gulf City phone book hanging beside a booth. I looked up the name Valerie Wilson; she had said she was in the book. I knew before I looked that it was a waste of time. She wasn't listed.

I wondered if anything she told me was true. The beach-party yarn certainly wasn't. She hadn't waded out into the shallows and hidden behind a piling to look me over. She was out there before I came along, hiding from somebody. And at first, after I spotted her, she hadn't wanted my help. She had changed her mind after the car with the spotlight drove past.

One of the last things she told me was how she happened to think of pearl-handled automatics. Maybe she lied about that, too. Maybe she had a much more interesting chain of thought leading to the subject of guns. Well, she needn't come around asking me for a penny for her thoughts. If she had unpleasant thoughts about guns, I'd pay her five bucks to keep them to herself.

I dropped the empty paper of matches into a trash can, put the compact into my pocket, and, after a moment's thought, decided to save the stamps, too. No use wasting them; I could soak them apart someday. That left the small white coin purse. I opened it. It contained twenty-two dollars and fifty cents, and a door key attached to a plastic tag stamped with the number eight. Probably it fit the door of her room in a small hotel; a large hotel would have its name stamped on the tag. I looked at the money and shook my head. Valerie should have stayed to listen to my character analysis. My statement that she didn't pay enough attention to details might have reminded her she was sneaking off without her money. All she had, I suspected, was the two loose nickels I had picked up and handed to her. I hoped that her hotel wasn't far away. She wouldn't enjoy a long walk in bare feet.

Until I opened the purse I hadn't decided what to do. Maybe she was in trouble, maybe not; at any rate, she had hinted that I was about as desirable to have underfoot as a patch of sandspurs. If I hadn't found the money I might have returned to Joe Baldwin's Moorish palace and tried to forget everything that had happened. But the money gave me a legitimate excuse to try to find her. I didn't want her to vanish from my vacation quite so fast, and I wanted very much to know whether or not she was in as much trouble as I suspected.

Chapter Two:
FOOTPRINTS IN THE SAND

The janitor in the bus station told me that police headquarters was around the corner, and I left my car parked where it was and walked to the place. Gulf City was only a town of fifteen thousand, and the police merely rated a couple of rooms in the big white frame house used as City Hall. I entered the room labeled *Chief of Police—Samuel Tinsman.* A young guy in a khaki uniform was sitting at a desk, rubbing his knuckles in a crop of whisk-broom hair. He wore a small gold badge and a large frown.

He glared at the patrolman standing beside the desk and said angrily, "More slugs in the parking-meters! Davidson, you got to bear down on this." He poked irritably at a small pile of lead slugs on his desk pad.

The patrolman shuffled his feet. "Yeah, Chief," he muttered, "but people slip 'em in when I'm not around."

"Well, you got to be around! Trouble is you don't check those meters often enough; you're in some drugstore lapping up coffee. Man puts a slug in and it shows in the window of the meter until somebody else puts in a coin. All you have to do is get around often enough and look in the windows of the meters and when you find a slug wait around and nail the guy when he comes back."

"Okay, Chief. I'll bear down on it."

"Good." He watched the patrolman leave the room, and then turned to me and said in a worried tone, "Evening. Anything wrong?"

"Oh, I don't know," I said cautiously. "Does much go wrong around here?"

"Take these slugs," he grumbled. "A buck's worth, just in one day. You might think people had no respect for law and order."

"I can see it must be irritating, but it isn't very big stuff, is it? I don't suppose you have anything big happen in a quiet town like this."

"That's where you're wrong," he said glumly. "A burglar broke into the Richards Building one night last week and stole some gold inlays from a dentist's office. I haven't been able to crack that yet. I just got made Chief a few months ago and I don't know what City Council's gonna say if this goes on."

"If anything big did happen you'd know it fast, wouldn't you? I mean, if one of your prowl cars saw something, they'd call in right away?"

"Sure. We have two-way radio. So I'd get a report right away if something broke."

"Is the far southern end of the beach in city limits? And do your prowl cars ever take a run along the beach down to the pass?"

"Yeah, it's in the city. But we don't go down there unless we get a call. Don't think one of my cars has been there in a month. Has something happened?"

"I don't think anything has yet," I said. "I'm trying to locate a girl named Valerie Wilson."

"What do you mean, you're trying to locate her? When did you see her last?"

"I was with her tonight. And she sort of, well, vanished."

"Vanished, huh?" he said in a shocked tone. He pulled out a notebook and wet the stub of a pencil and printed in big black letters: *Missing Person.* "Age and address?" he asked.

"She's in her twenties. I don't know her address. I don't think all this is necessary, Chief."

"I got to get the facts. Color hair?"

"Couldn't see it. She wore a red bandanna. Now, look—"

"Color eyes?"

I gave up trying to head him off. When he chose a course he plodded along it like a loggerhead turtle trundling down a beach. "I don't know the color of her eyes. She wore a white shirt and gray slacks. Bare feet. Height about five five. Weight around one ten. Nice figure. I wouldn't call her pretty."

"Plain, huh?"

"Oh, no. Just the opposite." I was beginning to warm up to the subject. "I don't know if I can describe her face. But maybe I can give you an idea. Look, if you were walking in a garden at night and you met a girl who had a nice low, husky voice and sort of a tantalizing laugh, but you couldn't really see her, you'd hope she looked the way this girl does. What I mean is, her face would go nicely in a Caribbean travel ad."

"Pull yourself together," the Chief said reprovingly. "All you're doing is giving out with a long, low whistle. You got no lead to where she lives?"

"Only this," I said, opening the coin purse and explaining how she had lost her money and key and the numbered key tag.

He examined the key and its tag, and said, "We can trace her through this. Just a matter of calling all the hotels and rooming-houses. Maybe first you better tell me who you are, and the whole story."

I decided it was all right to talk. If Valerie was in trouble, it wasn't with the police. I gave him the full story except for censoring the part about Valerie breaking speed limits and going through red lights and bucking traffic on one-way streets; I was afraid that those details might distract him from the main point.

When I finished talking, he sat for a moment stacking the parking-meter slugs into neat piles. "Tell you what," he said in a flat voice. "You want to leave the purse and money and key and her compact here, I'll try to see she gets them. I guess I got no right to take them away from you."

"I want to take them back myself."

He looked at me as if I were a suspect in the gold-inlays case. "Yeah," he said, "I thought so. This is a police department, not a lonely-hearts club. Why don't you let the girl alone?"

"Let her alone? I'm trying to help her!"

"You met a dame on the beach. You got in her hair. She decided she'd rather cuddle up with a good book. So she ditched you."

I said angrily, "What about the car on the beach? What about the car tailing us into town?"

"I hope you always go straight, Stuart," he said severely. "You can't get away with stories like that. If I put a lie detector on you, I bet you'd blow out the fuse."

"The girl may be in trouble! You can't laugh it off like this."

He drew a thick black cross through the notebook page that he had titled *Missing Person*. "Go away and write a poem about girls you meet in gardens. I got other things to worry about."

I believe strongly in law and order, but at the moment I felt an urge to start a crime wave. I picked up Valerie's belongings, and took a dollar bill from my wallet. "You're carrying too big a burden," I said. "Let me buy you a good night's sleep." I put the dollar bill on his desk, scooped up the parking-meter slugs, and walked out.

Behind me the Chief said, in a voice filled with longing, "I only hope Davidson catches you putting one of them in a meter."

I returned to my car and found a note stuffed under the windshield wiper. I reached for it eagerly; perhaps Valerie had changed her mind. I unfolded it, and gave a snort. Sinister characters might chase people all over Gulf City, but nobody was going to get away with parking in an Unloading Zone. The note was a summons.

As I stared at the thing my eyes narrowed to cold hard slits. "Cops," I said, out of the corner of my mouth. I tore the summons into confetti; let them try to locate me through my New York license. A little more of Gulf City's police department and I would turn into a gunsel and a hood, whatever gunsels and hoods were.

I climbed into the car and pulled out from the curb. Something flashed in the rear-view mirror. Headlights. A car half a block behind me was pulling out from the curb, too. It could be coincidence. I swung around the corner, and a few moments later a gray sedan made the turn, too. I drove slowly around the block; that should dispose of any coincidence. It did.

The gray sedan followed. Once when it slid under a street light I saw the car had a spotlight. A chill the size of a small jellyfish oozed down my back. I had been an idiot to leave my car parked in the open. After Valerie fooled the driver of the gray sedan by going through the red light and zipping down the one-way street against the arrows, the driver of the gray sedan had cruised around looking for a convertible with the top lowered. This was great, I thought; if I wanted to turn gunsel maybe I could get a free lesson from the guy tailing me.

Valerie's racetrack driving hadn't done any good, and I had even less confidence in my driving. I turned onto the main street and headed away from the Baldwin place, thinking hard and sticking with a couple of other cars for company. We left the business zone and the two cars ahead of me speeded up. That gave me an idea. I stepped on the gas, passed one car, slowed and let him get by, speeded up and passed both cars, slowed and let one pass, and so on. Within a mile I shuffled my car with the other two like a pea in a shell game.

The driver of the gray sedan tailing me wasn't close enough for his head-lights to identify my convertible, and by now he ought to be very confused as to which taillight was mine. Eventually one of the cars turned left off the main road and I took the next turn to the right. I hit thirty-five and forty miles an hour on back roads, heading for town. No headlights flick-ered in the rear-view mirror.

I drove through town and out to the beach residential section and swung into the palm-lined driveway of the palace that fifteen percent commis-sions on advertising built. I parked at the garage and got out, swaggering slightly, to open the doors. I felt very successful.

Then I noticed an odd light on the driveway just behind my car. I walked around to the rear. The right taillight was okay, but the left one was send-ing out a white glare. I examined it. The red glass was missing and only the naked bulb was left. That is, nearly all the red glass was missing. A few fragments still clung to the frame. The jellyfish-size chill began to crawl down my back again. It felt slightly different this time, however. More like a small octopus. It wasn't likely that the thick red glass had broken while I was driving. Maybe somebody had purposely smashed it while the car was parked at the bus station. That would make my car easy to follow at night. Maybe somebody had a good laugh watching me try to shuffle that white taillight with the red taillights of other cars. Of course, I hadn't seen any headlights following me after I turned off the main road and started back to town, but the driver of the gray sedan might have switched off his headlights. Or he could have dropped far back and still followed my white taillight.

My heart began thumping as if it needed a carbon and valve job. I crept down the driveway to the street. A gray sedan was just easing away, its engine purring like a cat with cream. Undoubtedly I was the cream.

Without wasting time putting my car away in the garage, I hurried into the house and went into the study looking for a telephone. The study was filled with sheeted chairs that sat around like ghosts waiting for a call to haunt somebody, and its walls were covered with mounted specimens of the big toothy fish that old Joe Baldwin loved to catch. A sawfish swam high in the shadows against the far wall, and near by a barracuda watched me with a cold glass eye. A cheerless room. I saw a telephone and walked toward it, hoping it was not disconnected. It wasn't. As I stretched out my hand, the thing suddenly rang. I picked it up nervously.

"Bill?" a cool voice said. "Bill, this is Valerie."

"Don't bother me," I growled. "I'm busy reading a book on how to string women up by the thumbs."

Her laugh rustled softly from the receiver. "You were nice and I acted very rudely. I'm sorry."

"How did you know where to phone me?"

"You told me about the Casa del Mar, remember? I've been calling and calling without getting an answer. I only have two nickels and I've almost worn them out in the telephone coin slot. You found my money, didn't you?"

"Uh-huh. Twenty-two dollars and fifty cents. And your room key."

She said in a coaxing tone, "Could you forget how nasty I was and bring the purse to me at the bus station? It's two miles to where I'm staying and I was going to take a taxi. But I didn't realize I'd lost my money until you drove away, and now all I have left is one nickel."

I said grimly, "If I go to all that trouble, I could use a small reward."

"What—what kind of reward?"

"Answers to a few questions. As a start, how did you manage to disappear so fast?"

"I was hiding in the phone booth in the bus station. You stood right beside me looking up something in the book. I was afraid you were going to make a call."

"I was looking up the name Valerie Wilson. Not much chance I'd be making a call, was there?"

"I'm sorry," she said faintly.

"Valerie, do you know anything about a little pastime called the shell game?"

"I—I don't think I do."

"The operator has three English walnut shells, and a pea. He shuffles the pea back and forth under the shells, and suckers bet which shell is hiding the pea. But meanwhile the operator has palmed the pea, and the suckers can't win. I've been betting on empty shells and I'm tired of it. Now, what's the score? Who's been following you, and why?"

There was silence for a moment at the other end of the line; then she said breathlessly, "I didn't want to tell you because it makes me seem like such a fool. I met a man while I was having dinner tonight in a restaurant. He seemed nice, and I went for a drive with him. He stopped his car out near where you met me, and went native. I had to jump out of the car, and he chased me, and I lost my sandals running through the sand."

"And he trailed us back into town?"

"Yes. I didn't want him to find out where I live and I was afraid maybe I hadn't thrown him off, so I wanted to stop at the bus station and take a taxi."

"Did you happen to think of telling the police a guy was bothering you?"

"Well, yes, but—"

"I thought of it, too. And I did something about it. I told the Chief of Police everything that had happened and he decided I was the guy who had been bothering you. He threw me out. Fun, huh?"

"Oh, Bill! I'm awfully sorry I got you into all this."

"In regard to your new story, I think I'm betting on another empty walnut shell. However, I'll bring down your stuff. I have your purse and money and key and compact and a pair of stamps stuck together and the guy who was tailing you."

"You *what?*"

"Yes, I picked him up, too. He followed me home. Probably outside right now. He's not very good company and I'll be glad to let you have him back along with your other belongings."

"Bill," she said, "don't come down. I won't be here. I—" Her voice trailed away.

"Wait a minute," I cried. "I didn't mean to scare you. I only wanted to get the truth. I— Hello— Hello." There was a click at the other end of the line, silence. I kept saying, "Hello," and finally the operator cut in and told me my party had disconnected. "All right," I said. "Get me the police station." In a short time the Chief's voice came over the wire, and I said, "This is William J. Stuart. I was talking to you about a girl maybe a half hour ago."

"Now, listen, Stuart," he said wearily. "I have no time to spare. A couple things came up and—"

"I have another missing-person case for you," I said cheerily. "Name of missing person, William J. Stuart. Address, Casa del Mar, the Baldwin place. Color hair, brown. Color eyes—"

"Stuart, I ought to run you in as drunk and disorderly. The only thing missing about you is your common sense. Go home and sleep it off."

"I am home, Chief. Look, I admit I'm not missing yet, but maybe I will be. And you'll save a lot of trouble getting these facts from me before I turn up missing. You won't believe this, but the car I mentioned tailed me home. And Valerie Wilson called up a moment ago to ask me to bring her money and stuff back to the bus station, and when I told her about being followed she said in a faint voice not to come, and hung up. Shall I stop now and let you have a good laugh, Chief, or do you want my color eyes?"

The Chief cleared his throat. "Stuart," he said, "maybe I've been too hasty. A couple things came up since you left that kinda tie in with your story. I got reports there's a tough character loose in town. You sit where you are and I'll come right out."

"Chief," I said coyly, "this is so sudden."

He yelled, "Don't make a joke of this thing just because I've been slow catching on. I'm serious. Something queer's going on in this town and I want to break it up before there's real trouble. You sit there like I said, see? Don't go outside or let anybody in till I come. I'll ring three times. Okay?"

"Yeah, sure," I said. "I'll see you."

I hung up. I didn't feel quite as gay and sparkling as I had felt when I started talking to him. I wished he hadn't been quite so worried, or at least hadn't mentioned a tough character loose in town. I glanced around and saw the barracuda staring at me as if I were a mullet. Why a man would want a thing like that hanging in his study, when he could have decorated the walls with a nice cheerful set of advertising layouts, I didn't know. I crossed the room to a gun rack and examined the shotguns and rifles. They weren't loaded, and I opened a cabinet beside them looking for ammunition. One drawer held a forty-five automatic and a box of cartridges. I filled the clip and carried the forty-five into the dark living-room and sat near a window to wait.

Darkness did unpleasant things to familiar sights and sounds. Outside the window an old bougainvillaea vine squirmed over its arbor and dangled the silhouettes of hangman's nooses against the night sky. Palm fronds reached for the house with dripping black fingers. The huge mottled leaf of a Pothos aureus lurked in a patch of starlight like a Seminole face streaked with war paint. A big insect, crawling on the copper screen, imitated fingers prying to release the hooks. It seemed as though I waited a long time, but actually it couldn't have been more than half my life expectancy. I heard no footsteps, saw no lights. And so, when the Chief rang the doorbell, he might just as well have stabbed me three times.

I moved weakly to the door and opened it. The Chief brushed some twigs from his khaki uniform, came in, put his revolver in its holster long enough to shake hands. Then he took out the gun immediately.

"Stuart," he said earnestly, "I want to apologize for the way I treated you. This thing is hot." He turned back to the doorway and called, "Come on in, Al."

A big guy with shoulders like the fenders of a jeep sauntered into the house. He wore two-toned sports shoes and a light blue suit and dark blue shirt. He had wavy black hair and the kind of rugged good looks you sometimes see on fighters who haven't soaked up too many left jabs. He flicked a glance up and down me, and I got the impression that he picked up everything from my shoe size to how much I tip barbers.

He said casually, "I don't go in for forty-fives, myself. Especially not when the clip's not shoved in all the way."

I said, "Huh?" and stared at the automatic in my left hand.

"Like this," he said, taking it from me. He tapped the base of the clip and I heard it click up into place. "They don't pick up bullets from the clip if you don't get it seated," he said pleasantly, handing it back to me.

The Chief said proudly, "This is Detective Sergeant Al Leonard."

I said, "I didn't know I rated a detective sergeant. Matter of fact, I didn't know Gulf City rated one."

"Al's a visitor from up North," the Chief said. "Dropped in just after you were around to say hello, talk a little shop. Not often we get a big-city detective down here. I asked him to come along for the ride."

"Sounded interesting," Al said. "I'm not used to vacations. Getting restless."

Things were looking up, I decided. With a real cop around perhaps I could get some action. "Glad you came," I said. "What's the dope? Found anybody?"

The Chief said, "Al and I, and two of my boys, have been searching the area for half an hour. Haven't got your man yet, but we will. I'd say you called me just in time. We found his car. We were hunting for it even before you phoned. After you left, the damnedest bunch of reports began coming in on that car."

"That's a relief. I'll be glad to get that gray sedan off my rear bumpers."

"Gray sedan? No. This is a green convertible with New York license—"

"That's my car," I said irritably.

"Right out by the garage?" the Chief asked, frowning.

"Sure."

"You admit it's yours?"

"I not only admit it, I insist on it."

"Well," he said slowly. He looked at his revolver and replaced it, rather doubtfully, in the holster. He brought out his notebook. "At nine thirty-two p.m.," he said, "a Mrs. Minnie Hall, of nineteen ten Valencia Street, walking home from the movies, saw a green convertible driving at a high rate of speed east on Hibiscus Avenue. When she arrived home she phoned a complaint to our switchboard. At nine thirty-six Officer Jennings, on duty at the corner of Main and Harding Streets in the business section, saw a green convertible with a New York license, which he was unable to read, go through a red light and turn against the one-way traffic on Harding Street."

"The girl was driving," I snapped. "She was trying to shake off that gray sedan. I told you about it."

"You didn't report these traffic-law violations. At ten-o-two Officer Davidson, having just left police headquarters, ticketed a green convertible with your New York license for parking in an Unloading Zone in front of the bus station."

"Half a block down the street was a gray sedan he should have tagged."

"At ten-eighteen," the Chief went on, "a Mr. Joseph Hatch, of twenty forty-eight Hacienda Place, who had entered the bus station to look up timetables, saw a man of your description approach the green convertible. Mr. Hatch, who recognized the paper under your windshield wiper as a summons, watched to see your reaction. He stated that you looked coldly at the summons, said, 'Cops' out of the corner of your mouth, tore up the summons, and drove away. Mr. Hatch stated it as his belief that you were a New York City gunman."

Al Leonard yawned and said, "I wish I worked in New York. All the hard guys in my burg know how to put a clip in a rod."

I growled, "Do you blame me for tearing up that summons? I'm being chased all over town by thugs and when I stop to yell, 'Help, police!' I get a parking-ticket."

"Suppose," the Chief said, "I finish. At ten twenty-five Officer Davidson saw the same green convertible driving west on Main Street near Harper and took its license number again for violation of—"

"Now, listen," I said. "At ten twenty-five I was driving west on Main Street near Harper. But I was not speeding or bucking traffic or—"

The Chief said triumphantly, "You were driving with a broken left taillight."

"The guy in the gray sedan broke it while I was parked, so he could follow me more easily."

"It's too bad nobody else ever saw this gray sedan."

"The girl saw it. If you'd quit directing traffic and find her—"

The Chief asked, "What do you think of all this, Al?"

Al massaged his blue-shadowed chin with a big hand. "Too big for me," he said. "I only handle homicide."

"What I think is this, Al," the Chief said. "We get a lot of traffic cases, on account of we enforce the law in this town. You'd be amazed the stories people cook up, to get out of fines. What I think is, this Stuart and a girl did some wild driving and then Stuart worries about his license number being taken and cooks up this yarn." He turned to me. "You got anything to say to that, Stuart?"

"Chief," I said wearily, "I'll end all your troubles. I stole those gold inlays from the Richards Building. Look." I opened my mouth so he could peek in.

"Traffic court," he said, "is at ten tomorrow morning. I'll see you there."

"I'll try to clear myself before then. Will my corpse do?"

The Chief said, "About that forty-five you got. Discharge of firearms within city limits is prohibited."

"I'll put it away," I said. "I'll stay on the right side of the law and use knives."

The Chief said coldly, "Good night."

"So long," Al said. "Don't take any wooden coffins, pal—I mean wooden nickels." One side of his mouth twitched in a grin, and he followed the Chief out of the house.

I walked slowly to the study and replaced the forty-five in the cabinet. The whole business was maddening. It was like seeing a big black fin cruise toward a swimmer and screaming, "Shark!" and running up and down the beach trying to get help and having a lifeguard grab me for disturbing the peace. I didn't know what else I could do. Probably I'd be smart to bring in the shells I had collected earlier in the evening and start cleaning them. That was the only kind of shell game I was qualified to play.

I turned to leave the room, and saw light glinting in the cold glass eye of the barracuda on the wall. For some reason the thing didn't look interested in me any more. The big grim jaws seemed to be yawning, as if the fish had decided I wasn't legal size and ought to be thrown back onto the bank. It was all in my mind, of course; I was acting like a minnow and trying not to admit it to myself. Because, I knew, there was one action I could take that might clear up a few things. It involved pretending that I wasn't a minnow, and swimming out by myself into deep water. It meant going alone to a deserted beach and trying to find out what had happened before I found the girl hiding behind a piling of the abandoned pier.

I didn't care for the idea. On the other hand, I didn't like strangers hinting that I was a frightened idiot, and showing me how to put clips in automatics, and telling me sarcastically not to take any wooden coffins. I looked at the barracuda and decided that it had almost as ugly a jaw as Al Leonard and that they could both go jump in the Gulf. I went outside and climbed into my car and headed for the southern end of the beach road.

For the first few minutes I kept peeking at the rear-view mirror and wincing every time I saw headlights. I told myself to stop that stuff; it was only eleven-thirty, and it was natural for other cars to be on the road. The Chief and his bunch had searched the area around the Casa del Mar without finding anybody. It wasn't likely that the gray sedan was still riding my taillight. But if it was, I couldn't do anything about it, and I was just as safe or unsafe prowling the beach as sitting alone in the big empty house. I made myself concentrate on trying to remember the tide tables for the southern end of the beach. As nearly as I could recall, I had met the girl perhaps an hour and a half before dead low tide. The water would be coming in now, but every footprint that had been on the beach before ten that night should still be there.

I parked at the end of the road and turned on a flashlight and began following the girl's footsteps and mine to the place where we waded ashore. On the way I crossed two sets of tire tracks, both apparently made by the car that had cruised along the beach using its spotlight. I couldn't be sure, but it looked as if the car had stopped on its return trip to let somebody jump out to examine our footprints. If my guess was correct, the driver of the gray sedan had picked up our trail at that point.

The first problem was to find where Valerie had entered the water. I hunted up and down the beach, starting from the pilings, and located her footprints a hundred yards to the north. I began backtracking. The trail led me off the beach into sand dunes. Something about the tracks was different up there. As I studied them my heart began thudding in a heavy dull rhythm, like a bell buoy in the swells before a storm. I got the answer. The marks looked different because she had been running hard.

I pushed on through a tangle of sea grape, breathing as if I were climbing mountains instead of ten-foot dunes. The sand was too soft now to hold a clear print; all I could see were vague hollows. The beam of my flashlight glowed on an object half buried in the sand. I picked it up. It was a red sandal. I plodded on and squirmed through a final thick mass of shrubbery and saw a small beach cottage twenty feet away. It was brightly lighted and a radio was picking up soft rumba music from a Cuban station and just outside the back door lay another red sandal. I crept to a window and peered into the living-room.

There was a color inside that matched the girl's red sandals. The color had seeped out over the white shirt of a man who was lying dead on the floor.

Chapter Three:
THE CORPSE IN THE COTTAGE

My first impulse was to get in my car and see how fast it would really travel. My next few impulses were the same, but I waited and at last had a faint urge to find out something more. I moved around the cottage peeking into windows. The man with the stained shirt had the place to himself. I picked up the red sandal outside the back, not quite knowing why I did, and opened the back screen door and went in.

An empty ice-cube tray was on the kitchen table beside a bowl in which the ice had melted. I sidled into the living-room and tried to work up interest in details like a couple of overturned highball glasses and a half-empty fifth of bourbon and a small canvas sack that had dribbled water onto the floor beside the couch. A few cigarette stubs that showed lipstick marks rested in an ashtray. The tray also held charred paper matches that probably fit the folder Valerie had dropped from her shoulder bag. I didn't look directly at the man on the floor, but little things about him kept registering in my mind—sleek black hair, thin face, lips drawn back in a frozen grin.

The Cuban dance music pulsed in a slow sickening beat from the radio. I edged across the room, reached for the knob to turn it off.

Behind me a voice said, "Let it alone, pal. I like music while I work."

I swung around and saw Al Leonard and the Chief of Police. Al had made the remark; he was looking at me with a puzzled expression, as if wondering why I wasn't home in bed with the covers pulled up over my ears. If that was his thought, I could understand it; I was wondering the same thing. Apparently the Chief wasn't playing with any complicated ideas. His square, honest face couldn't have been set more sternly if he had caught me throwing rocks at stop signs, and the revolver he was pointing at me looked big enough to need a prime mover.

I said faintly, "Let me know what you consider a false move, so I won't make it."

"Cool, isn't he?" the Chief said in an awed voice. "Al, I sure owe you thanks. If you hadn't said there was something queer about this Stuart and maybe we'd better watch his house for a while, we'd never have trailed him here. Who would have thought the guy's a killer?"

"I don't know," Al said. "Maybe nobody will." He moved softly into the room and looked down at Exhibit A, or whatever cops call bodies.

The Chief complained, "What do you mean, maybe nobody will think he's a killer? We caught him red-handed returning to the scene of the crime, didn't we?"

"Yeah, sure," Al said. "He knocks off a guy and then spends all evening coaxing you to come look at what he did." He bent and picked up two cartridge cases. "One minute he can shoot the stitches out of a guy's shirt pocket with a thirty-two-caliber automatic and the next he don't know how to put a clip in a forty-five."

"Thanks, Al," I said. "Now if you'll tell the Chief to put away that cannon before we have another corpse stretched out here—"

The Chief grumbled, "He could have been setting up an alibi."

Al shrugged. "If you want to make it stick," he said, "you ought to coax him to wander around and put a few fingerprints on things. Maybe I shouldn't have stopped him from turning off that radio. The volume knob will take a nice print." He grinned at me and said, "How about picking up that glass and making yourself a nice highball, pal?"

"I just went on the wagon," I said.

"Well, if he didn't do it," the Chief said glumly, "who did?"

Al looked around slowly. His glance flicked over the red sandals I was carrying and the lipstick marks on the cigarettes in the ashtray and finally came to rest at a point near the ceiling. "I wouldn't know," he said. "I'm on vacation."

"Now, look, Al, you got to help me on this. We never had a murder in this town."

"I don't mind helping," Al said, "but you got to do the work. If I get too mixed up in this, I'll get nailed to testify and maybe have to sit here the next six months and back home somebody eases into my job. Don't let this thing throw you. What was that case you had last week?"

"The gold inlays swiped out of the Richards Building?"

"Yeah, the gold inlays. Okay, pretend you don't care who knocked this guy off, you just want to find who swiped the gold inlays from his teeth."

The Chief looked happier. "I get it," he said. He peered at the red sandals I was carrying and asked, "What are you doing with those?"

I said coldly, "I'm making extra footprints with them to confuse you."

"That's what you always run into," Al said. "No cooperation from the public."

"What do we do with him?" the Chief asked.

"If I was running it," Al said, "I'd wrap him up in a nice little cell. He's a material witness in a murder case. I'd get a judge to set some nice high bail. Let him run around loose and you can't tell what might happen. He might start digging up bodies all over town."

"I kind of like the idea," the Chief said.

"So do I," I said heartily. "Then the reporters won't have any trouble finding me. I have a swell story for them. All about how I knew something was wrong but I couldn't get a cop because they were too busy tagging my car for traffic violations."

The Chief looked at me sadly. "You wouldn't do that."

"Yes, I would. Jails bring out the cop-hater in me."

Al said, "Your first idea of tagging him with this was a good one. He's gonna be hard to handle."

"It's a nice modern jail," the Chief said. "I'd make sure you were comfortable."

"I'd make sure you weren't."

"What do you want to do, then?" he cried. "Skip back to New York? You know I can't let you do that."

"I'm not going to skip. I want to hang around and see what happens. Maybe I can help."

"We're not running a public peep show here," the Chief said sternly. "This is a matter for the police to handle."

"Good," I said. "Then let's get some police here, shall we?"

Al said, "Chief, if you want to smack him, I'll look the other way. In the stomach don't leave any marks."

The Chief breathed heavily a few times, and said, "I don't go in for smacking people around. Now, look, Stuart, I got off on the wrong foot with you. I've been fumbling the ball every time you handed it to me. I admit it. Now can we start clean?"

"No jail?" I asked.

"No jail."

"No tickets for speeding and wrong turns and parking and broken taillights and all that?"

"No tickets."

"All right," I said. "Then as far as I'm concerned, I reported that stuff to you at the police station and you came right out here with me to see what was wrong and we found this."

"Thanks," the Chief said. "Now, about those sandals—"

"Before we go into this," I said, "let's have another understanding. Let's not pin this thing on somebody just because she wears red sandals."

"You like that girl, don't you?"

"I like a lot of girls. I just want her to get an even break."

"You don't think she did this?"

"All I know is I found one red sandal back in the dunes when I was following her trail, and one red sandal outside the back door. I can make lots of guesses if you want. I can guess these sandals came off the tootsies of a Chinese girl named Limehouse Blues who was being held prisoner here by an opium ring. I can guess that a girl named Valerie Wilson wore them and happened to pass by this cottage and saw something that scared her and started running and lost them. Those guesses are just as good as the one you're aching to make."

"The guy's right," Al said.

"You admit anyway we have to find this girl, don't you?" the Chief said in a coaxing tone. "You been after me all evening to find her."

"Sure I want to find her. But I'm a lot more interested in you finding that gray sedan that tailed us."

"If there was a gray sedan."

"Of course there was! I saw it."

"Uh-huh. You happen to have that girl's purse with you?"

I brought it out reluctantly and handed it to him. He opened it, took out the numbered key, and went to the telephone. "Fingerprints?" he asked Al, pointing to the telephone.

"Maybe," Al said. "I wouldn't worry about it, though. Place ought to be lousy with prints."

"I don't have two-way radio in my car," the Chief said. "This will save time." He picked up the phone and called his headquarters and began whipping out orders to check all hotels and rooming-houses, and to have a fingerprint outfit and camera and the doctor who handled police cases sent out right away. He sounded efficient; now that he was thinking of the murder as just another gold-inlay job, he seemed to have something on the ball. I thought it would be just as well, however, for me to stick around and keep nagging him about gray sedans.

While he was telephoning, Al sat on the couch watching me curiously. I suspected that he couldn't understand why a minnow like me would be playing tag with sharks. "What do you do in New York, Stuart?" he asked finally.

"Advertising."

"On vacation, huh? How do you fill in your time here, when you're not playing body, body, who's got the body?"

"I collect sea shells."

"That's interesting, Stuart. Know what I'd do if I were you, Stuart? I'd make a deal with the Chief to come back to testify if I was needed, and I'd spend the rest of my vacation looking for shells at Coney Island."

"You can't find shells there."

"You might not collect any shells," Al said, "and you might not collect any bullet holes."

Something the size of a small rock went down my throat. Probably just a gulp. "I don't get it," I said uneasily.

"Pal, right at the moment you're the only person can tie that girl in with this cottage. You're the only person can tie a gray sedan in with this cottage. It's things like that getting around that make a guy unpopular."

"Thanks," I mumbled. "I'll keep it in mind."

"Just a hint," Al said, yawning. "It don't mean anything to me personally. But maybe the Chief feels he's got enough bodies right now to keep him happy. If you do stay, don't go for many walks alone at night."

The Chief hung up the telephone and heard Al's last remark and wanted to know what it was about. After Al explained, the Chief said he'd put a man on duty outside my house and that anyway the case would probably be cleaned up by morning.

A siren wailed up to the cottage, and Gulf City's police department swung into action as grimly as if setting a trap for speeders. The Chief and his boys were slow but thorough. They photographed the body from all angles. They almost sifted the sand outside looking for footprints, although the sand was too soft to hold clear impressions of feet. They filled the house with a blizzard of fingerprint powder. Al Leonard helped them with the fingerprints. They found prints on one of the highball glasses and the bottle and radio and on a dozen other things around the cottage. Merely as a formality, the Chief explained smoothly, they took my fingerprints and compared them with the others, fortunately without finding any similarity.

Most of the prints around the cottage had been made by the murdered man, but the highball glass and radio and one place on the back screen door carried a different set. At that point the Chief asked me for the girl's compact, and dusted it with fingerprint powder. Inside it, on the back of the small hinged mirror, he found the print of an index finger that matched the ones on the highball glass and radio and back screen door. The Chief put the compact in a box with the red sandals and the cigarette butts marked with lipstick.

The phone rang, and the Chief answered it and said, "Yeah, speaking.... That's good.... Okay, get out there fast and pick her up." He replaced the phone and told me, "We traced the key tag. A girl named Valerie Wilson is registered at room number eight, Beachcomber Court. We'll have her in fifteen minutes."

"That's fine," I said politely. "And how soon will you have that gray sedan?"

"The way you talk about gray sedans you might think this guy here on the floor had tire marks across his shirt. Relax, will you?"

"Yeah," Al said, "the way the car market is nowadays, you can't expect one the moment you put in the order."

I said doggedly, "This car tailed us from— Are you listening to me or not?"

Nobody answered, so apparently they weren't. I shut up for the time being. Al Leonard searched the pockets of the dead man, and found a wallet containing money and a driver's license. The license was made out to Edward Jones, and the address given was the beach cottage. The Chief checked with the telephone company and learned that the phone was listed under the name Edward Jones. Following that the police doctor had his turn and, after examining the body, guessed that Mr. Jones had not been using his phone after about 8 or 9 p.m. The doctor had a stretcher brought in, and took the body away. That seemed to relieve everyone but Al Leonard. The boys started taking the place apart as happily as volunteer firemen working on a burning house, but they didn't find much. You might almost have thought that the late Mr. Jones had decided that if he was ever murdered he wanted the cops to have a tough time finding out how he liked his eggs and who his best friends were.

During the search, the Chief opened the small canvas sack that had been dripping water onto the floor beside the couch. He poked around inside it and said disgustedly, "Bunch of sea shells. You want these, Stuart?"

"Probably junk," I said, peering into the bag. "No, wait, maybe I will take them. That looks like a good king's crown on top."

Al chuckled and said, "You want to watch that. You see what happens to guys who go in for collecting sea shells." He jerked a thumb at the dark red stain on the floor.

"Don't scare him like that," the Chief said. "Nobody ever gets hurt if they stick to collecting shells, unless maybe they cut their feet on them."

"As a matter of fact," I said, "there is an authenticated case of a shell collector being killed by a small shell. It was a member of the conus family, a type that has a little hook it uses to inject poison into its prey. The cone jabbed the poisoned hook into the collector's thumb, and he died."

The Chief yawned and said, "Where was this tragedy, Stuart?"

"In Australia."

The telephone rang, and the Chief said, "In Australia, huh? Excuse me while I handle a murder case in Florida." He picked up the phone, and didn't like what somebody on the other end told him. "Well, sit there, then," he growled, and hung up. "She's not in her room at Beachcomber Court," he said to me. He seemed to take it as a personal affront, as if Valerie Wilson had broken a date with him. "What about that, Stuart?"

"I have a radio transmitter in my wrist watch," I said. "I tipped her off to lie low until you find that gray sedan."

"Well, she can't go far," the Chief grumbled. "No money, no shoes. I wish it wasn't too late to put something in the paper. They only print one edition and they lock it up around eleven at night. If her description was on the front page, she couldn't move a step. Now I'll have to scatter men all over town looking for her and we only have fourteen on the force."

"Fifteen," Al said. "I'll help."

"So will I," I said. "That's sixteen."

"Fifteen," the Chief said coldly. "Well, let's get out of here. You go home and take it easy, Stuart. I'll keep a man outside your place. And don't go playing detective, understand?"

I picked up the bag of shells and started toward the door. "It is sort of like play, isn't it?" I said cheerfully. I tapped Al on the shoulder and said, "Don't take any wooden coffins, pal—I mean wooden nickels." I twitched up one corner of my mouth in a grin, and got out of there just in time to avoid something regrettable in the line of police brutality.

I didn't feel quite as gay and carefree as I had been acting. In fact, my thoughts would have fit nicely into a soap-opera program. The way things were shaping up, the next time I wanted to see Valerie Wilson I had better come calling with a box of candy in one hand and a habeas corpus in the other. The case against her looked bad. She had visited a man named Edward Jones early in the evening, and they had a couple of drinks and Valerie tuned the radio to a Cuban dance band and smoked a few cigarettes and something happened and Mr. Jones made the error of standing at the wrong end of a gun when it went off. There was no evidence that a third party was involved.

No evidence, that is, except tire marks on the beach that might have been made by fishermen, and the flicker of headlights in my rear-view mirror, and the sight of a gray sedan easing away from my house. The more I thought about the gray sedan the less I liked it as an alibi. I pictured a tough prosecutor getting me on the stand and asking if I was a nervous person and often imagined things. If he was smart he would say, "Boo!" when I wasn't expecting it, and win his case right there. I didn't know what I was doing mixed up in a shooting; I liked having my vacations on a beach, not a beachhead.

I walked to my car and drove home. A police car chaperoned me all the way, and paused at the Casa del Mar long enough to drop off a cop who turned out to be Davidson, the beagle of the parking-meters. I invited him in for a cup of coffee but he refused; he was very happy that he had been promoted from slugs that fit meters to slugs that fit guns, and he planned to stay on the alert outside the house until he was relieved.

I carried the bag of shells that the late Mr. Jones had collected into the house, and dumped the contents onto a kitchen table. I already knew there was a good king's crown in the lot, but I was surprised to see fourteen other moderately rare shells, all in fine condition. There was a Scotch bonnet, a tiger clam with a complete halo of purple around the lips instead of the usual broken markings, a yellow cockle, a nice lace murex, a lettered olive, and a good set of sunray shells. Only an expert could have walked along a beach littered with millions of shells and picked up that collection. The shells were still damp, indicating that they had been gathered on the beach earlier that evening. I wondered idly why there had been no other shells in the cottage; the average shell collector would have filled the place with them.

The telephone rang while I was thinking about that. I went into the study and picked it up, expecting to hear the Chief tell me some news about Valerie Wilson. The news was about her, all right, but it came first-hand.

"Hello, Bill," she said in a tired voice. "My feet hurt."

I would have felt slightly less upset if the late Mr. Jones had been calling me.

Chapter Four: UNEXPECTED COMPANY

"That's great," I said huskily. "I mean, that's too bad. If I sound incoherent it's because my head hurts. Where are you?"

"I'm at the bus station. You'd better come down after all. Now I don't have any nickels left."

I didn't quite know what kind of a shell game she was operating this time. "Let me get this straight," I said cautiously. "About three or four hours ago you wanted me to come down, and then you changed your mind and hung up after I said a gray sedan had tailed me here. Now, what's the idea?"

She said mournfully, "I walked all the way home, Bill, and just before I got there I thought I saw a gray sedan, but I couldn't be sure. So instead of going into where I'm staying, I hid outside and watched, and maybe an hour later I saw lights in my room and somebody prowling. That scared me and I walked back here and started trying to call you. I think I'd better stay at a hotel downtown tonight. But I need my money to do that."

I wondered how to say tactfully that the Chief of Police would take care of the housing problem for her. "There has been a little trouble," I said. "The cops picked up that guy you had the date with. And your name came into the conversation and the cops found where you live from that key tag you dropped."

"Oh, heck," she said angrily. "That spoils everything. What did they pick him up for, speeding?"

That was a little more innocence than I could take. I said roughly, "They picked him up for being dead."

There was a long pause and I thought she had hung up, but finally she asked in a weak voice, "How do you mean, dead?"

"You know the way a guy gets dead when he stands too close to a few bullets? Dead that way. In his beach cottage."

"It couldn't be!" she gasped. "Are you sure it was Eddie? Eddie Patrono? Slick black hair, thin face—"

"This was Eddie Jones. You ought to learn a man's name before you go up to see his shell collection."

"All right, Eddie Jones. That was the name he was using here. But how could he be dead? He was the one chasing us in the gray sedan."

"The only ride Eddie Jones took after nine p.m. was in a hearse."

She said faintly, "Who do the police think did it?"

"There was one vote for me on the first ballot. But in the runoff I was snowed under. You're elected. It was unanimous."

Once again I thought she had hung up, but at last she said, "Bill, how did you vote?"

"What difference does it make? I'm not a cop or a county prosecutor or a circuit-court judge or even a guy who might be called for jury duty."

"It does make a difference," she said breathlessly. "You're the only person who can help me. I don't have a penny or a place to go or a friend in town."

"The police station is right around the corner from you. I'll meet you there and do my best to see you get a square deal."

"Bill, I can't clear myself if I'm in jail! I've got to have time. I think I know who killed Eddie. But it won't be easy to prove. Please come down and at least listen to the whole story."

"No," I muttered.

She said wistfully, "I could walk out to your house. My feet aren't so very bad."

For some reason that made me angry. I couldn't figure whether I was angry at her or at myself. "There's a cop outside watching the place!" I shouted. "I don't know whether he's supposed to be seeing I don't get hurt or don't get away. If I went somewhere he'd want to come, too. If you came out here he'd nail you. The police know what you're wearing and about your bare feet and everything."

She said softly, "Thank you, Bill."

"Thanks for what? I haven't done anything for you."

"What you said means that anyway you're not going to turn me in."

If this went on, the next article my tailor made for me would be a strait jacket. "I didn't mean anything of the kind! I may call the cops the minute you hang up."

"I wish you'd make up your mind."

"Before I make up my mind," I said bitterly, "I have to find where I mislaid it."

"Poor Bill. Here you are mixed up in a murder case when all you want to do is wander along a beach picking up shells and girls."

"From now on I only want to pick up shells."

"Bill, promise me one thing."

"No. Absolutely not."

"It's just a little thing. Will you stay home between eleven and noon? I have an idea. If it works out and if I don't get caught, I want to phone you about it."

"I won't make any promises. If you have any good ideas, you'd better tell them to the cops."

"Good night, Bill," she said. "Pleasant dreams."

"Wait a minute. How are you going to get along until eleven? You can get a bad infection walking around on bare feet if they're cut and blistered.

You can— Are you paying attention?" There was no answer. The line was dead.

I wandered around the house for a few minutes kicking the lighter articles of furniture, and then sneaked out to the garage. I didn't know whether or not I intended to get in my car and drive to the bus station. As it turned out I didn't have to make a decision. When I reached the garage, Officer Davidson popped up from behind a bush. He looked so young and happy and full of hide-and-go-seek spirit that I almost expected him to shriek, "Five-ten Bill Stuart!"

He called cheerily, "Going somewhere, Mr. Stuart? I got orders to stay with you."

I muttered, "Just getting something from the car."

I shuffled back into the house. It was three-thirty and I felt as if I had spent the evening in a cement mixer. I went to bed and dreamed that I was walking barefoot down Main Street in Gulf City, and every time I wanted to rest Officer Davidson made me move on because I didn't have any nickels to put in his parking-meters. I awoke once, and wondered how Valerie was going to telephone me between eleven and noon. She had used both her nickels. I couldn't work out the answer to that question. Probably it was just as well. If I had suspected what the answer was, I wouldn't have managed to get back to sleep.

When I awoke it was ten-thirty and the sun was shining and mockingbirds were singing their silly heads off. I scowled. I was in a mood for rain and buzzards. I cut myself shaving and broke a shoelace and banged my head against the second-floor overhang as I went downstairs. That was Valerie Wilson's fault, because I was thinking about her and not about what I was doing. Probably she was in jail by now. All right, there were worse places to be in than jail.

"Oh, are there?" I said aloud, pausing at the foot of the stairway. "Okay, name three."

A rasping voice said, "I give up, pal," and Al Leonard sauntered in from the living-room.

"What are you doing here?" I growled.

"The Chief and I thought maybe you might be bored just talking to yourself, so we came in."

The Chief moved into view and said apologetically, "We only got here a minute ago, Mr. Stuart. The front door was ajar and I thought somebody might have broken in so we stepped inside."

"Personally," Al said, "if I was a material witness in a murder case I wouldn't want to leave doors open when I hit the hay. Good thing the Chief left a man on duty here. What was that name-three game you were playing when you came downstairs?"

"I don't know that it's any of your business," I said. "But I was feeling upset about Valerie Wilson and I tried to tell myself she could be in worse places than jail and then I wondered if there were and told myself to name three."

"Oh, yes," Al said. "And I had to give up. How did you make out on it, pal?"

"Don't be funny."

"I'm not being funny. I thought if you had any idea of worse places she might be in, it might be helpful. Because she sure isn't in jail."

For some ridiculous reason I began to feel more cheerful. "Haven't found her, huh?"

"About all the Chief's boys have found," Al said, "is their way home."

"Now, look, Al," the Chief protested, "it's not as easy as you think. Maybe up in your city it would be a snap to spot a woman walking around with bare feet, but this is a resort town and you see all kinds of funny outfits even in the business section. And plenty of women wear gray slacks and white shirts and bandannas."

"What your boys want to do," Al said, "is go up to any dame dressed like that and say, 'Pardon me, baby, is your name Valerie Wilson?' If she says yes, they got her."

The Chief grumbled, "The trouble is we never had much to practice on here except traffic cases."

I said brightly, "Then I have a case right down your alley. It concerns a gray sedan."

The Chief sighed. "Okay," he said, "let's go into this gray-sedan business. When did you first see it?"

"On the beach right after I met the girl."

"Oh, no, you didn't. Not a *gray* sedan. On account of I waded out to the pilings where you met the girl, and had a patrol car drive along the beach, and nobody could swear it was gray or red or green or pink."

"Are you going to tell me it was a fisherman driving south to the pass? Did you check how far his tire marks went?"

"Yeah. They didn't go all the way to the pass, but that don't mean anything. High tide could have washed out the marks. Now, when did you think you saw it again?"

"On the road into town. Tailing us."

"You saw a couple headlights in the mirror. They could have been on a ten-ton truck."

I said irritably, "You can't claim that I didn't see a gray sedan when I drove away from the bus station. I even went around the block to find out if it followed. It did. I saw it again outside the property here when I got back."

"How do you know that wasn't coincidence, Stuart? Plenty of gray sedans in town. Maybe the one near the bus station only went around the block looking for a friend. The one out here was a guy taking his date to look at the Gulf."

"Then why was Valerie Wilson so upset when she saw the headlights back of us? Why did she do all that racetrack driving?"

The Chief looked as happy as if he had just forced somebody to confess all. "Got you on that," he said. "Look. This Wilson girl is having a party with Jones and for some reason shoots him. She doesn't realize nobody's in any of the near-by cottages. She gets scared, thinks people heard the shots. So she runs. You come across her and offer her a lift. On the way in town she realizes you're getting suspicious. She's driving fast because she's getting away from the scene of a murder, and you think it's because somebody's chasing her. She decides maybe that's a good alibi. So she starts driving as if a car's chasing her. That way, in case she ever gets tied in with the murder, she can claim somebody sneaked into the front room and shot Jones while she was in the kitchen mixing drinks, and she ran and the murderer chased her. She ditched you at the bus station because she wanted to break her trail there, in case you went to the police when the murder was discovered. She figured on being well out of town by then. Not bad, huh?"

"You're overlooking three things," I said. "The first is that I'm not a one-hundred-percent idiot."

Al said lazily, "What percent would you give yourself, pal?"

I ignored him. "The next thing is this. After I came home, she called up to ask me to bring her money to the bus station. But when I told her I'd been followed home, she said not to come, and hung up."

"You also told her," the Chief said, "that you'd been to the police. That's why she hung up. Probably that's why we couldn't find her at Beachcomber Court, too. She walked out there and hung around in the shadows and finally saw the patrol car drive up and cops going into her room."

I didn't care for the answers the Chief had worked out, "Okay," I growled, "I imagined the gray sedan. And I imagined that someone broke my left taillight so it would be easier to follow my car."

"Someone did break it," the Chief said. "Valerie Wilson. She figured it would help you along in your worries about being tailed."

It all sounded very neat and precise and deadly. There didn't seem to be any real flaws in his case, once you granted his basic premise that I had a jittery imagination and wasn't too bright. I suspected that a lot of people would go along with him on that. Of course he didn't know about Valerie's second telephone call, but he could easily fit that into the story. He would claim she called to find out if she was wanted for the murder, and to try to coax me into putting up getaway money. I hoped he never learned that I could have tipped him off where to pick up Valerie at three-thirty that morning. He might think I was playing on the other team. The fact was that I didn't want to play on either team. I didn't even want to sit in the grandstand and watch.

"I don't hear any more comebacks out of you," the Chief said.

"You have a good case," I muttered. "Only I can't make up my mind she did it. She didn't act like a killer."

"You go right ahead and think that, Stuart. And when the time comes you get up in court and say she didn't act like a killer and tell the jury how all the killers you've known did act."

"Why do you keep harping on the Wilson angle all the time? Why don't you look into the background of that Jones guy?"

The Chief said glumly, "He's got no more background than a crab has fur. He rented the place a year ago, always paid up on time. Nobody around town seems to know him, although he's been seen in bars now and then. The Wilson angle is all we got and anyway it's plenty of angle for me. And I need some help from you on it."

"What for? The way you have things set up, all you need now is a guy to dust off the electric chair."

"Well, it turns out we need the murder weapon and the girl. Couldn't get a single lead out of that room she had at Beachcomber Court. Plenty of fingerprints, of course. They match the ones on the compact and where the guy was killed. But no letters, no diaries, no address book, nothing but clothes. If this was a big city I could send guys all over the country and find where she bought the clothes, but as it is I'm licked. Now, did she drop any hints who she knew around town? You have any idea what she might be doing today?"

I found myself staring at the clock. It was after eleven. She was going to call me soon, and undoubtedly the call could be traced. "How would I know?" I said. "You think she called me up and told me her plans?"

"No, I guess not," he said regretfully. "About the murder weapon. You said she spilled stuff out of her shoulder bag in front of the bus station, so she could skip while you picked it up. You didn't happen to see a gun in her bag, did you?"

"What kind of a gun?"

"Thirty-two-caliber automatic."

I said, without thinking, "A pearl-handled job?"

The Chief snapped, "Listen, Stuart. All we know is the guy had a pair of thirty-two-caliber slugs in him. How would I know whether the thing had a pearl handle or was set with diamonds?"

Al Leonard asked, "What brought pearl handles to your mind?"

I winced. What brought that to mind was remembering Valerie had said it was just as well she spilled the contents of her bag, because it would stop me from wondering if she carried a small pearl-handled automatic. "I thought women always used pearl-handled guns," I said.

Al looked at me in disgust. "Sometimes they use wooden-handled meat cleavers."

"Well, anyway, she didn't have a gun."

The Chief shrugged and said, "That means we comb the sand dunes and beach for it. There's just one thing more, Stuart. Take this description you gave me of the Wilson girl. You described her clothes okay. But outside of the clothes what was she like?"

"I don't know. Unfortunately she wasn't outside her clothes. She was inside them."

"Very funny," Al said.

The Chief growled, "I want a description of her face. If she manages to change her clothes, we got nothing to go on."

"I never saw her in a good light," I said. "Can't the people at Beachcomber Court describe her?"

"The desk clerk only saw her a couple times since she checked in a few days ago. He's one of these guys sees nothing but legs. He says she had good legs. Legs! I can't pick up every dame in this town with good legs."

"It's a nice idea, though," Al said.

"I got to have facts!" the Chief said angrily. "Put your mind on it, Stuart! What color were her eyes? Blue? Green? Brown? Gray?"

"Let me think," I said. I concentrated so hard on the problem that I didn't hear the taxi swish up to the entrance or the rapid click of high heels on the walk outside the front door. "Maybe they were gray," I said.

At that instant a gorgeous creature came into the house and skipped across the room and flung her arms around me and cried, "I couldn't stay up in New York any longer, darling. I had to come down to be with my husband." She looked up into my face and I saw that I was wrong about the gray eyes. Because, under the brim of her perky hat, Valerie Wilson's eyes were soft and frightened and brown.

Chapter Five: TEMPORARY WIFE

I stood there wondering if anybody in the room knew how to give artificial respiration, because I was about to need some. Valerie tilted up on
her toes and kissed me. Her lips were quivering, and long smooth shud-
ders went through her body. Her mouth clung to mine as if she wanted
desperately to keep me from speaking, from saying the few small words
that would let the Chief wind up his case. I wondered dizzily if she
thought she could get away with it. All the evidence said she had killed a
man fifteen hours earlier. The fact that I had a few doubts didn't rate as
evidence. She must be crazy to think I would go for this.

She drew back slightly and looked at me with wide fearful eyes and said,
"Well?"

I took a deep breath. She wasn't crazy, after all. I was. "Hello, dear," I said.
"Did you have a nice trip?" The words came creakily out of my throat.
With them came an odd, strangled sound. I didn't worry too much about
it because it was probably just a death rattle.

The fear flicked out of her eyes and she gave me an impish smile and
whirled away from me and cried gaily, "I didn't see you had company or I
wouldn't have rushed in like this."

The Chief had been looking politely out of the window, and Al Leonard
had been looking at Valerie's legs. I mumbled, "This is Sergeant Leonard
and this is Chief of Police Tinsman."

Al said, "Hiya," and the Chief said, "Morning, Mrs. Stuart."

"Oh, dear," Valerie gasped. "Police? Oh, Bill, I hope you haven't been getting into any trouble."

"I've been trying hard," I said grimly.

"Usually he never does anything wrong," Valerie said in a confidential
tone, "but once he was thrown out of a fashion-show audience for suddenly giving a wolf call when the models came on in negligees, and if he
has more than two drinks in a night club he's likely to yell 'yippee!' and
start chasing the cigarette girls. He's so quiet ordinarily that I suppose he
has to break loose one way or another." She turned to me and said, "Darling, bring in my suitcase and pay the taxi driver, will you?"

I gave her a look that should have steamed the curl out of her eyelashes,
and went outside. I asked the taxi driver how much I owed and what bus
my wife had arrived on. He said she had arrived on the eleven-o'clock
train, and that I owed ninety-five cents, including a quarter tip he had
given a porter at the station because my wife had no change. I paid him,

wondering how Valerie had worked all this. In eight hours, in spite of not having a penny, she had acquired a perky white hat, gray suede pumps, a gray skirt belted with a black-and-white sash, an expensive looking suitcase, and a haggard-looking husband. She still wore the white shirt and carried the big white plastic handbag, although she had removed the shoulder strap from the bag. I hoped she had also removed any small, pearl-handled automatics.

As I re-entered the house she was saying happily, "—and so I thought he could just forget his nasty old shells for a few days and pay some attention to me, and, besides, the girls seem to be wearing perfectly disgraceful bathing-suits this year and if he insists on leering at anybody it might as well be me. What do you think?"

"Yes, ma'am," the Chief said. He sounded groggy. "If we could take a minute to finish up our business with Mr. Stuart we won't have to bother you any more. It's just a little matter of describing a girl he met on the beach. We're trying to find her."

"Well!" Valerie said, looking at me indignantly. "Give the Chief of Police the girl's telephone number and let's get it over."

"Just a description is all we want," the Chief said. "Uh, you said she had gray eyes, Mr. Stuart?"

"Brown," I snapped. "With a shifty look in them." That ought to show the girl she couldn't push me around.

Valerie said coolly, "At least you're true to the color of my eyes."

The Chief asked, "Don't you have some idea about the color of her hair?"

Valerie took off her hat and fluffed out her hair with a casual gesture. It was reddish-brown, with lights in it like a Gulf sunset. She smiled mockingly at me and I lost my nerve. I mumbled, "She was wearing a red bandanna and I couldn't see her hair."

"Now, about her face," the Chief said. He paused, cleared his throat. "I kinda hate to bring this up in front of Mrs. Stuart."

"Please go on," Valerie sighed. "I'm used to it."

The Chief consulted his notebook and said in an embarrassed tone, "You said if you were walking in a garden at night and met a girl who had a nice, low, husky voice and sort of a tantalizing laugh, but you couldn't really see her, you'd hope she looked the way this girl did. You said her face would go nicely in a Caribbean travel ad. Now, that isn't a very clear description."

"It's clear enough for me," Valerie said. "I don't think I came a moment too soon."

"Let me add something to that description," I growled. "If I saw her face in a Caribbean travel ad, I'd take the Fall River Line to Boston."

The Chief cleared his throat again. "Yeah, well, I see your point," he mumbled. "This first description sort of confuses my boys, but I guess I better stick with it. Thanks for the help, Mr. Stuart. We'll be getting on."

"But I want to know what this is about!" Valerie cried.

"I'll let Mr. Stuart explain," the Chief said, and left hastily.

"I'd like to stay for this," Al said, "but I see enough homicide as it is. So long, pal."

I watched them get in the police car and drive away. I shut the front door, turned to the girl. She was sitting on the edge of the living-room table, swinging her lovely bare legs and watching me like a cat waiting to see which way a mouse will jump. "It isn't enough," I said bitterly, "that you make me an accessory after the fact of murder and force me to harbor a fugitive, but you also go out of your way to blacken my character. Wolf calls at fashion shows! Chasing cigarette girls! I never did anything like that in my life."

"That's the trouble with you," she said. "Repressed."

"Okay. Keep on telling the cops things like that and they won't wait to pin the accessory and harboring charges on me. They'll toss me in jail as a sex fiend."

"But I had to say something to explain why you pick up strange girls on the beach, in spite of having such a charming wife."

"Valerie," I said, "you'd better start suit for divorce fast. On grounds of wife-beating. I'll be happy to provide the grounds. You deliberately set out to frame me. You picked a time when the police were in here and—"

"I didn't know the police were in here. That just happened. But you told me a policeman was on guard outside and I knew he'd see me arrive and obviously you'd have to tell him I was your wife. Otherwise he'd think it very odd for me to be staying here."

"What gave you the idea I'd let you stay here?"

"The fact that you didn't turn me in right away. And it's too late for you to back out now. How would you explain to the police what you've done?"

"I don't know," I said sullenly. "I can't even explain it to myself."

She jumped down from the table and moved close to me and dialed one of the buttons on my shirt as if it were a radio and she expected to get Bing Crosby. "You're really very wonderful," she said softly. "And you did it because you knew I didn't kill that man and you wanted to give me a chance."

"I bet nobody's going to give me a chance. When you walked in here and pulled that stunt, you almost had another corpse to worry about. What if I had told the Chief I wasn't married?"

"I would have had to blacken your character some more," she said cheerfully. "I'd have said it wasn't the first time you pretended to be a bachelor, so you'd have more freedom to chase girls."

"Had everything planned, didn't you? Right down to the last nail in my coffin."

"Not everything," she said, peeking up at me. "I didn't know the police would be here and so I hadn't planned to kiss you. I decided to do that on the spur of the moment. It was," she said thoughtfully, "a rather nice moment, come to think of it."

A blush the size of a small forest fire burned over my face. "Let's not have any more of that," I said gruffly. "In case I decide that there's nothing to do but let you stay here, I want it distinctly understood that I do not intend to take any advantage of the situation."

"You mean it's all right if I do?" she asked, dialing another button on my shirt.

I took a firm step backward. "It is not."

"Oh, dear. Married fifteen minutes and already a kissless bride. And I had such hopes when I heard that lovely description of me you had given the police. What was it? If you met a girl like me walking in a garden at night—"

"If I ever do again," I said, "I will start an Anti-Garden Club. Do you mind taking a few minutes' vacation from blackening my character and twisting off my shirt buttons to answer some questions? Where did you get that outfit you're wearing? You claimed you didn't have a nickel."

"It's a long story and I'm awfully hungry."

"That's too bad. Murders take away my appetite."

"Well, I had done all that walking in my bare feet and after that second time I called you I simply had to rest and so—"

"Wait a minute," I said. "At least that's one point I can check. Take off those shoes and let me see your feet."

She sat down obediently and eased off the gray suede pumps. I looked at the bottoms of her feet, and shivered. I didn't see how she had managed to come skipping happily into the house. With feet as cut and blistered as hers, I would have come in walking on my hands. I told her not to move and went upstairs and brought down a basin of warm water and cotton and antiseptic and clean white socks and my bedroom slippers.

As I started to work I said angrily, "Don't blame me if this hurts. It's your own fault."

She wiggled her toes and said, "This is nice. I like having men at my feet."

"You'll be lucky if you don't have a surgeon at them. Why didn't you tell me right away how bad they were?"

"I don't understand you," she sighed. "I've dragged you into an awful mess and you ask questions about my feet."

"That's because you told me the truth about your feet. I'm afraid to go into any other subjects."

"I told you the truth about my name. And about not killing Eddie Patrono."

"Do you mind if we call him Eddie Jones? I wouldn't want to make a slip in front of the police and say Patrono. Might get them curious. Who was this Eddie Jones?"

"A small-time thug. We came from the same city up North."

"What city?"

She hesitated, and said, "Can't we skip that?"

"Valerie," I said wearily, "it wouldn't be much harder to trust you if you pulled out a thirty-two-caliber automatic and began cleaning the inside of the barrel."

She gasped, "Was that what killed him? Did they find it?"

"They found the cartridge cases outside him and the slugs inside him. I don't hear you saying what city. A suspicious person might think you don't want to be traced when you leave town."

"Bill, you've trusted me so much. Can't you trust me a little more? I'm trying to be honest about everything. I didn't have to ask you to skip where I come from. I could have said Boston or Cleveland or Chicago or Little Wampum, Minnesota, and you couldn't have proved I was lying."

"Okay. We skip it."

"I'm on vacation. Back home I'm a reporter on a newspaper." She stopped and looked at me.

"Go ahead. You're a newspaper reporter. I'm practicing trusting you. I'm not going to ask what *etaoin shrdlu* means or what happens on a copy desk."

"I could tell you, though. The top line of keys on a linotype machine gives you the letters *etaoin shrdlu*. A copy desk is where a bunch of bitter old men take out their Jack-the-Ripper complexes on the stories I write."

"All right, you work on a paper. You'd make more money writing advertising copy."

"I like being a reporter. Well, I came down here on vacation and happened to bump into Eddie. We had a reform wave in town last year, and Eddie was one of the boys who thought they could help it along by getting out of town fast. Nobody had anything on Eddie; he merely didn't want to get called up before the Special Grand Jury and maybe have his friends worrying about what he said. For some reason he always thought I was his type, so when I ran into him here I thought I might coax some inside stuff from him."

"In addition to advertising paying better," I said, "you meet a nicer class of people."

"Eddie coaxed me out to his place last night by hinting that he was ready to talk. It turned out his idea of talk was saying, 'How about it, baby?' He had a few drinks and began to act rough and I broke away and ran. And honestly, Bill, I didn't know anything happened to him. I thought he was the one driving along the beach and following us into town."

"Now, who do you think was tailing us?"

"A man named George Lawrence. He had a piece of the numbers business back home, and Eddie ran errands for him. They both came down here to sit out the Special Grand Jury, and Lawrence kept Eddie on the payroll. Eddie told me that much. I also got the idea that Eddie figured he was getting paid off in box tops. Maybe they had a fight and Lawrence was just waiting for a chance to kill Eddie. Or maybe Lawrence recognized me and thought Eddie was going to talk too much. Anyway, all I have to do is find George Lawrence."

"And after you find him he breaks down sobbing and tells all. Don't be foolish. What can you pin on the guy?"

"But it's my only chance!" she cried. "The way things are now, it looks as if I had a date with Eddie and shot him. There aren't any other angles. But if I can find George Lawrence, I can prove he was Eddie's boss. I can prove they were both in the rackets. Maybe I can prove they had a fight, or find the gun Lawrence used to kill Eddie, or something. Don't you see? It opens up a new angle that the police can't simply laugh off."

"I'm getting convinced that woman's place is in the home. If this story looks so good to you, why don't you tell it to the cops right now and let them find Lawrence?"

"I'm just a simple barefoot girl from the city," she said, "but I've covered enough crime stories to know that when the police have a bird in the hand they don't waste much time chasing possible birds in theoretical bushes. I have to be able at least to give them a few feathers and twigs."

"I could use a few more feathers myself. How did Lawrence happen to be at the cottage last night?"

"I don't know. Maybe he suspected Eddie was having a date with me. Or maybe he happened to stroll down the beach to see Eddie, and spotted us. So he stayed outside, listening. After I ran away he decided it was too good a chance to miss, and went inside and shot Eddie. Then he took Eddie's car and followed me. He wanted me to see the car and think Eddie was chasing me, so I'd keep on running."

"Why did he follow me home from the bus station?"

"You worried him by going to the police. Maybe he planned to go back to the cottage and get rid of the body and make it look as if Eddie had disappeared. But he didn't know what you were up to. By the way, what did you do after the first time I telephoned?"

I told her what had happened.

"You see?" she said. "Lawrence hung around here until he saw the police

come, and then decided to go home and take it easy. If anybody got tagged
for the murder, I would be it."

"Why did you hang up on me that first time you called? The cops think
it was because I told you I'd been to see them."

"I thought Eddie had followed you home. I didn't want him tailing you
back to the bus station and finding me again. He didn't know where I was
staying. He was drunk and nasty and I was afraid of what he might do."

I put a final dab of antiseptic on her left foot, and said, "That takes care
of the feet. Now all you need is a wheel chair and you can rush right out
looking for this man Lawrence. And, of course, you haven't any idea where
to find him."

"Poof," she said. "I could probably dance all night, the way you've fixed
up my feet. About Lawrence, I do have some ideas where to look for him.
Eddie told me he lives in another place on the beach. All I have to do is
wander around and keep my eyes open. I know Lawrence when I see him."

"Uh-huh. And he knows you. Would you care to make me the benefici-
ary of your life insurance?"

"Oh, fiddlesticks. He doesn't know I'm hunting for him. I've just got to
be smart and spot him first."

"I hope you don't expect me to play hide-and-go-seek with a killer."

She patted my cheek and said, "If you'll just let me stay here and wear
your slippers when I come in from the hide-and-go-seek, I'll think you're
wonderful."

"Personally," I grumbled, "I don't believe half that story. But I suppose I'll
have to trail along after you to mop up the bloodstains. Now do you want
some breakfast?"

She pulled on my white socks and wriggled her feet into the slippers.
"Breakfast?" she said. "I couldn't eat a thing more than a few pounds of
steak."

"I pity the guy who marries you. Have you looked up the current quota-
tion on steaks?"

"I will settle for a few dry crusts of bread thrown to me under the table."

"I can do better than that. Fruit, cereal, bacon, eggs? Any of them appeal
to you?"

"All of them," she said, linking her arm gaily through mine and clop-
clopping beside me into the kitchen. "Now, you sit down and I'll have
breakfast ready in a moment."

"You sit down. I know my way around kitchens."

"You mean to say you cook your own meals?"

"Certainly I do."

"No wonder you look so starved. Men don't know how to cook."

"That," I said, "is a racket dreamed up by women back in the Stone Age.

I can see a cave man sitting by his fire ready to sink a fang into a nice rare aurochs steak, and a cute little number coming up and taking the steak firmly away from him and telling him it needs charring to bring out the vitamins, and pretty soon the dope is hunting for two and wondering why he never got indigestion when he was a bachelor."

"How do you like your eggs?" she said.

I saw it was no use arguing. She was beginning to rush around the kitchen with milk bottles and pans and eggs and oranges and paring-knives. It looked safer to stay out of her way. "Soft-boiled," I said wearily. I could hardly bear to watch what was happening. She cut her finger getting the oranges ready for juicing and almost scorched herself lighting the gas stove. She brought water to a furious boil and prepared to drop in the eggs. "No, no, no, no," I said. "You can't guarantee soft-boiled eggs that way. You turn off the gas, move the pan off the burner, drop in the eggs, and put on the lid a fraction of an inch off center so a little steam can escape."

She dropped the eggs in the boiling water and said cheerily, "Why don't you clear those shells of yours from the table, and set it? Did you collect all those last night?"

"No. Eddie did."

"Eddie!"

"Yes, Eddie. They were in a bag by the couch in the cottage, and the Chief said I could have them. He must have collected them a short time before you came, because they were still wet."

She looked at me with startled eyes. "Look," she said. "Eddie's interest in conchology was limited to oysters on the half shell."

"That's ridiculous. He must have studied shell collecting. He was hot stuff at it, judging from this bunch."

"He didn't know a thing about them! That was one of his gripes about his boss. He said the way Lawrence collected shells you might think they all had pearls in them. He said he was sick of playing caddy for a lousy shell collector, and if he had to sit around Lawrence's place listening to one more lecture on shells he'd go nuts."

"Oh-h-h. You think Lawrence left them at the cottage."

"I know it. He was wandering along the beach at low tide collecting shells, just as you were, and decided to drop in on Eddie, and saw me there and listened. After the shooting he was so busy following us that he never had a chance to go back and get his shells."

"Hmm."

"Bill, you don't think I left them, do you?"

"No. One of the first things you said to me was that as far as you were concerned, shells make an excellent surface for secondary roads. So you and Eddie felt the same way about shells. I thought it was queer there weren't any other shells around that cottage. A man who is nuts about shells ought to have his place filled with them, when he's living in a collector's paradise like Gulf City."

"Then why did you say, 'Hmm,' in that funny tone?"

"I had an idea. Maybe a shell collector like me could find a shell collector like Lawrence."

"Oh, Bill, you don't even know what he looks like!"

"We could fix that. I used to do a lot of sketching before I became art director for Baldwin and Bond. Give me a good description and hang over my shoulder while I sketch, and we can work out a likeness. Then maybe I can find people around town who know a shell collector who looks like the sketch."

"It wouldn't work," she said. "Lawrence was hiding out. Of course, Eddie was, too, but Eddie wasn't important and there wasn't any warrant out for him as there was for Lawrence. So Eddie ran all the errands and did all the shopping. Lawrence wouldn't have shown himself around town."

I argued, "If Eddie didn't like shells or know anything about them, I bet he didn't run any shell-collecting errands. Lawrence must have bought books on shells. He must have wanted to show off in front of other men who collect shells. Listen. If I wanted to catch a murderer who was nuts about tarpon fishing, I'd talk to charter-boat captains. If I wanted a murderer who is nuts about shell collecting, I'd talk to shell collectors."

"It's sweet of you to want to help," she said earnestly, "and I think shell collecting is a nice little hobby, but let's be practical. You collect shells and I'll collect Mr. Lawrence. Now, sit down and drink your orange juice. It has vitamins."

I shrugged and pulled up chairs to the kitchen table and sat down and drank the orange juice. "In addition to vitamins," I said, "this orange juice also has seeds in it. I always strain it."

"That takes out some of the goodness," she said. "And besides, I hate washing strainers." She began crunching her way happily through a box of cereal, and asked, "Can't you think of any more questions? You give up easily."

I thought for a minute. In some ways her story sounded good; in other ways, it had holes big enough to drive a prowl car through. For example, why hadn't there been anything to identify her or to indicate where she came from in her room at Beachcomber Court? And why, before she claimed to know of the murder, had she thought of pearl-handled automatics when she spilled the contents of her shoulder bag? I didn't think I would take up those points; I might get answers that would worry me. The thing for me to do was to keep reminding myself that no matter how many holes there were in her story, there *had* been a third person at the cottage and there *had* been somebody following us into town.

There were, however, a few small points I could take up without fear of getting answers that might haunt me. I said, "What about your new outfit and the suitcase? Did you happen to have the suitcase in a check room somewhere?"

"Well, no," she said hesitantly. "It wasn't as easy as that. Probably you won't approve of what I did. But just remember, I had to come here and see you, and I didn't dare try to sneak in for fear that policeman you mentioned would catch me. I had to come openly, which meant I had to get a new outfit because you had told the police how I was dressed. Of course, I couldn't get a new outfit until the stores opened, so I needed a place to hide until morning. So I went to the Civic Center and used a bobby pin to unhook a screen, and climbed in."

"I see why you said I wouldn't approve. That's called breaking and entering. It's illegal."

"I had to have a place to sleep, Bill. I woke up before anybody came, and washed and sat on the porch with my feet tucked under me and a newspaper in front of my face. I had already thrown away the red bandanna. An ad in the paper gave me an idea. It was for a shoe clearance this morning, and the most important thing I had to do was get shoes. So I took a chance that a policeman might see me, and went to the store when it opened. Fortunately there were quite a number of women waiting for the sale, and luckily my slacks were so long that they almost hid my feet. If you took a quick look you might have thought I was maybe wearing sandals. So I went in and got those gray suede pumps."

"I hope you didn't charge them to this address. If the cops—"

"Oh, no. I didn't do anything stupid. Women were milling all around and grabbing shoes from the clearance tables and trying them on, and I planned to put on a pair and simply walk out."

"That's stealing!"

"Well, I didn't do it, after all. A salesman came up just as I found a pair of gray suede pumps in my size. I told him the shoes were just what I wanted and please put my old shoes in a bag. And what do you think? When we looked for my old shoes, they were gone. The manager was called and he laughed and said some woman must have picked them up and bought them, thinking they were on sale. He naturally insisted that I take the gray suede pumps without charge. So was that stealing?"

"It's called obtaining goods under false pretenses."

"I suppose it was," she sighed. "Well, anyway, by then I was a hardened criminal, so I went to a hat store that didn't have any customers and only one salesgirl, and picked out a hat a little too small for me and asked the girl to put it on the sizer and stretch it. When she went in the stock room to use the sizer I called that I would be back in a minute, and picked up that cute white hat and left."

"You went through this town like the James boys, didn't you? Don't you have any sense of right and wrong?"

"I certainly do," she said firmly. "It's wrong for me to be arrested for a murder I didn't commit."

"But you won't mind being arrested for crimes you did commit. I refer to breaking and entering, obtaining goods under false pretenses, and larceny."

"But, Bill, I'm going to pay those stores every penny I owe. And I'm going to pay the Civic Center for that curtain, too."

I groaned and said, "What curtain?"

"Well, after getting the hat and shoes, I went back to the Civic Center. I borrowed a needle and thread and scissors from the woman at the tourist desk, and went in the ladies' room and made over my gray slacks into a skirt. You'd be surprised how good I am at making clothes. I ripped out the inner seams of both legs of the slacks, and cut them off and sewed them together and hemmed them and—"

"I'm more interested in the curtain."

"Oh. It was just a black-and-white curtain. I thought it would make a cute sash. And you might as well stop frowning at me. I had to change my appearance. It's all your fault for describing me to the police."

"If I had really described you to the police, they would have called out the National Guard. Did you find any other breakable laws?"

"Of course not. Because I only borrowed that suitcase at the station and I'm going to return it to whoever owns it right away."

"Ah, yes," I said. "Now we come to the train-robbing angle."

"I had to pretend I was just arriving in town, didn't I? I wouldn't come without baggage, would I? I went to the station and when the eleven-o'clock train came I mixed with the passengers and grabbed a porter and told him to take that suitcase from the little baggage truck, you know, the one that picks up luggage from the passenger cars and you don't need a claim check, and I had him carry it to the taxi. Then I told the taxi driver I was out of change and would he please give the porter a quarter and he did and here I am."

I sighed. "At least I don't have to worry about that quarter. I settled with the taxi driver."

"What I'm going to do," she said, "is send the shoe store and hat shop and Civic Center each ten dollars in a plain envelope. And I'll find out from the station who reported a suitcase missing and we'll deliver it. And you have my money, don't you?"

"I have twenty-two dollars and fifty cents."

"That won't be enough, will it? And I can't get the money that was in my room. I don't suppose you'd take a check, would you?"

I tried to conceal the gleam in my eye. "Well, yes, I will."

She studied my expression, and giggled. "I see. I take a blank check and write in the name and address of my bank and then you know where I come from. No. Could you lend me the money?"

"Anything you say," I muttered.

"Don't act so depressed about it. You really ought to be paying me a salary. Look what you're getting, a housekeeper, a cook—"

"Speaking of cooks," I said, glancing at the stove, "let's have those hard-boiled eggs."

"Oh, dear. I did forget them, didn't I? But if you put a little milk in them and mix it around they'll seem soft-boiled."

I shuddered. "Can I pay you not to cook?"

She said gaily, "The trouble with you is you're a bachelor and set in your ways. I expect having me around will grow on you."

"It will grow on me, all right. Like a rash."

I ate my hard-boiled eggs silently, thinking about what had to be done and not paying much attention to Valerie's chatter. I decided that she was right about sending money in plain envelopes to pay for the shoes and hat and curtain; going in person to pay for them would require embarrassing explanations. On the other hand she couldn't wear the shoes and hat and black-and-white sash because they might be spotted as stolen property. The safe thing to do was to get her a completely new outfit. I told her that. She looked at me as coyly as the wolf closing in on Little Red Riding Hood, and asked me for paper and a pencil and began happily making a list. The length of the list horrified me. Clothing this woman from finger wave to toenail polish was going to create serious national shortages. However, it had to be done.

Chapter Six: CLUE IN THE SAND

After breakfast we prepared the envelopes to be mailed to the shoe and hat shops and the Civic Center, and I phoned the railroad station to ask about missing luggage. I explained, without identifying myself, that my daughter had accidentally taken the wrong suitcase, not realizing that I had already put her baggage in the car. The man at the other end of the line was very pleasant about it, and gave me the name and address of a woman who had reported her suitcase missing. We left the house and drove to the address, and I parked the car where it couldn't be seen from the house and sent Valerie up to the door with the suitcase. That worked out all right, and we headed downtown to start our buying wave.

Two hours and a couple hundred dollars later we finished shopping and went to a drugstore because Valerie thought she could do with a milk shake and a few sandwiches. Apparently it took a continuous supply of consumer goods of all kinds to keep her going. We sat at a table and I drank coffee while she ate. I was tired but rather pleased with myself. It was the first time I had taken a girl shopping, and it turned out, as Valerie admitted readily, that I had a good eye for line and fabric and color. Of course an art director for a big advertising agency has to know about such things, but there is a difference between two-dimensional art work and three-dimensional girls. It had been flattering to see how eagerly Valerie took my suggestions.

I studied the effect I had created. She wore a pale yellow hat that accented the faint reddish highlights in her hair, a yellow and gray print dress with a wide gray belt to emphasize her slender waist, and the gray suede shoes. I didn't approve of the shoes, not on artistic grounds but because they linked her with the trail of crime she had blazed through town that morning; however, Valerie said she couldn't bear the thought of breaking in another pair of shoes until her feet were better.

Our only disagreements had been about the shoes and about a bathing-suit she had insisted on buying. It seemed to me that the bathing-suit had been placed in the women's section by mistake and should actually be on sale with infants' wear, but Valerie said, with a giggle, that I was starting to act like a husband and that the two-piece suit contained at least a yard of material and that I would be amazed when I saw how it covered her. I agreed that I would probably be amazed.

I was thinking about the bathing-suit, and wondering whether I ought to buy her a barrel to wear outside it, when a hand grabbed my shoulder and a man said roughly, "Gotcha. You're through, Stuart."

My Adam's apple bounced up and down like a pingpong ball in a fast rally, and I looked up. Al Leonard and the Chief loomed over me. Al was gripping my shoulder, and his eyes had a hard glint that reminded me of handcuffs. I remembered that the costumes being worn in Florida this season included uniforms with gray and black stripes. "I'm—through?" I said weakly.

"Yeah," Al said. "Through with your coffee, aren't you?" He laughed heartily and turned to the Chief and said, "Guy's as jittery as a bookie who can't pay off."

"Don't jump at him that way," the Chief protested. "Mr. Stuart's been through a lot."

I said gratefully, "I certainly have. Will you sit down and have something?"

"Well, I'll sit down for a minute," the Chief said, pulling up a chair. "Uh, does Mrs. Stuart understand what's going on, now?"

"Oh, yes," Valerie said. "That will teach Bill to pick up strange girls."

"No real harm in what he did," the Chief said. "Just gave a helping hand to the girl, was all. Hope you won't blame him too much."

"She's doing okay," Al said. "She got some new clothes out of it." He looked Valerie over like a corner lounger studying a pretty girl. "Nice outfit, too," he said.

"Do you like it?" Valerie said happily. "Bill picked it out."

"I still say it looks good," Al said lazily.

I frowned. Ordinarily I try not to take violent dislikes to characters as big and tough as Al Leonard, but the guy was starting to bother me. I didn't care for his two-toned blue sports outfits or the precise waves in his hair or the way his beard showed blue under his clean-shaven skin or his slightly off-center grin or his definitely off-center remarks. From the moment we met he had been getting off those cold-war cracks at me. I didn't like his practical jokes or the cool, appraising way he looked over another man's wife. Of course Valerie wasn't my wife, and I felt no more possessive about her than I would about a time bomb, but Al didn't know that.

Okay, I told myself, *you don't like him concentrating that tough-guy charm on Valerie. So what are you going to do about it, Stuart? Poke him in the nose and see if you can change it to a shape you like better? No,* I told myself frankly, *I am not going to try to change the shape of his nose. I am going to change the subject. It will probably work out better all around.*

I said, "I picked up a lead for you in that murder case."

"I already have leads," the Chief grumbled. "But you can't throw a lead into jail and charge it with murder. Don't let me discourage you, though. What did you pick up?"

"I picked up a bag of shells last night at that cottage."

"That's nice," Al said. "Built any sand castles lately?"

I ignored him, and told the Chief about the rarity of the shells and the fact that they were still wet. "It proves," I said finally, "that a third person was around when Jones was killed. In fact, there's the driver of that gray sedan you keep shrugging off."

The Chief said, "You're parking overtime with that gray sedan. Either the girl or Jones picked up the shells."

"I was collecting shells when I met her," I argued. "The way she sneered at me you might have thought I was picking up cigarette butts. And there weren't any other shells around the cottage, so it wasn't Eddie Jones's hobby. Whoever collected those shells knew his stuff. He was a nut about it, like me. I have shells all over the Baldwin place."

"Why do you say *Eddie* Jones?" the Chief asked. "He could have been called by other nicknames."

I gulped. In some ways the Chief was too alert. I would have to be careful in the future not to let out bits of information I wasn't supposed to know. "He just seemed like an Eddie type to me. Let's get back to the main subject. A third person was at that cottage."

The Chief yawned. "All right," he said. "Go find him."

"If you mean that, maybe I will."

Al asked, "How would you go about it?"

I thought about the facts Valerie had dug up on Lawrence, and reminded myself not to pull any rabbits out of hats. "I'd go along the beach looking for a third person's footprints. I'd try to trace them."

The Chief said, "Unfortunately we have tides on the beach."

"People don't always walk below high-tide mark. Anyway, if I lost the trail I'd start finding out who are the expert shell collectors in town."

"Then where are you?" the Chief asked.

"Well, I don't know. But there's no harm trying, is there? Maybe you'll find out something about Jones that will tie him in with one of the shell collectors I locate."

"Waste of time."

I took a chance and said, "Maybe this third party lives in another beach cottage. It would be a logical place, if he's so interested in shells. I could go along the beach looking in cottages for shell collections and—"

The Chief said, "If there is a third person in this case, which I doubt, he could be living anywhere in town."

"You don't mind if I stroll along the beach and keep my eyes open, do you?"

"Okay by me. But don't keep them so wide open you get turned in as a Peeping Tom. Look, Al, we better start out to the cottage."

Al said, "Why don't you tell them about the lead you picked up?"

"Oh, I don't know," the Chief muttered. "I feel pretty dumb about that."

Valerie said, "I bet you weren't dumb at all. Please tell us."

"Well, in one way I was smart," the Chief said. "But I was smart too late, which comes to the same thing as being dumb. I could have nailed that Wilson dame this morning."

"Very interesting," I said, trying to make my voice sound hearty.

"The trouble was, I was so sure we were going to pick her up around Beachcomber Court that I didn't cover all the angles. She was barefoot, see? The first thing she had to do was either steal or buy a pair of shoes. I should have had every shoe store in town on the lookout this morning."

Valerie seemed to lose her appetite for her second sandwich. "Would you really have caught her?" she asked.

"Yes, ma'am. After I left your place this morning I got to thinking about it. So I made the rounds of the shoe stores, asking if a barefoot girl had been in to buy shoes. I figured any shoe clerk would remember that. Well, nobody remembered a girl like that, but the manager of one store told me about a funny case this morning. He's having a clearance sale, and while some girl was trying on shoes, a clerk must have sold the pair she had on when she came in the store. So they had to give her a pair of shoes. Three guesses who pulled that stunt."

"Valerie Wilson," Valerie said in a faint voice.

"So right now," the Chief said, consulting his notebook, "she's wearing a pair of gray suede pumps with two-inch heels, size six and a half."

In the silence that followed I heard the thud of my heart and a tiny scraping noise as Valerie edged a pair of gray suede pumps, size six and a half, farther under her chair.

The Chief drummed his fingers on the table in a slow chain-gang rhythm. "Also she has dark brown hair," he said. "I'll get her."

Al said, "She's probably in Tampa or Miami by now."

"Not without money she isn't," the Chief said. "The fact she had to pull that trick on the shoe store instead of just buying a pair proves she hasn't any dough. She's still around. For all we know, she may not even think she's tied in with the murder. Okay, she saw the police at her hotel last night, but she could figure that's only because Mr. Stuart reported she seemed to be in trouble. She wants to hang around to find what the score is. You interested in what I'm going to do?"

Valerie said weakly, "Yes."

"I haven't told the newspaper anything about her or about you, Mr. Stuart. All I've given them is that one of my prowl cars saw lights late at night in the cottage and investigated and found the body. That way I won't scare this Wilson girl. If I thought it wouldn't worry her, I might tell the paper that the police expect an arrest momentarily. Think that might scare her, Al?"

"It won't scare anybody who knows cop talk," Al said. "When a cop tells the papers he expects an arrest momentarily, it means he don't know where the hell he's at."

The Chief said stubbornly, "I know where I'm at. I know what shoes she's wearing. Before long I'll find out if she chiseled anything else from stores, and where she went. Come on, let's get out to the cottage, Al."

Al got up and stretched his eighteen-inch biceps and said, "The Chief has two guys combing the bushes around the cottage for that thirty-two automatic. We're going out." He tilted an eyebrow at Valerie and added, "Maybe you'd like to trail along?"

"I'd love to," Valerie said. "But I'll have to stop at the house first. It might be interesting, Bill. You could look for footprints on the beach."

I nodded slowly, wondering if Al had suggested it with the idea of getting a chance to make time with Valerie.

The Chief said, "Don't seem right to have outsiders around for an official investigation."

"Don't be stingy," Al said, grinning. "Stuart isn't an outsider. But for him you'd still be running down slugs in parking-meters instead of slugs in a corpse."

"Okay, then," the Chief said. He looked at his watch. "It's four now. You better get out soon. We'll be leaving the cottage before dark."

He and Al tramped out of the drugstore. Valerie and I looked at each other. "If you want to quick-freeze anything," she said, "I'll lend you my feet."

"Thanks. I'm already quick-frozen. Do you still think you can't bear the idea of breaking in some different shoes?"

"They used to have a medieval torture called the boot. I believe I could even break in a pair of those."

"When we get into the car, you change into those white sports shoes we bought. That was close! We'll have to get rid of that whole outfit you wore to the house this morning."

"Do you think we have to be so careful, Bill? The Chief isn't that good. He's just a small-town policeman."

"Have you ever watched a starfish work on a shell?"

"I don't know what you mean."

"A starfish is a shell's worst enemy, but there's nothing brilliant or dashing about the way he works. He clamps himself around a bivalve and starts trying to pull the two halves of the shell apart. At first the soft little animal that lives inside the shell isn't worried. It thinks it's hidden. But the starfish just sits there in his dull small-town way, pulling and pulling, and after a while the soft little animal in the shell can't hold the valves closed any longer and gets forced out into the open and the starfish eats it. The way the Chief works reminds me of starfish."

Valerie shivered and said, "You win."

We went out to the car and drove off. On the way home I said, "Do you think it's wise to hang around these cops so much? I mean, like going out to the cottage now. If we ever make a slip in front of them—"

"We have to keep track of what they're doing."

"I can tell you what Al will be doing if he gets a chance. Making a pass at you."

"Oh." She peeked at me sideways. "He's quite handsome, isn't he? I could almost vote him the Cop I Would Most Like To Be Arrested By."

I said coldly, "In case he does appeal to you, let me make one thing clear. While you are posing as my wife, you will act as my wife." She giggled, and I added quickly, "In public, that is."

After we reached the Casa del Mar I collected her perky white hat and black-and-white sash and gray suede shoes and the made-over gray skirt, and locked them in a closet upstairs. It wasn't likely that the Chief would find out about the stolen hat and the Civic Center curtain, but there was no use taking a chance. I went downstairs and found Valerie in the study. She was peering through a small hollow cylinder of blue steel.

"What's that?" I asked.

She put it on the table beside a spring and some oddly shaped bits of metal. "It's the barrel of a forty-five Colt automatic," she said, starting to fit some of the pieces together. "I found it in that cabinet beside the gun stand."

"What are you doing with it?" I said uneasily. "And how did it come apart?"

"I field-stripped it to make sure it works."

"Just a little homemaker, huh? Can't stand having any dust on the forty-fives around your house."

Her fingers assembled the weapon rapidly. "I did some stories back home about the police pistol team," she said. "They taught me how to shoot and take care of a gun. I thought we might put this in the glove compartment of the car."

"Nothing I like better than an outing with a girl and a forty-five. Why are we taking it?"

She finished assembling the gun, worked the slide a few times, released the hammer, and snapped the loaded clip into the handle. I noted that she got it all the way in. "We may be on the beach after dark," she said calmly. "It's just a precaution."

"I can think of a better precaution. It involves not being on the beach after dark. So let's start right away."

We drove to the beach cottage and found the Chief and two of his men busily raking sand and crawling under bushes, looking for the murder weapon. Al Leonard was standing idle, watching the activity the way a Dead End kid with a pocketful of stolen lighters might watch Boy Scouts starting a fire by friction. As soon as we arrived he moved in on Valerie. I wanted Valerie to help me hunt footprints on the beach, and Al wanted to tell her how he handled a gang killing up North. The gang killing seemed to appeal to her more than my project. I would have stayed to listen if I had thought the yarn ended with the gangsters beating up Al and getting away clean, but I decided that there was no hope of such a happy ending and so I went to the beach alone.

I walked north along the water's edge for a quarter mile. High tide had scrubbed half the beach clean. In a couple of places above high-tide mark I saw footprints leading south, but they might mean a lot or nothing and I couldn't work up much interest in them. In fact I couldn't even work up much interest in an excellent banded tulip shell that I located under a bit of seaweed. I kicked the tulip shell until it broke, and headed back to the cottage. Perhaps Valerie had finished helping Al solve the Northern gang killing by now, and was willing to pay attention to the case of the State of Florida vs. Valerie Wilson.

She and Al were no longer in a huddle when I returned. Al was condescending to help look for the missing thirty-two, and was poking through the sea grapes in front of the cottage. For a moment I couldn't locate Valerie; then I spotted her moving through some high bushes off to the left. I worked my way toward her, stooping to avoid branches. She didn't see me coming, and so when she gasped suddenly I thought I had startled her. I was wrong. She was gasping at the sight of an object lying in a clear space between two masses of sea grape. The object gleamed dully, like a coiled rattler. It was just as deadly.

I watched with sickening fascination as she crouched and scooped a hole in the sand and buried a thirty-two-caliber automatic.

Chapter Seven: SPOTLIGHT ON DEATH

I must have made a slight noise. Valerie's head snapped around and she saw me. Sunlight coming on a long slant through the sea grapes painted a leopard pattern of light and shadow on her crouching figure. She looked lithe and graceful and dangerous. This wasn't the same girl who had giggled as I worked on her bruised feet and who squeaked in fright when the gas stove in the kitchen popped. She was a stranger. Her eyes were bright, watchful. I felt that if I moved abruptly she would either vanish in the underbrush or snatch out the buried gun and whip it around at me. I didn't budge.

She blinked and then smiled and turned back into the girl who squeaked when gas burners popped. "Oh, there you are," she said. "You startled me."

"Did I?" The words came up my throat like sandpaper.

"Some darned old sandspurs are in my shoe and I was trying to get them out." She stood up and limped toward me and said, "Could I borrow one of your nice broad shoulders to hang onto while I shake out my shoe? I know I keep hanging all kinds of burdens on your shoulders, but—"

I said, "I don't think my shoulders will take this one," and brushed past her and kicked at the sand over the gun.

She was up beside me with panther quickness. "Bill," she said. "Don't." Her fingernails bit into my arm.

I kicked the gun clear of sand. "Funny," I said. "It ought to have a pearl handle, as advertised. But it just has a plain old blue-steel grip."

"Bill, it wasn't in my handbag. It wasn't!"

"Not when you spilled it at the bus station. But it had been. That's what brought that remark about pearl-handled automatics to your mind."

"Let me bury it again," she begged. "Oh Bill, please!"

I stared at the lovely upturned face and watched her eyes widen slowly with fear. I shivered. No matter what I did, I wasn't going to enjoy thinking about it afterwards. But there really wasn't any choice. "No sale," I said. She bent and tried to grab the gun, but I yanked her up. "Let it alone," I snapped.

"At least let me wipe it off! I handled it a moment ago. My fingerprints—"

I shook her roughly. "Whose fingerprints were on it before then? Come on. Let's have it."

"I don't know! Maybe the man who shot Eddie. But if they find my prints on it now, I won't have a chance!"

"Your prints were all over the cottage. What does another set matter?

The only important thing is did this gun do the killing?"

"I don't know," she wailed.

"Well, the cops can get that answer. And maybe they can get another one. Do I have to wait for them or will you tell me? I won't take a don't-know on it, either."

"All right. It's my gun."

"Is that the works? It's just—your gun? Nothing more?"

"I was afraid of Eddie. I took it in my purse last night, and when he got rough I grabbed it. But I wouldn't have shot him. I couldn't! He must have seen that. He made a lunge and knocked it out of my hand and then I ran out the back. But, Bill, the police will never believe that! You've got to let me hide it." She blinked her damp eyes and smiled and said, "It's easier to hide a little gun than a girl who eats as much as I do, isn't it?"

"That's an odd thing, it isn't easier. I helped hide a girl who wanted a chance to clear herself. But I won't hide a gun that may prove she can't."

"And what do you think the police will hand you, if everything comes out? The keys to the city?"

"Could be," I said grimly. "But I bet they won't fit my cell door."

"Bill, the whole thing might be a frame-up. Lawrence could have picked up my gun and shot Eddie. He threw it out here for the police to find, so everything would be pinned on me."

"He may have—if there is a man named Lawrence."

"The bag of shells—"

"All I have is your testimony that Eddie hated shells."

"And the gray sedan—"

"The Chief says I had a bad dream."

"And what do you say?"

I muttered, "Let me borrow a phrase from you. I don't know."

"And while you're making up your mind, what happens?"

"I'm sorry. I guess this happens." I called loudly, "Chief! Al! I found a gun." There was an answering shout from the Chief and a choked cry from Valerie. She twisted from my grasp and flashed away into the thick green brush. I made no move to follow. I waited, with a hangover throb in my head, until the Chief and Al and the patrolmen arrived. I pointed to the gun. "That's it," I said.

"Man, that *is* it!" the Chief said. "Did you touch it?"

"Only with my foot."

Al looked at me curiously and said, "This Stuart is quite a guy. Finds the body, finds the gun. How about finding the dame for us, pal?"

"Any day now," I muttered. I wondered if I should have let Valerie wipe off the gun. But if the police proved that the thirty-two was hers and that it had fired the slugs found in Eddie, the absence of fingerprints wouldn't clear her. If somebody else had used the weapon, there was a faint chance that his prints might be on it.

The Chief picked up the gun carefully. He sniffed at the muzzle, eased out the clip, and peered at the bullets showing through the perforated sides. "It's been fired not too long ago," he said. "Three bullets in the clip. One probably in the firing-chamber. Two in the dead guy. Makes six all told."

Just to make a noise as if I were alive, I asked, "How many should the clip hold?"

"Takes seven, but that's hard on the spring. Six is better. Anybody knows guns will hold it to six."

Al said, "You don't have a ballistics lab, do you?"

"Nope. But I'll do a rush job on the prints and fire a slug in a bunch of rags and send that and the two slugs from the body to the FBI. If we hurry I can get off the package air mail on the night plane. Have an answer day after tomorrow. Let's go. It's way after six now."

"Okay," Al said. He started to follow the Chief, then turned back to me and asked, "Where's Mrs. Stuart?"

"She wandered off somewhere."

"That's odd. She was around here not long ago."

Sweat oozed down my face. "Maybe she saw footprints, and followed them."

His eyes had the cold blank stare of gun muzzles. "Funny she didn't hear you call out about the automatic."

"If she's a few hundred yards away, these bushes would muffle the sound."

"Uh-huh. It's gonna be dark in an hour or so. You want to make sure these bushes don't muffle any sounds that might not be nice."

I said in a choked voice, "What do you mean?"

"I wouldn't say a shot was a nice sound, would you? Not if you were sitting on the bull's-eye. And you certainly got your tail parked right on it, pal."

"What are you getting at?"

"You better round up Mrs. Stuart and trundle home. Won't be any cops here in a couple minutes. Won't be much light in an hour or so. If this Valerie Wilson ever gets a load of what you're doing to her, she may not play cute."

I didn't know whether I felt relieved or not. For a moment I had been afraid that Al was adding things up. He wasn't. But the idea he did have was not pleasant. I said hoarsely, "We won't stay."

From someplace near the cottage the Chief called, "Hey, Al! Come on."

"Right away," Al yelled. Then he said, "That tip I gave you about trying the beach at Coney Island still goes."

"I'll give it some thought."

"Well, anyway," Al said, "you found the thirty-two. So if you stick around maybe you won't have to worry about finding *that* caliber hole in your guts."

He walked toward the cottage. I followed, and watched him and the Chief and the other two cops drive away in their cars. After the hum of their engines faded it seemed very quiet. Around the deserted cottage a breeze whispered furtively in palm fronds. A gull's shadow whipped across the sand and startled me. Over the Gulf a cloud picked up the same red color that had stained Eddie's shirt. I thought about Al's remark that now I didn't have to worry about thirty-two-caliber holes. I went to my car and opened the glove compartment with trembling fingers. My flashlight and the big Colt automatic were gone.

The hardest thing I had ever done in my life was forcing myself to stay there and look for Valerie.

I didn't want to stay. I wanted to jump in my car and take Al's advice about Coney Island. Instead I hung around with my pores squeezing out ice cubes. Every sound made me flinch—the whisk of a lizard through dry fronds, the heart-stopping squall of a heron, the secretive flutter of leaves closing behind me. Everything indicated that Valerie was guilty. She came out here this afternoon not to look for footprints but to get her automatic before the police did. I messed up her plans. Well, she didn't have to put out much energy to clear things up for herself. All it required was a gentle pressure on the trigger and grip of the forty-five. That one slight action would buy her a car and money, and a lot of silence from me.

There was still a possibility that she wasn't guilty. But so what? She lied to me from the start. She had a fast answer for everything, whenever she was forced to give answers. Even now I probably didn't know half her story. She didn't want me as a helper; she wanted a stooge.

I peered in the cottage and searched the low green jungles of sea grape and mangrove and palmetto. Now and then I called softly. There was no answer. The sun went down. In the west, colors darkened and long purple clouds cruised along the horizon like sharks. A breeze came in from the Gulf; leaves and fronds whispered behind my back, and on the beach waves snickered and chuckled. I searched for another hour and then returned to the car and drove slowly toward home.

Anyway I had proved, at the cost of a down payment on a nervous breakdown, that Valerie only wanted to worry about one shooting at a time. I was still alive. Perhaps that didn't mean much to anybody else in Gulf City, and so it might be smart to get out of town. Valerie had no more use for me; Al thought I would find Coney Island restful; and the Chief would sleep better if I were in New York instead of in Gulf City digging up bodies and yapping about gray sedans. Of course, running back to New York wouldn't solve everything. If the police caught Valerie they would want me back to answer one little question, did I want to plead guilty or not guilty?

I shrugged. All right, so I would get maybe three to ten years. That would be no fun. On the other hand, neither was a hole in the head. I thought I would go back to New York.

As I finished settling that problem I dimmed my lights for an approaching car. The other driver didn't return the courtesy. His long-range beams hurt my eyes and I slowed and pulled over to the edge of the road. The other car roared up and for a split second its glaring lights seemed to jump right in my car, then it was gone. As I drove on, an ugly thought prowled into my mind. Was I imagining things, or had a light really jumped into my car? A spotlight, for example? A spotlight on a gray sedan?

The steering wheel began to feel damp and slippery under my hands. I started arguing with myself. *Look, Stuart,* I said, *that could have been a delivery truck in pink and orange just as easily as a gray sedan. You admit that? Good. Now,* I said coaxingly, *let's think about that spotlight. Maybe there wasn't any spotlight, merely long-range headlights. And if it was a spotlight, so what? Look,* I said, *millions of cars have spotlights. A guy wants a new car and the dealer says how about a nice spotlight along with the white sidewall tires and radio and heater and other accessories, and the customer says sure, he'd even take a battery of Yankee Stadium floodlights to get the buggy. Then the guy gets on a road in Gulf City and wants his money's worth from the spotlight and so he slaps it in my eyes. Look, Stuart,* I said, *be reasonable about these things. Only an idiot would take a million-to-one chance that it was a spotlight on a gray sedan heading out to the beach cottage. Only an idiot, see? Uh-huh. Meet William J. Stuart, local idiot.*

I put on the brakes and turned the car around.

The road back to the cottage stretched emptily before me. When the concrete ended and the shell road began, I switched off the headlights and drove cautiously. The small colony of cottages fringing the end of the road slid by in darkness. There were no lights, no trace of the car that had blazed past me. I parked at Eddie Jones's place. It was black and silent. Exactly twenty-four hours ago the windows must have glowed and ice clinked in highball glasses and feet jerked to the swish of rumba music. And then there had been angry voices and patter of feet and slam of the back screen door and finally the whiplash crackle of shots. Or had the slam of the door merely been an echo of the shots? I wished I knew.

I went to the beach and walked south until the pilings of the old pier loomed against the black sequin glitter of the Gulf. It almost seemed that events were repeating, and that I could wade out and hear a girl's soft, husky voice jeering at me for bothering with sea shells. It was hard to believe that she could have scoffed at me so lightly and coolly a few minutes after shooting a man. Of course that didn't prove anything, except, perhaps, that my knowledge of killers was limited. I sighed and turned back. She wasn't out there tonight, and there was no car stabbing at the pilings with a spotlight.

To the north the beach stretched in a long hazy crescent to the headland a couple of miles away where the main beach residential section began. Lights gleamed from houses on the headland, but the beach curving to it was dark. No, wait, not entirely dark. A firefly point of light danced far down the sand, danced and faded. There were no houses along that sweep of beach. Nothing but dunes and sea grapes and the tall black plumes of Australian pines. So it was not a light flickering in a window. A car would have sent out a longer beam. It might be a flashlight. I hurried back to my starting point and looked for new footprints on the sand. During my search for Valerie I hadn't checked the beach for footprints after sunset; it had seemed a waste of time when I didn't have a light. And so I had missed something. I had missed the line of footprints coming from a dense mass of bushes near the cottage and winding north along the beach. Where the sand was packed just right, heels had sunk deeply and now trapped shadows. A woman's heels. She had walked north, zigzagging along a day-old trail partly erased by the tide.

I didn't think she was going to find the end of the trail. Because, as I traced her course, I saw that at one spot near the water her footprints vanished for a few steps. They had been mashed flat by tires. I ran for my car. Local idiot William J. Stuart had won his million-to-one chance. Or maybe lost it.

At the end of the shell road a rutted stretch of sand led between dunes to the flat beach. I started the car and swung into the sandy ruts. My headlights picked out new tire tracks that swept down close to the water and then curved north. I turned off the lights, and followed. My tires spun across damp sand with a faint rising wail that blended with the hiss of air and the surf-beat of blood in my ears. I didn't dare go too fast; the noise might alert the driver up ahead. The car skimmed along as silently as a pelican riding updrafts over dunes, dipping and rising and dipping. I stared ahead, fingers cramped and aching on the wheel. Light pricked the darkness for a second. A flashlight, not too far ahead.

Then I saw the gray sedan.

It was drifting along like smoke a few hundred yards away, closing in on the spot where the light had twinkled. I slammed the accelerator to the floor. The car leaped under me. Up ahead a spotlight beam lashed out from the gray sedan. It picked up a tiny figure that ran and twisted like a rabbit dodging hounds. I watched helplessly, knowing she couldn't dodge fast enough. A spurt of orange flicked out from the sedan. Another. I couldn't hear the shots over the howl of my engine. But I saw the figure, larger now, trip and tumble and roll and lie still.

The gray sedan picked up speed lazily. The driver hadn't heard me. The spotlight centered on a limp, sprawled figure and the gray car went down the beam like a train on tracks. He was going to make sure. His wheels would jolt and shudder, and he would have no more worries about Valerie Wilson. He needed about five seconds. He only had three. I came screaming down on him from the up-beach side and crashed into his car and we rocketed together past the girl.

I should have swung my wheel harder, smashed him into the Gulf. I didn't get two chances. Flame stabbed at me and shots crashed above the shriek of twisting metal. As I ducked, his car wrenched ahead and cut into my front fender and I went whirling out and hit and kept on falling through blackness.

Chapter Eight:
THE MYSTERIOUS GRAY SEDAN

Goblin faces swung over me against the black sky. A gasoline lantern hissed on the sand, lighting the faces above it so that they looked like Halloween masks. A grandfather's clock ticked loudly and solemnly in my head; it was a most unpleasant clock, and I suspected that when it struck the hour a cuckoo would pop out and tell me in a hoarse, confidential tone that it was later than I thought. The right side of my face, and my right shoulder and knee, felt scalded. My stomach had apparently been used as a backstop in batting practice.

I said weakly, "Where's Va—"

A soft hand slid over my mouth and a finger tapped my lips warningly. "I'm all right," her voice said. "Don't try to talk yet."

I turned slightly. My head was resting in her lap. Her face was a dim white blur and stars were tangled in her hair. It made a nice effect, one that I would use in a layout if we ever managed to steal the De Beers Consolidated Mines diamond account from N. W. Ayer & Son, Inc. "You shouldn't be all right," I objected. "What about the—"

Her hand pressed my lips again. She bent lower, and her hair made a silky tent around my face. She whispered, "Those bullets didn't hit me. I dropped to make him think I was hit. Be careful what you say in front of all these people. The police are coming. How do you feel?"

"I'll live," I muttered. "Or will I? Let me sit up and see what falls off."

I sat up and twisted my head and flexed muscles. There were a few creaks and twinges, and the sting of sand burns where I skidded along the beach, but I had come through fairly well for a Model-T guy driving in a fast league. Beyond the circle of faces my convertible lay on its side. Apparently it had flipped me out when it swung broadside. There was no sign of the gray sedan. A quarter mile away the houses on the headland pasted yellow windows against the darkness.

A voice from the circle of faces said, "He's all right. Wind knocked out of him, was all."

A woman said shrilly, "Maybe it knocked some sense into him. I ran out when I heard those cars backfiring. Racing each other on the beach at night! And no lights! Young man," she told me, "I think you're crazy."

"That," I said wearily, "makes two of us who feel that way." I got up and limped to the car.

Valerie joined me, and said, "It turned completely over in the air, but it hit on its wheels and then tilted over. I think it can still run."

"I wish I could," I muttered.

Several men helped me push the car onto its wheels. The left side, which had smashed into the gray sedan and hit the beach, looked as if a pile driver had been patting it. I climbed behind the wheel and tested the engine. It worked, sort of. There was nothing wrong that couldn't be fixed by trading it in for a new car.

A siren sang mournfully and a pair of headlights swung down the beach and stopped near us. The Chief jumped out. In his efficient way he took first things first, in this case our license number, before looking to see who was in the car. He jotted down the number and then did a double-take at it. He sighed, put away the notebook, and came up to the side of the car. He put his foot on the battered running-board as if it were a brass rail and he needed a drink badly.

"Mr. Stuart," he said, "could I pay you to finish your vacation in Maine?"

"I like it here," I said. "No chance to die of boredom. Too many quicker ways."

"Reckless driving again. Do you figure this counts as part of our deal?"

"No. I want you to arrest the other driver and me."

He blinked and said, "Where is the other driver?"

A voice from the crowd called, "He didn't stop. He turned off the beach by my house and drove away on the boulevard."

"Anybody get his license number?" the Chief asked. Nobody answered. He shrugged and said to me, "What was the other car like?"

I said sweetly, "It was a gray sedan."

That, I thought, would teach him not to make cracks about paying me to finish my vacation in Maine. The way things were going I would probably finish it in the local cemetery. I heard a couple of gulps plunk in his throat. He walked away to look at tire marks, his feet shuffling like a fighter walking uphill to his corner. He returned finally and said in a low voice, "What's the story? Don't talk too loud. I don't want it all over town."

I said, "We spotted footprints that looked worth investigating. They looked as if they had been made by somebody walking to the cottage last night. We were driving along slowly, picking them out with a flashlight wherever they hadn't been washed off by the tide. We heard a car coming up behind us and got worried and put on speed. We didn't start fast enough. A guy in a gray sedan shot at us and sideswiped our car and we turned over. Now I'd like to see where those footprints came from."

The Chief jerked a thumb at the crowd and grumbled, "They come from every house within a half mile. Stuart, if you'd tell me about these things before you mess them up—"

"I love to tell you about things. Once upon a time there was a gray sedan."

"Oh, shut up. If this heap can still move, I'll trail you to your place. If it won't, I'll drive you home and call for a tow car."

I said I thought we could make it. We started off with the Chief following closely. Valerie listened to the rattles and clinks from my car, and said with a nervous laugh, "All we need is a Just Married sign. It already sounds as if the old shoes and tin cans were tied on behind."

"Any time I start on a honeymoon with you," I said, "it will not be in a light convertible. It will be in a light tank."

"I'm awfully sorry about what happened to you and the car."

"Don't worry about me. I can grow new skin for free. But this car is going to make some mechanic's fortune."

She said humbly, "After this is all over, I can get some money and pay for it. And I haven't thanked you yet. Bill, I think he was going to kill me!"

"The idea battered its way into my head, too. But you don't owe me any thanks. You ought to kick me, for thinking you shot Eddie Jones and for going off and leaving you."

"But you didn't go off! You looked and looked, and twice I thought you were going to step on me. And besides I could very easily have shot Eddie. Why, when he jumped at me I could have squeezed the trigger and—"

"Don't," I said.

"Were you going to turn me in if this hadn't happened?"

"That depended on whether or not your gun shot Eddie, and whether or not I could coax you to tell me the full story. How about letting me in on a few facts right now?"

"What—what kind of facts?"

"I know so little about you that any old facts you can spare would be nice. For example, you might tell me about your high-school love affairs and whether you like chocolate nut sundaes and why you really came here to Gulf City."

She thought about that briefly and said, "I think it's better this way, now that you trust me."

"I trust you about as far as I can heave a howitzer. You realize, don't you, that now your playmate must suspect you're hiding out at my place? We may not have long to clear this up before he tips off the police. So I ought to know the whole story."

"I don't think he wants me talking to the police. He wants to scare me out of town."

"He's making progress as far as I'm concerned."

She grabbed my arm and cried, "You mustn't get upset! The Chief will keep a guard on the house. And Lawrence is just one man. If he comes near the house he'll be caught and that will settle everything."

"Now I know how a shrimp feels, dangling on a hook in the water. Okay, you won't tell me the score. Let's get you on a subject where you won't hedge. Did you start running on the beach because you heard my car? I forgot to switch on the headlights or blow the horn."

"I heard one of the cars. The moment I did, I started running for the dunes. But I hadn't taken two steps when the spotlight hit me."

"Too bad you didn't get out that forty-five and print your initials on his car. I thought you knew how to shoot."

"I didn't have time." She gave a little jump and asked, "Did you know I'd taken the forty-five? And you kept on hunting for me? Oh, Bill! Didn't you think I might shoot you?"

"You couldn't have hit me in the heart. It was up in my mouth."

She ducked her head against my shoulder and made queer little sounds. She was either laughing or crying. If she had any brains she was laughing, and in many ways she seemed to be a very bright girl. At last she lifted her head and murmured, "Now what do we do?"

"We arrive home, and we remember we were together in the car all the time, and I talk about gray sedans and make the Chief wish he had joined the fire department."

We started to carry out that program nicely. Among other things, I pointed out to the Chief that what had happened confirmed my theory that the killer lived in a house on the beach. Otherwise, I said, he would not have been so worried when he saw us backtracking the footprints. If he didn't live right on the beach, his footprints would end on a road or pavement and we would lose the trail.

"So," I said triumphantly, "the thing to do is forget about Valerie Wilson, and find a killer who is a shell collector and lives on the beach."

"Oh, yeah?" the Chief said. "What do I do about those Valerie Wilson fingerprints that were on the gun?"

I scowled. That was a niggling point for him to bring up. It could be explained so easily if I only dared tell him the whole story. But I didn't dare. He might come up with a theory that accounted for everything and kept Valerie on the spot. I grumbled, "You don't even know if that gun did the killing."

"I'll know in two days. Meanwhile would you care to place a small bet?"

I peeked at Valerie and saw that she wasn't in a gambling mood. I said irritably, "How can you possibly tie Valerie Wilson in with the bag of shells and the footprints on the beach and the gray sedan?"

"She or that Edward Jones or both of them collected the shells. The footprints on the beach don't mean anything, just a casual stroller."

"Then why did a guy in a gray sedan try to knock me off tonight?"

The Chief looked at me fondly. "On account of you're gonna be such a swell witness against Valerie Wilson. In fact, maybe she was even driving that gray sedan."

I was so scandalized that I almost blurted out the truth. "She was not! A man was driving. I saw his face." I had not, of course, really seen his face.

"Can you describe him?"

"Well—um—maybe, if I think about it."

"Can you prove she wasn't in the car?"

"Uh, not right now. Be sensible, will you? You claim she had an accomplice. Then why did she have to chisel a pair of shoes this morning?"

"She was broke and couldn't get in touch with the guy right away."

"She had a nickel left after she called me. She could have telephoned the accomplice or even walked to his place."

The Chief looked smug. "The way I work it out," he said, "is the accomplice lives in a hotel. She used the second nickel trying to call him, but he wasn't in. She was afraid to march into his hotel barefoot and wearing an outfit that had been described to the police. So before she could contact the guy she had to get a new outfit. How does that sound?"

It sounded too close to the facts. I snapped, "If the accomplice didn't know she was in trouble last night, why did he trail us from the cottage to the bus station, and then trail me home?"

"Nobody trailed you to the bus station. That was just your imagination, and the girl working up an alibi for herself. A gray sedan did trail you home from the bus station. It was driven by a person who'd seen you visit police headquarters and wanted to find out what you'd do next. Guess who it was? The Wilson girl. The reason she took you to the bus station was her gray sedan was parked near it."

"Gotcha!" I said. "If she had a car, why didn't she make a getaway last night? Or why didn't she drive to her boyfriend's hotel and park outside and call him when he appeared?"

"On account of she had no money and ran out of gas."

I groaned.

The Chief winked at Valerie and said, "Got him on the ropes."

"I bet she's left town," I said faintly.

"Yeah? I bet you been so close to her tonight on the beach you could almost have touched her."

I shivered. If he kept on this way he would save me the trouble of introducing him to Valerie Wilson. The devil of it was that he could probably twist his theories around to make me the accomplice, if and when he found out the score. He might claim that Valerie and I faked the accident on the beach, with Valerie driving the gray sedan and hiding it after the accident and running back to join me. He might claim that I produced the murder weapon to try to keep him from suspecting us.

The Chief rose to his feet and said, "It was a tough fight, Mom, but I won.

I'll call Al Leonard if you don't mind and tell him what happened and how I figure things." He picked up the telephone and called the downtown hotel where Al was staying. Valerie and I looked at each other and shrugged helplessly. The Chief told Al what had happened, outlined my theories and his own, and started to have a good chuckle with Al over my ridiculous ideas. Then he stopped chuckling, and looked worried. He listened to Al and said, "Yes, but—" and, "Well, but—" and finally said, "Oh, all right!" and hung up and looked glumly at me. "What do you pay that guy?" he growled.

I said, "It was a tough fight, Mom, but I won."

"Yeah, well, he thinks you maybe have something and I don't."

"Let's compromise then and do it my way."

"No, I won't," he said stubbornly. "I'm going ahead with my ideas. But I'll give you a chance to try out yours. You want to check beach cottages for shell collections. Okay, I'll let Davidson go with you tomorrow, and put Clark on duty outside here tonight. Al wants to go with you, too. We have a car raffle coming up for the Police Pension Fund, and you can take tickets around from door to door. That'll give you a good excuse for calling."

Valerie said, "I bet the only reason you're doing this is to get some tickets sold."

"You're not kidding," the Chief said. He took out his notebook. "I'll send some identification cards out with Davidson in case people want proof you're really working for the Police Pension Fund. So I better get your first name, Mrs. Stuart. What is it?"

The question came so suddenly it caught us off balance. We had never agreed on a first name for her to use in public. Without thinking I said, "Betty."

At almost the same instant Valerie said, "Jean."

There was a moment of silence in which you could have heard either a pin or William J. Stuart drop. The Chief said, "Betty Jean. Cute name." He wrote it in his notebook and told us not to wander out of Davidson's sight the next day, and departed.

Valerie giggled and said, "They don't come any closer than that. When we each popped up with a different name I thought I'd die."

I muttered, "I think I did."

"Know what I could do now?"

"I know what a sensible girl would do. Start shopping for a good slick lawyer. But since it's you, you probably want to eat."

That was correct, and we moved to the kitchen. Valerie toyed with a stack of bread and cheese and cold cuts until there wasn't anything left on the plate. I toyed with a glass of milk and two crackers until there wasn't anything left but a glass of milk and two crackers. Then we went upstairs and prepared a bedroom for her. The procedure embarrassed me, and Valerie took advantage of the situation. She tested the lock of the door with melodramatic care. As we made the bed she tried on a hunted look for size; it didn't fit well but she wore it anyway. Now and then she cringed against a wall when I happened to pass near her. I didn't understand how, with a murder rap hanging over her head, she could enjoy herself so much. Apparently if a hurricane caught us offshore in a sailboat she would want to have a water fight.

"Oh, stop it," I said. "You're as safe from me as if I were in Alaska. In fact, I wish I were."

She murmured, "It's just that you're so big and I'm so little."

"You're little, huh? So is a hand grenade." I walked angrily into the hall.

She called from the doorway of her room, "You forgot something."

"Hm? What's that?"

"You forgot to kiss me good night."

The expression in her slanted topaz eyes reminded me of a cat I once owned. It used to look at me in the same demure, calculating way while it honed its claws in my ankles. "Valerie," I said earnestly, "I plan to kiss you just once more. I am looking forward eagerly to the moment. It will be when I kiss you good-by."

I turned and walked away. I wished I had merely come to Florida to collect coral snakes.

Chapter Nine:
DODGING A MURDER RAP

It is amazing what a good night's sleep can do. When I awoke the next morning I felt fine. I did my setting up exercises in front of the mirror, admiring the way muscles peeped out shyly under my bronze skin. Anyway, it was bronze where it wasn't freckled or peeling. I shaved and dressed and started downstairs. Odd sounds were coming from the kitchen; apparently Valerie was getting breakfast. A piece of china tinkled as it fell in the sink and shattered. The teakettle gave a loud whistle and blew out its stopper. A chair fell over; probably Valerie tripped over it as she dropped the piece of china and ran to the stove to rescue the teakettle. Mingled with these sounds were Valerie's gasps, squeaks, and yips. She seemed to tackle housekeeping with a rather touching faith that things wouldn't boil over or burn and that china wouldn't break or furniture get in her way when she was in a hurry.

The previous day those sounds would have made me wince, but at the moment, for some reason, they seemed cheerful and homey. I hurried downstairs, getting hungrier every moment as I sniffed the aroma of burning bacon and slightly charred toast.

I burst into the kitchen and grinned at Valerie and said, "Gosh, I feel good. I can lick anybody my size in the house."

From the corner a flat voice rasped, "What size are you, pal?"

I turned and saw Al Leonard balancing on two legs of a kitchen chair. "Oh, hello," I said distantly. "What are you doing here?"

"I'm gonna help you look for shells today, remember?"

"That's right. You thought I had a pretty good idea, didn't you?"

"I thought you had a lousy idea, pal. You don't have a chance of finding the killer. But I thought he might find you. I told the Chief it was a good idea just so you could get some protection."

"Isn't it nice of him to come?" Valerie said. Then she held up a finger and said mournfully, "I burned it with bacon grease."

"Kiss it and make it well," Al said tonelessly. "I won't look."

His twisted grin and the metallic rasp of his voice were beginning to spoil the day for me. I said, "Why don't you go in the living-room and play cops-and-robbers until we finish breakfast?"

"I got invited to breakfast by Mrs. Stuart. You don't mind if I accept, do you, pal?"

"Well, try to scatter a little sunshine around, instead of making cracks."

"Sorry, pal. I only scatter sunshine when I'm on duty. This is my vacation."

Valerie said, "Are men always like this before breakfast? I wish you'd carry things into the dining-room and start sinking your teeth into food instead of each other."

"Sorry," Al said. "It's just I don't like to play nursemaid."

We went into the dining-room. Al and I sat on opposite sides of the table and ate silently and grimly, while Valerie fluttered around us and made soothing comments like an observer from the U.N. I didn't understand why Al was in such a bad temper; after all, he had invited himself to go on our expedition. The way he growled through his food you might think he was used to being fed horsemeat on the floor of a cage. He ate his fried eggs and beat me to the extra pair on the platter and nodded grumpily when Valerie asked if he wanted more.

After Valerie went to the kitchen to fry the eggs, I decided to try to put things on a friendlier basis. I said, merely by way of extending an olive branch, "You know that bag of shells I got at the beach cottage? You're good at fingerprints. Do you think there might be any on the shells? I haven't handled all of them."

My question seemed to interest him. He massaged his anchor-shaped jaw for a while, and said, "You know anything about fingerprints?"

"Don't believe I do."

"People leave fingerprints because they have oil and sweat on their skin. A guy goes along a beach picking up wet shells, and getting sand on his fingers and wiping it off; he won't make a good print even on a good surface. Shells don't have a good surface, anyway. Most of them are too rough."

"Oh. I see."

"What you need is a nice smooth surface like this," he said, picking up an unused glass standing beside the milk pitcher. "I have a can of fingerprint powder with me. The Chief and I were using it last night on that gun. I'll show you."

A twinge of uneasiness went through me. Had I brought in that particular glass, or had Al? Or had Valerie? And did it matter anyway? "Don't bother," I said. "Your eggs will be ready in a second and they'll get cold."

Al looked over his shoulder. The swinging door into the kitchen was closed, but beyond it sounded the crunch of a knife opening an eggshell and the crackle of the egg dropping into hot grease. "We have a couple minutes," Al said. He took a small can from his pocket, held the glass delicately by the rim, and dusted it with the powder. He tapped it lightly on the table and most of the powder sifted off. "There," he said. "You see?"

Three prints showed clearly on the side of the glass. I stood up. There was no reason to worry, of course. No reason for my legs to feel as brittle as dry mangrove branches. "That's very nice," I said, holding out my hand for the glass. "I'll take it out and wash it and see if your eggs are ready."

"No hurry," Al said. "Sit down. Maybe Mrs. Stuart might want to see how I did it." He looked at me and asked, "What do you keep standing there for?"

"The—the eggs."

"Look, pal, why all this sudden interest in my eggs? Up to now you acted like you hoped I'd starve. Why don't you sit down?"

I lowered myself into the chair as if it were equipped with electrodes.

Al leaned back comfortably and held the glass up to the light. "Don't know when I ever took nicer prints," he said, studying the glass like a connoisseur admiring old wine.

I tried to relax. After all, it was only my guilty conscience playing ghost with me. It was nothing but my imagination that made me think Al's fingers were tightening on the glass, that he was slowly tensing, that his eyes were narrowing to thirty-two caliber.

"Yeah," he repeated, "I don't know when I ever took nicer prints."

"You said that before," I chattered. "You said that before. You—"

"Your needle's stuck, pal."

I stared at him in horror. There wasn't any doubt now. The expression on his face as he studied the prints made me think of a wolf spotting fresh deer tracks. I couldn't seem to move or talk.

"Like meeting an old friend," Al said. "I—I don't get it." The wolf eyes looked at me. "I think maybe you had a visitor last night."

"What visitor? What do you mean? I—"

"And it could be," Al said, "that she stayed all night." He leaned forward and showed me a mouthful of teeth in what he thought was a grin and said softly, "Don't rush out to get my eggs, pal. Let Valerie Wilson bring them in."

Now that it had happened I felt oddly cool. In a few moments Valerie would push open the swinging door and walk innocently into the room. I had to warn her. In a Western movie I would have upended the dining-room table on Al, and shouted to give Valerie a chance to escape. But this wasn't a very good movie. The prop man had handed me a table I couldn't budge, and the script gave the guy across the table all the hair-trigger impulses and steely muscles. If I let out a warning yell, Al would be in the kitchen before Valerie could trip over the nearest chair. There was only one chance of warning her. It meant talking fast and saying things that gripped Al's attention.

The thoughts flashed through my head, and I started jabbering in a tense whisper. "You got to listen," I said. "I know it looks bad for me, but I had my reasons. Sure, I could have turned her in when she walked in here yesterday in front of you and the Chief. But so what? You didn't have the real goods on her then. You got to remember this dame gave me a real runaround. I don't let women get away with that. So I figured if I played along I could get the rest of the goods on her before turning her in. Like the gun, see? You didn't have the gun."

I caught a breath, lifted my voice a notch. "You don't think that was just luck I stumbled on the gun, do you? I knew she'd be looking for it. Yesterday out there at the cottage I watched her." I raised my voice again. "Just what I thought. She found the thing, tried to bury it. So I pretended to kick it accidentally out of the sand. Listen, I made things easy for you there."

I was putting on more volume all the time. Valerie ought to hear. My voice was a couple of notches above normal already. "I'd have turned her in right then," I gasped, "but she's got some guy working with her. I wanted to spot him, too. I don't know why she wanted to hide out with me instead of him. Anyway, she and the guy staged that beach accident last night. He didn't try to kill us at all, just tried to make her look good as far as I was concerned. I didn't fall for that. I didn't fall for anything. I just wanted to get her and her boyfriend but good. You've got to believe me! You got to!" I ran out of breath and sat there panting.

Al was leaning forward to listen, eyes glittering. "What a rat," he said admiringly. "What a rat!"

The kitchen was quiet. Not a footstep, not a dish clinking. I didn't know whether she had fled or not. I couldn't hold him much longer. It was incredible that I had held him so long. I cried, "You got to give me a break! I wasn't helping her, I swear it! Finding the gun for you proves I wasn't. I just wanted to get all the dope on her. Far as I'm concerned Valerie Wilson can rot in jail."

My last words came out in a yell that should have ripped him from the chair for a dash to the kitchen. Instead, he gave me that wolf grin and said calmly, "You don't have to yell. She can hear you okay."

The kitchen door swung open. Valerie poised there, her face white. She said fiercely, "That's the dirtiest trick I ever ran into."

"He really pulled one, didn't he?" Al said. "Meet William J. Stuart, the noted rat."

"I mean you, Al Leonard!" she cried.

Al sat up, frowning. "I did it to bring you to your senses," he growled. "You were hanging onto the guy like he added up to something. I wanted to put him on a spot and show you he was a weak sister. I didn't know he'd rat that bad."

I stopped thinking. What was happening put too much overload on the circuits in my head, and the fuses blew. I got up mechanically and walked around the table and threw a right at Al's face. It didn't land. A big hand flicked out, caught my wrist, whirled me around in a hammerlock.

Al's voice rasped into my ear. "Don't lead with your right, pal. Get the guy off balance first with a left, see? Like this." His right hand tightened the hammerlock until pain shrieked up my arm, and his left hand slapped my face.

"Al!" the girl cried.

His left hand halted in the middle of another slap. "Yeah?"

"Hit him again and I'll break this pitcher on your head."

Al's right hand whirled me around again, shoved me across the room. "Pack him away in cotton before he gets hurt," he said.

I couldn't get any other ideas so I started back for him. I thought of trying that tip about leading with my left.

Valerie jumped between us and grabbed my shoulders. "Bill," she gasped. "Stop it! You two will wreck everything. Oh, please stop!"

"Tell him to get out," I said thickly. "I don't know whether he's a cop or a crook or what. But I want him out of here."

"I'll go fast enough," Al said. "But I won't leave her here with a rat like you."

"What she does is up to her. But you're going. If I can't throw you out I'll get the guy on duty outside here to help. So if this is a shakedown it won't work."

"Shakedown!" Al said bitterly. "I'm in this thing as deep as anybody. Boy, I'll look good in striped pants on one of these Florida road gangs."

"Turn the record over," I said. "It doesn't make sense on this side."

Valerie said, "Please listen, Bill. I can clear it up in two minutes."

"Why didn't you clear it up before?"

"Because I was afraid to! Because I needed your help so badly. And one of the things you told me that first night was you didn't want any part of women who were hunting bargains in trouble. I was afraid if I told you everything you'd—you'd—"

Al snapped, "She was afraid you'd run like a rabbit."

"You see," Valerie said faintly, "I came down here hunting for trouble. And I still am."

"And, baby, have you found it!" Al said.

I sat down and tried to steady a match long enough to light a cigarette. "Look," I said, "is this the five-star final version of your story this time? With all names spelled correctly and no typographical errors? If not, I don't want to waste time listening."

"This is it, honest," she said. "And anyway, there are only a couple of things you don't know."

"Little things," Al said. "About the size of bullets."

She looked at him angrily, then told me, "I'm not here on vacation. I came down because Eddie Patrono, or Jones, got sore at his boss. I used to string Eddie along back home. He thought it was because I went for him in a big way, but my real reason was that sometimes I got a good news lead from him. He telephoned me long distance a week ago and said why didn't I run down here and cheer him up. I said it was sweet of him but I couldn't. He said it might be worthwhile for both of us. I asked why. He said maybe certain people would pay plenty to locate a guy he used to work for. I knew who that meant. I tried to find out more, but he wouldn't tell me. He said if I could work a deal with those certain people I was to come to Gulf City, Florida, and get in touch with him through a post-office box here. After he hung up I told my editor. He talked to an organization called the Committee of Thirty that was behind the Special Grand Jury cleanup, and they decided I ought to come down."

I said, "Couldn't you trace Eddie's call?"

"We tried. But he made it from a pay station here in Gulf City. So that didn't help any more than the post-office box."

"And you came down alone?"

Valerie shrugged. "Nobody knew whether Eddie was on the level or not. If I found things looked good, I was to yell for help. So I came down alone and took a room at that little beach hotel and left a note for Eddie at the post-office box. I bribed the desk clerk at a downtown hotel to take any phone calls or messages that came for me from Eddie."

I asked, "Why so much caution?"

"I was afraid if Eddie found out where I was staying he might search my room for the money I was supposed to bring. And I thought he might turn mean if he suspected anything."

"How much money did he want?"

Valerie took a deep breath. "Fifty thousand dollars."

"Fifty thousand bucks!" I cried. "For turning in a guy named George Lawrence who merely had a piece of the numbers racket in your city?"

Al said, "You wanted names spelled right, didn't you? Let's clean this one up for you. The name is not George Lawrence. It's George Lane, L-a-n-e. Maybe you heard of Champ Lane?"

My vertebrae turned into a stack of ice cubes. Now I knew what city Valerie and Al Leonard came from. When you said Champ Lane you identified the place, just as Nucky Johnson used to mean Atlantic City and Tom Pendergast meant Kansas City. The boss. The big shot. The man who sat behind the scenes and pulled strings. He had even made the New York papers a year ago when he vanished one jump ahead of an indictment.

"Fifty grand," I said hoarsely. "Sounds like a bargain."

"Yeah," Al said. "Fifty grand to buy a city. Eddie was a cheap skate. And so was the Committee of Thirty for not coming across. Fifty grand and they owned the town."

Valerie snapped, "The Committee isn't buying the town. They want to give it back to the people who live in it. They don't pay bribes."

"They put up a couple hundred thousand bucks for the investigation," Al said, "and wouldn't pay fifty grand to Eddie to make it stick. Maybe I'm wrong. I'm not a businessman."

I said, "That brings up the interesting question of just who you are."

"I used to be captain of the Vice Squad. That was a year ago. When our girlfriend here decided that perhaps Eddie had something, they sent me down to try to pick up Lane."

I did some quick figuring and got an unpleasant answer. "You headed the Vice Squad a year ago? Wasn't Lane still running things?"

"Uh-huh," Al said, without much interest.

"I merely come from New York City," I said. "We never have any racket troubles there so I don't know the score. So maybe I'm off base in asking why they sent Champ Lane's Vice Squad captain on a secret mission to arrest Champ Lane."

Valerie said, "Al did as honest a job as he could with the Vice Squad. And when the Special Grand Jury started work, Al slipped them all kinds of information."

"Just a Boy Scout at heart, huh?" I said. "And you never got anything out of it?"

Al said, "Sure I got something out of it. Lane's crowd busted me from captain to sergeant, and threw me off the Vice Squad, and made me grounds-keeper of the city stables. We have sixteen of the cutest horses you ever saw and we only use them in parades and we only have about ten parades a year. They figured I'd get fed up and resign, and they were pretty near right. Of course, I was lucky. If they'd known what I told the Special Grand Jury, instead of only suspecting it, they'd have demoted me to a slab in the morgue."

Valerie said, "Al doesn't have any reason to love Champ Lane. He's one of the few cops the Committee can trust."

"City isn't cleaned up yet?" I asked.

"Oh, no," she said. "There haven't been any real changes, except that everybody's lying low. That's why the Committee had to be so careful in picking a man to send here. If they'd gone to the Police Commissioner for help, Champ Lane would have known in an hour. Al isn't here officially. He's on vacation. But he has a secret warrant for Lane."

"You mean Lane's still running the town?"

Al said, "When Lane pulled out, he left word that if he was nailed he'd make sure everybody else got nailed with him. They say he took all his records. Probably got them stashed away down here, maybe in his house."

Valerie said, "The Committee thinks that Lane phones his orders back home from here."

"Well," I muttered, "that only leaves one thing to clear up. When you got in a jam, why did you come to me instead of to Al?"

"I didn't know Al had arrived. It was only the night before Eddie was killed that I decided Lane was really here. So I called my editor and told him, and later that night I got a call back from him saying the Committee would send Al Leonard down and that Al would contact me at my hotel. I didn't expect him here so soon."

Al said, "I flew down that next afternoon. Got here at six, checked in at a hotel, tried to contact Bright Eyes at her hotel. No luck."

Valerie said faintly, "I was out with Eddie."

"Yeah, that was great," Al said. "Couldn't have waited, could you? Had to try to wrap it up all by yourself."

"I had made a date with him and didn't dare break it! How could I know what was going to happen? After we reached the cottage, Eddie wanted the money. He wanted it right then. He figured we would skip off together with it. When I stalled for time he got horribly suspicious. He said I was either going to pay off both ways, or find myself holding up a couple of tons of sand." She shuddered and hid her face in her hands and said, "Then you know what happened."

"Yeah," Al said. "Can't say I blame you, either."

Her head snapped up. "You don't blame me for what?"

"Forget it," Al said.

"You think I shot Eddie!"

"Look, sister," Al said, "I'm for you. It don't matter what I think. Eddie asked for what he got. You want to pin it on Lane, we'll try to pin it on Lane. I don't doubt he was around then or later. But it'll be hard to get around the fingerprints on that gun. You'll be smart to scram and let these hick cops chase their own tails. They'll never trace you."

Valerie looked at me as if she expected me to say something. I didn't know what it was. The only thing that came into my mind was to ask Al why he had visited the police the night Eddie was killed.

Al shrugged. "I couldn't locate Bright Eyes here. So I thought I'd meet the local law and see if I could figure on co-operation in case I needed it. Then the riot started. I figured Valerie was in on it, but I didn't know where to find her. When she walked in on you yesterday morning, I had to play dumb. Out at the cottage yesterday afternoon was my first chance to talk to her."

I got up slowly, my joints working like rusty hinges. "Well, Al," I said, "drop in and see me at Coney Island. I think I'll pack now."

"You're smartening up, pal."

"Whoever is on duty outside won't try to stop me from leaving, will he?"

"It's Davidson," Al said. "He was going with you on that beach trip, but he don't have any orders to keep you in town. It was only on the first night that the Chief gave him orders to stick with you. Tell Davidson you got called back suddenly to New York and give him your address there."

Valerie said tonelessly, "Will your car get you home all right?"

"It's just body damage. I'll stop at a garage and have them hammer out the fenders so they won't scrape the wheels. What about you, though? It'll look funny if Davidson sees me drive away without you."

Al said, "I rented a car today. You leave with her and I'll trail you and pick her up on the outskirts of town."

I nodded and went upstairs, trying to keep my mind a nice neat blank. Valerie came up and went into her room. I collected all my stuff and sorted it methodically into piles. After a while Valerie came to the door. Her face was emptier of expression than a model showing off a high style outfit, and you almost have to have no face to beat one of them.

She watched me put my shirts in one compartment of the wardrobe suitcase and my underwear in another. "You're very systematic, aren't you?" she said.

"A place for everything and everything in its place."

"And your place is in New York, of course. Let me help you pack." She collected an armful of socks and began putting them into the suitcase. Then she stopped and studied one pair. "There's a hole in the heel of this one," she said. "Do you want to take time for me to mend it?"

"Don't bother, thanks."

"It's just as well," she said in a bright, artificial voice. "I'm terrible at darning things. Probably I would have sewed two socks together. And was my cooking really as bad as it seemed to me? I love kitchens, but nothing I cook seems to come out right."

I thought about that. "Your cooking horrified me at first," I said. "But when I became more used to the idea it wasn't so bad. The unexpected things that happened sort of gave me an appetite. It was like having a floor show with every meal. I mean that in a nice way."

"I really think you do. That's the first time anyone ever said nice things about my cooking."

I shut the wardrobe suitcase and locked it and packed the rest of my stuff neatly in a smaller bag and closed it.

Valerie said, "Don't you ever have to jump on your suitcases to close them? I always have to jump on mine."

"You ought to arrange articles so you don't have to jam them together. By the way, are you packed?"

"Oh, yes. I've already jumped on the suitcase you bought me. And I'll pay you for everything as soon as I can. I don't think I have enough now in my checking account. But I'll get the paper to send me some money here."

I nodded and picked up my bags and walked toward the door. Then her last remark registered on me and I dropped the bags. "What did you say?" I asked. "They'll send the money *here?*"

"Oh, yes. They won't mind sending it."

"Wait a minute! You can't be planning to stay here!"

"Not in this house, of course. But in Gulf City."

Al's flat voice came from the bedroom doorway. "You're not staying, sister," he said.

I said irritably, "What's the idea of haunting us?"

He looked at me without expression. "I thought I might carry your bags, mister."

Valerie said coolly, "I'm not leaving Gulf City and you can't make me leave."

I frowned and said, "I thought that was all decided."

"Somebody forgot to ask me about it," she said.

"You can't stay in Gulf City," I growled. "It was one thing when it looked as if you only had to locate one ordinary guy to clear yourself, but it's something very different now. If a man like Lane began to feel crowded, he could get a gang of thugs here tomorrow."

"You're not kidding," Al said. "Probably the only reason he hasn't done it yet is he's not worried. He has Bright Eyes here ducking a murder rap. He figures she can't locate him by herself and that she don't dare yell for help for fear the murder rap will catch up with her. But if he gets worried—"

I cried, "He could bring in two gunmen for every cop on the Gulf City police force."

"You're listening to a smart cookie," Al said. "He knows the score. That's why he's dusting out of here."

"Wait a minute," I said. "That's not why I'm leaving. I admit it's a good reason, but—"

"Just why are you leaving?" Valerie asked in a strained voice.

"Well, first, because you are."

"But I'm not! Do you think I'd go back home and live the rest of my life with a murder charge hanging over my head?"

"At least you'd be living," Al said.

"And that's not even half of it," she said angrily. "The main reason I'm staying is to make sure Lane gets caught. He's been hiding almost a year now. And witnesses are disappearing and the reformers are losing interest the way they always do, and in another few months Champ Lane can walk back into town and laugh off that indictment."

"You can't help by staying here," Al said.

"Oh, no? If I can't do anything else, I can act as bait."

Al said softly, "You know what sometimes happens to bait."

I looked at the firm set of her chin. She didn't seem to scare easily. I said, "Where could you stay? If the cops spot you after I leave, they may get ideas."

"Al can find me a place. If he won't do it, I'll find one myself."

Al shrugged. "Okay, if you want it that way. Matter of fact, I decided last night I better rent a shack near the beach. Be handier in looking for Lane, and not so public. Know what that dumb Chief of Police did last night? He called my hotel and had me paged. I was in the bar having a quick one and here comes a bellhop yelling for Sergeant Al Leonard. A little more of that and Lane will have me pegged. For all I know he has stooges in town. So I'll rent a shack at the beach and you can stay there, too."

I said indignantly, "You can't ask her to stay alone with a man."

"And just what are you, pal? A small boy? She's been staying here with you."

"Yes, I know, but—"

"You mean if she burns a finger you don't trust me to kiss it and make it well?"

"I wouldn't trust you with anything in skirts."

He tilted a grin at me. "She looks cute in slacks."

"Oh, stop it," Valerie said. "I'm old enough to make my own decisions. Bill, you said the first reason why you were leaving was because you thought I was leaving. What's the second reason?"

I muttered, "Do we have to go into that?"

"Don't embarrass him," Al said. "He has a right to think about his health. What sensible guy wants to live at the wrong end of a shooting-gallery?"

"I don't like either end of shooting-galleries," I said. "But I told you before that wasn't the reason." I looked into Valerie's clear brown eyes and dropped my glance and mumbled, "I don't suppose you have much use for me, after the way Al proved I would sell you out in a second if things got rough."

"You mean that trick Al pulled on you in the dining-room?"

"Yes. That's it."

"Isn't it queer?" she said. "I had the impression you did all that talking for just one reason. So that I'd hear you and have a chance to run."

Suddenly I stopped feeling old and tired and full of aches. I was nine feet tall and fifty inches around the chest. "You mean you really understood? I was trying to hold Al's attention and to raise my voice without tipping him off what I was doing, and—"

"You're not going to fall for that stuff, are you?" Al cried. "Look, baby, he was ratting! I've heard plenty of them do it. They raise their voices because they're scared. He'd do it again if he got in another jam. Don't be dumb! Any cop would tell you I'm right."

Valerie said, "And any cop would tell you I shot Eddie Patrono. What's your guess, Bill?"

"I'm not guessing. I know you didn't shoot him."

She gave me a smile that made me dizzy. "We wouldn't make very good cops, would we, Bill?"

"Personally," I said, "I always wanted to grow up to be a train engineer. Know something? I don't think my car can get back to New York without a complete overhaul."

"That's a shame. You might have to stay here several days."

"Might take a week or more."

Al said, "What goes on here?"

I said, "I would certainly hate to stay here with holes in my socks and no appetite for meals."

"I darn socks beautifully," Valerie said. "And my popovers are so light you have to keep windows closed so they won't float out of the house."

I turned to Al. "Boy," I said, "I believe you said you came upstairs to carry the bags. Take Mrs. Stuart's things to the Blue Room."

For a moment I thought I would have to call the fire department, but Al finally stopped burning and said, "Well, now I've seen everything. Anybody got a nice hard wall I can bash my head against?"

Valerie skipped over to him and put a hand on his arm and said, "Please don't be upset. You've been wonderful and I know we've caused you a lot of trouble."

I frowned. It was nice that she had sympathetic impulses, but she shouldn't let them carry her away.

Al said, "Well, I'll drop in now and then to see how you're getting along. Take it easy."

"But where are you going?" Valerie cried. "You said you would help us check beach cottages."

"Baby, I'd just as soon march along the beach carrying a sign saying, 'Champ Lane Unfair to Committee of Thirty.' He has you and your boyfriend pegged. The only chance we have is to keep him from pegging me. If he sees us together on the beach, he'll remember who I am, and school will be out. I work this alone, my way."

"But we could help!"

"The question in my mind," Al said, "is who this Stuart is helping."

"You might explain that crack," I said.

"Okay. You pick her up on the beach right after Eddie was shot. How do I know you aren't working for Lane?"

Valerie gasped, "Don't be silly! Then why would Bill hide me? Why did he save me last night on the beach?"

"That stuff last night could have been faked. The whole idea could be to get your confidence. To find out who's back of you, who's working with you. Then Lane can have everybody knocked off at once like pins in a bowling alley, and not leave any splits standing in the back corners."

"I can't buy that," she said. "Bill isn't the type."

Al grumbled, "I admit Lane usually goes in for tough guys, and Stuart sure isn't that type. But the only other way I can figure him is he'd have to study hard to get in a school for backward kids."

I smiled. A minute ago, Al had been taking it on the chin and Valerie had been all sympathy for him. Now I was being put through the wringer, and she was back squeezing my hand in a comforting way.

"Bill has a very good brain," she said firmly.

"Yeah?" Al said. "Then he must have forgot to pack it when he left New York City. All he's been for you is bad news. He starts off by giving the cops your description. He finds a body for them and proves to the cops you were there and hands them your room key so they can locate you fast. He digs up that rod you buried and won't even let you wipe off the fingerprints. And downstairs today in the dining-room—jeez, the guy was crazy!"

Valerie said, "I thought he handled that dirty trick of yours very cleverly."

"By ratting, huh? Well, leave that lay. What I mean is this. You're wanted for murder, baby. Your fingerprints are all over this shack. So what does this idiot do but coax me to give him a fingerprint demonstration?"

I said, "I tried to head you off."

"Yeah, but you couldn't. And if you had pulled that stunt on this one-cylinder Chief of Police, you couldn't have headed him off either. He took a mail-order course in fingerprinting. He likes to show how good he is."

Valerie said, "Now, look, Al, you can't kid me the way you kidded Bill. I know a little something about fingerprinting. I know you can't just look at a fingerprint and say who made it. You have to compare it with prints that you have already identified. So where was the harm in Bill asking about fingerprints?"

"It just happens," Al said, "that the Chief is carrying around a photograph of your fingerprints, sister. So don't coax him to show off."

I said, "All right, I've been pulling boners. What bright things have you been doing?"

Al said wearily, "I come down here looking for Champ Lane and I spend all my time keeping Bright Eyes out of jail. After you find the body, I sit around the cottage wiping off every place where I think she might have left prints. I even wipe off one highball glass. It turns out it's Eddie's glass, but I don't know that and I don't get a chance to wipe off the other one. You take her downtown in a pair of shoes that will identify her to the Chief as Valerie Wilson, and I have to keep blocking him off so he won't see them. After you find that rod, I go along with the Chief hoping for a chance to wipe it off, but he never lets it out of his hands. Anyway, I tried. I keep telling him Valerie Wilson has left town. I keep telling her to get out of town. Handing her that advice is the brightest thing I've done."

Valerie said, "I can't see it that way. But I do appreciate everything you've done."

"Well, sweet dreams," Al said. "I'll have a hideout ready for you, if you change your mind before it's too late."

I said stiffly, "I'll look after her."

"You better," Al said. "Because if you don't, do you know what's gonna happen to you?"

"No."

"That's just as well," he said softly, and flicked his hand in casual salute and left.

Chapter Ten: FACE OF A FUGITIVE

I had high hopes of finding a clue to Lane's hideout during our expedition that day. As it turned out, however, we would have had just as much luck hunting along those Gulf of Mexico beaches for a shell called the Glory of the Pacific. Valerie and Officer Davidson and I spent all morning and afternoon peeping into places along the beach, looking for an impressive shell collection that Lane might have made. Sometimes we found people home and sold them tickets for the car raffle for the Police Pension Fund and got a good look inside their living-rooms, and sometimes no one answered the door and we sneaked around looking in windows.

The checkup went faster than I had figured, because there were only a couple hundred houses along the six or seven miles of residential beachfront, and now that the season was over more than half of the places were closed and boarded up. Of course, Lane might be living in one of the boarded-up houses, but we had no way to check them.

We started at the southern end of the beach and headed north, working separately but making sure that we kept each other in sight. Shortly after noon we reached the only beach place that I could prove had a shell collection; unfortunately it was the Casa del Mar, temporary residence of William J. Stuart and his temporary wife. We had lunch there, and went on. Davidson was having a wonderful time in spite of not finding my mystery man; like everybody else on the Gulf City police force he loved to hand out tickets, even though they were merely for a car raffle.

I found myself enjoying the day, too. It was pleasant to saunter along the beach watching ripples twinkling on the Gulf and gulls figure-skating against the blue sky. Valerie seemed to have forgotten the serious purpose back of our walk. She skipped along like a school kid starting vacation, her eyes bright and the wind combing her hair back from her face. She even took time to poke through some of the drifts of shells we passed. For a while that made me hope she was getting the shell-collecting fever, but later I realized that she was merely looking for shells that would skitter nicely when she scaled them over the water. I watched her for a time, and decided that she ought to be restrained. Her activity was not only slowing our man hunt but also might result in the loss of rare shells.

I said, "If you run across any Junonias, please don't throw them away."

She looked startled. "What's a Junonia?"

"It's a shell. A univalve, with rows of squarish brown spots on an ivory background. They're quite rare and sometimes people look for years before they find one. I don't have any in my collection."

"I think," she said, laughing, "that you'd be just as happy finding a Junonia as finding Mr. Lane."

"I would not! But there's no harm in picking up a shell or two while we're looking for the guy."

"That explains something for me, Bill. I could never understand why, if Mr. Lane was suspicious of Eddie and was heading for the beach cottage that night to spy on him, he took time to gather shells. But now I see he was merely acting like a real shell collector. He saw no harm in picking up a shell or two while he was on his way maybe to shoot a man."

"Go ahead and laugh. You may yet be glad you have a shell collector on your side."

"I'm already glad, Bill. Tell me about Junonias. Do they build islands, like coral, or make pearls or anything? Do they have exciting lives?"

"Well, no. They live quietly in crevices in rocks and coral reefs, and try not to get into trouble."

She said reflectively, "I've met people like that. Sometimes they're surprisingly lively and nice when you get them out in the open."

"I can't imagine it."

"Fact, though," she said. "Well, I won't throw any away."

"Thanks. And keep on the lookout for Lane. We only have a mile more to cover."

"Are you still hopeful, Bill?"

I wanted to say something confident but there was no use kidding. "No," I said. "Looks as if my hunch was no good."

"I'm glad you had it, though. It's been one of the nicest days I've ever spent. And we might stir up something in this last mile."

"No one," I said, "will be more surprised than I."

As a matter of fact no one *was* more surprised than I, because I did stir up something a short time afterward. Not that it meant anything. It turned out to be nothing more than one of Al Leonard's rather grim practical jokes, like the time he sneaked up behind me in the drugstore and grabbed my shoulder and said, "Gotcha!" But for two seconds it provided all the excitement I could handle.

It happened at a small cottage on a lonely stretch of beach. I walked up to the place, noting that the shades were pulled down and that it had a vacant appearance, and knocked on the door. No answer. I knocked again, waited, started to turn away. At that moment the door whipped open behind me and a powerful hand yanked me inside and another hand clamped over my mouth.

A voice growled, "Looking for Champ Lane, are you? Okay, here I am. What are you gonna do about it?"

He was gripping me so I couldn't yell, and I couldn't break away. I was considering doing something about it by passing out on him, but I suddenly realized that the voice was familiar. It was Al. I stopped struggling and relaxed.

He began laughing, a flat staccato sound like a submachine gun letting off bursts. He let me go and said happily, "Caught on finally, did you? Only took you five seconds and two heart attacks."

"Very funny. Remind me to give you a cigar loaded with dynamite."

"Aah, don't get sore. Just a gag." He went to the doorway and yelled, "Hey, Mrs. Stuart! Davidson! Come here, will you?" He left the doorway and began snapping window shades up to their rollers. "Just rented this joint for two weeks. How do you like my shack? Not bad, huh?"

"You'll wreck the shades that way. I hope the owner put a damage clause in the lease."

"Come on, cheer up, Stuart. I didn't hurt you. I got in here about half an hour ago and saw you people heading this way and thought I'd see what you would do if you actually ran across the guy. What would you have done?"

"We were all supposed to keep an eye on each other. One of them should have seen you yank me in here."

"Isn't that cute?" he said, chuckling. "Only it happens that Bright Eyes was playing with shells and Davidson was too far away, and for all they knew some magician stuffed you back in his hat like a white rabbit."

Valerie and Davidson arrived just then, and Al had another good laugh explaining his joke to them—without, of course, mentioning Champ Lane's name. Valerie looked displeased, but Davidson said admiringly, "The Sergeant's a great kidder." Al insisted we had to stay for a drink. He opened his suitcase and unpacked a fifth of rye, and brought glasses from the kitchen and apologized for having to serve warm tap water with the rye, due to the fact that the refrigerator hadn't frozen any ice cubes yet. He played host as expansively as if the rather bare four-room cottage were a mansion; apparently he only needed a few simple pleasures, like scaring people half to death, to put him in a good humor. Probably back home he had a high old time scorching fellow cops with the hot-foot trick.

I hated to admit it, but I saw his point of view about me. He had been sent to Gulf City on a dangerous job. Picking up Champ Lane would have been a tricky business even without complications, but Al had run into a pair of complications named Valerie Wilson and William J. Stuart. He was playing bloodhound along a cold trail, and we kept stirring up nests of fire ants in his path. I thought about the troubles he was having, and worked up enough sympathy for him so that I didn't protest when he invited himself to dinner at our place.

After that we finished our investigation of beachfront houses, and counted up results for the day. We had found no clues leading to Champ Lane, but we had sold seventy-one tickets for the Police Pension Fund car raffle. I was sorry that I couldn't coax the police to raffle off the mysterious gray sedan; maybe that would induce them to find it.

For dinner that night I made biscuits and Valerie charred a steak delicately and Al warmed over a few of his favorite murder cases. He served us a gang knifing with the fruit cup and a hatchet murder with the steak. The latter case won him my steak, as he had undoubtedly hoped. After dinner, when we were having coffee and an arsenic slaying, I said rather acidly, "You solved all those gory cases so easily that I don't suppose you'll have any trouble with this plain old shooting we have here."

"I'll clean it up," Al said. "That is, if you two will keep out of my hair. That dumb stunt today of parading along the beach may make it harder."

I said, "Well, you don't like my ideas. How about giving me a chance to sneer at yours?"

Al looked as happy as if I had asked him for his autograph. He loved talking about himself. "People write a lot of baloney about how a big-time cop works," he said. "You get your best results with three methods. One, you get a pigeon who tips you off what you want to know. Two, you know how the guy you're chasing operates, and you set a trap for him. Three, you keep a good set of Rogues' Gallery photos filed away in your head, and you keep your eyes open for the guy you want. That's all there is to it."

"And how does that fit this case?"

"We had a nice pigeon," Al said. "We had Eddie Patrono. But Bright Eyes here fixed that. So now I only have two ways to work. We know Champ Lane hangs out somewhere along the beach; Eddie told Valerie that. I'm down on the beach now and I stay under cover and keep my eyes open. Lane can't stay in his hideout forever. He hasn't got Eddie to run errands now. He'll have to run some himself."

"You skipped over that second method," I said suspiciously. "I mean about setting a trap."

"Think I'm holding out on you, huh? Well, pal, I won't keep it a secret. You two make good bait for a trap."

"I don't like that idea," I said angrily.

"Don't blame me. I been telling you to beat it."

Valerie said, "What would happen, Al, if you went to the Chief of Police and told him you're looking for Champ Lane and maybe he's connected with the murder?"

Al shrugged. "They can't find a dame who's right under their noses when they have a lot of leads to go on. How can they find a guy who's really hiding when they don't have any leads?"

"Might still be worth trying," I said

Al shook his head. "Tell them about Lane and it would be all over town before you could say Police Pension Fund. You can't keep a thing as big as that quiet. And Lane may have stooges in town. If he's still here, the only reason is because maybe it's a lot of trouble moving his records and bank accounts and stuff like that, and he figures he only has to worry about a couple amateurs who don't dare yell copper because they'll get tagged with a murder charge."

"Then do we just sit here?" Valerie asked plaintively.

"Next to leaving town, it's the best thing to do," Al said. "The last idea Stuart had was that one you tried today. Got any more dumb ideas, pal?"

If he hadn't sneered at me in quite such an irritating way, perhaps I wouldn't have thought again of a certain idea. "Matter of fact," I said, "I do have another." I went upstairs and collected a few sheets of drawing-paper and a box of colored pencils. When I returned to the dining-room I said, "I always carry around some sketching stuff, in case I get an idea for an advertising layout. I just thought up a swell one. At the top it says, 'Wanted,' in invisible ink, and at the bottom it says, 'For Murder,' in invisible ink, and in the center is a nice sketch of Champ Lane. Come on, tell me what he looks like."

"Guy's nuts," Al said. "We just finished saying it would wreck everything to advertise Lane is here."

"I'm not going to advertise it. I told you I'd use invisible ink for the 'Wanted for Murder' part."

Valerie said, "Bill, didn't we talk about this once before, and decide it wouldn't work?"

"You decided it wouldn't work. You told me to run along and play with my shells. But I still like the idea. I want to make a sketch and take it to places in town that Lane might have visited."

Al said, "From what Valerie says, Lane stayed under cover and let Eddie run errands."

I said, "Eddie hated shell collecting. Lane is nuts about it. So I bet Eddie never ran any errands about shells. I want to take a sketch of Lane to bookstores and see if he ever bought books on shell collecting. I want to take it to that big shell shop, and to shell experts. Maybe someone will recognize him and know where he lives."

"And maybe," Al said, "they'll recognize him as Champ Lane and then everyone in town will hear about it."

Valerie said, "I don't think they would spot him as Champ Lane. He didn't like photographers. There were very seldom any pictures of him published, so his face isn't well known."

Al argued, "But that's only one of the things that can go wrong. Now, listen. All along, Stuart's ideas have been getting you deeper in this mess. I got a hunch this idea is booby-trapped, too. So let it alone, will you?"

"I vote we try it," Valerie said.

"Okay," Al said wearily. "Here we go again."

I began working on the sketch. It wasn't easy to do the job from oral descriptions, and sometimes Valerie and Al disagreed on the shape of Lane's nose or the color of his eyes, but eventually I finished. An interesting face stared up at me from the drawing-paper. Bald head, thick black eyebrows, gray eyes, nose built like a meat cleaver, wide firm mouth, heavy chin. I decided that the Florida sunlight had probably bleached his eyebrows and tanned his face, so I made those changes. I studied the face again. It was not one I wanted to meet in a dark alley. Without conscious thought I had given his gray eyes a bleak stare. They kept watching me. It was silly to let that bother me. Whenever you draw eyes looking straight forward, they always seem to be watching you.

"It's good," Valerie said.

"You're asking for grief," Al muttered.

"I don't know why," I said. "If I take this around to enough people, I may get a real lead. You were talking about big-time police methods. Well, I always heard they do a lot of pavement pounding asking hundreds of people the same questions. You didn't mention that system. It's what we did today checking those houses for shell collections. It's what I want to do with this sketch. It's what the Chief of Police is doing, trying to find Valerie."

"Well, it's one way to work," Al grumbled. "But it's not as good as the others and you need trained cops to do it. You and this Chief of Police are amateurs. He just stumbled on that business of Bright Eyes chiseling the pair of shoes. He won't find out a thing more. He—"

The doorbell rang just then. Valerie opened the door, and the Chief of Police bounded in like a big puppy retrieving a ball.

"Guess what?" he said happily. "I almost got my hands on Valerie Wilson!"

Valerie, two feet away from him, flinched.

Al said, yawning, "You better reach right out and grab her, then." I glared at him; the remark was in bad taste.

The Chief said, "Well, I have a little way to go yet. But I've been getting results today. I went back to that shoe store to see if I could get a better description, and guess what? They received a plain envelope in the mail today, with no letter or return address, containing a ten-dollar bill."

I had an awful suspicion what was coming. That was one of the three envelopes Valerie and I had mailed, to pay for the shoes, hat, and curtain she had swiped. "That doesn't mean anything," I said, without much hope.

"Oh, yes, it does," he said. "Yesterday a hat was reported stolen from the La Mode Hat Shop. I didn't know about it until today, and I went to the La Mode and hanged if they hadn't received ten bucks in the mail the same way. The description they gave me of the girl they think took the hat tallies with the description of the Wilson dame. Must have been she sent both stores the money. That means she's still in town. Somebody's helping her now, or she wouldn't have money and a new hideout. Not bad, huh?"

"Is—is that all?" Valerie asked.

"One thing more," he said cheerily. "I figured if she had picked up shoes and a new hat, maybe she picked up some more stuff to wear. So my boys and I checked every store in town to see if they received any mysterious money in the mail, and one of them happened to be talking about it to his girl at the Civic Center and I'll bet you won't believe this!"

Al muttered, "I'll believe anything now."

"Yes, sir," the Chief said, "the Civic Center received ten bucks this morning, too. We checked all around the place and found they were missing a black-and-white curtain. And the woman at the tourist desk remembered a girl borrowing a needle and thread and scissors yesterday morning. A girl who answers the description of Valerie Wilson. What do you figure she would have done with that needle and thread and scissors and black-and-white curtain?"

I said, "She made herself a sarong."

"I don't think you'd make a good detective, Stuart. What the girls at the Civic Center figure is, she made those gray slacks over into a gray skirt, and used the curtain as a sash. Matter of fact one of the girls even remembers a dame dressed like that. So that gives me a complete description of what she wore. Now I only have to find people who saw where she went in that outfit."

"Amazing," I said, giving Al a dirty look, "what you can do by pounding the pavements."

"Can't beat it," the Chief said. "Well, Davidson tells me you didn't make out so good pounding the beach today, except for selling tickets. Any other ideas on the fire?" He peered at the table where I had been working, and said, "What's that picture?"

Al picked up the sketch and started folding it and said casually, "Just a little drawing Stuart was doing."

"Let me have it," I said.

"Now, look," Al said, "you don't want—"

"Yes, I do," I insisted. "My confidence in pavement pounding has just been renewed. Maybe this is a good time to start." I yanked it out of his hand and showed it to the Chief. "My wife and I have been working on it," I explained. "You see, we both got a look at the man driving the gray sedan on the beach last night. So we tried to work out a rough sketch of him."

"A rough sketch!" the Chief cried. "You couldn't have done as good with a camera and flash gun! This is a real guy you drew!"

"Yeah?" Al said in a toneless voice. "You ever see him?"

"Well, no," the Chief said. "I mean this could only be one particular guy and not anybody else. But I don't understand how you did this thing. You mean a guy comes crashing into you in the dark on the beach and you saw him this good?"

Three people in the room held their breath. Then I said hastily, "Don't forget we had a flashlight. We were using it to follow the footprints. My wife swung the beam in his face."

Valerie let out a small sigh and sank into a chair.

"Oh," the Chief said. "That explains it."

"I'm going to take it around to shell experts tomorrow and see if they know him," I said. "Good idea, huh?"

"Yeah, not bad," the Chief said. He looked at me fondly, not at all like a man who was about to set off the booby trap under me, and said, "And you can do me a sketch of Valerie Wilson. Good idea, huh?"

The hush that followed seemed long enough for a reading of the burial service. Valerie huddled in her chair. Al stood motionless, his eyes as cold and watchful as the eyes in the sketch I had done. Finally, out of desperation, I began talking. I said I couldn't possibly do a sketch of Valerie Wilson. It had been dark when I met her. I hadn't seen her clearly. I was too tired to do another sketch. My hand was cramped. The light was bad and I needed a new set of colored pencils.

The Chief brushed aside my objections as casually as if he had the goods on me and I was pleading not guilty. He pointed out that I certainly had a better chance to see Valerie Wilson than I'd had to see the driver of the gray sedan. I met her on the beach when I had a flashlight. I sat beside her in my car. I saw her under street lights at the bus station. If I was tired he personally would keep me supplied with coffee. A little massage would fix my cramped hand. If the light and the colored pencils had been good enough for my first sketch, they were good enough for this one. If I had forgotten any details of Valerie Wilson's appearance, he would be delighted to refresh my memory. At that point he hauled out his notebook, in which three pages were now filled with descriptive details.

I couldn't head him off. He kept plowing ahead like a bulldozer clearing out clumps of palmetto. At last, for fear that a continued refusal would make him suspicious, I gave in.

"Good boy," he said. He winked at the others and said, "I knew he'd come through. Little temperamental was all. Got to expect that from artists."

He and Valerie and Al stood over me in a sort of deathbed grouping as I started to work. The Chief wanted a full-length job. I set my jaw grimly and drew him a figure that had all the glamorous lines of a bag of cement.

The Chief tapped my shoulder. "Nooooo," he said reprovingly. "You can do better than that. Get in there and pitch some curves."

"That's the way I remember her," I mumbled.

"Let me jog that memory of yours." He leafed through his notebook and said, "Height about five five. Weight around one ten. Nice figure. I'm quoting your original description, Stuart. I'm no artist, but that isn't any nice figure you drew."

I erased the lines with a trembling hand and started again. I tried hard to get off the track, but the Chief was horribly alert. When I finished the figure and outline of the head, the result was entirely too close to Valerie's actual appearance; the only changes I had managed to sneak in were at the shoulders, which I had made narrower, and at the hips, to which I had added a few extra inches.

"Now the face," the Chief said. "And after you finish this full-length job, draw me just the face alone on another hunk of paper."

"I didn't see her face clearly," I protested.

The Chief began quoting from the notebook. "'If you were walking in a garden at night and met a girl who—'"

"I know I said that! But it isn't a description you can use for a portrait."

He looked at his notebook again. "Well, okay. But you have to draw me a face that would go nicely in a Caribbean travel ad. You said that."

I groaned, and went on with the job. I sketched for several minutes without interruption. Then a hand touched my shoulder. I looked up at Valerie. Her eyes were wide and startled, and she shook her head slightly. I peered at the sketch and saw to my horror that my hand was tricking me. The half-completed face was beginning to look like Valerie. I held my breath and carefully changed lines and shadows until the resemblance faded. The Chief didn't say anything.

Finally I stretched my aching fingers and said, "That's the best I can do."

The Chief studied the full-length job and the head-and-shoulders sketch. "Give her brown eyes," he said. "That's what you said she had."

I obeyed, making the eyes several shades darker than Valerie's.

"Now," the Chief said, peering at his fiendish notebook, "give her nice soft hair, about two inches less than shoulder length. Make it brown with reddish lights in it."

"I didn't tell you she had hair like that!"

"No, but the girl who works in the La Mode Hat Shop said so."

I forced my shaking hand to work. "Is that all?" I muttered.

"Just two or three little things," he said pleasantly. He opened his notebook to a very accurate sketch of the perky white hat Valerie had stolen, and laid it before me. He produced a small newspaper ad showing the gray suede pumps she had taken. "Put these on her," he said, "and draw a black-and-white sash around her waist. Here's a sample." He dropped a bit of material on the table. "They let me cut that from another curtain at the Civic Center," he explained.

I followed instructions. When I finished I shut my eyes. I was afraid to look at the result.

"Well," the Chief said, "the face is kind of hazy, but maybe we can do better after I go back to those shops and the Civic Center and see what they suggest. Figure is good."

I opened my eyes and stared at the sketch of a pretty girl in a perky white hat, white shirt, gray skirt, black-and-white sash, and gray suede pumps. I shuddered. Even with the narrower shoulders and plumper hips, it was too good.

"Funny thing," the Chief said. "I could swear I saw a girl dressed like that. But I can't remember where."

Al said, in a voice like a file on metal, "You probably saw her in your sleep."

"Yeah? I was wide awake yesterday morning and that's when I think I saw her. You know doggone well I was awake. You were with me."

"Sure, she came up to us on the street and bummed a light."

"Anyway," the Chief said, "now I really have something to go on. Mighty nice of you to help out, Stuart. I know it was hard work. You look dead tired."

"I don't feel that good, though," I said.

"Well, take it easy. I put Clark on duty outside here until midnight and then Lawson takes over. So don't worry. Good night." He waved his hand to us and strode out jauntily with his two sketches.

After a moment Al said, "So don't worry. Ha, ha."

Valerie said ruefully, "You ought to give up advertising, Bill. You have a future doing portraits."

"He has a future doing time," Al snapped. "Stuart, I'd tell you to blow your brains out, only they're too small a target to hit."

I muttered, "I'm not the only dope. Who was it said you can't get anywhere pounding the pavements?"

"How did I know you mailed ten-dollar bills all over town in plain envelopes? Even a moron like the Chief couldn't miss that. People get ten bucks free for nothing in the mail and they're sure to talk about it. Why did you do it?"

Valerie said, "Bill and I thought it was right to pay for the things I took."

"Look, sister. If they catch you, nobody's gonna worry about bringing larceny charges. But that's not the point I started to make. I said right from the beginning that the idea of sketching Champ Lane was booby-trapped."

"It was just bad luck the Chief came in," Valerie said.

"But that's the only kind of luck this Stuart has! I tried to cover up the sketch and he wouldn't let me. If the Chief hadn't come in, I bet Stuart would have taken the sketch to him, and it would have worked out the same way. You know what we're getting into now? The same kind of set-up we had this morning when Stuart coaxed me to play fingerprints with him. And if the Chief ever starts thinking with his head instead of his feet, he'll catch on. Then we'll see if Stuart rats on us."

"Cheer up," I said. "I'll claim I don't even know you. I wish it were true, too."

Al said, "This may be your last chance to skip, Valerie."

"Sorry. Bill and I have a date to see shell experts tomorrow."

"Okay," Al said. "Have fun. Nice picture you did of her, pal. Almost as good a likeness as the police photographer will get. So long." He stamped out of the house.

I slumped in a chair and waited for Valerie to say something. She didn't. She moved quietly around the room straightening furniture and putting my colored pencils back in the box. I said, "If you want to stab me with one of those pencils, the jury will probably call it justifiable homicide."

She came up behind me and twined her fingers in my limp hair and gave it a little tug. "You're tired," she said. "I bet you have a headache."

"How can a guy who doesn't have a head on his shoulders have a headache?"

"You have a very nice head. I like it."

"You mean you're not sore at me for being stupid tonight? You don't hold anything against me?"

"Only one thing. And that didn't happen tonight."

"What was it?"

"Yesterday morning the Chief was reading that lovely description of me and he came to your statement that my face would look nice in a Caribbean travel ad. And you snarled that if you saw my face in a Caribbean travel ad, you'd take the Fall River Line to Boston. I still hold that against you."

"Well," I grumbled, "you needn't. That body of water we were walking beside today didn't look like Long Island Sound to me."

"Wonderful! Coming from you, that's practically a proposal of marriage." She bent suddenly and kissed me.

I sat up, startled. "Why did you do that?" I asked nervously.

"Coming from me," she said, "that means I accept." Then she laughed and skipped upstairs.

I shook my head. I couldn't figure her out. Anyway, it was nice she didn't think I was an idiot. If she was right, perhaps one of my ideas would click and we would get out of the mess. If she was wrong, when we went on trial we could both plead insanity.

Chapter Eleven: SHOCKING PICTURE

Valerie and I started out early the next morning with the sketch of Champ Lane. I had prepared a story to explain our search; I was an artist on vacation, and met a man on the beach who was an expert shell collector. After leaving him I decided that there was a market for a pamphlet on shell collecting. I wanted to do the illustrations and ask the collector to do the text, but I didn't know how to locate him except by sketching his face from memory and asking people if they knew him.

We went first to the book store. My story was accepted without question. One of the clerks thought he recognized the face, and said he believed the man had bought a number of books on shell collecting six months earlier. He didn't know the man's name or where he lived. Next we tried the Shell Shop. Once again the sketch brought a faint stirring of memory, but that was all. The owner of the shop, however, gave us a list of the leading shell collectors in town, and we got busy locating them. Two of them were sure they had exchanged comments with the man, while collecting shells on the beach, but they had no idea where he lived.

It was early afternoon before we picked up a lead, and it was such a slight one that for a time I paid little attention to it. We ran across it while visiting a real-estate man who was on the Shell Shop list of experts. He had a small office in the business section, and his window was filled with an excellent shell collection instead of the usual photos of houses for sale and rent. He studied my sketch and said the man had been in to see him a number of times, originally to ask for help in identifying a rare specimen and later just to talk about shells. The man's name was Lawrence, George Lawrence, and he lived in a house somewhere on the beach.

That was getting close, but it was no more than Valerie and I already knew. I said, "Don't you have any idea where his house is?"

"Well, he isn't listed in the phone book and he never seemed to want to talk much about himself. He let something drop once, but it doesn't really tell where his house is."

"It might help me."

"He came in here once with a mighty nice bunch of shells he'd collected the day before. It was right in the middle of tourist season, when the beach gets pretty well picked over, so I asked him how he managed to get such nice shells in one day. It turned out he'd been diving for them."

"Diving?" Valerie said. "I didn't know anybody collected shells that way."

"Yes, ma'am. That's how the very best shells are taken. Like spiny oysters and such. Up at Tarpon Springs the sponge divers always keep their eyes open for shells. Sometimes they pick up a spiny oyster worth more than a day's take of sponges. Of course, that's deep-water diving. This man Lawrence had been diving off the beach in only eight or ten feet of water. That way he got shells before they'd been broken or chipped by waves washing them up on the beach."

I asked, "What has that to do with where he lives?"

"Well, I was still curious to know how he found a couple dozen nice shells in one day. You could spend a week diving some places off the beach and come up with nothing but seaweed and sand dollars. Well, he told me he had found a sand bar a few hundred yards offshore that stretches out at just the right angle to trap shells every time we get a good blow from the southwest, and he goes out and dives for them. He said it was mighty convenient because the sand bar was right offshore from his house."

"Then where's the sand bar? Did he say?"

The real-estate agent grinned and shook his head. "You know how shell collectors are. If they find a good private place to get shells, they won't tell where it is. Like fishermen keeping quiet about a real nice spot for reds or snook. Of course I could make some guesses where that sand bar is, if it hasn't shifted any in the past few months."

"Good," I said. "Where do you figure it is?"

He pointed to an aerial photograph hanging on a wall of his office. "That's a photo-mosaic of the beachfront. You know, a lot of aerial photos fitted together. I use it in selling and renting beach property. You can see the sand bars showing offshore."

I stared at the mosaic of photographs. There were many shadings in the water off the beach, the dark curves of channels, pale shallows, an occasional white streak where a sand bar lifted from deeper water.

The agent said, "I figure one of these might angle out just the right way to trap shells." His finger traced four of the white streaks. "You understand, though, it wouldn't be only the angle that makes Mr. Lawrence's sand bar such a fine trap for shells. First there have to be shells coming in to be trapped. I figure there must be some good colonies of shells out beyond his sand bar, on account of feed or water conditions being just right, and comes a good blow from the southwest it roils up those colonies and washes in some of the dead shells. So you see, here are four sand bars all going out at about the same angle, but maybe there aren't any colonies of shells out beyond three of them and so they wouldn't trap shells no matter what."

I studied the photograph. Three of the sand bars were rather long, and located in front of solidly built-up sections of beach front. One was small, covering an area of beach that seemed to have only one house. I shrugged. Lane might be living in any one of fifty houses. It would be a waste of time to check all those places casually; we had done that the previous day. And it might take weeks to check fifty houses carefully. We didn't have weeks. The way the Chief of Police was digging up Valerie's trail we might not even have days. If we could narrow the area of search to ten or even fifteen houses—but there was no way to do that.

We thanked the real-estate agent, and left to hunt for other collectors on our list. An hour later we crossed off the last name, without having picked up any more information.

"Does it seem to you," Valerie asked sadly, "that we're sunk?"

"Sunk, hmm?" I said. "That gives me an idea. Sand bars are sunk, too. I'm beginning to think more fondly of sand bars."

"But, Bill, we agreed we could never check carefully on fifty houses."

"We could check carefully on four sand bars. Remember how he said maybe there wouldn't be any shells to speak of on three of the sand bars? Can you swim?"

"Certainly. Do you think I bought that cute bathing-suit to wear in a bubble bath?"

"It might look more appropriate in one. Okay, we dive for shells tomorrow."

We bought a chart of the beach area, then returned to the real-estate office and explained that we wanted to inquire for Mr. Lawrence at houses facing the four sand bars. That gave me an excuse to mark the locations of the sand bars on my chart. After that I made arrangements at the boatyard to use a cabin cruiser that my boss, Joe Baldwin, had said I could borrow, and finally we went to a sporting-goods store and bought a couple of diving goggles.

We were walking along the main street, after completing our errands, feeling much more hopeful than we had any right to be, when we were hailed by the Chief of Police.

"Just the people I'm after," he said, with an unfortunate choice of words. "Let's have a Coke or something. I have something to go over with you." He ushered us into the drugstore where, two days earlier, he had almost caught Valerie wearing the notorious gray suede pumps. I wished he would pick his words and his drugstores with more regard for our feelings. "First," he said, settling himself in a booth, "I had a wire from the FBI saying the test bullet I shot from that thirty-two-caliber automatic matches the murder bullets."

Valerie said huskily, "There isn't any doubt?"

"Not a bit. That keeps things nice and simple. I ought to be able to clean this business up in a day or two, and then you people can relax."

"I can hardly wait," I said.

"Yeah, sure, I know how you feel. Now let me tell you about those sketches you made. Mighty helpful, Stuart. Know where that girl went after she got her new outfit? To the railroad station."

Under cover of the table, Valerie's fingers tightened on mine. She said, "That means she left town, doesn't it?"

Her wistful suggestion had no effect on the Chief. She might just as well have tried to stop a steam roller by tossing a posy in its path. "Mrs. Stuart," he said, "you don't understand how this girl's mind works. First place, we know she didn't leave town that morning. The envelopes in which she sent the money to pay for the things she swiped were mailed at a downtown box between the two- and four-o'clock collections that afternoon. Nope. She either went to the railroad station to make me think she'd left town, in case I trailed her that far, or—can you guess?"

I said feverishly, "That reminds me of the Russian who said, 'Ivan tells me he's going to Omsk so I'll think he's going to Tomsk when all the time he's going to Omsk.' Maybe she gave you the idea that she was going to catch a train so you'd think she wasn't going to catch a train when all the time she was going to catch a train. She could have asked a porter to mail those letters."

"I got no interest in how the Russian mind works, Stuart. This is America. If you can't make a guess, I'll tell you. Maybe she went to the station to meet somebody coming in on the eleven-o'clock train."

I felt slightly relieved. His theory was far enough away from the truth to be harmless. I decided to encourage him, "Maybe you have something there," I said. "If a friend of hers came in on the train, that would account for her being able to get money and a place to stay."

"Uh-huh. And that brings me to the point where you can help. So far I haven't found anyone who saw her leave the station. They look at those sketches you made and can't quite make up their minds whether they saw the girl or not. That's because the face you sketched is so vague. I need a real sharp job done on the face."

"I've already done the best I can."

"I don't know. Once last night when you were working on the face it started to look like a real person, but after you finished it was blah. Not that I blame you. You didn't have enough to work from. What you need is a real live model, like artists always use. Right, Mrs. Stuart?"

Valerie let out a squeak that seemed to satisfy him.

A waitress brought coffee and Cokes, and I tried to dampen the inside of my throat, which felt like a wool sock. "Where," I said hoarsely, "would I get a live model?"

"Right here in this drugstore."

The wool sock in my throat began to suffer from shrinkage. "I don't understand."

"This is the idea, Stuart. The people at the Civic Center and shoe store and La Mode Hat Shop are not artists, see? They can't sketch me a chin that's like hers, or eyes or nose or mouth. But if they had some examples to pick from, we could maybe put together the right set of features." He unfolded a sheet of paper and brought out a pencil. "Here you are," he said coaxingly. "There are half a dozen good-looking girls in here right now you can use as models. You draw me a bunch of real chins and noses and eyes and lips, and I'll take them around and let people pick which ones come closest to the way Valerie Wilson looks. Start with that cute kid making a sundae back of the counter."

Under the table Valerie twisted the fingers of my left hand into pretzel shapes. "Go ahead, Bill," she said.

I went to work. The Chief was alert, as usual, and complained whenever my sketches weren't accurate enough. I did a collection of six different chins.

"Very nice," the Chief said. "Just for luck, add Mrs. Stuart's chin to that bunch, will you?"

"That's going too far," I cried. "I won't have my wife—"

"Now, now," he said soothingly. "Don't get upset. There's nothing in that belief criminals look different from other people. It might happen that the Wilson girl has a chin like Mrs. Stuart's. Nothing wrong with that. Do you mind, Mrs. Stuart?"

She tilted her chin up bravely and said, "I don't mind at all. Sometimes I think Bill isn't quite as anxious as he should be to see you catch that girl."

"Yeah, I thought that a couple of times," the Chief said. "Not," he added tactfully, "that I think your husband fell for her or anything like that, but he's too softhearted. Well, come on, Stuart. We're both against you."

I sketched her chin. The Chief watched my pencil like a Florida real-estate promoter getting a signature on the dotted line. I didn't dare try any tricks. Our only protection now was the fact that the Chief's mind was much too sane and orderly to suspect that Valerie Wilson and Mrs. William J. Stuart were the same. But our protection was horribly flimsy. A thoughtless word or action might bring the unthinkable idea into his head. That would be curtains for us. So I drew Valerie's chin with photographic accuracy, and the Chief was pleased.

Of course after that I knew he would want her eyes and nose and mouth sketched, when the time came. I didn't care to have her features lined up at the bottom of the page, because if the Chief's jury voted for several of her features the Chief would remember who was the model. To avoid that, I scattered my sketches of her eyes and nose and lips around the page. It was an odd feeling to look into her grave brown eyes and draw them, knowing that it might be just the clue the Chief needed, and to watch her lips smiling at me while I sketched them. I didn't understand how she could smile at a guy who had done the things to her that I had.

I completed the job finally and pushed the paper across the table to the Chief. "Take it away," I growled. "It gives me the creeps to see all those eyes and noses and things floating in space. You won't get anywhere with it."

"I don't know. It may give that Wilson girl the creeps. Now there's just one little thing more."

"You always have one little thing more."

"It will only take you a moment," he crooned, bringing out the full-length sketch. "The consensus," he said, "is you made the hips a little too big. Take off a couple inches, will you?"

I obeyed mechanically, like a member of a chain gang.

The Chief didn't stay long after that. He asked how we were doing with my sketch of the mystery man, and didn't think highly of our program for investigating sand bars the next day. He asked us to stay home that evening, so he could show me how his art jury voted and get an accurate sketch of the girl's face. Then he left.

Valerie murmured, "Remind me not to marry an artist."

"Yes," I said, "I certainly landed you in an awful mess."

"I was joking, Bill. I dragged you into the mess, remember?" She giggled, with a touch of hysteria, and said, "I'm glad you took those extra inches off my hips. Just think, if they catch me those sketches will probably be published all over the country and you'll be famous, and pictures you do from then on will be in terrific demand."

"You mean those pictures I do showing sunrise through a barred window?"

"Do you think it's that bad, Bill? And would it help if I went somewhere else?"

"Do you want to?"

An odd change came over her face. A few minutes earlier, when I had been making sketches that might send her to jail, her chin had tilted up and she had smiled. Now her chin quivered and her smile wilted at the corners. "I don't want to," she whispered.

For some reason that upset me. I said harshly, "Maybe you ought to think it over. How do you know that the Chief won't come around tonight and point out the sketches I made of your chin and nose and eyes and mouth and tell me to draw a face with those features? How do you know I won't go to pieces? How do you know I won't turn rat the way Al says I will?"

"Bill, are you saying those things because you're angry with me?"

"I'm not angry with you! I'm sore at myself because I don't know how I'll act in a spot like that."

Her chin stopped quivering and she said in a surprisingly calm voice, "If that's all that's bothering you, you can stop worrying right now. I know how you'll act."

"I wish you'd let me in on the secret. I don't have any idea how to handle it."

"You'll think of something. You always do. And it may not come to that after all. Do you think there's much chance people will pick my features?"

"I don't know. I never heard of anybody trying to piece together a face that way. What worries me is I did your features better than any of the others. I was afraid not to, with that fiend watching me. Maybe they'll choose your nose, for example, because it's better drawn than the others."

She said lightly, "It also happens to be a better nose. Let's leave before the Chief comes back with some more cunning ideas, shall we?"

When we returned home Valerie said we ought to tell Al about our plans for the next day. He had given us the number of the telephone in the place he had rented, so I called him and gave a report. I didn't tell him about our meeting with the Chief because I didn't want an explosion in my left ear. It was bad enough just listening to his comments about sand bars. His place was only three miles up the beach from us, and I could probably have hung up the phone and heard him perfectly. He asked if we had made arrangements with the Chief to lend us Davidson or anybody. I said no, and Al blew up again. He said he didn't have anything better to do than play nursemaid for us and that he would go along on the boat to make sure we didn't run into trouble. I arranged to pick him up the next morning at the new fishing-pier on the beach.

After that was settled, I wandered around the house in a slight coma, thinking about what might happen when the Chief visited us later in the evening. Valerie began cooking dinner. I said I didn't want dinner and Valerie said she really didn't either but that we had to eat to keep up our strength. So we had dinner and Valerie kept up her strength and acquired what was left of mine. It was amazing how nothing affected her appetite. Afterward I went into the living-room and tried to relax, but none of the chairs had edges that were really comfortable to sit on, and I decided that it might help pass the time to clean some of my shells.

I prepared a solution of water and a commercial bleach, and dropped my uncleaned shells into it. Valerie began asking questions. I explained that few shells look their best in a natural state; you have to soak them in a bleach to remove some of the surface discoloration, and then use muriatic acid to cut off the crust hiding the natural color and markings. I took a heart cockle and a spotted clam and a lion's paw that I had previously bleached and showed her how acid brought out their hidden beauty. Her interest was stimulating and I even began to wonder if, with proper encouragement, she might turn into a real sheller. I became so interested in teaching her that I forgot my worries. At nine o'clock the doorbell reminded me of them. It made a whirring noise like a big Glades rattler and I jumped a foot.

When I opened the door the Chief marched in as if leading a parade. "The vote's in," he said. "Now let's see what she looks like."

I glanced at the sheet of paper filled with the disembodied chins and eyes and noses and lips. There were check marks beside some of the sketches. As I studied the things my stomach began to do loops and roll-overs. The jury hadn't brought in a unanimous verdict, but it had done all right. If I followed the vote, we could trade in the guard outside the house for a turnkey. I didn't believe that the jurors had recognized Valerie's features in every case; I thought they had been influenced by the fact that her features were drawn better than the others. But that was no defense. I couldn't explain it to the Chief without putting the unthinkable idea into his head.

I dropped the sketches on the living-room table and said, "I'll ask my wife where she put my drawing stuff." I went into the kitchen and told Valerie, "The Chief hit the jackpot. Get my car keys and beat it. I'll stall as long as I can."

She held a shell that she had been drying up to the light, and said, "They do have lovely colors, don't they? And why should I run and leave you holding the fort?"

"It won't help if both of us are arrested. Come on. Hurry."

"Did everybody vote for me, Bill?"

"It's unanimous for your eyes and nose. Two votes to one for your mouth. One and a half for your chin, with the opposition splitting the other one and a half votes."

"I do have lovely eyes, don't I? I'm not going."

"Don't be stupid! I can't handle this."

"Of course you can. Remember that the pen is mightier than the sword."

"Unfortunately he doesn't have a sword," I snapped. "He has a thirty-eight-caliber revolver."

Valerie giggled and went into the living-room. I followed with dragging feet, picking my drawing stuff from the dining-room sideboard and carrying it to the table in the living-room. I sat down and took a fresh sheet of drawing-paper and sketched the outline of a girl's head.

The Chief leaned over the back of my chair, breathing like a locomotive getting up steam. "Don't forget to copy the hair exactly from that other sketch," he said.

"I will. And sit down somewhere, will you? Makes me nervous to have people crouching over me."

He grumbled but sat down across the table. After I finished he would undoubtedly make sure that I had copied the winning features accurately. Behind him, Valerie perched on the arm of a chair and swung her legs. She had lovely legs. She saw me looking at them and tilted an eyebrow at me and pulled up her skirt an eighth of an inch. I couldn't help grinning. She was the most charming idiot I had ever met. Somehow the incident gave me confidence, and an idea crept shyly into my head and I went to work.

Twenty minutes later I shoved the completed sketch across the table. The Chief pounced on it. I sat back and watched with grim pleasure as blood scorched into his face. He gave me a nasty look, grabbed the sheet containing the sample features. He made careful comparisons. Finally he looked at me again. He couldn't have been madder if someone had ripped out his parking-meters and installed slot machines.

I said, "Copied them exactly, didn't I? Put a micrometer on them if you don't think so. I told you it wouldn't work."

"What's the idea?" he said hoarsely. "What's the idea, Stuart?"

Valerie sidled up to the table and looked at the sketch, then fled to the sofa. She curled herself up tightly and clamped a hand over her mouth and shook with silent hysterics.

"Hideous, isn't it?" I said.

"It's not a person at all, Stuart. It's a zombie! If you ever met a girl like this on the beach your feet would only touch every other sand dune getting away! What did you do to this?"

I pulled the sketch back to my side of the table and looked at the face admiringly. The eyes were as huge and dazzling as the ones Salvador Dali sometimes puts in his surrealist paintings. The tiny nose looked as if it might wander forlornly away at any moment. Under the nose were large and fiercely luscious lips, and below them drooped a small tired chin. I was pleased with the effect. I had merely transferred the sample features to the face without bringing them into proportion, and added a few shadings to emphasize the result.

I said, "You admit I copied the features exactly, don't you?"

"But you didn't make them come out right! You got to make the eyes and mouth smaller and the nose and chin bigger!"

I brought out my best brand of artistic double talk. "I can't do that," I said loftily. "A face is an esthetic unity. It is a synthesis of flesh tones and features and curves and planes, all interrelated and adding values to each other. You can't hand me a nose and pair of eyes and mouth and chin and tell me to make a real face out of them. Where is the synthesis, the unity, the interrelation of shadows and flesh tones and curves and planes? Where are the subtle values that each feature gives to the others?"

The Chief said in a dazed voice, "They sure aren't here."

"Well, I told you it wouldn't work."

He said pleadingly, "I don't follow all that art talk. But can't you do something to this?"

"Sure," I said. I drew a neat mustache on the nightmare face. "I am noted," I said, "for my work on posters in the New York subways."

The Chief made a strangled sound, and crumpled the sketch and threw it across the room. He turned to Valerie, who managed to snap out of her hysterics in time. "Mrs. Stuart," he said earnestly, "I appeal to you."

"Yes?" she said in a choked voice.

"Mrs. Stuart, I haven't wanted to mention this. I hate to give you any cause for worry, but I don't think your husband is co-operating. The reason is this Wilson girl. She made an impression on him, and I have a hunch he doesn't want her arrested."

Valerie stared at me solemnly. "Bill," she said, "is that true?"

"Of course not. She doesn't mean a thing to me."

The Chief said, "Mrs. Stuart, will you do me a favor? Will you work on your husband about this? I'm sure he'll co-operate better if you work on him."

"Indeed I will," Valerie said.

The Chief gathered his two original sketches. "And don't think this business is a joking matter," he told me angrily. "It happens there was a prowler around here last night, and whoever it was saw Lawson on guard and ran. Think that over, Stuart. Good night." He gave me a long, hard look, and left the house.

Valerie retrieved the crumpled sketch. She smoothed the paper and said in an awed tone, "I've never appreciated you properly. You did a fiendish thing to the poor man."

"People can only push me so far," I said. "Then I either get mad or fall down. Fortunately in this case I got mad."

"You were wonderful. I said you could handle it."

"You must enjoy betting on long shots. I didn't have an idea until I started sketching."

She said lightly, "Is it true that this Wilson girl made an impression on you?"

I studied the bland expression on her face and wondered what was going on in her busy little brain. Any number of thoughts might have prompted her question. It was safest to assume, however, that she had a lazy feline urge to twine around my ankles for a few moments and then hone her claws delicately in me. I wasn't the only person in the room with a talent for fiendish tricks. I said, "Indeed she did make an impression on me. I still have the marks of her gray suede pumps up and down my back."

"Umm," she said, looking at me thoughtfully. Apparently my ankles were moving around too fast for her. "Let's take a stroll in the garden," she suggested.

"What for? I've given up walking in gardens at night and meeting girls who have nice low husky voices and tantalizing laughs. It leads to trouble."

"You're a suspicious creature. I just want to see who's on guard and find out if he knows any more about that prowler the Chief mentioned."

"In that case," I said, "okay."

We went outside and found our old friend Davidson on the early shift. He didn't know much more than what the Chief had told us; in the early morning hours Officer Lawson had seen a shadowy figure approaching the house. Lawson tried to sneak up on the prowler but stumbled over a fallen palm frond and the shadow vanished. Lawson searched the grounds, but merely found footprints where a man had jumped from the seawall onto the beach.

"Don't worry about it," Davidson said. "Nobody's gonna get away with that tonight. We have orders now to call out if we see anyone, and if the person starts running we shoot."

"Please make sure it isn't one of us," I said.

"Oh, I'll make sure. Are you and Mrs. Stuart going to be outside very long?"

"We'll just stroll around for a few minutes," Valerie said.

Davidson sighed. "It's a swell night to be out with a girl," he said. "I have to keep an eye on you two while you're outside, to make sure nothing happens. But if you were looking at the stars or something and, well, I know how a guy can feel, Mr. Stuart, and what I mean is if you feel romantic I'll look the other way."

Valerie laughed softly, and I said, "Thanks," in an embarrassed tone. We strolled away to look at the place where the prowler had jumped down from the seawall. There was nothing to see but a couple of hollows in the sand. We stood there silently for a few minutes. The beach was a veil of misty tulle edged with the sequin glitter of the Gulf. Palm fronds swayed against the sky like huge Oriental fans. There was fragrance in the air that might come from oleanders or jasmine or from the girl standing beside me. A mockingbird sent his incredible notes swooping and tumbling through the garden. I wished Davidson hadn't put ideas into my head.

Valerie murmured, "The stars are making quite a night of it, aren't they? I've never seen so many millions of them."

I took a deep breath and said, "You can't possibly see millions. With the naked eye you can only see about thirty-five hundred stars at one time."

"Do you have to be so practical, Bill?"

"Yes," I muttered.

"What a shame. Think how disappointed Officer Davidson will be."

"What do you mean?"

"He thinks we're a young married couple and he expects us to act romantic. Do you think it will make him suspicious when we're not romantic?"

My heart started beating out a jungle rhythm.

"I don't know," I said huskily. "We might be taking a chance."

Her slim body swayed toward me. "Why take a chance?"

I caught her in my arms and gasped, "Of course, this is just for his benefit."

"Of course, darling."

Her body tightened against mine and her lips were warm and soft in the darkness and I felt her long slender legs trembling against mine and my heart rattled up and down my ribs like a stick on a picket fence and skyrockets whished and flared in my head. Davidson should have been very happy.

She drew back finally and said in a weak voice, "Don't forget you can only see thirty-five hundred stars with the naked eye."

"I was wrong. I can see millions of them."

"Bill, please! We're only playing house, remember?"

"Sorry," I mumbled. "You're right." Then I grinned and said, "But don't you think Davidson might still be just a little suspicious?"

"Maybe just a little," she sighed, and came back into my arms.

For the next few moments I forgot our troubles, and had fantastic dreams of what the future might be like. It was just as well that I couldn't look ahead, because the next day wasn't going to bring me any more moments like that. And if I had wanted a prophetic dream of the future I should have ordered myself a nightmare.

Chapter Twelve: DIVING INTO DANGER

The next day got off to an unpleasant start about 3 a.m. with target practice under my window. Valerie and I caromed into each other in the hall and rushed downstairs. Clark, who was on duty, gave us a depressing report. He had seen somebody outside the kitchen door. When he called a challenge, the shadowy figure whirled and shot twice at him. Clark made a dive for cover before shooting back. That gave the prowler a chance to run. Clark sent a couple of slugs at a dim form flitting away through the shrubbery, but didn't score. After telling us what had happened, he phoned in a report, and reinforcements came out and searched the neighborhood. All they found was the mark of a jimmy on the edge of the kitchen door.

I went back to bed finally to catch up on my insomnia. I couldn't have been more restless if I had spent the rest of the night being tossed in a blanket. Things were getting out of hand. The Chief was moving in on us from one side and Champ Lane, who might have imported a few thugs, was crowding us on the other. Unless we did something fast, we had the future of a nut in a nutcracker.

At breakfast Valerie didn't seem at all like the girl I had held in my arms such a short time ago. She kept up a bright, impersonal flow of talk, as if we were strangers who had just met at a cocktail party. We packed a picnic lunch, collected towels and bathing-suits and the diving-goggles, and drove to the boat yard. The dockmaster had the cabin cruiser ready for us. He checked over the controls with me to make sure I could handle the boat and gave me some pointers on following the channel that led to the Gulf. When he heard we were going to dive for shells, he lent me a couple of gadgets he used in dragging for scallops, a glass-bottomed bucket for looking down into the water, and an iron contraption like a clam rake that could be attached to ropes and towed slowly over the bottom.

We cruised through the narrow inland channels and out the pass at the southern end of Gulf City's beach and up the shoreline. We slid by the isolated group of cottages where Eddie Patrono had been murdered and the deserted beach where I had crashed into the gray sedan, and rounded the headland marking the beginning of the main beach residential section. A solitary figure waved to us from the new fishing-pier, and we swung in and picked up Al Leonard. Valerie told him about our latest troubles with the Chief of Police, and about the shooting early that morning. That gave Al a chance to run through his list of synonyms for the word "idiot"; he hadn't learned any new ones since the last time he talked to me.

I showed him how to handle the boat, then took my chart and went forward to look for the first sand bar. It made a lemon-colored streak against the green of deeper water. It was one of the three big sand bars marked on my chart. I rigged up buoys with fishing line and sinkers and kapok seat cushions to mark its outline. We studied the bottom through the glass-bottomed bucket without seeing anything of interest. Then we attached ropes to the scallop drag and hauled it back and forth over the area. We brought up two empty clam shells, some seaweed, and an irritated crab.

That didn't prove the sand bar was really barren, so we anchored and prepared to do some diving. Valerie went into the cabin first to change into her bathing-suit. When she came back I wondered if she had forgotten something—her bathing-suit, for example—but it turned out that she was wearing one. It was a strapless two-piece job that fit her lovely body like suntan.

Al said, "Wear that at the trial and they'll never convict you, baby."

"Not," I said, "unless there are women on the jury."

Al and I got into our bathing-suits. He had the build of a good fast light-heavyweight, and he posed around in his bathing-trunks as if he were weighing in for a crack at the title. I had to admit that he and Valerie were a handsome couple; I ought to revise my Caribbean travel ad to include Al, because it would give women readers the notion that they too, like Valerie, would meet a guy with dark and dangerous good looks on their cruise. I wondered where I fit into the tropical-cruise picture. Perhaps I could use myself in an illustration captioned *How to Abandon Ship.*

It gave me some pleasure to discover that Al was strictly a beach-and-deck athlete. He could stay afloat, but he was clumsy in the water and swam as if trying to slug somebody into the ropes. As a result, Valerie and I used the goggles and did all the diving. Al was in a playful mood and spent his time trying to romp with Valerie and to start water fights. That delayed our work, and by the time we finished a fruitless survey of the sand bar we had to pause for lunch. After eating we cruised north and located the second big sand bar and spent a couple of hours working over it, without result. It was late afternoon when we reached the third sand bar, which happened to be the small one located off a relatively undeveloped stretch of beach. I only saw one small cottage ashore, half hidden by a green froth of palms. Because it was getting late and the sand bar was so small I decided that we could save time by diving at once, instead of dragging it first.

When I announced that program, Al said, "Look, pal, we already had a nice swim today and you've had fun trying to pick up more shells for your collection, so do we have to play this game any more? It's late."

"I haven't been trying to get shells for my collection," I snapped. "I've been trying to find where Champ Lane lives."

Valerie said, "Of course, I'm willing to go on trying, Bill, but it does seem hopeless. We haven't even found one good shell."

"I know all the arguments against us," I said. "But that isn't going to stop me from checking all the sand bars."

I switched off the engine and let the boat drift toward the spot where I wanted to anchor. Al went below and came up with a towel in his hand. He followed me to the bow, watched me pick up the anchor.

"I still don't understand," he said, "what you'd do if you stumbled across Lane. Suppose the guy swam out here and sneaked aboard and pointed one of these things at you?" He spoke so quietly that for a moment I didn't realize he was working up to another grim practical joke. Then I got the idea. He had dropped the towel. Under it he had been hiding a revolver. It was pointing at my stomach. "What would you do, huh?" he said. "Defend yourself with that anchor?"

I looked at the anchor in my hand, and at Al's feet. He didn't know very much about boats. Nobody who knows boats will stand inside a coil of an anchor rope that is about to be released. I hated to do this to him, but I was fed up with his jokes. "What would I do?" I said mildly. "I'd just drop the anchor overboard."

I dropped it. Rope hissed into the water and the coil locked around Al's ankle and he gave a startled yell and went overboard.

The moment it happened I was sorry. An anchor rope can be as nasty to wrestle with under water as an octopus, especially if you don't start out with a lungful of air. Al had used up his breath yelling. I didn't waste any time. I jerked the rope off its cleat and dove in after him. Below me Al was flopping in the apple-green water like a big, pale frog. His struggles were merely taking up the slack in the anchor rope and keeping the loop tight around his ankle. He was already in bad shape. I yanked the upper end of the anchor rope, got some slack, dragged the loop off his ankle, and hauled him to the surface. He had just enough strength left to hang onto the side of the boat. I climbed aboard and with Valerie's help pulled him into the cockpit. He coughed and choked for a minute.

"Great stuff, pal," he said finally. "Trying to drown me?"

Valerie said, "Bill didn't know you were standing in a coil of the anchor rope."

"I knew it," I muttered, "but I didn't stop to think what might happen."

"Oh, Bill!" she said reproachfully.

"He was playing one of his lousy jokes on me," I said. "Like the time in the drugstore when he grabbed my shoulder and said, 'Gotcha!' and the time he pretended he was Lane and yanked me into his cottage. He pulled a gun on me, up at the bow, and said what would I do if Lane pointed one at me."

"It was just a gag," Al said. "You didn't have to get sore."

"Well, what I did was just a gag, too, and you don't have to get sore."

"Where did you put my gun?"

"I didn't put it anywhere. You dropped it overboard."

"You mean my gun's in the water?" Al cried. "Listen, they don't give those things away for box tops! And what happens if we run across Lane when I don't have a gun?"

I told him we'd try to find it, and we spent half an hour diving for the thing. Unfortunately I had dropped the anchor before we were squarely over the bar, and the boat had swung around on the anchor rope. That forced us to search a big area that included several spots too deep for diving. We didn't find the gun. By the time we gave up it was five o'clock. Al wanted to quit and go home; he seemed to feel undressed without his revolver. I insisted on staying a little longer to look for shells, and moved the boat into a better position over the bar.

Valerie and I began diving. Al made a couple of tries and then merely floated around on top of the water, glaring at me every time I popped up. Apparently he wasn't going to forget what I had done to him. I didn't realize, however, that he was waiting for a chance to pay me back. I came up after a dive and found him right beside me.

"Now let's see how you like it," he snapped, and grabbed me.

Probably he thought I wouldn't have time to catch my breath. I did, though. I gulped a lungful of air and went limp and let him clamp on a headlock and push me under the surface. Perhaps he forgot that if two people start wrestling in the water both of them go down. Maybe he was counting too much on the fact that I'm not a champion swimmer and look as if I'd have trouble wrestling my way out of an undershirt. He didn't know that I have one aquatic talent—I can hold my breath under water for more than two minutes. So I relaxed and sank, and Al sank with me.

On land, he would have tossed me around as if shaking dust out of a rag, but it's not easy to shake out a rag under water. He worked hard on me for about fifteen seconds. I waited quietly and let him burn oxygen. At the twenty-second mark he began to weaken. At twenty-five seconds he let me go and tried to reach the surface. I hooked my fingers in his bathing-trunks and sculled toward the bottom. At thirty seconds he forgot all about headlocks and flying mares and half nelsons, and clawed wildly at me. He grabbed me in a front strangle hold. I bent his fingers, broke the grip, and swung him around facing away from me. In a few more seconds bubbles gushed in a silver fountain from his mouth and he went limp. I towed him to the surface.

Valerie swam up to me and gasped, "Oh, Bill, not again!"

"He decided to hold me under water and—"

"But, Bill, do you always half drown people when they scuffle with you in the water? What's come over you? You've never acted like this before."

"All right, it's my fault," I snapped. "I always go berserk in the water. It's because I was bitten once by a rabid shark."

She looked at me as if I had slapped her, and didn't say anything more. We towed Al to the boat. The process of hauling him aboard forced water from his lungs and stomach, and in a few minutes he was able to sit up. He stared at me with cold glazed eyes.

"Too bad I lost the gun," he said. "You could have saved time and shot me."

"I'm sorry it happened. If you'll just stop jumping me—"

"Pal, I will sit here and be quiet as a mouse. Can we go home now? All you're bringing up from this sand bar is my body."

Valerie said hesitantly, "I found something on my last dive." She picked up a lettered olive shell and explained, "I saw a funny little ridge in the sand, and scooped this out. It's alive. So do you think we ought to stay a while?"

"Live shells don't mean anything," I said. "Only empty ones that have been washed up on the bar."

"How about this one, then?" she asked, showing me an empty cardita.

"Might be a good sign, might not."

"I found it off there," she said, pointing to a spot about thirty feet away. "I thought I saw a couple of others, too."

I said to Al, "Okay with you if we try it?"

"Sure, go ahead. I'll stay in the boat just to play safe."

Valerie said, "You could use the glass-bottomed bucket and tell us if you see anything on the bottom."

"It's an idea," Al said.

I moved the boat to the spot Valerie indicated, and dropped anchor. In the meantime Al had been dressing in the cabin. He came up and leaned over the side and studied the bottom through the glass-bottomed bucket.

"Something right down beside the boat," he said. "Might be a shell."

Valerie and I climbed onto the stern transom and plunged in. She hit the water a split second ahead of me and I had a glimpse of her slim body, inlaid with pearly bubbles, sliding down into pale green shadows and vanishing. I wondered if she would vanish from my life just as quickly and completely. It seemed likely. None of my ideas for helping her were any good, and my scuffles with Al had made her think I was meaner to handle than a catfish.

I tried to forget about it, and swam around near the bottom looking for whatever Al had seen. The slanting light was no longer much good for working at a depth of eight to ten feet. I couldn't spot anything but a starfish writhing jerkily over the sand. I looked up to check my position. Above me the surface glittered like the silver backing of a mirror, with a break where the dull red hull of the cruiser wedged down into it. Beside the boat hung a huge pale eye, watching me. For a moment I was startled; then I realized that it was merely the glass bottom of the bucket. I pushed up from the bottom and broke water near the boat.

"Couldn't find anything," I said.

"Right down under me," Al said.

I nodded, did some force-breathing to pile up oxygen, and went under. As I swam down I thought about the way Al had stared at me. His cold, black eyes couldn't have looked nastier if they had been peering at me over revolver sights. I didn't like it. He hadn't forgiven me for the anchor rope incident, and now he had another score to settle, too. I made a turn in the water, stared up. The big pale eye of the bucket watched me. It looked cold and inhuman, like the eye of a giant squid. I didn't think I would come up right beside that bucket. In fact—

My body chilled as if I had hit ice water. An idea prowled into my head. An unthinkable idea. The sort of idea I had been hoping that the Chief of Police would never get about Valerie. Now I had one—about Al. I tried to shove it out of my head. It wouldn't budge. The trouble with unthinkable ideas was that they began to seem horribly logical the moment you got them. I paddled in what I hoped was a casual way along the bottom until the curve of the boat's hull hid me, then swam forward and eased up to the surface and crawled quietly aboard the cruiser at the bow.

Back in the cockpit, Al said, "Right below me, baby," and water rustled as Valerie made a surface dive.

I crept back along the port side. Al was bending over the starboard gunwale, peering down into the water like a big sleek cat crouched over a goldfish bowl. I shivered. If my idea was right, we had been playing tag all afternoon with murder.

I lowered myself inch by inch into the cockpit. My muscles were dead as old rubber bands and felt as if they might let me drop at any moment. My toes touched planking. Al's back was only a few feet away. I tried not to breathe, but my lungs weren't in the two-minute league any more. If Al hadn't been concentrating so hard he would have heard the hiss of air in my throat. I groped quietly below the port gunwale, remembering that a gaff was clamped there—a big gaff with a three-foot metal handle and a wide sharp hook, the kind used for boating tarpon. My fingers touched metal, eased it from the holder. Al leaned farther out, staring into the water. Muscles twitched like snakes in his right arm. Valerie must be coming up. He tensed. His right hand flicked into view, the fingers gripping something short and dark and limber. It could be a blackjack.

His hand poised for a second. The gaff made a sheet-lightning glitter in the air. The shaft smacked his arm. The small dark object flew out of his numbed fingers, splashed out of sight. He whirled around and faced me. Against his white face the stubble of beard looked like pin feathers on a dead duck. Beyond him in the water Valerie stared in horror at us. Al froze, the bright point of the gaff an inch from his throat.

"Don't move," I said. "I'll rip your throat out."

Al gulped. If he could have seen how close that brought his larynx to the needle point he wouldn't have done it. "Guy's gone bats," he said hoarsely. "Talk him out of it, Valerie."

"Bill!" she cried. "Bill, what's the matter? Please—"

"Shut up," I said. "Climb aboard. And don't get in my way. He tried to blackjack you."

"Gone crazy," Al said.

"I saw it in your hand."

"Hunk of driftwood. She was coming up under it. I yanked it out of her way. Take a look and you'll see it."

"I'd rather watch your throat."

"Don't be scared, pal. You broke my arm." He lifted his voice as he heard Valerie climbing aboard. "Hear that, baby? He broke my arm. Call him off."

Out of the corner of my eye I saw Valerie moving toward me. "Don't touch me," I said. "So help me, I'll let him have it just to be on the safe side. He tried to blackjack you. He was going to smack me, too, but I came up behind him instead of in front."

"Hunk of driftwood," Al said. "Just getting it out of your way."

"Bill, please. Look at the shell I found."

"Don't humor me," I said. "I'm not crazy. In fact I just started to get some sense. Al's working with Lane. He's out to kill us."

"It's impossible!" she cried. "It can't—"

"Sure," I said. "Impossible. It's been right under our noses all the time and it was so impossible we never thought of it. Like the Chief not being able to think that Valerie Wilson and you are the same person. Impossible like that."

Al said, "I sell out Lane to the Committee of Thirty and get busted to the city stables so I'm working for Lane."

"I'll prove it with his own words," I said. "Remember him talking about how big-time cops operate? Remember System Number One? Quote, you get a pigeon to tip you off what you want to know, unquote. Lane needed a pigeon the Committee would trust. Al is it. Did he ever give that Committee any really hot dope? Or was it just minor stuff that didn't really matter?"

Valerie said breathlessly, "You're wrong, Bill. I don't know what Al told the Committee or the Special Grand Jury, but they trusted him completely."

"Yeah. So the cleanup didn't work and Lane got away."

"Yeah," Al said, "and so Lane's crowd busted me as a reward, and I keep right on working for Lane. Get that hook away from him, baby. I've seen these nuts before. He'll use it on me."

"You're not kidding," I said. "Think a minute, Valerie. Who tipped Lane you were down here?"

"Nobody tipped him," Al said. "He happened to walk to the cottage that night and saw her with Eddie and knew what that meant."

"Who was on the job right after the murder? Al was. You think that was chance?"

Al said, "I got the assignment from the Committee at two a.m. the day of the murder. I had to wait until ten that morning to get my leave okayed. I caught the first plane down here, got in at six, checked in at a hotel, couldn't locate Valerie, decided to see what the local cops were like. I can prove where I was every second."

"Can you prove Lane didn't know where you were staying? Can you prove he didn't phone you after trailing us downtown that night? Can you prove you didn't hop right over to the police station to see why I had gone there?"

"I can prove you're crazy."

"Valerie," I said, "you mentioned once that when you returned to your hotel that night you saw the gray sedan, and so you stayed outside. But that was before the cops knew where you lived. Before anyone in town knew except Al. So how did the guy in the gray sedan locate you?"

"But, Bill, I didn't actually see that car! I only thought perhaps I did. I could have imagined it."

"Maybe your imagination is as accurate as mine. You remember everyone said I was imagining a gray sedan following me. Who was right?"

"You were, Bill, but—"

Al said, "If I was working against her, I could have tipped off the local cops."

"And then," I said, "they arrest her and she tells them about Lane. No. You had a quieter way to handle things."

"Why did I go out of my way to protect her, then? Why did I wipe off all her fingerprints I could find at the cottage and—"

"Up to a point you had to protect her. You didn't want her caught. But I don't go for that fingerprint stuff. Enough prints were left to pin it on her. And who invited us out that afternoon to hunt for the murder gun?"

Valerie said, "Al had to find a way to talk to me alone."

"Maybe he also wanted a chance to plant that gun where you'd stumble on it. He wasn't far from where you found it. Lane used the gun and wiped off his prints and wanted yours on the thing. Al knew you'd pick up the gun and try to hide it."

Al gave a flat laugh. "Did I know a guy named Stuart would catch her hiding it and turn it in?"

"That was a break for you, wasn't it? But it didn't mean much. You were hidden in the bushes, watching. One way or another you'd have made sure the cops found it. And look, Valerie, who else but Al and the local cops knew we were alone at the cottage after they left? Who tipped off Lane about that? Who came out in the gray sedan to nail us? Lane or Al? Or was it both?"

"I was with the Chief," Al said. "I can prove it."

"Can you prove you didn't sneak away to telephone?"

"We're back again to me proving you're crazy. How did Lane learn you were out there alone? Simple. He's keeping an eye on the setup from somewhere down the road. He sees the police cars heading back to town. Your car doesn't come along. He tails the police cars part of the way downtown to make sure they aren't coming back. He waits until dark, then drives toward the cottage. He sees your convertible. The top's down; he flicks his spotlight in and sees that Valerie isn't with you. What's the answer? She's still out there. Give me a tougher one, pal."

"I'll grant him one thing," I said. "He didn't want to kill us if he could scare us out of town. You wouldn't be much bother from then on, Valerie. Not with a murder rap hanging over you. But we wouldn't go."

"I can't believe it!" she said. "Al could have killed us a dozen times."

"Oh, no. Not if he wanted to get away clean. Every time he's been in our house, a cop outside knew he was there. The one time we were in that place Al rented, Davidson was along. But who tried to break into our house last night?"

"Lane did," Al said scornfully.

I went on stubbornly. "Today's the first real chance he's had. He made sure we weren't taking a cop with us before he offered to come along. He suggested that we pick him up at the new fishing-pier, where nobody was likely to see him join us. I thought he was kidding when he pulled that gun on me. He wasn't. He was going to shoot us both. The beach is lonely along here. We missed that by the thickness of an anchor rope. After that he turned cautious. He doesn't like working without a gun. He didn't want to tackle us both at once; something might go wrong. He was going to drown me in the water that time, but it didn't work. So he got his blackjack. He didn't care which of us he tapped first, because he knew he could handle the other. How does that sound?"

Valerie cried, "I don't know how it sounds! I can't think, you've made me so dizzy. But I can't believe it. I—"

"Look, baby," Al said, "I can turn that whole argument around on him. Like this. He's working with Lane and this is the first chance he's had to knock me off. He doesn't want to kill you because you're a cute number and he likes the idea of owning a dame who don't dare walk out on him. He tried twice to drown me, but you were watching too close. He just missed breaking my head with that steel gadget and only broke my arm. I could say all that. But it saves time to just say he's nuts. Take your pick, baby."

"I can't," she wailed. "I've got to think!"

"Go right ahead. As long as you're thinking, Stuart won't dare let me have it."

I said, "And while you're thinking, get up the anchor and start the boat. If the anchor's too heavy, untie the rope and throw it away."

"Bill," she said faintly, "I really did find a shell. You ought to look at it."

"I wouldn't take my eyes off Al for a million bucks."

"Got him scared," Al said. "Even with a broken arm."

"Let me make a sling for his arm, Bill."

"Do what I told you," I growled. "I'll believe his broken arm when I see the X-rays. And don't jostle me as you go by. That point moves an inch and it'll be in his throat."

For a moment there was no sound but the snicker of little waves along the hull. Then I heard Valerie suck in a quivering breath and edge past me. I could imagine the way she shrank against the gunwale to avoid touching my back. Probably I looked as nice to touch as a water moccasin. In a short time I heard the anchor clunk on deck, then the whirr of the starter and mutter of the exhaust.

"Where do we go?" she asked.

"Fishing-pier," I said. "Al can swim ashore when we get there."

"With a broken arm?" Al said. "You better swim ashore with me, Valerie. We'll both be safer."

"I—I'll see when we get there," she said.

I tried to ease my muscles. I hadn't budged since Al first whirled around. Pain burned slowly up my right arm. The point of the gaff wavered slightly. Just beyond it, the big artery in Al's neck pulsed and writhed, like a worm trying to avoid the point of a fishhook. That artery was all I had seen for ten minutes. Its wriggling was making me sick. I glanced up at Al's face. His eyes looked blank and shiny.

He smiled and said, "Getting tired, pal?"

"Shut up."

"You're not going to stick me just for talking. Your arm's tired, pal. Your brain's tired."

"Shut up."

"I think you're coming out of that fit you had. You're beginning to wonder if you made a big mistake. Why don't you sit down and be sensible?"

I didn't answer. The devilish thing was that the guy was right. I was beginning to wonder. I hadn't expected that he would have such fast answers to every charge I made. And the fact that I hadn't been able to convince Valerie had shaken my confidence. After all, I didn't know what had gone on in her city. I didn't know how much help Al had given her damned Committee of Thirty. Maybe Al was on the level.

Yeah, and maybe he wasn't. I couldn't take a chance. If he was Lane's man, and if his arm wasn't broken, the only life insurance Valerie and l had was the inch separating the point of the gaff and Al's throat.

I waited motionless, listening to the endless tap of waves on the hull and the quiet snoring of the exhaust. "Valerie," I said finally, "how far to the pier?"

"We've only gone a quarter mile. The pier is several miles farther. Bill?"

"Yeah?"

"Can I at least look at Al's arm? The boat will steer itself for a minute."

"Well, go ahead. Don't get in my way, though."

Her feet pattered on the deck. I kept watching Al's throat. I couldn't see his right arm clearly. It was lying across his lap. Valerie moved into the edges of my field of vision. Her hair was a soft blur of color as she bent over his arm. I blinked. If I could look at her hair for a while, it would rest my eyes. The throbbing glitter of the gaff made them ache.

"Bill," she said, "his arm *must* be broken. You can see the bruise. Look."

I glanced down. Something flickered. I looked back at Al's throat. The gaff point wasn't there. I gazed stupidly at my right hand. Its fingers were still clenched, but now they were gripping an imaginary gaff handle. I tried to move the fingers. They didn't respond. My whole right arm was dead. I looked at Al and saw his left hand toss the gaff overboard. Then he smiled at me.

"Nobody can hold things at arm's length very long," he said pleasantly. "I been expecting your arm to drop off."

He brushed Valerie casually aside and came up from the seat and smashed a right hook into my face. It slammed me back against the stern. I sagged there and watched him dully. I licked my lips. They felt numb, too.

Al poised two steps from me. "Think of that," he said. "I hit him with a right. Dear, dear, how quickly arms knit these days." He went through an elaborate process of cocking his right fist.

Valerie flung herself on his right arm. "Stop it!" she gasped.

"I'm not gonna hurt him much," Al said. "But I can't leave a nut like him stay on his feet. Next thing he'll be at me with a boat hook or a bobby pin or something."

I shook the fog out of my head. "Valerie," I said, "get away from him.

Jump overboard. Swim ashore. Because if what I told you was right, you're next on the list."

"Don't sound so brash now, does he?" Al said. "You heard that 'if,' didn't you? Stand back, baby. I been promising myself this for a long time. I want to hear him rat again. Come on, pal, rat for the lady."

"Let him alone!" Valerie cried. "Let him—"

Al swept his right arm back almost lazily, flung her away. "That first smack was on the mouth," he said. "Maybe the nose this time."

I looked at Valerie. She was crouched against the cabin, making no effort to escape. She didn't believe me. There wasn't time to argue. A couple more socks would put me away. And then, if I was right, it would be too late for her to do anything. There was only one way to make sure she would be safe for the next few hours. I pretended to sag as Al stepped forward, then whirled and flung myself over the stern into the water.

I came up gasping, and began swimming toward shore. It wasn't far away; Valerie had cut in close to a point of land. I skipped a couple of strokes to look back. Al was shoving Valerie away from the controls. Water boiled up at the stern and the boat swung in a fast turn. He was coming after me. My dead muscles dragged me slowly through the water. The beach was a hundred feet away. I would never make it unless the cruiser grounded. Some places along the beach it would have grounded already, but here it was deeper than average. Finally my toes hit bottom. I started wading. It wasn't even as fast as swimming. The water shoaled with maddening slowness. I would never make it. The cruiser only drew two and a half feet and it was so close that the bow looked like an enormous ax blade slashing toward me.

Valerie shrieked at Al. "Let him go! Let him go or I'll think he's right and I'll jump in, too!"

For a second the boat boiled toward me. Then it swung a few points to port and the big bow wave knocked me down and the boat rushed by. I staggered up again and floundered the rest of the way to the beach. The cruiser swung around and idled back, fifty feet offshore. Al had one hand on the wheel and the other on Valerie's shoulder. I wished I knew whether that was a casual pose or whether he wanted to be ready to grab her if she tried to get away.

"What a rat," Al said. "Says I'm a killer and then jumps overboard and leaves you with me."

"Why bother with him?" Valerie said.

"I only want to tell him he'll find this crate at the pier. You hear me, rat?"

I licked my lips. Salt was stinging away the numb feeling. If I was right about Al, it might help Valerie if I played rat some more. If I was wrong, well, she wouldn't have much use for me anyway. I called hoarsely, "Look,

Al, I'm sorry I went off half cocked. I didn't think. I see now I must have sounded crazy."

"Isn't that cute?" Al said. "Sit up on your hind legs and beg and I might save you a long hike to the pier."

I backed away. "No," I said. "I don't want a lift. You might hit me again. I know you got a right to but—"

"Come on, Al," Valerie said. "I couldn't stand being in the same boat with him."

"Valerie," I said miserably, "I—"

"Stick to shells on the beach from now on," she cut in. "Quit diving. You might meet a really tough minnow. Here's a shell for your collection." Her arm whipped back and something spun through the air and skittered twice on water and hit sand near my feet.

Al rattled out a laugh, and the exhaust echoed the flat, metallic sound, and the boat leaped away. I watched until the wake faded on the darkening water. I aimed a purposeless kick at the shell Valerie had tossed ashore. Then suddenly prickles of excitement jabbed my skin and I grabbed the shell.

Maybe, at the last moment, Valerie had made her decision. Perhaps it wasn't what Al and I thought. And perhaps she knew her decision came too late to save both of us and so she set her firm chin and made sure I escaped. Maybe. Perhaps. The answer to the riddle was locked in the lion's paw shell I was holding.

The previous night Valerie had watched me cleaning shells in the kitchen. Among them had been a lion's paw. She had watched muriatic acid cut the dull red crust from the lion's paw and bring out its hidden color. The shell that now lay in my hand was a remarkable specimen, but not merely because both valves were perfect and the hinge was intact. It was remarkable for another reason. Probably it was the first lion's paw shell in history that had been brought up from a fathom and a half of water already perfectly bleached and cleaned.

That might be a crazy coincidence. Another explanation sneaked into my thoughts; it was just as crazy as the answer of coincidence, but it gave a deadly meaning to everything that had happened. Unfortunately I couldn't sell anyone that explanation without proof. I could prove it one of two ways—by going out again to the sand bar or by stopping a slug from a thirty-eight. Either way, it wouldn't take much time.

Chapter Thirteen: CORNERED

An hour later I reached a spot from which I had a good view of the fishing-pier. Sunset colors were burning on the Gulf, and against them the pier looked bleak and charred. The cabin cruiser rocked gently at the end of a mooring line. It seemed to be deserted, and Al's car was gone. I watched for a few minutes, then turned back to the Baldwin place a mile up the beach. I had no intention of working alone. The apparently deserted boat might be a trap. If my wild ideas were right, Al had let me escape only because he couldn't handle Valerie and me at the same time. But he wasn't going to wave good-by to me unless I happened to be leaving in a coffin.

I was relieved to find Davidson on duty on the grounds of the Casa del Mar; at least I didn't have to worry about a trap in the house. I telephoned the Chief of Police and said I had to have his help for a couple of hours.

"I'm busy," he said. "Take Davidson."

That didn't appeal to me. Davidson was a nice kid but too great an admirer of Al. "He's not smart enough," I said. "I need you."

"Get Al Leonard."

"Al and I had a scrap."

"You wouldn't play ball with me last night, Stuart. Why should I drop everything now for you? Might interest you to know I found out plenty today. In about two hours I ought to know where to pick up that Wilson dame. What have you on the fire any hotter than that?"

"Give me two hours and you can pick up Valerie Wilson *and* the driver of the gray sedan."

"That will be quite a trick, Stuart. On account of he's dead."

"He's what!"

"He's 'd' as in drowned, 'e' as in exit, 'a' as in all gone, 'd' as in defunct. D-e-a-d, dead."

"Where did it happen? What does he look like?"

"I guess he looks like that sketch you drew. Haven't got the body yet. Don't know we ever will. About five a.m. today a man fishing on the next island to the north saw headlights whip onto an old wooden bridge over the pass, heard a crash, no more headlights. Car went through the rail. About ten feet of water there and the tide was going out fast. Crew from the sheriff's office hauled the car out this afternoon. Nobody in it. The door was open. The driver was either dead or stunned, and got swept away by the tide. Gray sedan. Registered in the name of our other corpse, Eddie Jones. Kind of a bad-luck car."

"Maybe the accident was faked."

"Always got a different idea from me, don't you?"

I said desperately, "Whether it was faked or not, I can still take you to the key man in this whole business. You can't let me down! You used to laugh at me about the gray sedan, didn't you? Well, who was right? The only way you'll ever see Valerie Wilson is by coming with me."

He didn't answer right away. Finally he growled, "I'll pick you up in ten minutes. But this better be good."

I hung up, changed from bathing-trunks into clothes, and squinted at my face in the mirror. It wasn't very pretty. I shrugged. The thing to remember was that it hadn't been very pretty even before it met Al's knuckles.

A siren whimpered into the driveway. I ran out and climbed in the Chief's car. He peered at my face and said, "I see what you mean. You and Al had a scrap."

He seemed to be waiting for an explanation, but I merely said, "Yeah, we did." I didn't dare throw any charges at Al until I could make them stick.

"Where's Mrs. Stuart?"

I said, without thinking, "Upstairs with a headache."

He nodded, and drove to the gateway where Davidson was standing. "I'll be back in a couple of hours," the Chief said. "Keep your eyes open. Mrs. Stuart is still in there."

Davidson blinked in surprise, and I went cold. Davidson had seen me come in alone. A word from him might wreck everything. "Mrs. Stuart?" he said. "Why, she—"

"Just keep your eyes open," the Chief cut in. Gravel spurted back from the wheels, and the car jumped ahead. "That Davidson," he said. "Always got some comeback, like you. Where are we headed?"

I took a moment to catch up on my breathing, and said, "The new fishing-pier. My boat's there. I want to take you a couple miles up the beach in it."

"You mean that dizzy sand-bar idea of yours worked?"

"Just about. It'll only take a few minutes to make sure after we get there."

"Stuart, if you waste my time when I almost have this case wrapped up—"

"If I waste your time, throw me in jail and I won't squawk. How's that?"

He frowned thoughtfully, and I wished I hadn't spoken those words. He didn't have a brilliant mind, but it kept clanking away as busily as a slot machine on Saturday night. By the law of averages he ought to hit the jackpot pretty soon. I had better stop feeding him ideas about throwing me into jail. His mind clanked around a few times on the impetus of my remark, and then turned up a row of lemons. "I can't throw a guy into jail for having dumb ideas," he said.

"Good. Then I'll spring another dumb idea on you. When we reach the pier, flash your spotlight around. And have that cannon of yours ready, in case anybody is on the boat waiting to jump us."

My tone must have impressed him. "Okay," he grunted. "If there is anything to this business, I guess a guy could have seen you fooling around off the beach and followed you back to the pier."

We parked at the pier and the Chief fanned his light around. We saw nothing unusual. We moved out cautiously along the pier. Nobody was on the boat. I started the engine and headed up the coast. It wasn't as dark as I would have preferred. Stars were picking holes in the blackness overhead. The moon hung in the western sky, thin as a knife scar. I hoped we couldn't be seen from shore.

The Chief said, "You didn't ask me what else I found out today."

I was more interested in figuring how to locate the sand bar. "Yeah?" I muttered. "What?" He started telling me something, but for a time his words didn't register. I studied the chart in the dim light from the control panel, trying to remember landmarks that would be helpful in the darkness. There was a cottage on that lonely stretch of beach. If it was lighted—

Something the Chief said rang an alarm in my ears. "What was that again?" I asked nervously.

"Why don't you pay more attention, Stuart? I told you that after I learned about the stolen suitcase I knew Valerie Wilson didn't go to the railroad station to meet anyone. She went there to grab a suitcase and make it look like she just arrived in town. With a suitcase she'd have to take a taxi, see? So it was just a matter of asking the porters and taxi drivers did they see her. Your full-length sketch came in handy."

"You—found the porter?"

"Yeah, sure. And we got a double check on the identity because the girl claimed she had no change and asked the taxi driver to tip the porter for her. Of course we know the Wilson girl had no money."

I stared at him. There was a smug look on his square honest face. I couldn't believe that he was playing cat-and-mouse with me; Al would have done it, but the Chief wasn't the type. I asked the question that would prove it, one way or another. "Did you find the taxi driver?"

"Well, yes and no. We found who he is. But it just happens this is his day off and he's out fishing. I have one of the boys waiting at his house with the full-length sketch of Valerie Wilson. Soon as the guy comes back, we'll know where he took her. That's why I didn't want to come with you tonight."

I muttered, "You won't miss anything," and changed the subject fast. I was afraid to let him feed any questions about Valerie's hideout into that slot-machine brain of his. He didn't really need to ask the taxi driver where he had driven Valerie. All he had to do was ask himself where she could have gone when she had no money and apparently no friends in town except a guy named Stuart. If he had trouble working that out, he could get the answer an easier way, merely by remembering that Mrs. William J. Stuart had arrived in town on that 11 a.m. train and had taken a taxi to Mr. Stuart's residence and on arrival had asked Mr. Stuart to pay the taxi driver. So he had two chances to hit the jackpot. If he did, our little cruise would stop right there. After catching me in such an enormous lie, he wouldn't believe anything I said.

I tried to keep him busy over the chart and watching for landmarks. It was a maddening job, because his thoughts wandered back frequently to the taxi driver and I had to think up remarks to get him off the track. By the time we cruised into position off the lonely stretch of beach I was soaked with sweat and my heartbeats felt like kicks in the stomach.

A light glittered ashore in the half-concealed cottage. I switched off the boat's running-lights and used the cottage to orient myself. I couldn't locate the small sand bar exactly so I attached the iron scallop drag and towed it slowly at a depth of ten feet.

The Chief said restlessly, "You're not going to waste my time by dragging for shells, are you? I thought it was something big."

"It is big. Wait and see."

"A body?" he said with more interest.

"You'll see. Handle the wheel while I use this drag, will you? And keep circling slowly until we locate the bar."

I stood at the stern and held the drag ropes. It was like a weird new kind of fishing. The boat muttered back and forth over the slow dark swells. The drag ropes vibrated in my hands as if alive. Ashore, the light of the cottage seemed to wink mockingly. If my guess was right, Champ Lane was sitting there.

The rope jerked suddenly as the drag hit bottom. It raked over sand for a few seconds, swung free. We had cut across the bar. I called directions to the Chief and we turned and located it again. I dropped a weighted line and a kapok cushion overboard, and placed a lighted flashlight on the cushion. That gave us a good marker, and we cruised up and down the length of the bar. Twice I thought we hit something, and brought up the drag, but it had only collected seaweed. My arms started aching. The Chief was grumbling again. I didn't know how long I could hold him. I didn't even know if it was worth while. Perhaps finding the lion's paw shell had been coincidence. All my other ideas had been washouts. This probably was too. It—

Down in the black water the drag bucked and quivered. It couldn't be weed this time. I yanked at the ropes. The drag lifted heavily from bottom.

The Chief heard me panting, and cut the engine and ran back to help. We gave a heave. The drag broke water and bumped up over the stern and then, as I held my breath, tilted and spilled dozens of small clattering objects over our feet.

The Chief switched on his light and looked at our haul and grumbled, "Just a bunch of shells."

I began laughing like an idiot. Just a bunch of shells, huh? Just a bunch of banded tulips and jewel cases and Junonias and paper figs and flamingo tongues and even a gorgeous left-handed whelk. Just a bushel of perfectly bleached and cleaned specimens worth several hundred dollars. The funniest thing was that I didn't deserve to find them. My ideas really had been washouts. But people had taken me too seriously and had gone out of their way to make sure my ideas wouldn't work. They had gone out of their way a little too far, and so they had served up Champ Lane to me on the half shell.

"What's wrong with you?" the Chief snapped. "Is this all you wanted? I'm through with this shell game."

I stopped laughing and said, "So am I. So let's go ashore to that lighted cottage and clean up the case."

"The cottage, huh? Is that where your mystery man lived? But he was drowned this morning. Finding his hangout don't clean up the case. I want the Wilson dame. My boys may mess up the job of grabbing her. I ought to get back."

I still couldn't tell him the whole story. He might not believe any part of it except my confession about helping Valerie. I pictured him slapping handcuffs on me and turning the boat back without a glance at the cottage. A lot of things might go wrong if that happened. I gave him the only argument that was sure to work, although I didn't know whether it was the truth or not. "Save yourself a roundabout trip," I said. "She's in that cottage."

"Then let's go," he said, taking out his revolver and checking the cylinder.

I took the wheel. We picked up the cushion and flashlight, and turned toward shore. A hundred feet off the beach I cut the engine and eased down the anchor; I didn't want the boat so close to shore that it would immediately alarm anyone glancing out of the cottage. I told the Chief we might hit some deep spots. He wrapped his revolver in an oilskin chart cover, and we paddled quietly ashore and crawled to a clump of sea grapes and studied the cottage. It was quiet. No one moved back of the lighted windows.

I whispered, "Place looks familiar. Maybe I was the one who visited it, that day my wife and Davidson and I spent on the beach."

"There's something I don't understand," the Chief muttered. "Why should the Wilson girl be here? It don't make sense."

"Why doesn't it?"

"Well, it just don't. Why would she go to all the trouble of pretending to arrive on that eleven a.m. train if she was only coming here?"

My knees began wobbling. He was playing around with the jackpot again. "Come on," I said. "We're wasting time."

"Let me think this out. I figured she swiped that suitcase and pretended she came in on the train because she was going to a hotel where she had a friend. She had to put up a front for the room clerk and people in the lobby. But if she was coming out here, she didn't need to put up a front. She didn't need a suitcase. She could have walked out here and not taken a chance with a taxi."

"This is a swell time to argue. The answer's twenty steps away. If you're not going, I am."

He grabbed my arm and said irritably, "Don't rush me. I'll go with you, all right, but I want to figure what we're stepping into. And it don't make sense that this is her hideout. She never went to all the railroad-station trouble just to come here. So by God she didn't come here. Then why would she be here now?"

"If you'll take a look—"

"You think she came here. I thought she went to a hotel. Could be we're both wrong. But then where would she have gone?"

I stood up, almost dragging him up with me. His slot-machine brain would pay off in about two more questions. His revolver was in its holster. I wondered if I could grab it away from him. I didn't want to bet I could. I chattered, "The whole thing happened days ago and doesn't mean a thing now."

"Oh, yes, it does. If she wasn't going to a hotel, why did she pretend she came in on the train? Only one possible reason. She was going to walk into a friend's house where she might meet strangers. But why worry about strangers? No reason to put on a front for them. Unless—"

"Unless we hurry she'll get away. We—"

"Wait. Listen. I got it. No reason for her to put on a front for strangers unless they were cops. But where would she run into cops? Where—" His fingers suddenly locked hard on my arm and he said, "You bastard."

I said desperately, "I'd have told you in ten minutes. Now listen to the rest of it. She—"

"Tell it to your lawyer. You better get a good one. I know the rest of the story. She's not home with any headache."

"No. If you'll let me—"

"You bet she isn't. You knew I was getting close. She's on her way North.

You tricked me into coming with you tonight to give her a few extra hours. Sure, if she gets clean away, I'll have trouble proving she was Valerie Wilson. But maybe now I can block her off upstate. How did she go? Come on, talk."

I would go crazy if he stopped me this close to the cottage. If I got him there we might see Champ Lane or Valerie. "Take one look at the cottage," I gasped. "Then I'll spill everything."

"Anything to waste time, huh? Maybe she took the night plane. That hits Jacksonville around ten. If I hurry I can call the Jax police and have her nabbed there. Okay. Don't talk. Hold out your other hand."

He flipped out a pair of handcuffs with his left hand. His right was gripping my left arm. I swung my arm against the grip of his thumb, broke loose, ran for the cottage. My back felt icy and I tensed for a shot. There was none. I heard a grunt, the hiss of feet racing over sand behind me. I reached the porch, yanked open the screen door. A thought whipped through my mind. I had almost made another horrible mistake. No wonder the cottage looked familiar. It was the one Al had rented. But that was all right, because Valerie lay bound and gagged on a couch in the living-room. The Chief couldn't laugh that off.

I yelled, "Here she is," and swung around to let him in.

But I had made a final mistake, after all. The man chasing me leaped onto the porch. A grin twitched his mouth. It was Al Leonard.

"Yeah, here she is," he said. "Nice of you to drop in, pal."

Chapter Fourteen:
BORROWED ALIBI

I didn't quite click on what had happened. I got ready to dive at him the moment the Chief appeared. But no one moved in the shadows behind Al. He crouched slightly and watched me. The gun in his right hand leveled at my stomach. A sock filled with something heavy sagged in his left hand.

"Come on, if you want it that way," he said. "Which hand do you take?"

I said hoarsely, "What did you do with him?"

"The Chief? He got delayed. A sock filled with sand makes a nice black-jack. I thought I'd split a gut back there, laughing at you two dopes arguing. Gave me a swell chance to sneak up on you. I slugged him just as you broke away. Probably saved your life, pal. The guy don't shoot bad."

"You can't get away with this."

"Want to try stopping me? The only reason you're on your feet right now is I need a guy to carry some two-legged baggage when I leave here. I elected you redcap. What do you want to do, play porter or play dead?"

I looked at the gun. "Porter," I said.

"That's a good boy. Let's go back and pick up the luggage I dropped."

I glanced back into the room and saw Valerie staring at me with big, sad eyes. Perhaps for a moment she had thought the Marines were coming to the rescue. Instead it was only a small boy named William J. Stuart in his sailor suit. I shuffled across the porch and walked ahead of Al to the clump of sea grapes. The Chief lay on his face, still gripping the handcuffs.

"Just a moment," Al said. He collected the Chief's revolver, hauled his wrists together, and snapped the handcuffs on them. "I ought to cuff you together," he said, "but then you couldn't handle him and Valerie. Okay. Get him back to the cottage."

I swung the limp body across my shoulders and heard the slow thud of his heart. "He's still alive," I said.

"You don't think I handled a blackjack ten years without knowing how to pop a guy, do you?"

I carried him back to the cottage and lowered him gently into a chair. I looked at Valerie. She still wore the scanty bathing-suit. There were bruises and scraped places on her smooth body, and red welts where ropes cut into her wrists and ankles and knees. Every time she took a breath, a corner of the towel gagging her fluttered up against her nose and cut off air.

"Let me fix the towel so she can breathe," I said.

"Okay. Take it off if you want. But don't touch those ropes. I had enough trouble tying her up after we left you. Might think she was all fingernails and elbows."

I lifted her head and untied the towel. Her lips moved numbly, trying to form words.

"Mind if we talk?" I asked.

"Talk. Sing. Whistle. No yells, though. Otherwise write your own ticket. Make a pass at her if you want. I don't think you ever got to first base with her before, so maybe you can do better when she can't move. I'll just sit back and enjoy the show."

I wondered what was in his mind. Perhaps he merely wanted a little sadistic fun. Perhaps he had some deeper reason for waiting. I didn't know. As far as I was concerned, however, anything that postponed the final settlement was all to the good. While there's life there's hope. I wished I knew what to hope for.

I told Valerie, "I'm sorry I messed things up again."

She tried to smile. "It was my fault, Bill. You've been wonderful."

"Yeah," Al said. "We're all proud of you, Stuart."

"I didn't think fast enough," she said. "I wasn't sure you were right until he started to run you down with the boat. And then it was too late. It was too late the moment he grabbed the gaff."

"That gaff!" Al said. "I've ducked some nasty gadgets in my time, but just thinking of that gaff gives me a sore throat. I wonder would you have used it."

"I don't know."

"Well, I figured to play it safe. I knew your arm would die on you. What did you do after you left us, pal?"

I started to tell him, but just then the Chief groaned and stirred.

Al told me to get over to his chair and make sure he didn't come out fighting. "I hate to hit a fellow officer," he explained.

I went to the Chief and worked on the back of his neck to help clear his head. He opened his eyes and brought them into focus on me and went for my throat. Even with his hands manacled I had trouble holding him. I talked fast and finally managed to get the score across to him.

He glared at Al and said, "You can't get away with this."

"I know," Al said. "Stuart told me the same thing. I feel bad about it. That shot you just heard is me committing suicide." He gave a clacking laugh.

"But what's it all about?"

"You tell him, Stuart," Al said. "I'll fill in anything you don't know."

I began outlining the story, with Al straightening out points now and then. It turned out that almost every charge I had made against Al was well founded. He went to the Committee of Thirty and to the Special Grand Jury on Champ Lane's orders, and got in solidly with them by handing them a lot of minor stuff. When the Committee told him to try to find and arrest Lane in Gulf City, he phoned Lane and warned him. Al arrived in Gulf City and couldn't locate either Lane or Valerie right away. But at a little after ten, the night of the murder, Lane telephoned Al and told him what had happened.

Al said, "After I warned him, see, he knew what Eddie was up to. So when Eddie said he had a date with a girl and wouldn't be around that night, the boss figured Eddie was dating Valerie and might take her to that cottage down the beach. So the boss took a hike down the beach, collecting those damn shells on the way, and looked in at the cottage and saw Eddie's scrap with Valerie. It seemed like too good a chance to miss, so when Eddie wobbled out to the kitchen door after Valerie, the boss walked in the front and picked up her rod and let Eddie have it when he came back in."

"Then he took Eddie's car and followed us," I said.

Al nodded. "That's right, only it wasn't actually Eddie's car. It belonged to the boss and Eddie was just a chauffeur and errand boy. The car was in Eddie's name so if there was an accident or anything the boss wouldn't appear."

It was weird sitting there listening to him. If there hadn't been any guns or ropes or handcuffs, you might have thought we were a group of friends hashing over the latest murder in the papers. Al leaned back and smiled pleasantly at us and even let me have a cigarette. I couldn't figure him. Probably, like a lot of other people, he enjoyed talking about how smart he was, but that didn't account very well for our round-table discussion on murder. He wanted to know how I trailed him to the cottage, and I explained about the shells.

"Very nice work, pal," he said. You might have thought he was going to pin a medal on me.

The Chief said, "I don't understand about this cottage. Stuart thought he was finding Lane's hideout. Instead it turns out to be Al's place."

"I have it figured now," I said. "This *was* Lane's hideout. Right?"

"On the nose," Al said.

"I had that screwy idea about checking every cottage on the beach," I said. "Al and Lane took my idea too seriously. They decided they either had to close up this place so it would look vacant, which might make us suspicious, or else hide Lane's shell collection. Well, after getting rid of the shells, somebody had the idea of Al moving in here and inviting us to look around. That would cover up perfectly. It was pretty smart."

"My idea," Al said modestly.

The Chief asked, "Why did they drop Lane's shell collection on that sand bar? Why not just bury them, or throw them in the woods or something?"

I said, "You bury them and maybe a kid comes along digging in the sand and says, 'Mama, look at all the pretty shells,' and they take a bunch home and somebody who knows shells sees them and wonders why anyone would bury hundreds of dollars' worth of rare shells. The same argument works against tossing them anywhere. A guy finds a Junonia worth ten dollars out in the woods and he's going to talk. Maybe he'll even get a line in the newspaper about his find."

"That's it," Al said. "The boss figured that pet sand bar of his was a perfect place. Anybody happens to find one there, what's more natural? And he can always get most of them back, when things clear up. I liked to died when you found out he had a pet sand bar and went looking for it. Tell me some more how you worked it tonight."

I gave him some more details, and said, "Just out of curiosity, Al, were you hanging around the pier tonight looking for a chance to pick me up?"

"I sure was, pal. But you played mighty hard to get. And for all I knew, when you and the Chief drove there, you had a carful of cops following you. Did you?"

"No," the Chief said disgustedly. "Just us. I don't suppose it would have done any good if Stuart had given me the whole story. I wouldn't have believed him."

"Right now," Al said, "your boys probably have the taxi driver's story and are all over Stuart's place and everywhere looking for you."

"All over everywhere is right," the Chief muttered. "They got no idea where I went. I still don't know one thing. Where is Champ Lane?"

Al lifted an eyebrow. "You don't think he's living here?"

I said, "I'm beginning to wonder if he's living anywhere."

Al chuckled. "Don't let that gray sedan going through the bridge fool you."

"I never went for that," I said. "That was faked, to throw us off the trail. You jumped before it hit the bridge. Well, it didn't work. You must have realized that about eight o'clock tonight, when you saw us go out in the boat. So after you returned here I figure you elected Champ Lane Corpse Number Two."

Valerie gasped, "But, Bill, I haven't heard anything. No shots or—"

"Keep quiet, baby," Al said. "Let him talk. He's got me interested."

"A sandbag doesn't make any noise," I said. "Look at the spot Al's in. He can ease you and me out of the way, Valerie, and not worry. It will look as if you killed Eddie and I helped you afterward and when things became rough we skipped town. But the Chief doesn't fit into that picture. If he disappears, there's hell to pay and maybe Al is stuck with the check."

"You're not kidding," the Chief said. "My boys will take this town apart. And the FBI will say it's kidnapping, which gives them an in."

"I see what you mean," Al said.

"So," I said, "the Chief can't disappear. He has to be found dead in the line of duty."

Al said, yawning, "You and him could shoot it out and all three of you be found dead."

"That's messy," I said. "It's not often that three people shoot it out and all wind up dead. Might not look right. But Champ Lane could knock us off and Al could rush in at the last minute and plug Lane. If the guy's still alive, he's tied up somewhere waiting for the ax."

Al lit a cigarette. His eyes reflected the tiny flame and glowed like the eyes of a big cat. "Just where would that get me?" he murmured.

"Come on," I said. "You have it all worked out. That gets you headlines. You're a hero. Back home the Committee of Thirty says you ought to be Police Commissioner. Lane's crowd can't squawk because you have all Champ Lane's files. You claimed he had them here."

"Uh-huh," Al said. "Every closet in the house is packed with them. That's why we couldn't hide the shell collection in closets. Go on, pal."

"What else is there? You're a hero to the reformers. You have the goods on Champ Lane's crowd. Six months with that setup and it'll be Al Champ Leonard."

"Bossing the town, huh?" Al said lazily.

"Sure. You couldn't miss."

Al looked at me and laughed. Something in his expression told me I had guessed wrong again. It didn't matter, of course. Anyway, my talking had used up a few more minutes. If I kept going long enough maybe somebody would come around to read the electric-light meter and get shot, too.

Al said, "Stuart, you have the nastiest mind I ever met." He raised his voice. "Hey, Mr. Lane! Come on in."

Footsteps sounded back of the half-closed door into a bedroom. The door swung open. The man who stood there was astonishingly like the sketch I had made. Bald head, thick black eyebrows slightly faded by the sun, big nose, heavy chin, bleak gray eyes. The chin was jutting angrily and the eyes were even colder than I had drawn them.

"You dumb ox," he told Al. "I ordered you to keep me out of this."

"But what could I do?" Al said, grinning. "A guy has to protect his reputation."

"You didn't have to sit here jabbering for half an hour."

"I had to find out something, Mr. Lane. You know, when you get a bunch of suspects in to detective headquarters you don't always try to sweat stuff out of them. Sometimes you act calm and friendly and let them have cigarettes and get them talking. You'd be surprised how people open up sometimes."

"What did you want to find out?"

"I had to find out if any of the Chief's boys knew where he went tonight, and did anybody but Stuart know the whole score. I couldn't sweat the answer out of them because they would have lied. So I coaxed them to talk and found everything is okay. Seemed like a smart idea to me."

"Well, it's the first smart one you've had," Lane said. "All right, get them out of here."

I said huskily, "Mr. Lane, you don't want to be responsible for three more murders."

"Get them out of here," Lane repeated, without looking at me.

Al said, "Don't embarrass Mr. Lane, Stuart. He don't like to know about nasty things. Look, Mr. Lane, what do you suggest?"

"They left their boat anchored just off the beach. Take them away in that. It's your business what you do with them."

"What about that FBI-kidnapping angle about this cop here?"

Lane snapped, "Use your head for a change, and figure out something. You've messed this thing up from start to finish."

"I thought I did pretty good."

"Pretty good! Every time you listened to this man Stuart he put a new idea in your head. And every new idea got us in a worse spot. First it was moving in here. That slapped a ball and chain on both of us. It meant if they suspected you, they'd find you never rented the place at all. They'd find a George Smith bought it a year ago, and the man I bought it from can probably identify my face. Then you turned panicky and threw my shells right where Stuart was going to look for shells."

"You had the sand bar idea, Mr. Lane. That was an idea Stuart put in your head."

"I didn't know the idiot would visit every shell expert in town and hear about that sand bar. You should have known what he might do. You kept telling me not to worry about him."

Al looked at me almost fondly. "This Stuart is quite a guy," he said. "I never saw a man with so many ideas. He shoots them off like fireworks. Most of his ideas are lousy, but he shoots off so many that he keeps putting ideas in other people's heads. Look how he kept putting ideas into the Chief's head about Valerie, without meaning to."

"He put a dumb one in your head today," Lane said. "Walking right into your hands, wasn't he? So you messed up things on the boat and gave him the whole picture."

"I got him and Valerie now, didn't I?"

"You also have a local cop."

"Did I do anything else wrong, Mr. Lane?"

Lane gave a short, hard laugh. "Plenty," he said. "For two nights you tried to sneak into Stuart's house and both times you were chased away by hick cops. You went out on a routine job today and not only flubbed it but also lost your blackjack and revolver. I thought once of making you Police Commissioner. Now I'm not even sure you can run those city stables."

"I'll do better from now on, Mr. Lane."

"See that you do. Now get these people out of here. And leave me my gun. You can use the one you took from this local cop."

"Okay," Al said. He slid one of the revolvers across the floor. It spun to rest at Lane's feet. "There you are, Champ," he said.

Lane's face went purple. "Don't call me Champ," he snarled. "It's Mr. Lane to you. And come here and pick up this gun."

Al got up lazily. "Yes, sir, Mr. Lane," he said. Then he looked at Lane and smiled and didn't move.

The room was suddenly very quiet. The air felt heavy, hard to breathe, like air before a hurricane. I wanted to yell to clear my lungs. Valerie curled up into a tight ball. The Chief leaned forward. Light glittered from Al's eyes. Across the room the purple stain faded from Lane's face and left it dull gray.

Lane muttered, "And when you get out in the boat, don't let Stuart put any more crazy ideas into your head." He stooped slowly toward the gun.

Al said, "I kind of like the last one he gave me." His right hand tightened on the Chief's revolver, and sound crashed against my ears three times, and Lane crumpled.

One moment we were all figures in a stiff tableau, like a jigsaw puzzle fitting neatly together on a card table. The next instant, Valerie kicked the card table and pieces flew all over the place. Her drawn-up legs lashed out, caught Al in the back. He lurched forward. The Chief chopped down with his manacled hands. Metal crunched into Al's wrist. He yelled. His gun clattered to the floor. There was a blur of motion as he and the Chief dove for it. I leaped across the room, grabbed Lane's gun. I swung around, praying I could shoot straight. I didn't have to. Al had missed the other gun. He wheeled, crashed into the screen door, vanished.

"His car!" Valerie screamed. "It's out back."

The Chief ran into the kitchen. Window glass shattered. I saw him crouch, twist his left hand down against the handcuffs to give his right hand more play. Flame spurted twice from the revolver.

He ran back, gasped, "Missed him. Scared him away from the car, though. Give me that gun, Stuart."

He jumped out to the porch. I followed. Down on the beach a figure swerved and darted like a broken-field runner, heading for the water. The Chief fired slowly, three times. Al ran on. Spray flashed as he hit water, struck out for the boat lying offshore.

I started running. Behind me the Chief yelled a hoarse warning. I didn't stop. I raced out into the shallows and churned on until water hit my waist and then swam. Ahead of me a dark head bobbed. It turned. Al's teeth showed white in a snarl. A fist lashed at me. I gulped a breath that hurt my lungs, and dove and caught his legs. Fingers raked my hair and knees battered my ribs. I held on, felt us sink slowly in the black water. I was very happy. Maybe I could hold my breath three minutes this time.

Chapter Fifteen:
AN IDEA THAT WORKED

I came out of a pleasant daze and felt someone shaking me. I growled and hung onto the limp object in my arms.

"Let him go!" a voice howled in my ear.

I opened my eyes and blinked. I was back in the shallows. The Chief was yanking at my arms, trying to tear me away from Al.

"Hello," I said.

"Jeez, you're a hard guy to handle," the Chief gasped. "Like to drown me, too. And you kept growling like a dog with a bone. Come on. Drag him ashore. Think you can bring him to?"

I shrugged. I had only a mild interest in the matter.

"Well, see what you can do," he said severely. "It would be nice if we could have one trial in this town instead of just a lot of funerals. Wait. First get these cuffs off me. Key's in my watch pocket."

I unlocked the handcuffs and the Chief promptly snapped them on Al, muttering something about taking no chances. We dragged Al to the beach and I started to work on him. The Chief went back to the cottage and released Valerie and telephoned for help. In about fifteen minutes everything in Gulf City that had a siren or bells—police cars, ambulances, and fire engines—converged on us. A fireman took over the artificial respiration from me and finally fixed things so the Chief could have his trial.

There was a lot of running around and talking after that, but the excitement was over. The Chief drove us back to our house. He didn't say much, and I suspected that he wasn't happy.

He let us out at the door and mumbled, "You did a nice job, Mr. Stuart. Stick around and they'll probably make you Chief of Police."

"What for?" I said. "They already have a good Chief of Police."

"Don't give me that stuff. I walk around for days with your girlfriend right under my nose and I never tumble to it."

"What about us?" I said. "Al was right under our noses and we didn't catch on. Lane was there, too. And we knew a lot more of the story than you did. We had plenty to go on. You didn't have a thing. I say you did a swell job. It certainly gave me nightmares."

"You're not kidding?"

"No, indeed. And I'm going to tell the reporters what a swell job you did."

His solemn face cracked in the first smile I had ever seen him use. It made him look like a cutout Halloween pumpkin. "That's mighty nice," he said. "I like this job. And I know how much I owe you two. Of course, you got to stay for the trial, but if you come down this way again some other year collecting shells, count on me for anything you want." He stopped, thought a moment, and then said in a worried tone, "Of course, you might find the shelling better at Sanibel and Captiva than here."

I grinned and said, "I know what you mean."

The worried look left his face, and he waved and drove off.

Valerie said, "It was nice of you to cheer him up."

"He's a good guy. But I never want him on my trail again."

She looked out over the grounds of the Casa del Mar and said with a little sigh, "It seems queer not to have anyone on guard."

"Yeah," I said. It was odd that last night the garden had been full of magic and now there was none. The palm trees looked like old feather dusters, and a mockingbird was imitating a cracked phonograph record.

"Well," she said, "we'll both have to stay for the trial, but that shouldn't take long. Al has no defense. Then what will you do, Bill?"

"Go back to the job, of course."

"Oh, yes," she said brightly. "Back to the Long Island Railroad and penny-ante poker and nice girls your friends want to marry off to you and coffee with two lumps of sugar."

"Yeah, I guess so."

"Bill, I'd better move to a hotel tonight. I couldn't very well stay here now."

"No. No, of course not. Going to phone your paper first?"

"I almost forgot that. It is a terrific story, isn't it? And of course I'll get terrific stories out of the trial."

"What will you do after the trial?"

She gave a tiny laugh, flat and brittle as a spoon clinking on china, and said, "Go back to my job, naturally. There will be a lot of big stories to cover."

I glared at her. "You're going to walk back into that mess?" I cried. "You're going to play around with thugs and gunmen after the lesson you had here? I thought you'd picked up some sense!"

"From you, I suppose."

"All right. From me."

"Well, I haven't," she said angrily. "I'm going back home and get into as much trouble as I want to and I'm going to burn all the toast I feel like burning and soft-boil eggs my way and wear any kind of bathing-suit I want to and—"

"Wow," I said. "I pity the guy who marries you."

"Oh, shut up," she said in a broken voice.

"Why should I shut up?"

"Because if you keep talking about people marrying me, you might even put an idea into your own big dumb head."

I said coldly, "If it will give you any satisfaction, that idea has been in my head for days."

"About—about marrying me?"

"Yes. Go on and laugh."

The next instant she was in my arms and the palm trees started whirling like pinwheels and the mockingbirds began giving the Philharmonic a lesson in music.

"What do you know?" I said dizzily. "One of my ideas finally worked."

THE END